BLUE SUEDE SHOES

a novel

DEBORAH REARDON

RIVER GROVE
BOOKS

Published by River Grove Books
Austin, TX
www.greenleafbookgroup.com

Distributed by River Grove Books

For ordering information or special discounts for bulk purchases, please contact River Grove Books at PO Box 91869, Austin, TX 78709, 512.891.6100.

Design and composition by Greenleaf Book Group LLC
Cover design by Greenleaf Book Group LLC

Publisher's Cataloging-in-Publication Data
(Prepared by The Donohue Group, Inc.)
Reardon, Deborah.
 Blue suede shoes : a novel / Deborah Reardon.–1st ed.
  p. ; cm.
 Issued also as an ebook.
 1. Murder–Wisconsin–Fiction. 2. Women bankers–Wisconsin–
Fiction. 3. Wisconsin–Fiction. 4. Mystery fiction. I. Title.

PS3618.E27 B48 2012
813/.6

LCCN: 2012948963
Print ISBN: 978-1-938416-11-8
eBook ISBN: 978-1-938416-12-5
First Edition

With the support of Mike

To Steven
On the wings of our Maxine
For the inspiration to write Blue Suede Shoes *during those precious*
years in New Berlin, Wisconsin.

ONE

C lare had finally gotten deep into the Sunday newspaper late in the evening, and she might not have noticed her childhood friend Derek Watkins at all had she not accidentally glimpsed his truck headlamps lighting up the edge of her driveway over the top of the newsprint. It was a sight that wouldn't have ordinarily fazed her—he stopped by often enough—but it was so late on a Sunday, and he hadn't called. Through the filmy sheers covering the window, she saw him crossing the porch. She didn't lounge and wait for him to knock; something in his demeanor made her run to the door.

"Good Lord, Derek, what happened?" Clare demanded. His shirt was torn, he was soaking wet, and there was mud and dried blood all over him. Without waiting for an answer, she struggled to yank all 240 pounds of him inside; whoever had done this to him might be close behind. As soon as he was in, she bolted the door.

"You're hurt!" she said.

"I'm not." She reached out to check him for injuries; he resisted.

"You've got to listen to me," he said, and he grabbed hold of her shoulders. "I'm not hurt, Clare! It's about Mary. I just got done at the police station; it's a really big mess."

Clare froze. "What are you saying? Did they find Mary?"

Weeks had gone by since four-year-old Mary Martin had vanished. Her disappearance had been weighing heavily on their tight-knit town of Danfield, Wisconsin, a small community of 5,500 citizens outside of Milwaukee, many of whom had sprung into action to help the authorities when the news first broke. Clare was still reluctant to consciously accept what she felt deep down: time was no longer on Mary's side for survival. But maybe her shaken friend had brought news that could finally help the traumatic case move forward.

"Come on Derek, take a breath! What happened?"

"I was fishing," he said. "Just fishing. I was getting ready to leave when Coach started barking and running around frantically. And, and I found the spot where Mary might have died . . ."

He wasn't making sense, and he must have realized it, because his gravelly voice trailed off in disbelief. He shook his head and kept talking. "Damn, Clare! She was the sweetest little girl—what kind of monster could have done this? Can you imagine what her parents are going through? Russell and Courtney will be heartbroken . . ."

Clare's heart plummeted while she privately repeated the word monster, a term that had been universally invoked since Mary had disappeared. The beloved little girl had become the poster child for the community, smashing its reputation as one of the safest places anywhere to raise a family.

She stood there silently with him, letting him calm down, as water dripped to the wood floor from his soaked clothes.

"Let's get these wet things off you and go sit down," Clare finally said. "I'll get some coffee going."

"It'll have to be stronger than that," Derek argued.

The two had frequented each other's homes over the years since grade school, so Derek felt comfortable peeling off his soiled jacket and flannel shirt. He hung both on the coat rack and then unbolted the door and stepped back out front to leave his muddy boots on the porch. Clare tossed him an old pair of his sweat bottoms that she let him keep in the hallway closet for days when he'd come to help shovel the walkway after the worst storms.

In the stress of the moment, Clare was overcome by the familiar tug of their youth that had been abated by careers, adult responsibilities, and her time away at Northwestern University. Their closeness had been somewhat marred when she grabbed at the opportunity at twenty-five to pursue a long-desired degree in law enforcement in Chicago and made too big a deal about the chance to shed her small-town roots. But their connection, resumed upon her coming back to Danfield, was irrefutable, as evidenced by his choice to lean on her tonight.

"Grab a garbage bag if you could, Clare," Derek called and stepped into the hall bathroom.

While he scrubbed down to his dry duds behind the hall bathroom door, Clare let him ramble and get the story straight in his head. He had been a longtime employee and manager of Marwood's Hardware, and he was telling her every detail of how he'd tweaked his October work schedule in order to nab some late-afternoon fishing at the end of the season. She wanted to know what had happened and would have been annoyed by these tidbits if they had been coming from anyone else. But instead she worried; it wasn't like Derek to be this rattled.

The bathroom door opened. "Give me a towel," Derek said, motioning to the mess on the floor.

"Not now, Derek," she said. "I'll get that later; this is not the time to be a neat freak. I know this is painful, but I've got to know what happened."

Clare brought a couple of beers, and the two of them went to the couch. He was finally putting substantive sentences together.

"Like I said, I was fishing," he began again. "I kept saying, Coach, come on, let's go! He didn't even look at me."

Derek's breath got shorter with every detail.

"It was getting later, and I was cold," he pressed on. "It had been drizzling, and I'd left my raincoat at the truck. The temperatures started dropping so quickly, so at first I turned up the path so that I could get it and stay longer, but as I kept walking I decided it felt too late to stay and Coach and I should just go home. And you know Coach always follows me, but tonight, when I was halfway up the path to the truck, he suddenly shot back down to the creek toward the spillway."

He trailed off again.

"I'm listening; it doesn't sound like Coach." Clare said.

Derek wiped his sweaty forehead and changed the subject. "Clare, this is really awful. I shouldn't be here throwing all this at you. But I went by my house and it was surrounded with reporters."

"What? Don't be ridiculous; I would have done the same thing. And I can't imagine your mom's reaction if you'd have brought the media hounds over to her house."

Her favorite denim shirt had been soaked, earlier, when she had helped him in the foyer, and it now lay cold and clammy against her chest. She began to shiver from the dampness, but the discomfort was a small inconvenience, given what Derek had just gone through.

"I could see Coach moving and jumping around from a distance," he said, a bit more animated now. "He was growling . . . but he wouldn't even look up when I tried to get his attention. That just wasn't like him."

Clare wished he could get past the dog part of the story, but Coach's behavior also struck her as odd. Derek and his dog had been virtually inseparable since he had found the mangy, homeless collie mix dragging a floating piece of bark out of the lake. His instinctive reaction to scrub and nourish the poor mutt had grown into the colossal efforts he'd undertaken to return the dog—who right from the beginning he'd nicknamed Coach—to his rightful owner. The two of them, man and canine, had hobbled about town hanging posters, inquiring with neighbors, and checking the local kennels before they'd finally called an end to the search.

"How did you get Coach's attention, Derek?" Clare prompted.

"I was freezing, but instead of continuing to get my jacket, I had to chase Coach . . . I was just freezing," he repeated. "I accidentally slipped down the creek bed at one point and my boots got soaked."

He was staring at the rug in the entryway, caked with mud and soaked with water.

"Please don't worry about that right now," Clare pleaded. "It'll get clean."

"If you could have seen her little underwear, Clare," Derek said, "and Coach had grabbed her shirt and was shaking it . . ."

His voice was emotionless; it was like he'd gone into a trance.

"There was so much blood . . . and her body wasn't anywhere. Clare, it appears she's gone," he said.

Her stomach was getting more nauseous with each sickening detail, but she had to know; tomorrow everyone would be talking about it.

"She's gone? Is that what the police say?" she asked. "Did you talk to the chief?" She was personally curious about how Chief Jared Grady would handle this new development in the most notable case in Danfield's history.

"Jared came out to the crime scene and to the interview at the station," Derek said. "I can't even think about all this, Clare . . ." Sweaty moisture zigzagged the wrinkles on his cheeks, minor creases that were now noticeably pronounced crevasses, evidence that the evening had taken its toll. Derek had always been renowned for his calm, rational temperament, and she knew how uncomfortable he must have been with this sort of outward expression.

From that point, his story was all about his running to his truck and out to the road to flag somebody down for help. He remained pinned to his truck until the emergency team found him. He didn't make eye contact with Clare until she nudged him sideways.

"Where's Coach now?" she asked.

"They got him. The police said he could have evidence on him. They're going to inspect him and clean him up, I guess. I can bring him home in a couple of days. I'm sure he's freaking out right now." Derek clutched his calloused hands again.

Clare embraced his large shoulders and pulled him close; her five-foot-seven, 135-pound body seemed miniature in comparison. His restlessness subsided, and he was speechless except for his hollow wheezing. The two childhood buddies sat glued together. Clare was utterly horrified for Derek's misfortune, but she still felt some relief. It had been a tremendous break for the investigation. She resisted any urge to talk about what the impact might be on Mary's parents, their grade-school friends Russell and Courtney. Instead, she focused on a spot on ceiling and thought about the eerie first moments at her mother Yvonne's house, when they had first heard the news that Mary had gone missing.

Yvonne had no sooner joined Clare at the kitchen table with a bowl of green beans and clutched her daughter's hand for the dinner prayer when the phone rang. Yvonne had sprung to grab the corded phone in the other room.

"Mom, just let it ring," she remembered insisting. She remembered it so vividly because it had been one of their eternal sore points, one of a laundry list of annoying traits that had ravaged her mother since the disappearance of Clare's father Ray Paxton when Clare was just seven. No note, no trail, no nothing; he had just dropped from sight, and here they were dealing with the aftermath of his leaving over two decades later.

She had begun to eat without her mother when she heard Yvonne shout. "Get in here, Clare!" She figured it was her mother being her neurotic self, so she took her sweet time moving to the living room. It took only a glance at her mother's face for her to realize that something was very wrong.

"Here, listen to Vivian," Yvonne said, nervously offering Clare the phone so that she could turn on the TV.

Clare waved away talking to Yvonne's friend Vivian Fox, engrossed by the television images that appeared: Russell and Courtney Martin huddled front and center on the police station steps, pleading frantically for the return of their daughter Mary. For some time they had been estranged, and this was an extraordinary display of unity amid the uncertainty of their bitter divorce, Clare remembered thinking.

"What a terrible thing!" Yvonne rattled to her friend on the other end of the line, looking ten years older than her forty-eight. "It's just frightening to think of what could have happened to that precious little child . . ."

Clare held up her hand to shush her mother's endless chattering with Vivian and motioned for Yvonne to hang up so that she could hear the news anchor continue with the breaking story. Courtney had returned to the house from working with the gardeners on a flowerbed arrangement. One minute little Mary Martin had been napping; the next she was nowhere to be found. The hair was immediately up on the back of Clare's neck. Her mind began to turn over any number of crazy inferences, an inevitable reflex spawned by her high-school summer jobs at the Danfield police station and by the few short years she had spent working on her criminal psychology degree in Chicago.

Aside from the obvious frightening fact that a well-known small child was missing, there was something extraordinary that Clare could not put her finger on that first night of Mary's disappearance. That extraordinary feeling came back to her in force now, sitting next to a shocked and silent Derek on her couch.

She felt the heaviness of his breathing and sat feeling tense beside him, wondering whether she dared turn on the news. Neither had moved much for a while, and her left arm was almost completely numb from clutching his shoulder when the phone rang. She scrambled to pick it up, nearly spilling one of the half-consumed, warm beers.

"Yes?" Clare whispered.

Clare listened to Derek's father's frantic request for his son.

"Oh . . . Mr. Watkins! He's here. We should have called sooner."

Like Clare, Derek was an only child, and so he stayed very close to his parents, despite his independent and resourceful nature. She could see Derek waving his arm for the phone.

Mr. Watkins was relieved and then continued to ramble about his quest to find his son, all the phone calls, and the news. His TV was playing in the background.

"It sounds pretty horrible," she said before he could keep going. "But we're under control now. And he's already finished at the police station and they kept Coach for evidence or something. I'm guessing he'll just crash here . . . "

She felt a nudge. Derek took hold of the phone. "Hey Dad, don't take everything miss busybody has to say too seriously," he said.

Clare rolled her eyes.

Derek paused, listening.

"We can go over all the details, Dad, but not over the phone." Derek's voice cracked slightly. "Yeah, there was a little media troop out in front of my house . . . sounds like you have some visitors in your neighborhood as well, if you don't recognize the vehicles."

While Derek carried on the conversation, apologizing over and over for not calling, Clare cleaned up an earlier mess in the kitchen. She rummaged through the hallway linen closet, organizing the amenities for Derek to stay in the guest room downstairs, and then darted upstairs to get ready for bed. When she came back down to say good night, he was off the phone. She eased through the living room to the larger-than-life version of the little boy she'd befriended in the fourth grade. He was leaning back in the corner of her couch, propped against two couch pillows with one arm resting across his forehead.

"What did you decide after all that?" she asked. "I assume you're staying put for the night?"

"How long has it been since I stayed over because we drank too much? Remember those days? If I still drank tequila, I'd be skunked by now."

"This is a bit different. You're staying clear of the cameras. The guest room is all set up." She folded her body into the armchair beside the couch where he sat drained of all emotion. Derek had the most moderate personality of all her male friends growing up, neither hot-tempered nor overly softhearted. From the first moments when he had entered the classroom mid-semester, she could see the teachers and male classmates instantly start to size him up for his future football and basketball potential. Ultimately,

Derek participated in sports quite gamely throughout the years, but he didn't have the same raw desire for competition and focus on athletics as those who suited him up. Instead, he channeled what desire he had into his engineering mindset and his talent for building things. He wasn't quite geeky enough to make fun of, and he wasn't inclined to pound his chest with the rest of his testosterone-laden male counterparts, so in the end, he blended in without fanfare.

Once his ten-year-old classmates had dared him to pinch off the tail of a stray cat they found, and he was strong enough do it with just his thumb and his forefinger. Yet he had been so overwhelmed by his horrific act that he had secretly nurtured the cat back to health. She knew him well enough to know that the events of tonight could eat him alive if he couldn't make it better or let it go, but at the same time, Clare felt oddly uneasy by his listlessness.

"Clare, you go on up," he said finally. "I'll probably sneak out in a while. Not sure yet."

"I am going up," Clare tossed a couch throw to Derek that was barely long enough to cover him down to his knees. "You might as well stay here and head home in the daylight. The guest room is all made up."

His nod was almost imperceptible.

"Good night," he said.

Clare turned off the stairwell light, Chief Jared Grady on her mind.

TWO

Clare had already hit the snooze button twice, but even in her groggy state, she was sure that the person on the other end of the ringing phone would be her mother Yvonne. It was the morning after Derek's late-night arrival, and she had fallen asleep anxious about the fallout from the events of yesterday.

She picked up the receiver and before she had a chance to say hello, Yvonne began, "Clare, thank goodness! Don't know how I missed last night's news. I had the TV off and was fussing around the house. Vivian is out of town and nobody called me."

"Good morning, Mother," Clare responded sleepily.

"And I guess Derek is at your house?" she asked. "I just talked to Martha Watkins and she says Derek is with you. Clare, when were you going to call me?"

"Mother, it was late," she said, massaging her face. She slumped back under the covers while she digested the nagging from the other end of the line. These were the moments she wished she had caller ID.

"Is he okay, Clare?" Yvonne queried.

"Yes, Derek is here and he's okay," Clare confirmed. "Hopefully he's still sleeping and didn't hear the phone ringing."

She listened to her mother go on about the radio and television news, and the ugly photographs the *Danfield Press* had run on their front page.

Clare took the opportunity to get up, stretch, and begin looking through her closet for a suit to wear today. It was time to check on Derek.

"Nobody can imagine, Mother," Clare interrupted. "Look, I'll call you later, but I've got to go to work."

She hung up before she could tell whether Yvonne was still talking, prepared to hear about whatever her mother wanted to say later.

Anybody else would have called his or her mother at a time like this, but Clare and Yvonne were different. In their relationship, Yvonne was the one who needed mothering.

When Clare's father Ray left for good, those who knew the family well seemed to think it was a blessing. Clare's own memories were shadowed by Ray's raunchy voice in the middle of the night, by his hacking from the bedroom, by his terrible breath when he wandered home during breakfast before she went to school. She never shed a tear for his disappearance, for a guy who was thirty-one when he left, and who from her memory seemed ages older than Yvonne.

But instead of celebrating with everyone else, Yvonne let her physical appearance go and never stopped waiting for Ray to come back. That, to Clare, was more indefensible. No matter how much Clare doted on her mother, while trying to help repair her broken heart, Clare had forever sat second chair to Yvonne's clinging to her memory of Ray.

Showered and dressed, Clare peeked around the stairwell and found Derek sitting up on the couch. With his elbows on his knees, he palmed his face with his calloused, rugged hands. The blankets lay in a rumpled pile at the end of the couch.

"Man, what happened to me?" he asked, as soon as he saw her.

"Looks to me like you raided the closet instead of taking the guest room."

"You know I can't drag this filth to every room in the house."

Clare walked behind him and squeezed his shoulders before slipping into the kitchen to make coffee. "Eggs, toast, what can I get you?"

"Can't think of food right now, but I probably ought to call Franklin . . . Mr. Marwood before I head home to shower."

While Derek made the call, Clare scanned the neighborhood for unwelcome intruders from the press—no one—before she lifted the paper from her front porch. She waited until she was just inside the doorway before slipping it from the plastic wrapping to reveal the front page.

The picture of Mary Martin's blue suede shoes hit her like nothing Derek could have described. The missing child's shoes lay touching, the right shoe on its side and the left sitting upright. And a little limp shoestring was dangling off a boulder in the flowing glistening stream that surrounded it. The sight of those shoes weighed more heavily on her than any graphic crime scene she had ever visited or viewed. It was an obvious nightmare for the police that the newswire had gotten away with this photo.

Clare laid the paper in the pile by the fireplace hearth. She wasn't compelled to hand Derek the paper, nor did he ask for it. She sat down beside him and rubbed his back gently.

"How you doing?" she asked, breaking the silence.

"Mr. Marwood asked that I take at least one sick day . . . but we'll talk tomorrow to see. He was pretty shocked."

"How about you, Derek?" Clare nudged, heading for the kitchen to get the coffee.

"I'm okay, I guess," he said, in a tight voice, like he was gasping for air. "Tell me this was all a bad dream."

"I put a washcloth in the bathroom if you want to clean up," she said and brought his mug of coffee.

"Clare, this is ridiculous," he said, glancing down at the mud and blood still on his body. "What I really need is a long shower and a failing memory."

Derek had a penchant for tidiness and was obviously stressed out about his appearance. But beyond that, Clare knew people acted differently after they had experienced the effects of a crime scene. She hadn't the heart to tell him that it would take more than a washcloth or a quick shower for him to accomplish the kind of spiritual cleansing that he'd have to endure alone.

"Go slow today, okay?"

"Everybody's going to want to know something about what happened. You know all that detective stuff."

"All that matters is what the police want," she said. "Let Jared help you."

Clare was anxious to talk to Police Chief Jared Grady, who had been the most prominent figure enveloped in the thick of this, the most notable case in Danfield history.

A knock came and the front door cracked open slowly.

"Clare?"

She and Derek watched as his parents, Martha and Frank Watkins, invited themselves in. Frank Watkins came across the room to offer his son a handshake, and Martha gave Clare a grateful glance before going to huddle with her men.

"Son?" Frank asked.

"Dad, you didn't need to come," Derek said.

"I know that, son," Frank said, "but you ought to have an escort for the ride home in case it's a media mugging."

"Derek, just come stay with us a couple of days until the hysteria dies down a bit," Martha suggested.

"I'll be okay, guys, really," Derek insisted. "I just need to get cleaned up and to bolt the door for a day. I think they'll be more fixated on what the police are going to do than they will be on me."

Clare waited quietly while they lovingly argued and then said their good-byes as Frank hopped into Derek's truck with him and Martha got behind the wheel of the Buick. Cold exhaust sputtered from the tailpipes as Derek and his parents pulled from the curb. Clare watched from her porch for a long time, worrying about the toll last night would certainly take on her friend and the issues he would still have to deal with. But at least he had a strong family, unlike her fragmented experience. She had always

admired the three of them for their family love and unity. The
Watkins family had embraced her just as quickly as she had made
friends with their son. Frank and Martha's affection for her had
eventually led to them subtly encouraging a romance in Derek
and Clare's early teens. Clare had sensed that, but she was infatu-
ated with another boy named Parker and had thought of Derek as
a pseudo-sibling more than anything.

And maybe that had been the right way to think of him, as
family more than as an object of romance. She had rarely seen her
high-school sweetheart Parker since she had returned to Danfield,
but Derek still felt comfortable enough with her and the bond
they had shared since their childhood days to come here late last
night when he had needed a sounding board.

The bank president's assistant, LuAnn, was gripping the morning
news when Clare arrived at work.

"Thanks for getting everything open," Clare said carefully. "It
was an interesting night last night."

"Sure was," LuAnn said, eyeing Clare over the top of her bifo-
cals. She rustled the paper, ready to compare the skinny.

For the past twenty years—out of the thirty-five that Lee Graber
had been with the bank, taking an old savings and loan through a
considerable metamorphosis into the First National Bank of Danfield—LuAnn had proudly installed herself as her boss's lifeline.
Although LuAnn was a capable secretary, and Mr. Graber leaned
on her like crazy, Clare found her to be a busybody at times. Still,
it was protocol to keep LuAnn in the loop, and Clare, being the

chief operating officer of the bank, certainly knew how necessary it was to have plenty of underlings who managed the day-to-day and who could do so without the senior team in most instances, so Clare put up with her eccentricities the best she could.

"Does he have meetings this morning?" Clare grabbed a stack of reports and mail from a tray on LuAnn's desk and leaned in to Mr. Graber's darkened, empty office for verification.

"He just called to see if you had gotten here yet," LuAnn said. "He was sitting in the dentist's chair, finally getting that bridge-work done, when he heard the hygienist going crazy with the news about Mary . . ." LuAnn hesitated. "Well, you know . . . anyway . . . he must have missed it last night in the news because he goes to bed so early."

LuAnn rattled on about her boss as though she was the one who tucked Lee into bed. Unsubstantiated whispers about the two of them had become commonplace. They had come to know each other's quirks and idiosyncrasies over so many years of working together. Clare admired Lee in many ways but could be irritated by their office routine that included LuAnn's completing his sentences.

"If Mr. Graber calls again, let him know I might be in and out."

"Okay," LuAnn said, obviously wanting more; through all her earlier gibberish, Clare had felt LuAnn's inquiring stare. "How's Derek doing through all this? Of all people to stumble upon that mess; he's just so tame, for being such a big fella . . . Jared's the man for this, isn't he, though?"

The red-haired busybody had been making unapologetic inferences recently that Clare had a romantic interest in the police chief. She must have been convinced that Clare had gotten the inside scoop by now from Derek, and possibly more than that from Chief Grady.

"Derek's a pretty tough guy, LuAnn," Clare said, ignoring the Jared remark. "I suspect any of us would be in shock right now. Let's not blow this out of proportion until we know all the facts."

Rather than display her annoyance, Clare left it at that and headed downstairs to her first-floor office before LuAnn could pry any further.

She had just gotten started on covering her desk with the contents of her briefcase when there was a tap at her window. She turned to find Police Chief Jared Grady on the sidewalk of Main Street just outside, tapping his keys against the glass. She motioned Jared around to the back door.

Clare hustled by the gate blocking off the teller line, hearing the clatter and whoosh of the drive-through canister as it sent confidential customer exchanges to and from the kiosk. She flipped the deadbolt and opened the rear entrance to Jared.

"Hi," she said. "I figured it would be a fortress around you."

He smiled and leaned in as though he intended to engulf her, but they remained professional. She steered the thirty-eight-year-old Paul Newman lookalike back to her office, fielding the inquiring eyes and ears of the bank's lobby employees. In the eyes of Danfield, Jared was still earning his status as the new chief of police. At the same time, most of Danfield knew Clare was single and considered her attractive. The mere presence of these two together sparked rumors. But Clare was sensitive to speculation and eager to keep her private life under wraps.

"I'm actually headed home to clean up and get a couple hours of sleep," Jared said. "It's been nonstop."

"Can I get you a cup of coffee?" she asked. She moved to close her office door, keeping it open just a crack, and left the interior blinds open.

"I don't think caffeine is the answer at this point," Jared responded. "I just wanted to see you; I think that's what I needed."

Her smile acknowledged his sentiment.

"I know I shouldn't ask," Clare said, respectfully. "But any news on finding her body?"

"It's still an ongoing investigation," Jared said, "but you can take to heart the newspaper account that it's not likely that we will find any physical remains. I'm not confirming or denying anything, as you know."

"Those pictures already . . . those shoes . . ." She remembered the photo from this morning and felt creepy all over again.

"I was just furious that they got that photograph . . . I'm sure we pushed all kinds of free speech violations against the press on the scene last night. Hopefully now they'll all go away and leave the nitpicking to the nightly talking heads."

"Are you sure I can't get you something?" Clare asked. "I'd walk you down the street for breakfast, but that would be a madhouse."

He was fairly hardened by his trade, she'd learned by now, and it seemed that he had passed the moment of needing a shoulder to lean on and was ready to follow up on whatever other reason had brought him here today. He cocked his head slightly before he spoke.

"Clare, I'm sure that Derek said a lot of things last night," Jared said.

She could feel the hesitation in his tone; no doubt he was aware that Derek had spent the night at her house. Ever since

Jared Grady had met her and deemed her worthy, just after he'd taken over as chief of police a year ago, he'd been intensely interested in the status of Clare's close relationship to Derek. He was still confounded by the dynamics of small-town relationships that didn't appear to involve romance.

"Jared . . . he was more distraught than anything," Clare said. "You know he just needed to be with a friend."

"I know how he is with you," he said, speaking too quickly. "I had expected him to go right home so he wouldn't muddy the situation. That's all."

Jared put his hands on the desk and offered them to her. The office was in plain view of the lobby, and she politely leaned away. "The press was all over town and hanging around his house," she said. "You should be happy he avoided all of that." Clare restrained herself from accepting his gesture of affection in her office in plain view of the lobby.

He gave an understanding grin. "I just want to keep a lid on the gossip so we can handle this thing appropriately," he said and slid his hands off the desk and laid them securely on his thighs.

"You know I am not a gossip," she said. "And I suspect the phone was ringing off the hook at his house. He would have had a whole bunch of folks wanting to visit with him about it as well."

"I know that you're not a gossip," he said. "And I suppose he would have had a hard time ignoring the calls. I'm just saying we need to secure the flow of information."

"Good luck with controlling the chitchat around here," Clare said, and she pointed to the ceiling. "Folks like LuAnn are eagerly hovering by their phones. But just as you said when you got here, I know nothing more than what's in the news. Derek is my friend, and he needed a place to hang last night. Like all of us, he's been worried sick about Mary ever since she disappeared. Right now I imagine he would just love to get Coach out of your grasp."

Weakened from a night without sleep, he fanned his hand over the top of his sandy-brown locks, temporarily unable to muster the arrogance he was reputed to have.

"How about a quiet dinner this evening?" he asked. "We'll talk about Jamaica in the spring, or anything else you want."

He had yet to convince her to date him with any regularity, let alone get her to take a trip to Jamaica with him. But she was always intrigued by the prospect of taking their relationship to another level.

"I'll be flexible about dinner," she said. "But I suspect that you'll have trouble getting away."

"I'll call you," he motioned with a tap to the back of his chair.

Then he left her office and passed through the milling lobby of customers to the front entrance.

THREE

Around noon that day, bent over the steering wheel of the Jeep, Clare watched through the lowered passenger window as her mother Yvonne fluttered down her front walkway. Yvonne was carrying a paper grocery sack, a heavy one.

"What are you doing all dressed up?" Clare asked, pointing to the bag.

It was just five hours ago that she had hung up on her mother in order to get ready for work and get downstairs to Derek, and so this trip to escort Yvonne over to the Watkins' house was another chunk of time out of her workday, but a necessary one in this instance. A brisk breeze slapped Clare's face and she readied herself to lose her patience.

"I would have been fine going to the Watkins' alone, Clare," Yvonne said, folding herself in to the passenger seat of the Jeep.

"It's just a madhouse today, is all . . . I thought you should wait a day or two to go, until things die down," Clare said.

Yvonne's neurosis aside, this kind of media attention was clearly unfamiliar to Danfield.

"How did you know Derek was at his parents' house?" Clare asked.

"Very nice, Clare, that you can't imagine I'm in the know about anything. Anyway, I've made a nice potato salad and some of those pumpkin cookies Derek always likes."

"Mom, this is not a party or a funeral," Clare began and then stopped, instantly regretting her choice of words, given the circumstances. "We are stopping over at the Watkins' for a few minutes. We don't need to make a big social visit. I'm sure the last thing on Derek's mind is pumpkin cookies."

Yvonne gave her daughter a curt, determined look. "Clare, be nice. A big boy like that has got to keep his strength up. He's got that physical job . . . those police folks with the pencil-pushing desk jobs bothering him just don't understand how demanding this must be on him. Not the ones on the beat, mind you."

Clare sat tight while Yvonne issued her latest not-so-subtle dig at Chief Jared Grady and his cushy profession. She knew well that her mother's recent remarks in this vein—which weren't generally related to whatever topic was at hand—were strategically dished out to remind Clare that her mother knew about Jared's interest in her daughter. Yvonne seemed fine with Danfield's new police chief until she caught wind of the possible romantic link. Once Yvonne heard from the Danfield gossip mill that there might be an attraction between her daughter and the chief, she consistently characterized Jared as a paper pusher, an arrogant city slicker, and first and foremost, the antithesis of a Danfield-bred man like Derek Watkins. It bothered Clare. Even without any formal dating arrangement actually existing between her and Jared, her mother Yvonne wouldn't be her first choice of confidante about matters of the heart on any level.

She could have argued, against this most recent dig, that both brain and brawn were needed on the police force. Instead, she just said, "Don't start on that now, for heaven's sake."

"It's just a fact, Clare. Where would we be without *men*"— Yvonne emphasized the word—"to do the heavy lifting in the world?"

Clare knew the purpose of Yvonne's barbs: by *men*, she meant to shine a positive light on Clare's father Ray's career as a roving farmhand, which Clare knew had been lackluster at best.

"Where would *men* be without those pumpkin cookies," Clare whispered under her breath. Then, louder: "Let's not make a parade out of it. I'm just saying these are very crazy circumstances."

Yvonne burrowed securely in her seat and seized the bag a bit tighter as if Clare might try to snatch it.

"Anyway, I'm sure that Martha and Frank will be grateful," Yvonne assured her.

"No doubt they'll be grateful Mother, and Derek will be properly nourished," Clare agreed if merely to keep the conversation from escalating.

There was a very large, very unsanctioned group of media hounds laying silent siege around the Watkins' home. Clare drove the Jeep as close as she dared to them.

"See that crowd out on the sidewalk?" Clare motioned. "We need to move through it very quickly. No talking, no faces, no stalling, no anything. Do you understand?"

"Boy, you're bossy today," Yvonne responded indignantly. "They're not all bad people."

Clare could only take a deep reflecting breath, anticipating the inevitable photo op.

Small towns, while tending to be chatty at first, could be more tight lipped when it came to airing their real dirty laundry and were therefore wary of venomous outsiders. Thus, ever since the initial news of Mary's disappearance had died down, the press had been maintaining an innocuous distance, blending in and around the community and making whatever allies they could, all the while lying in wait for some morsel of news to drop. Now, before the citizens could have had a second to absorb the shock of the bloody clothing Derek had found, the *Milwaukee Journal Sentinel* and the national press corps had wasted little time in coming out of the woodwork to engulf three Danfield neighborhoods. It was not surprising that they'd already glommed on to the parents of the man who'd found the site where Mary may have perished.

Clare observed the press uneasily and then looked over at Yvonne, who was seemingly undaunted and eager to bring cheer with her pumpkin cookies. At least with Clare along, Yvonne wouldn't be fodder for the cluster of news-hungry wolves. She signaled Yvonne to sit tight and then circled around to open her mother's door.

"Again, just keep it simple," Clare reminded Yvonne. "We're just here to say hi and then I've got to get back to work."

Ignoring Yvonne's frustration, she linked her arm around Yvonne's elbow, put her head down, and moved quickly across the street, up the sidewalk, and onto the Watkins' walkway toward the door without making eye contact with the reporters. The instant their footsteps were detected, reporters were pushing microphones in their faces and peppering them with a chorus of questions about last night's events.

"Did Derek find Mary? . . . Will there be an arrest? . . . Let us help you catch the killer . . . " A cacophony of voices pleaded for a chance to break the real story.

"These are our good friends, they're good people . . ." Yvonne sang merrily, in Judas fashion.

"Mom!" Clare scolded.

Happily, Yvonne continued, "Derek is just the finest young man, my daughter and Derek have been . . ."

"That's enough!" Clare said as she took Yvonne's arm into a compliance hold, a trick she had learned during her teenage stints at the police station. By buckling her at the elbow and bending her at the wrist, she could inflict a momentary pain on her mother that made it impossible for Yvonne to utter as much as hello. She kept her mother in the hold long enough to get her up the porch steps without another word.

With their noses nearly pressing the front door, Frank Watkins peeled the screen door back a sliver to let them in. Once they were in the foyer, he sealed both the screen door and the wooden one behind it, drowning out the reporters who were still barking, but who remained miraculously restrained behind the artificial barrier of the sidewalk.

"You didn't have to do that!" Yvonne snapped at Clare.

Clare let her mother out of the compliance hold, but ignored her discomfort. Instead, she looked through the archway to the kitchen, where Derek appeared to be seated, poking his fork at a plate of food.

"He looks a little better now that he's cleaned up," Clare said in a low tone.

"He's okay," Frank responded. "First thing he took a shower, but understandably he's been very quiet most of the morning, except for during the visits from the sheriff and the DPD. I think he's more uptight about being pinned here by those hounds out in front of his house. For his mother's sake, we wandered back here, but he may bubble up soon and take a swat at the lot of them."

"I can't say that was pleasant, but I thought they were remarkably calm for the media. I figured I would have to do a little more blocking and tackling. Chatty here almost got them going."

"Clare, please," Yvonne said. She leaned into Frank. "She's gotta be the boss all the time. I wanted to give those people some good stuff about how kind and nice we are around here."

Frank smirked, and Clare feigned a loving tug on Yvonne. "Mom. I'll be right back. We're not staying."

Clare left her mother with a look that said, "don't wander," and then she walked into Martha's kitchen. Its yellow daisy wallpaper suddenly seemed garish for the circumstances. A mirror of Martha's florid personality, this childhood safe haven of Clare's and Derek's routinely spurred yummy reminders of hot summer afternoons at Martha's counter slurping up her hand-squeezed lemonade coolers and seemingly endless plates of homemade cookies with Derek and their grade-school buddies. She instinctively reached for the wall switch to dim the fluorescent glare in a room already awash in free-flowing natural lighting from the two bay windows.

"I should have got those lights Clare; good gosh, it's the middle of the day. It's been a morning hasn't it?" Martha Watkins was there in her matching daisy apron and fiery orange permed hair, fussing in the refrigerator. "I hope you'll join us for lunch," she said, and she placed a glass of iced tea for Clare on the table in front of a chair beside Derek.

"No, Mrs. Watkins, we just came for a minute. Mom wanted to see you guys—today of all days—but I've got to get back to work."

Martha waved a hand over a counter of neighborhood nibbles sent in light of their being pinned in. "We've got plenty, dear, if you change your mind." She gave Clare a forceful hug and went to join the chatter in the living room, returning just briefly to drop Yvonne's sack with the rest of the food. Then the two childhood friends were left alone.

Clare sat beside Derek in front of Martha's tea and immediately palmed his right hand.

"Hey . . . what can I do?" she asked. "This is crazy I know, but it'll die down in the next forty-eight hours or so. This is all about the Martins, not you . . . remember that."

He looked at her hands clutching his brawny knuckles and then gave her a brief bloodshot glance that was eerily empty.

"I've got so many images in my head that I can't get rid of," he said.

Only once could Clare remember this disturbing hollowness, and that was in the hospital several years back when Derek was waiting for the news following his father's heart attack. Derek usually had a knack for dusting himself off from life's calamities.

"I know you do, Derek," Clare said. "At least she's free from that . . . now." Her words seemed a small comfort.

Derek slipped his hand from her clasp. "Last night was awful," he said. "But I thought that it would become clearer today, that it would make some kind of sense, if that's possible. I figured the detectives would come and go and the people in front of my house would come and go. But I can't close my eyes without imagining her standing there in those shoes . . . " He waved over at a stack of newspapers on the kitchen table. "Dressed in her little outfit. The one that Coach was shaking around."

"If there is any bright spot . . . you found her clothes, you found something," Clare said. "At least there can be some answers, as horrible as that is. We have something now, Derek. Her dad, Russell, he can find some peace soon. I don't mean to sound callous, but the family has been at a standstill . . . we've all been waiting every day for anything, for any news that could put an end to this nightmare."

"I know. I've thought about all that. You're right . . . it just stinks!"

Derek hit the kitchen table hard. The chatter in the living room got quiet.

Clare whispered. "Look—you'll be picking up Coach soon. He's got to be missing you something terribly."

Talking about Coach was a better diversion than what she had been trying: smacking him around with needless jabbering about how he should feel wonderful in spite of the evidence of child murder that he had found. Derek breathed deeply, noticeably easing the taut muscles in his back.

"He's either scared or he's licking the crap out of the cops right now," he said.

Clare smiled. "I suspect the latter."

"Remember how he was when I first got him?"

"I do." Clare laughed quietly. "Nervous and shy and really, really smelly." She smiled again. "He's fine, Derek. No doubt they're being good to him; I'm sure of it. How about I meet you down at the station when you get him?"

"I can get the damn dog," Derek said.

His poorly delivered attempt at wit caught them both by surprise. They glared at each other for a second. Clare felt they were both on the brink of hysterical laughter. He massaged his face, as though he were tired of the whole mess.

"Okay . . . just asking," Clare said to bridge the moment. "Look, I wouldn't even be here if Yvonne hadn't had the urge to make you pumpkin cookies."

He smiled then, a little like the old Derek would, and Clare stood up. "This is tough, I know. But the best thing you can do, Derek, is get on with your life. Get back to work at Marwood's. I know there is a bunch of people out front, but they're harmless if you pretend they don't exist. And again—this is Russell and Courtney's issue, not a Derek concern," she counseled, regretting somewhat the motherly tone she was taking just after offering to help him get his dog. "You've got to let the Martins handle their own grief and heartache. With all the crap going on in that family, who knows how they'll end up?"

"It's not quite that simple," Derek reminded her softly, less on the brink than he had been moments ago. "And it doesn't matter what we all think of Russell and Courtney Martin. Could you imagine this happening to your daughter?"

"I can't . . . we can't," Clare concluded.

She knew Derek wasn't afraid so much as he was reticent. He didn't open up with strangers unless he was helping them in the hardware store, at which time visitors and vacationers had the small-town red-carpet service rolled out for them by a truly helpful handyman. Often people who stopped in for fishing supplies ended up buying tents, repellants, lanterns, and a host of outdoor amenities on Derek's recommendation. Derek's new customers hovered over the sales clerks while Mr. Marwood smiled gainfully from the registers. Derek just had that look of complete honesty and ruggedness all rolled into an unassuming large frame, and only with the occasional malcontent or transient thief did he exercise a show of strength. But he was very deliberate in the way he protected himself, and no doubt the whole idea that it was he who'd breached Courtney and Russell Martin's privacy was weighing on him.

"Go to work tomorrow, and just ignore all of them," Clare said. "They'll eventually fade away. The most important thing to do is to save all your discussions for the police and nobody else."

By "nobody else," she didn't mean herself, she thought, mindful of her earlier conversation with Jared. And she had a sinking feeling that she had noticed more than just Derek's misery last night.

Later, comforted by a Marlboro and a glass of wine, Clare huddled between the two tattered wicker chairs on her porch and absorbed the brisk, steadily declining temperatures. Since she'd returned to this city of blue-collar workers and subdivided farmland, this particular spot on the east side of her wrap-around porch had been her favorite. She sat and made a desperate attempt to unravel the hell out of the last twenty-four hours, including her lunch-hour trek, seemingly a lifetime ago, through the press line at the Watkins house. It was an almost seamless memory except for the ride back with Yvonne: her few chastising snips about Clare being so controlling, then her eager chirps about the compliments she'd received for her homemade eats. The meeting with Derek had depressed any inclination Clare might have felt to tussle with her mother's needless chatter, so instead she nodded and smiled.

Earlier after the Watkins visit and dropping Yvonne back at her house, Clare had managed to slip unobtrusively back into her office, avoiding the executive team altogether. She knew her staff would assess her mood and keep their distance, except maybe for LuAnn, whose inquisition Clare dreaded. Thankfully it never came. The afternoon dragged on pointlessly and unproductively, interrupted once by Jared's apologetic call to cancel dinner. She didn't emerge into the vacant, darkened lobby until 6:30 and nothing appealed to her more than going home to just crash.

Her TV was on but she sat outside to protect herself from the hysteria. The talking head feeding frenzy about Derek's discovery had reached its fever pitch. Sensationalized images of crime scene reenactment and unsubstantiated hoopla were seeping from her living room through the sound-muting double-paned windows. And though she could look away from the images through the window, Clare was helpless to turn off her own mental replay of Russell and Courtney Martin's recent statements before the discovery, which heaped even more resentment on top of the weeks of silent seething she and others had already done about the odd couple.

Even before Mary Martin had disappeared, Clare had brooded over the immeasurable damage she felt Mary's dysfunctional parents were inflicting on their daughter. In her short life, Mary had become the lightning rod for the couple's tormented relationship. Even the mild-mannered Russell had succumbed to their metaphorical war of the roses.

From the beginning, the match between Russell Martin and Courtney Richardson had promised torment and ambiguity for Courtney, the teenage snow queen, as well as bewilderment for citizens of Danfield. Certainly a bookie would have been writhing in ecstasy had he taken bets over whether the couple would ever say "I do."

The girl who'd been christened Courtney Juliet Richardson was cultured without regard to her surroundings. Her parents, Frances and Margaret, had justified their lifelong residency in the throes of a small town by gobbling up land from declining dairy farms and by developing a socially elite circle. Within their 10,000-square-foot mansion, which they had remodeled from an old schoolhouse, they built a cocoon for Courtney and her older brother Seth.

Clare remembered Courtney's contempt for their unsophisticated Danfield from early childhood, as well as the message she unyieldingly telegraphed to the world that she was destined for a big-city life. Courtney's carefully orchestrated life plan was to begin her reign in college, followed by a perfunctory stint in a big-city career that would ultimately culminate in a life as a big-city wife. But a crushing knee injury in her freshman year at Penn State sent her packing from the cheerleading squad. And though she was academically quite capable, she was emotionally unable to interact with anyone on campus without the crutch of her pom-poms, and so she returned and quietly completed her degree in

Madison. It was during this period that she had connected with Russell Martin.

In Courtney's mind, Russell was the poster child for everything she loathed and considered below her station in life; had they not connected, he'd more likely be the guy she would trust to clean her gutters rather than to father her children. Russell, Courtney's antithesis, was well skilled in carpentry but relatively primitive when it came to the finer things. Though he wasn't an A student he was considered capable and adept at animal husbandry because he grew up on the family farm. He'd talked of pursuing a veterinary degree, but after a couple of semesters at a local community college, Russell returned to building homes with a local contractor where he felt more comfortable.

Working with his hands, hunting season, and his Dodge pickup were to him the pinnacle of his desires. To Courtney, it was a nightmare. About the only thing they had in common was Mary, and even with her, each did his or her level best to protect Mary from the other's lifestyle.

Cheating on her occasional cigarette rule, Clare began dragging gingerly on her third. She set aside Mary's disappearance for a moment and grudgingly channeled her thoughts to the one small thing that she and Courtney had in common: their incomplete dream of ditching Danfield.

Three years ago, Clare, too, had returned after tasting two peaceful years attending Northwestern University in Chicago. Before that, she had gleefully left Danfield in the dust, driven by a lust for adventure and in pursuit of her long desire for a career in criminal justice. When Yvonne's medical issues brought Clare hobbling back to Danfield, it marked the disturbing possibility that she might not succeed in expanding her horizons, and that she had added three more unsettling years to her life. However filled with some successes those years had been—her career, the house she'd fixed up—she was still troubled by thoughts that this might be it.

Since then—sometimes prompted by the critiques of lifelong friends—she had struggled to define the initial impetus for her leaving. The fine line between adventure and resentment was as blurry as the innumerable excuses to ditch everything familiar for something that had no discernible connection to her past.

Then there was Chief Jared Grady. She blinked in the smoky haze of her cigarette; her heart was yet another matter. She acknowledged the spontaneous and mutual appeal they'd had for one another from the moment they'd met at his first town assembly, but that was as far as she had thought it might go. But it didn't take long, and over the past year, with him in his new job and her with one foot always out the door, they had slowly moved the romantic needle through coffees and dinners and wine at each other's houses. Clare was pleased with their slow-moving progress on many levels. Now, Jared was reaching out for more. Oddly, it triggered all her age-old fears about settling in Danfield.

Deluged with unwarranted guilt, she gathered the empty wine glass and her ashtray to call it a night. But as she was hanging her coat and scarf in the entryway closet, the opening segment of the 10:00 news that replayed an earlier press conference by Courtney and Russell Martin teased her. She'd missed it during her late evening at her office. Clare raised her hand multiple times to turn off the TV but she didn't. She couldn't.

As she looked on, it wasn't Russell's ill-at-ease demeanor at the podium or the fact that neither he nor Courtney appeared uncomfortable within twenty feet of each other that got her attention. What kept Clare hanging longer than she'd planned was the finality of their tone. They didn't come right out and say that they were folding the tent on the investigation. But Clare felt it. On one hand, they meekly pleaded for clues as to what happened to their daughter, on the other hand, they asked for prayers and offered thanks for all the support, saying they needed to put their daughter to rest.

Here Clare was thinking that Derek's discovery meant that they were headed toward the truth, and this stonefaced twosome gave a statement that indicated otherwise.

She turned the TV off this time and made the turn up the stairwell, fighting the urge for another cigarette, and making it all the way up to the landing.

FOUR

With a perfect grip on his .45-caliber Glock—standard issue police handgun—Jared permitted only infinitesimal flinches to his Heckler and Koch stance, flinches undetectable to untrained citizen eyes. He had obliterated the head and heart of his target, drawing the measured attention of Clare and the other officers on the range. In a characteristic show of flawlessness, he emptied and reloaded his third magazine in one seamless motion.

Jared could routinely be found here, preferably on the outdoor range when the weather permitted, fine-tuning his razor-sharp abilities on Saturday mornings. Today, Clare felt he was more intense than usual. The flickering ring of empty shell casings gathered at his feet was evidence that the sleepy villa of Danfield had raised the stakes for Police Chief Grady.

Though law enforcement matters in general intrigued Clare, it wasn't until Jared's arrival in Danfield that she had begun to turn a more judicious eye to the salacious headlines of crime reports in the newspaper. Jared had a quality that Clare now viewed as passion. In the eyes of others, it could look like an exhibition of superiority. Whether it was his unparalleled weapons expertise, the thoroughness of his defense and arrest training, or his super fit, well-proportioned body, Jared projected a bravado seldom found in worlds like Danfield.

Gnawing just beneath the surface, she knew, were memories of his former turbulent days commanding the operations, training, and patrol division of the Milwaukee Police Department. Initially admired for his ability to run a tight ship, Jared's cold, military-like methods of supervising his department earned him little praise with liberal politicians. He remained unwavering about the benefits of adhering to one standard of law and order, and he operated on the principle that the first order of business would be cracking down on crime with a heavy hand. The press chided him for his heartlessness with such fervor that his rehabilitation programs usually fell inadequately to the back pages. This, plus his uncompromising personality—especially when it came to matters that he perceived were driven by political correctness rather than by good police work—eventually cost him hierarchical support. The morale among his officers disintegrated, which his supporters attributed to fickle department heads not backing him up in the cleanup job they'd hired him to do.

Amid the political fervor and the rumors of demotion floating around the Milwaukee force, Jared was unknowingly earning brownie points from an unsophisticated neighboring Wisconsin town, where the bereaved city mayor and town council seemed hell-bent on revitalizing their lackluster police force. Danfield city officials were still reeling from the death of an officer at a local gas and food mart during a robbery shoot-out; a lack of adherence to real police procedure and sloppy investigative work had left them unable to catch the perpetrator, let alone develop even the tiniest of trails. The episode became the catalyst to totally revamp a department that hadn't seen a serious update in nearly forty years.

Thus another community's media nightmare provided the golden opportunity for Mayor Bernard Kohlhepp, who personally drove to Milwaukee to work out a deal, almost as if it were a professional sports trade. And thus Jared was sidetracked from his preordained candidacy as the next Milwaukee police chief to a posting in Danfield.

Clare waited by some benches near the firearms building until he left the range. He seemed relieved to see her.

"How long have you been standing here?" he asked and gently stroked her left arm.

"Long enough to think you need to step away from it a little bit."

"Just keeping my edge is all. Have to! It'll be a while before I'll see the light of day on this case."

He didn't even have to say the word Martin; Clare knew it was the only law enforcement game in town. She couldn't help but wonder how much of this was just a rerun of all the other gruesome cases he had dealt with in the past.

"I thought things would be wrapping up," Clare remarked, prying shamelessly.

"Just all rolled up in one tidy little ball, one would think, right, Clare?" he chuckled, still obviously tense.

"Just an interested citizen running through the news head-lines," she said. "There was enough hair and blood at the scene to indicate that she couldn't still be alive. According to the papers, all the suspects have evaporated, indicating a freak accident. Possibly she wandered off, and a wild animal got to her . . . " She got quiet with regret.

Further tidying his gear, Jared said nothing, and Clare accepted his silence. She studied him cautiously. After newspaper report-ers salivating to unearth familial connections to Mary's disap-pearance for weeks, Clare could not altogether reconcile herself to the notion that the parents—especially Courtney—could be altogether blameless. It had been five days now since Derek's find, and the whisperings of the community in the last few days hadn't lessened her reservations about Mary's mother. She had yet to really feel out Jared's take on the Martin relationship. He had been remarkably tight lipped on the smattering of sensational theories being bantered about in the press. The journalists' inter-est in Russell and Courtney had noticeably waned since the dis-covery of the scene at the creek. But Jared clearly wasn't acting as though he were merely going through the motions of confirming the inevitable.

"How about a cup of coffee?" Jared asked. "I just need a min-ute to clean up. Then we can discuss our make-up dinner plans for tonight."

Clare felt a bit patronized by the way he'd deflected even the most minuscule inquisition about Mary Martin. "That's awfully presumptuous, Chief Grady," she jabbed.

"Whatever it is, cancel it," Jared said. He gathered his weaponry and began walking.

"You're in luck," she said, pivoting in the opposite direction toward the parking lot. "I have an opening on my calendar. Got to skip coffee, though, so I'm putting myself in your hands for this evening's agenda. I've got a few Saturday errands and a quick stop at your station to sneak a peek while Derek picks up Coach."

Jared's facial expression abruptly sobered again. He turned back and took her elbow and guided her to another nearby bench closer to the exit, out of earshot of the other officers.

"The dog is fine," Jared said, tense again. "Derek will be fine."

"I know, Jared," she said, dismissing his attempt to take charge. "You know I'm just trying to be a good friend, is all. It's been a pretty crappy week for the guy, you have to admit."

He paused as though he realized he'd stepped out of bounds. "Just as long as he doesn't have to come to dinner with us tonight," he said.

"Who?" Clare asked. "Derek or Coach?" She got up to leave.

"You know, I've wanted to try Steven Wade's Café in Waukesha," he said, standing up as well. "Wear something a little dressy."

It was the push-and-pull moments between them and the slow burn in her gut that made her glance back to watch his confident march to the firearms building.

Amid the hoopla about Jared, the outsider with the braggadocio mannerisms, her attraction to him was still hard for her to define, though curiously intoxicating in these instances. A humming undercurrent about his chiseled good looks had fostered his reputation as arrogant and unapproachable with the townspeople, making him initially impossible for Clare to ignore, even if he hadn't tried to date her. But in spite of the tickle in the back of her mind, she had to give Jared credit for the peace and unity his no-nonsense approach to law enforcement had brought to the town of Danfield. That alone had earned him enough points to keep the mayor in an eternal good mood, the naysayers hovering at some distance from mainstream opinion, and Clare hanging around for one of his great kisses.

The leaves had fallen except for a meager handful that would cling steadfast until the first significant snow of the season yanked them down to join their fellows in slowly turning to winter compost. Though the shocking reds were less vibrant and the metallic yellows were losing their translucence, the loose, dry foliage still crisply tickled the pavement, sounding like hundreds of abandoned potato chips as she walked through them. The air's autumn bouquet drew Clare into a moment of joy. With each of her steps, the knee-high ground cover crumpled and sprang, not yet ready to disintegrate, as she headed for one of her routine holistic hikes though the wooded paths around Lake Waushara.

Content to be far from the nagging phone messages her mother had left for her while she was on the range watching Jared, she reflected on the reunion of Derek and Coach earlier. She'd caught up with Derek at his house after he'd returned from the station. He was scrubbing Coach generously in a large washtub in the backyard, and Clare had smiled, seeing the classic, unspoken mutual fondness that men often reserved for their dogs.

"Take it easy, Derek," she said. "It might be easier to just shave him."

"Naw, he loves this," Derek said. "We do this every now and then, don't we, bud?" He turned to Clare. "You disappeared at the station, but you weren't supposed to be there, we agreed," he said.

"Yeah, everybody looked a bit busy handing over Coach. You didn't need me hovering around. I just stopped for a peek."

"You'd have thought I was posting bail or something. Pretty crazy stuff just to pick up a dog."

He took to rinsing the suds with a Herculean grip on Coach's collar.

"I'll bet they're all over you about everything," she said gingerly. "Still interviewing you about stuff?"

Derek released Coach and started to back away, as did she, but neither of them were fast enough to avoid being peppered with the spray of his shaking.

"Hey!" Derek hollered. "Git!" Derek shooed him to run about the yard and began to busy himself with cleaning up the bathing area. "Not too much is happening," he said. "We've gone over the details a few times." He turned the washtub over to lean it against the tree and gathered rags and soap. "It's all just formalities at this point."

"Really? You'd think we'd be getting a more formal statement from the authorities, then, instead of this informal wrap up according to the papers. Did you see Russell and Courtney at the news conference?"

Derek stalled just long enough. "You know the chief. I suppose you've got the inside track."

Clare flinched a bit.

"Sorry," she said. "I don't want to revisit everything you've been through this week. Yvonne's been filling me in from her talks with your Mom. I figured you didn't need two of us poking at you."

"No, I'm sorry, Clare. I'm not lashing out at you. I just think we should be done with this."

"You don't really think I'm privy to police business, do you?" Clare asked.

"That was a dumb comment. Forget I said anything. Okay?"

Derek hugged her particularly firmly. When he let go, his tense facial expression had eased considerably.

"What would we do without Jared right now?" he had asked.

Now, entering the woods, Clare tugged the collar of her pullover around her neck against the wind and swirling leaves. She navigated a couple of fallen logs while realizing her relief that Derek's crisis might be winding down. She was still slightly agitated by his dispirited poke at her romantic link to Jared, as though that entitled her to know classified police business. He'd teased her mercilessly in recent weeks about her being a mole at the station, but playfully, and in a manner meant to show his approval of her dating again. After having been at her side for the twists and turns of her turbulent breakup with her high-school sweetheart so many years ago and her vow to not date anybody else in Danfield, Derek was hopeful she was accepting their small town. But now both guys were at it—just hours ago, Jared had hinted that her friendship with Derek should be relegated to an occasional hello on the sidewalk.

She stopped beside a log and stretched before picking up the pace, making an attempt to forget the two of them wrangling about her relationship with the other. Her attempt failed, and instead she stopped after just five minutes because of a cramp, feeling wheezy and winded from the run. Mountain bikers roared by on the trail unannounced, startling her; she skipped and then tripped into the ground cover.

Before she could yell at them or hear whether they had apologized, a couple of hikers called to her from an upper ledge: "Are you all right?"

"I'm fine," Clare said, waving them on.

She sat on a nearby stump, nearly in tears.

Unlike Jared, Clare knew the rules of small towns, though she struggled with her own demons when it came to total acceptance of them. On the bright side, her neighbors lived steeped in their decades of traditions, and they were commonly as nice as the hikers had been a minute ago. Except for the few Richardsons of the world, life in Danfield was a utopia. But it was the unwillingness of the people in Clare's little world to accept change or to explore the universe beyond their boundaries that had fed her appetite for something more than the simple life.

She remembered irritably that many of her childhood friends never saw the allure of an away football game or a class trip to the city for a cultural event; to them, these things were nothing more than an opportunity for a pre-pubescent dalliance. Bullet Broadmor threw eighty-yard passes as a freshman and rushed for more yardage as a quarterback than all the running backs put together in the first half of his sophomore year, yet his biggest dream was to take over his father's local real estate business. The college scouts went crazy with his shortsightedness while Clare did her own amount of rallying to get him to look at the bigger picture. But he insisted that he had the entire big picture he needed right here in Danfield.

Despite the dazzling landscape, fall always drew Clare into bittersweet reflections about the frailties of life and her ongoing tug-of-war with wanting to escape her country boundaries. She hungered for the natural talent and the opportunities that were bestowed on the likes of Bullet Broadmor. Instead, now she was always lying in the wake of her own lost dream, where her mother's cries for help were the lightning that had struck and brought her back to Danfield.

What if she had resisted her mother's irrational pleas about being abandoned during a time of failing health? Had Clare not succumbed, surely Yvonne's telephone tantrums would have subsided. In retrospect, her discovery that her mother's illness was largely mythical still ranked high in her roster of life's letdowns. But a greater letdown still—the outgrowth of that pivotal moment of her return—was how she had become immobilized, unable to pack her things up again or plead for mercy with the University for reinstatement. Her fear of returning had become a ghost bigger than living in Danfield.

Clare realized suddenly that while running, she had veered a considerable distance off the path she had chosen, which would normally wind back to the parking area. Gathering her breath, she leaned over to brace her knees and get her bearings. Quickly she honed in on a mile marker on a rustic log bench and a wooden post displaying multiple arrow signs. The first of these led to one of Derek's fishing spots, and another led to a pool created by the eddy of a creek where she and bunches of her friends had come to swim as kids. With a brief shiver, she realized how close she was to the Mary Martin crime scene. Mindful that she had forgotten the law enforcement warnings about hiking in pairs—particularly after Mary's disappearance—Clare scanned the wooded area. Nothing unusual.

Staying more observant than she had been, she picked the arrow that led her up to a forestry access road. She no longer felt her sense of private aloneness, or the bitterness she had been reflecting on when thinking about leaving school to return to Danfield. Moments ago, she had heard nothing because of her funk, and now suddenly the crackling leaves and the sounds of wild animals scavenging for the winter seemed magnified.

The natural chatter nearly distracted her completely until she stumbled upon the police barricades that blocked the untraveled slope near the path to the creek.

She spent little time rationalizing her next move, in spite of her uneasiness. She slid by the barriers and moved quickly down the slope, as if speed were synonymous with avoiding detection. She navigated the rugged, wooded terrain, moving through the dense pines, until a seven-foot rock ledge brought her to a halt.

Although she knew what it meant to secure the perimeter of a crime scene, she wasn't prepared for the mind-numbing effect of seeing the police tape hanging tree-to-tree. Her chest tightened like the sensations she'd heard Derek talk about. She looked around quickly, picking out the markers and surrealistically relived Derek's depiction of the blood pool, the location of Mary's clothing, and the rock where they had found her shoes.

She felt as though she was trampling over a religious shrine, and she slumped to her knees, overcome. But no sooner had she gripped her face in her hands than she jerked: there was a snapping sound, maybe footsteps. Real or imagined, she was at once aware of the darkening sky and the dropping temperatures, and then she became riddled with the chilling sensation that she was not alone.

The coming snowfall and the deepening shadows played on her paranoia enough to allow her to pry herself from her squatting position and to bolt back up the slope to the path, crossing the barricade again. Without stopping, she began to sprint the longer but more visible path back to her Jeep.

FIVE

Clare breezed unannounced through Yvonne's back door. She had yet to fully catch her breath; her adrenaline was still pulsing from her discovery and her escape from the woods. Yvonne and her childhood friend Vivian Fox were talking in the kitchen.

"For heaven's sake, Clare, don't you return your mother's phone calls anymore?" Yvonne, Clare knew, was eternally exasperated that her daughter was not always available at the drop of a hat.

"Hello Vivian," Clare said, tossing her purse and keys on the kitchen counter and then reaching out to Vivian for a hug.

"You see how much nicer she is to the company, Viv?" Yvonne intervened, trying to hand Vivian a cup of coffee between them; Clare ignored her and her needling comment.

"How's Carl?" she asked her mother's friend. "I hear he might make a run for city council?"

"He's been threatening for so long," Vivian said. "I think he just might go through with it."

"I'll be right there at the Fox campaign central when he's ready," Clare said gesturing.

"Carl would just love that!"

There were travel brochures on the table. "What's all this?" Clare asked, shuffling through a few of them.

"Your mother and I were daydreaming about going on a cruise," Vivian said. "Just the ladies, you know."

"You should do it—take a break from this place."

"You are certainly welcome to join us, if we ever really get brave enough," Vivian said and then spewed her famous laughter. Clare carried a fondness for Vivian that stemmed from the occasional sleepovers she had spent at the Fox house when she was a preschooler, as well as Vivian's magical appearances in the Paxton home and the milk-and-cookies moments Clare spent on Vivian's lap on the front steps. Forever a country girl, Vivian was the same age as Yvonne, but much less worn down. Clare always attributed Vivian's youthful appearance to her gleeful personality. Even after she and her husband Carl lost their four-year-old daughter to a rare form of leukemia, the two were remarkably comforting to others. The Fox family hadn't the heart to have more children themselves, and instead they played surrogate parents to their friends' children.

"Seriously, I think this is a great idea. I'll stay home," Clare suggested. "Carl and I will look after each other while you ladies are off sailing the high seas."

Yvonne inserted herself in the middle of their conversation again, this time to swoop up the papers and travel literature. "Clare, she's just kidding, you know. It's not all that serious."

"It should be, Mother."

"Where were you all morning anyway? You never answered my question."

"Do I need to?" Clare responded with much restraint.

"Clare . . . hey, the two of you," Vivian nicely intervened.

"I was hiking," Clare said. "Out getting fresh air and exercise, that's all. I'm here! What is so important, Mother, that it couldn't wait until now?"

Yvonne hurled a look of self-pity at Clare.

"I thought you might want to go to the grocery with me. Jewel Market is having a meat sale, and some of the Christmas paper is out now. Then you can stay for dinner," Yvonne added sheepishly.

More discomforted about having mentioned the hike than about Yvonne's lame excuse—why worry about Christmas paper when they hadn't yet thought about Thanksgiving?—Clare grabbed a Pepsi from the cases of soda in the laundry room and headed back to the kitchen for a glass. She tossed in the ice and tried to distract herself with the pouring and fizzing, the police scene at the creek still quite raw in her mind.

"Hey, Clare!" Vivian tipped up Clare's can to stop the overflow.

"Sorry," Clare said. "I got it." She grabbed a dishrag before the soda could flood over the edge of the counter.

"You look kind of flushed, sweetie. You feeling okay?" In a feeble attempt to play mother, Yvonne brushed the back of her hand against Clare's forehead.

Still reeling, Clare gave her hand a controlled push feeling it was more show for Vivian. She didn't have the strength now for this conversation.

"I'm not sick. I just stopped by to tell you not to plan on me for dinner."

"Now, honey—you have to stay. We're having something good tonight. I'm making bratwurst and mashed potatoes. I'll make you a nice little salad, the way you like."

A conciliatory tone didn't become Yvonne. Her mother made few food dishes the way she liked anymore, but Clare said nothing about the menu.

"Do we have to do this every time?" she began, but then she held up her hand for a chance to start over. "Mom, I have plans tonight, that's all. You like to sit here with your Saturday night television. I'd like to get out for no reason." She braced for the next comment.

"It's Jared, isn't it?" Yvonne asked.

Clare took another sip of the cool fizz first. "What does that mean?"

"You've got nice young hometown men like Parker Houghton around. That big-shot police boy is nothing but a showboat."

"Parker? What does Parker have to do with anything? That's high-school history." She paused to get her breath. "Vivian, are you following this logic?"

"You two are wearing me out," Vivian said. She began to gather her things.

"Vivian, don't go," Clare said. "I'm leaving. I'm sorry for chasing you away."

"Actually, Carl and I are going over to the Menomonee Harvest festival this afternoon," Vivian said and smiled.

Clare and Yvonne followed her to the door and waved her off at the front steps. At any other time, Clare might have welcomed the chance for a long overdue visit about her relationship with Jared. But after what she had just seen at the park, she didn't think she could handle it.

"Mother, it's just dinner," she said. "And if we want to make more of it, I'd like you to not make a big deal about it. We should listen to Viv. We don't have to go around and around about it. Most mothers would be glad that their single daughter has a date."

"He's trouble, that's all," Yvonne said, unrelenting.

"What he is, is a great police chief who's brought some much needed structure to our little Podunk police department! I'm happy to be making friends with him."

Clare thought silently for a civil period of time. Then, before Yvonne could speak, she said, "Mom, I have to go. I'll see you tomorrow for Sunday supper at one."

"Maybe I'll be here," Yvonne chirped.

She'd be there, Clare knew. She'd be there because she owed Clare for all the heartache she had caused her otherwise. Aside from their lifelong knocking of each other, Yvonne couldn't risk provoking her daughter to the point that she'd leave town again, and Clare knew it. So she clung to her worn, longstanding threat to bolt again, now prickled with curiosity as to whether Jared could be a factor in that decision.

Except for the lackluster terrain of Greenfield Avenue, the ambiance of Steven Wade's Café seemed cities away from the smallville flavor of Danfield. The quiet, petite surroundings, white table-cloths adorned with crystal vases, and fresh cut flowers were far more elegant than the dinner-wear options in Clare's closet.

Although she was still keenly aware of people who were more accustomed to the finer things in life, Clare had grown less intim-idated about experiences that brought her small-town girl self into contact with a pricier lifestyle. But her dalliances with sophisti-cation occasionally triggered memories of people like Courtney Richardson's family who drew clear lines between themselves and those who lacked in worldly possessions.

She'd dressed comfortably in a silk blouse and a calf-length wool skirt. Blessed with an abundant supply of healthy, wavy auburn locks, she'd grown self-conscious at times about admir-ers. Earlier at home, she had questioned the fashion value of her homemade updo. But now, reassured by Jared's adoring presence, she was feeling a sense of ease. Her tug-of-war with her upbringing was forever simmering below the surface, though, and as pretty as he could make her feel, Clare held back her natural inclination to remind him she'd be just as happy next to him at a ball game.

"This is a little over the top for a civil servant, even if he's the chief," Clare said, eyeing the menu without recrimination.

"You'd agree it's very difficult to spend my hard-earned civil ser-vant pay in Danfield, so I've been saving my pennies quite handily."

Squeezing a bit of lemon into his water glass, Jared disarmed her simply with his sturdy grin. They paused to accept their cocktails.

"We're certainly not at the Softee," Clare said, referencing their soft-serve ice cream and hamburger spot. "Not a single price on this menu."

"Never you mind about the expense; just enjoy. I thought you deserved a break from simple," he said, and then he leaned gracefully over the table and began to whisper. "And if at any time, I see you reaching into that lovely little handbag for anything remotely resembling currency, I'll have you arrested for bribing an officer of the law. By the way, you look gorgeous."

For whatever reason, his little displays of dry wit had been lost on others in town. Clare had found them quite alluring.

"Thank you," she said. "Apparently you think I'd mind being arrested."

Further fueled by the cocktails, their expressions flushed with an undeniable chemistry, and Clare was awkwardly aware of the developing sizzle.

"You spend all your money, then," she continued, to disrupt the tension. "I only brought enough to hail a cab anyway."

"What's with the cab money? How much better off could you be on a date than with a cop?"

"Even if he's a wise guy?"

"Wise guy or not, I know I'm in the company of a smart, beautiful woman," he said. "I look at you and I see the good in our little town."

"Our little town? Me—the good?" she said. "I'm not quite considered the epitome of our fair city. In any event, be careful . . . you just might find yourself liking it in spite of me. No traffic jams, homemade cookies that don't come from a grocery store shelf, kids who can grow up without all the worrying . . ." She shuddered before she could complete her thought.

"Clare?"

Her frothing emotions cooled to a simmer and her enjoyment of Jared's rugged good looks evaporated; she couldn't shake the ugly feelings from her mind. The frightening realities of urban life had crept into rural America with their cop shooting and now with the Mary Martin incident.

"Anyway, the pressures of life just aren't the same," she finished.

"Don't let me be responsible for those beautiful green eyes turning brown," Jared responded. "No serious stuff, okay? What's happening?"

Clare tried to recover. "Sorry," she said. "Just making an observation about the good stuff, is all."

"It's important to protect all that, isn't it?" Jared said, calmly. "All the more reason to have a well-run police department."

She could tell he was getting ready to say more.

"Speaking of which . . . you visited the crime scene today," he said. "I'd hoped to save that bit of news for another day."

He softly pulled her into his determined stare. She was speechless, unable to defend herself.

"For obvious reasons, we watch that area quite regularly," Jared said.

"The officer should have identified himself. He scared the hell out of me," Clare said, nervously raising her voice.

Jared appeared hurt by the shift in her demeanor. He took her hands as if to console her.

"Let's not do this tonight. Wrong place, wrong time," he said. "You're not in trouble. Except—you do know that it's a crime scene?"

Clare knew full well that he should have reprimanded her.

"You never answered my question this morning about continuing the investigation," she proceeded boldly. "At the press conference last night, the Martins made it sound like the case was nearing closure. You know . . . all that stuff about wanting to put their little girl to rest. They made it sound like they were all but waiting for a death certificate. And obviously you're still watching the area."

"Clare, it was very possibly an accident, an animal, or any number of mishaps, to quote the news accounts," he said, resigned. "But you know I can't say anything more because we are just not done yet. Tonight, I want to put all that aside and just have a nice quiet time together. After all this time, I don't even know what your favorite color is."

She ignored his attempt to change the subject. "That little girl didn't deserve any of this. And Danfield is one of the safest places to raise children because we don't get too many strangers running around here. So to my mind, it's scary that—if it turns out not to be an animal—the finger can be pointed pretty close to home."

They both knew she wanted to cast a harsher light on Courtney, if for no other reason than that Mary had been in her care at the time of her disappearance. Jared obviously didn't care to do that over a cup of coffee, let alone on their date. She looked for something in his quiet and justifiably unresponsive expression.

"Forget this case for a moment, isn't that statistically what happens?" Clare needed to satisfy her craving. "Family members are more likely to have caused harm to their children than a stranger? My God."

"Sometimes bad things just happen to good people," he spoke with authority "And when it happens to small children, it's so much more incomprehensible. And it's much more difficult to imagine healing that kind of a wound without having a neck to hang a noose around . . . don't I know that."

"Mary . . . she was a human tug rope between those two," Clare emphasized.

Before he could squeeze her hand tighter, she pulled free of his beautiful palms, though not without regrets. It would break her heart if she was hearing that he was just letting the idea of catching Mary's killer go.

"This is not great dinner conversation," she said. "Sorry."

"Courtney is nothing but an oversexed trust-fund baby who I think hates this small town worse than I've given the impression that I do, and worse than you do, for that matter. But I don't think we just box her up as a killer." He paused; he must not have wanted to make too many definitive statements. "Look at her parents," he continued. "Don't you think they would have done something if they thought she was capable of doing harm to Mary? Beneath all the money, however uppity, I think they are good people. Regardless of whatever they thought of Russell, Mary was their precious little grandchild."

"I've read many stories about people snapping," Clare said. "You've told me some of those stories."

She knew he had given her leeway that he wouldn't give anyone else, so she left it at that. His demeanor softened, and an iceberg melted beneath the lure of his sparkling eyes.

"Can it just be us tonight?" he whispered.

As if on cue, the waiter brought the wine and presented the label. Jared nodded. They waited in silence for the cork to be meticulously removed, for the wine to tumble lusciously into the wine glass, and for Jared's taste and nod of approval.

"Give us another minute," he said, putting the waiter at bay for the dinner order.

Clare weakened for the sake of the evening. "You're right about everything you said, and my interjecting tonight was not fair," she said. "But when is it a good time to get justice for Mary?"

She accepted his hand as the final gesture to end this discussion for the evening.

SIX

"You probably don't want to come in here," said Tom Pollenski, Clare's branch manager, who was leaning just inside the doorway of the meeting room prepared for Mr. Graber's monthly management huddle.

Tom managed some of the branch and operations personnel in Clare's chain of command. These people had apparently found their way to the sweets in the boardroom, where they hadn't been invited, but it was more than the brief invasion by the nonexecutive personnel that troubled Clare.

"What is this?" Clare asked, taken aback by the erratic chattering of her management peers from inside the conference room. "These guys are never here before me."

"I'm getting my guys out of the way here in just a second."

Tom said apologetically. "They just love it when LuAnn brings extra goodies."

"I don't mind them grabbing a few donuts, but the professional team . . ." Clare couldn't finish her comment in front of Tom.

Except for the coffee and donuts, which LuAnn had dropped off early, Clare had claimed responsibility for the business side of the meeting-room preparation. The emotional gyrations of the executive team and the invading staff during today's grab for coffee and donuts was as immediate a dismembering of their schedule as Clare had ever seen, fraught with patchy comments about Mary Martin and the community steeple and bell tower battle cropping up to plague their sleepy community psyche. She left the subtle queries aimed with Clare's personal friendships in mind largely unanswered, to protect Derek's privacy.

Clare saw her boss Lee's exasperated nods to her to reclaim the management team's territory, and she began to shoo the uninvited staff members back to work.

"Let's go, people," Tom motioned to his staff.

Clare caught Tom as he exited.

"I've never seen the managers this fired up before," she said.

"You know it's pretty crazy when Edmond stoops to chit-chatting with the teller staff," Tom agreed.

Already filtering through what had ended a delightful Saturday evening with Jared and a cautious yet uncontested Sunday dinner with Yvonne, Clare was as ill equipped for the emotional uneasiness as the rest of them. Learning about Mary's death after weeks of speculation as to her whereabouts had obviously not yet been properly absorbed by the bank staff, even given the whole week that had passed since Derek's discovery. As evidenced by the handful of yesterday's opinion columns strewn across the conference table, it appeared that the Sunday commentary on the situation had hit a nerve. In spite of her feeling standoffish, she was quietly buoyed by the idea that people still found something about the case worthy of debating. Mary's home life had some disquieting aspects that had for a long time been a nagging concern of Clare's, and so far she had failed to extract Jared's true analysis of that situation.

Lee Graber cleared his throat to signal some order to his team; then he launched into some semblance of his routine opening installment. Once the meeting itself began, he was peculiarly reticent, except for the tap of his pencil eraser on the boardroom table.

"Lee? Do you need me anymore?" Edmond asked. "Looks like the troops have gone haywire this morning, and I've got a ton of things to do today."

Lee Graber stared right through Edmond. Clare fingered the folder that contained her well-documented proposal involving the latest options in teller and platform systems. She deemed Edmond's request to be an attempt to escape hearing her presentation this morning. She had been formally delegated the responsibility of championing a technology upgrade for the bank, and she had yet to get Edmond's buy-in to spend the money. For a long time she'd advocated for intra-department integration and automation, but she had continually waged an uphill battle: her push for progress was a serious threat to an old-fashioned mindset that Clare despaired of curing. As was the case with many small, independent financial institutions, squeezing out the very last penny of profit was less important than flipping the switch at five or having a television and coloring books in the lobby for the children. While customers were pacified by these trivial benefits, Clare pegged them as symbolic of the mediocre mentality. To the old-fashioned mindset, archaic was somehow synonymous with mom and apple pie.

And so Clare looked over at Edmond for some logic behind his refusal to accept the upgrade that stemmed from something other than his inflated sense of self. As the chief financial officer, given his ranting about getting formidable returns for the shareholder and their pension funds, Clare was dumbfounded that he couldn't embrace modernization that might improve their profit margin in the long run.

"Clare, you're awfully quiet about this article that's gotten everyone shaken up," Edmond said, further infuriating her with his sarcasm about the town's collective trauma.

"What else is there to say?" she replied. "It's a mystery yet."

"Really—you're the mole here," Edmond smirked. "You have to know something the rest of us don't. The police department certainly isn't offering anything substantive in their press conferences."

Clare let Edmond's inference about a particular police chief go unchallenged and the meeting moved forward while she covertly disparaged her associates around the conference room. On any other Monday, there might have been modest rumblings, but they would have been guided by a principal agenda at Lee's insistence. He'd inevitably pull them to consensus amid the personality rubble. Instead, today, he was allowing them to flounder while he picked randomly through their agenda, saving Clare's piece for last.

Except for Christmas parties and summer picnics, Clare really hadn't developed deep personal ties with anyone besides Lee. Of her three male counterparts, Edmond Dutch—chief financial officer extraordinaire, as she referred to him—held a record in her mind as the most exasperating. He would give her moments, much like Yvonne, where she felt like she had a piece of tin foil stuck between her teeth. His penchant for opposition seemed purely driven by his unsubstantiated hypothesis that he had a higher IQ. Today was no different. As usual, Edmond picked his moments to sound stately before the audience of his own ego. John McNeil, who headed corporate sales, and Stuart Heyman, director of marketing, had beaten each other silly with guilt about Mary, but now seemed to have found solace in the sprinkle vs. chocolate donut discussion.

At last, Lee nodded to her to proceed with her presentation. Her eagerness to give the proposal about upgrading the bank's systems abated, she halfheartedly walked them through the bits and pieces while intermittently monitoring Lee's prayer-like expression and then his movement around the room during her presentation. He had ditched any semblance of his preferred dictatorial style.

"Thanks, Clare," he said, acknowledging her conclusion. He stood at the conference room window jingling his pocket change.

"Good day everyone," he said at last, dismissing them without so much as a concluding remark.

The team began to file out of the conference room with quizzical looks, and she began to go with them. "Clare, do you have a minute?" Lee asked.

"Certainly," she said.

She walked with him to his office in silence, stopping at LuAnn's desk to pick up messages. LuAnn tugged at Clare's sleeve as she passed. "He's not doing so well this morning."

"I can see that," Clare acknowledged. "I guess he's troubled about the Mary Martin thing? I don't know. Is there something else?"

"Not that I know of. Just take it easy is all. I'll get things straightened out," LuAnn said, speaking with authority.

Clare let it go when it came to these remarks; LuAnn's belief that she was the only one capable of diplomacy when it came to Lee.

Lee motioned to Clare to close the door.

"Good work on the project," he said. "But I suppose I should have kicked this week's agenda and called a special session."

"Not a problem," Clare affirmed. "Everybody was so distracted. I even felt cautiously optimistic that we could sneak in a consensus."

With a reluctant grin, Lee acknowledged that his managers sometimes tussled as if they controlled the International Monetary Fund instead of free toasters and holiday open houses.

"Sorry that I wasn't around much last week," he said. "I know you carried quite a burden. That dental stuff threw me for a loop, and then with all the bank's board activities, I just got swamped. Sometimes life just bites you in the ol' butt," he said, with a breathy emptying of his lungs. "Just when you think it couldn't get better . . . there's always something that brings you back down, isn't there? We have such precious little time on this earth."

"It has been an awful week, and there've been all these goings on about Mary, I agree," Clare said quietly.

Lee shuffled a few papers and then changed the subject, querying Clare with his superfluous thoughts about her earlier presentation. As tough as Lee was regarding business concerns, Clare was his occasional confidant on private matters, apart from the rumors about LuAnn. Clare could feel his implicit trust. He had mentored her through a banking career that had begun with her high-school internship in bookkeeping. Even without a degree, she had still risen to the rank of COO and cashier, and he had given her the responsibility of managing all the bank operations. Lee used her as a sounding board on more critical bank matters, even though he could aggravate her when he dug in his heels on age-old viewpoints. He and his wife had never had any children, and Clare sometimes wondered if she had offered them each a proxy familial lifeline. Without saying as much, she knew Lee was happy about her return to Danfield, even if it meant that she'd abandoned her pursuit of higher education and her love of criminal psychology.

Today, however, Lee's directionless discourse and doodling had squandered away another half hour. Clare snuck a peek at her watch when an intercom buzzed and LuAnn's squawking startled them both. Relieved by an awaiting appointment, Clare eagerly exited the stale atmosphere of Lee's office and veered straight for the rear exit and some fresh air.

Clare stood with a box of leftover donuts from the meeting, teetering at the garage entrance to Del's Auto Body—aptly named in memory of Parker Houghton's father—and admiring her high-school sweetheart from behind. In many ways, Parker still had the capacity to take her breath away. With his youthful physique, from her vantage point, she concluded that a stranger could have mistaken him for a lean twenty-year-old.

Seeing her in the doorway, Parker's employee Bart jerked himself out from beneath the belly of a Nissan. "Hey Houghton, more goodies!" he called, decked out in his paint uniform with his cracked fingernails and uncombed hair. One would never know from his rail-thin body that his diet centered on soda pop and pastries.

"Here, Bart, these are for all you guys," Clare said, handing him the box.

Bart eagerly snapped up the box as though he'd been awaiting the ice cream truck. He then nearly crashed into Parker, who was already approaching. Slightly irked by Bart's level of exuberance for her box of sugary snacks, Clare was too tired to show her irritation.

Her occasional unexplained goody-deliveries for the shop workers came mostly without her and Parker interacting. Often, if she was driving, she never got out of her vehicle. It was a ritual some of the management team performed for some of their clients. Today, for some reason unknown to her, she had come on foot.

"Thanks, Miss Paxton," Bart responded affectionately as Parker arrived.

Parker waved Bart on, ignoring his gesture to grab a donut.

"Do you think he'll ever stop calling me Miss Paxton?" Clare complained, grinning. "Feels like a little spinster jab."

"Can't help you feeling that way," Parker smiled. "You shouldn't think he gives it that much thought."

"Haven't seen you in a long while," Parker said while scrubbing his palms with an old cotton rag, pointedly referring to their years of estrangement. "How's your mom?"

Clare was keenly aware that theirs had become a ritual of across-the-street waves, when any number of subjects could have poked a hole in the dam between them.

"Mom is just great, what do you think? Ornery . . . I can't seem to get a moment's peace with her."

"So what brings you by?" Parker moved Clare a tad farther from the earshot of the garage.

She suddenly had no idea what had brought her to Parker's doorstep. A gust of wind whistled past the garage metal walls; Clare was awkwardly cognizant of the hollow humming. Her body stiffened from the biting wind chill.

"Nothing really," she said. "Just visiting a good bank customer."

"Hmm." Parker massaged the uneven stubble across his sturdy jaw.

She felt his questioning stare.

"Don't get me wrong, I'm appreciative of the donuts," he said, his signature throaty voice. "But where are we going here?" Parker was demonstrably amused by her transparency.

Clare lacked a reasonable excuse to back away. Sticky moments like these inevitably triggered memories of the merciless chastising she had received about town for dissolving their childhood-spawned romance. Although they'd managed to keep away from one another since, Parker still claimed a particular innermost spot inside of her. She was self-conscious about that familiarity, but no longer in pain from wishing he was something he wasn't.

From their first frightful kiss in a junior high breezeway between dances, Parker had been ready to seal his fate with her. He had found inspiration in his own surroundings, and he'd wanted Clare's hand in the journey. Parker had never fingered a map thinking about the things he had to see or the legacy he had to create; he wanted what was already in his own grasp. These were the characteristics that she'd come to appreciate and admire rather than selfishly disparage, the traits that had brought him to starting a successful business and to developing a phenomenal reputation across the county. These were qualities that belonged rightfully to the man who, in her mind, had chosen Danfield over her dreams.

"What, can't an old friend bring donuts to a good customer?" Clare asked.

"You know, John McNeil was just here Friday, dragging in some bagels. I suppose I should keep my mouth shut for the guys' sake, but the two of you are responsible for this extra ten pounds I'm packing." Parker patted his nearly rock-solid midriff.

Ready to burst with nervousness, Clare managed a grateful chuckle.

"Seriously," Parker added. "When your hazel eyes get that cinnamon brown color and that blue vein begins to protrude on your neck, I can tell something is eating at you." He gently touched a couple of fingers to the tender skin beneath her chin. She gingerly leaned away.

"Okay, smarty," she said. "These cinnamon eyes just get a little restless now and then, you seem to forget."

"Forget nothing. I got it loud and clear."

Engulfed by his scrutinizing stare, he was justified in that remark, Clare felt.

"It's just . . . what happened to Mary. I keep thinking about Russell," she said.

"Everybody is just reeling from that, aren't they?"

With her hands on the hips of her dress slacks, Clare shifted her stance.

"Things just get a little claustrophobic around here sometimes, you have to admit," she said. She looked at him for approval. "Don't you ever wonder . . . ?"

"Yvonne brought me up, didn't she?" he asked; she knew he wasn't really changing the subject. "Or should I say she brought up the entire wholesome Danfield male population. When are you ever going to stop letting her get to you?"

"It's a revolving door with us, Parker."

His eyes glazed, signaling his retreat.

"Got to get back," he said. "It's too cold out here to chitchat." Then he leaned in, brushed her cheek with his, and squeezed her elbow.

"Life is what you make of it," he whispered gently. "We are all going to get through this. You coming on Wednesday?"

She was unwilling to argue with him about anything.

"Don't remind me," she said. "We've officially gone mad around here with the whole bell tower thing as well."

Turning confidently, Parker treaded back toward the garage entrance. "It promises to be a great time," he called over his shoulder. "Oh, and thanks for the donuts. You're welcome any time, with or without gifts."

Enduring the frosty nip to her neck until his figure disappeared past the metal archway of the garage, Clare imagined herself running after him to duel it out with him at last over everything that had gone between them. More specifically, she wanted to rail at him for dredging up Yvonne and the reminder that her mother was at the center of the ruin of her ambitions. Clare's own culpability in everything barred her from contesting Parker's poetic but admonishing jabs. The idea that she could have ever walked away from Parker would remain a particularly perplexing quandary. She'd seen his offer of the quintessential small-town life as a choke hold, yet she was here, standing in Danfield, unable to articulate why she was here, standing in Danfield.

"Yeah, I'll be there," she said finally.

Whipped around by the wind, Clare lifted the collar of her wool coat, tightened her scarf, and waved even though no one was there to wave back.

SEVEN

Embarrassed by her meeting with Parker and eager to get back to her desk, Clare nearly missed Russell Martin walking across the street from her on her way back to the bank.

"Russell?"

He appeared to be languishing in front of a particular Main Street storefront, oblivious to her and the minimal traffic sloshing through the soggy main artery.

Clare was panicking about squandering the morning's work, but she hadn't seen Russell since the news had broken, and so she opted to check on him. When she got closer, she realized he was facing Riley Jean Ridder's specialty store full of antiques and collectibles.

He turned at the sound of her tripping the curb; his eyes widened with familiarity. As was typical of Russell, he was clad in a flannel shirt and hunting vest.

"Hi Clare," he said, and he backed away from the window.

"It's a little chilly out here. You have to be freezing."

"I'm used to it, I guess," Russell offered, brief as usual.

Tall and lanky, Russell was the definition of rugged, but he was also clearly anti-GQ in terms of style. His clothing was limited to a collection of boots—work boots, hunting boots, snow boots, any kind of boots—and a wide collection of items made of denim or flannel. In the summer, he broke out an assortment of cotton T-shirts that were typically white or earth-toned. Russell wasn't one to wear shorts. Even on the steamy summer days while sneaking Mary to the community swimming pool behind Courtney's back, he dressed in blue jeans and rolled them up before getting into the baby-wading pool. Clare still remembered the lone pair of cutoff blue jeans he had worn during their younger days of swimming in the lake. Because of the way he had grown upward rather than outward until his teens, his parents patched them for years until they could no longer be strapped together.

She was reminded once again that the differences between Russell and Courtney Martin were innumerable, from questions of basic attire on down to their shoelaces. But it wouldn't be the first time that a polished high-society woman broke ranks to carry on with a common man. Many looked on in amusement during their whirlwind love affair, giving it little chance to make it out of the parking lot of the local tavern it had started in. Folks were unanimously stunned when the two actually made it to the altar.

Clare leaned in and put her hand on Russell's shoulder.

"Russell, I am so sorry about everything you've had to go through. But at least now you are closer to finding her or getting to know what happened," she said with care. "Whatever you need, Yvonne and I would be happy to help."

Clare was actually impressed by his venturing out with the latest development in the case so fresh in the news and on the minds of the town. But without Mary in his quiet little life, it might have been worth braving the sympathetic pokes over solitary confinement.

"Thanks, Clare," he said and then paused for a bit. "It's tough," he finally said.

His eyes darted back to something in the store window again. She followed his glance to Riley's specialty doll collection.

"Mary . . . she really loves . . . these dolls," he said, more expressively than Clare was used to hearing from him. "Every time we come by this window . . . she . . . " He paused, his expression pained. "I always told her these were for bigger girls," he said.

Saddened, Clare squeezed his shoulder. "I know this is so hard for you . . . listen, I hope you don't think this is insensitive. But you could still get her the doll."

His head snapped up abruptly; she had obviously puzzled him with her suggestion.

"What I mean, Russell," she said quickly, "is just . . . if she comes home to you the doll would be a lovely homecoming gift. But if the time comes for you to have a service, you could send the doll with her. She could take a little present with her from her daddy. It's quite common to send a gift with a loved one."

He stood quietly but appeared to be mulling it over.

She hated herself for it, but she glanced at her watch because of how much time she had been away from the office and the mound of work that awaited her.

"Russell," she said, "would you like me to help you buy it?"

He nervously tapped the toe of his right boot on the concrete sidewalk.

"Yeah, I would," he said.

Clare welcomed the opportunity to step inside, holding back the store's storm door for Russell to follow her. She immediately removed her hat and gloves, desperately needing to thaw her hands and face.

Riley Jean Ridder was aflutter at the sight of Russell. Without a care that her gushing might intimidate him, she rounded the store counter to embrace him.

"Russell, Mr. Ridder and I have been praying for you every day. If there is anything we can do, you come to us."

A dairy farmer's daughter, the happily full-figured Riley had a small-town artistic flair that she poured into her dolls and her antique collections. Out from the back came Albert, her rail-thin better half who always seemed quite content to be socially over-shadowed by Riley.

"Son," Albert began, putting his hand on Russell's shoulder. "We loved that girl."

"Thank you, sir."

"Riley," Clare softly intervened, "Russell is just looking for something special for his little girl."

Without any hesitation, Riley nodded. "Yes, Russell, whatever you need," she said. "Just take your time. Can I help with some-thing in particular?"

Seemingly oblivious to all of them, Russell wandered to the

window display. He leaned over and seemed drawn to a little eighteen-inch doll with blond wavy locks. Interestingly enough, Clare noticed the doll was wearing blue shoes below her lacy pale blue dress. No matter what Mary was wearing—either dressy clothes from Courtney or tomboy clothes from Russell— she always favored the pair of blue suede shoes Courtney's parents had given her.

It reminded Clare of the funny remarks people had made when Mary first got them. It caused quite a little stir when she wore the "Elvis" shoes.

Russell reached to grab the doll and then pulled back. Riley shuffled toward him, stood beside him with a loving hand on his back, and gave him a nod of approval. He picked up the doll and cradled it, and then he began massaging the doll's feet. Clare felt haunted by the ghost of Derek's description and the newspaper photo of Mary's blue suede shoes.

"Are you okay?" Clare managed to ask Russell.

His calloused fingers completely engulfed the doll.

"This is . . . very nice," Russell said, stuttering uncomfortably.

He gathered himself, and he pulled out his straggly brown leather wallet from his back jean pocket.

"No, Russell . . . please," Riley said, shaking her head. "This is my gift. You take her . . . take her to your baby."

"Mrs. Ridder, I can't possibly accept this for free," Russell stated plainly and extended his arm with the cash to make the purchase.

"Russell," Mrs. Ridder balled up his extended hand with the cash and covered his fist with her motherly clasp. "Put your money away. I insist and I won't have it any other way. Consider it my gift to that sweet little baby of yours; may she come home safely."

There was that little sliver of hope again that Clare thought would linger unless and until there was a new discovery or there was a funeral.

As Riley wrapped the doll in tissue and placed it in a shopping bag, Russell appeared almost mortified by her charitable gesture. Clare knew he was a proud soul—just the appearance that through his marriage to Courtney, he was feeding off the Richardson family, topped the heap of his issues.

"Go ahead, son, it'll be fine," Albert instructed from the back office doorway.

Riley came back around the counter and handed the package to Russell.

"This is awfully kind of the both of you. I don't know what to say." He accepted the gift and clutched Riley's hand in gratitude.

Russell moved to the door, pausing before he left. He turned to Clare.

"Thanks, Clare," he said to her and tipped his ball cap. Then he was gone through the storm door.

The wind chill whipped Clare's backside when she leaned out of Riley's store to watch him ramble down the sidewalk with the bundle under his arm. Riley stood beside her in the shop doorway, wearing nothing but her short-sleeved housedress, somehow without goose bumps.

"Have you ever seen anything more sad in your life?" Riley asked. "It's just pitiful what's happened. Look at him . . . and that doll! How could I have charged him a penny?"

"All that complaining Courtney did," Clare said. "It would put her to shame to see him wanting that pretty little doll for Mary."

Clare's heart crumpled. It just seemed like yesterday that she'd looked at the front page of the Danfield newspaper and seen Russell zealously pumping his fist skyward while standing on the steps of the St. Christa Hospital after Mary's birth. Courtney, seated in a wheelchair, was covered up in the background of the photo that had been staged for a press release in the society pages. So the joyous image of Russell pumping his fist like he'd won a prizefight caused Courtney and her family to waste hours' worth of hair, nail, and makeup work. They had to scramble to publish a more suitable photograph of the mother and newborn daughter in a later publication that week.

Even tempered and impassive by nature, Russell was a completely different man when it came to his little girl Mary. When he wasn't pushing her in the stroller down the street, he could be seen tooling around town with her in his double-cab pickup. He had traded up from his single-cab so that he could place her car seat in the back.

Courtney seethed over the public display her husband and her daughter made, the way he outfitted Mary in little baby overalls and tennis shoes or kid's hiking boots. Russell was just as proud to dress her in frills and lace, but only for church, and special occasions. He and his wife fought about how to dress their daughter in the same way they fought about everything that had to do with their notions of an appropriate lifestyle. It was no secret that one of their rifts was over the exorbitant prices Courtney paid for Mary's clothing in high-end, specialty children's stores. It was a blow to his ego that such shopping required a Richardson-family stipend to support, and Russell contented himself that he could buy clothes that were just as nice, more sensible, and within his budget at K-Mart.

"I'll tell you one thing, Clare," Riley went on. "Mary's birth sure blew the bloom out of that couple's rose if there was one . . . and it sure turned that Russell into a man."

Clare agreed; if there could be a silver lining to the Martins' improbable alliance, she'd always thought it was the way that Russell grew a backbone when it came to anything involving Mary. Whether it was with a bat or a kickball, or a romp around the city park playground, he was determined to have some influence against his high-society wife.

"Got so much to do," Riley said, "and I just can't think much more about that whole issue right now. It'll about crush this town. Come back in here and have a cup of coffee with me, Clare. You look a bit chilled."

She pushed the door off of Clare's shoulder to move her inside. Clare bundled up instead.

"Thanks Riley," she said. "But I've been away from the office too long today."

"The town meeting over the bell tower should be interesting on Wednesday, speaking of sore subjects, shouldn't it?" Riley reminded. "We've got to stick together on this one. I'll bet Yvonne is all fired up."

Clare completely avoided a response about Yvonne or to offer her own two cents on the matter.

"Good-bye, Riley," Clare said. Riley looked in her face and Clare hoped she couldn't see the red at the corner of her eyes.

"Good-bye," Riley said finally.

With that, Clare drifted away toward the bank, not looking back in Riley's direction, thinking about Russell. It was all she could do to hold back her tears.

EIGHT

"Mom! Stop shoving me so hard, we'll get in soon enough . . . I can't move any faster. There's no room to go anywhere!"

"I told you to pick me up sooner, Clare! You knew how important it was for me to be up front."

"And you couldn't have gone without me?"

Yvonne ignored her. "Gotta look these bastards in the face."

"Mom, enough already," Clare said, trying to lower her voice in an attempt to tone down their arguing. "We're here."

Had it not been for the fluorescent bulbs frantically buzzing near overload, Clare might have checked her calendar to make sure it was the right century. It seemed that Yvonne was only one of many stuck in the past: the civic center mixed-use facility, a venue for large events and theatrical productions, had suddenly developed the personality of an Old West lynch mob at high noon. She scanned the room and the capacity crowds, their lips unable to declare quickly enough what had brought them here tonight.

Danfield's crumbling, hazardous, and abandoned chapel, with its signature red steeple and bell tower, sat high on a hill at the original center of the town, rising in dilapidated majesty eighty feet above its weary foundation, was in a standoff against a weathered but capable bulldozer and its supporting cast of demolition equipment. The battle to prevent the removal of the chapel was at the moment a hotter topic than the celebrated Green Bay Packers. She found the scene tonight much ado over a crumbling mass of brick and mortar. And after running into Russell on Monday, she wondered why the town seemed incapable of maintaining this level of rallying energy to solve a child kidnapping.

"Clare, I need to get to the front," Yvonne said. "You just need to move a little faster. If you'd just take a little interest!"

She continued jabbing Clare in the back.

"Stop with the 'you' already," Clare shot back. "I've got nowhere to go." She gestured to the shoulder-to-shoulder human trail in front of them.

Mrs. Hillman gave Clare an irritated look; she had received another shoe-to-shoe tap from Yvonne's momentum as she shoved everyone in her path.

"Look up there!" Clare went on. "They've got speakers all around the room. We're not going to miss anything."

"You could take this a little more seriously," Yvonne said.

"It's not like you haven't repeated that a hundred times," Clare said, growing more agitated.

"Just because you think this is silly doesn't mean I do. That building has been around this town forever."

"I never said it was silly!" Clare said. "How many times do we need to go over the same thing, again and again?"

"Okay, smarty," she said, her heated breath against Clare's neckline. "You've said several times how ridiculous I am for being sentimental."

Clare irritably stroked the burning sensation around her collarbone. Then, taking a firm grip on Yvonne's left tricep, Clare tugged her mother through ten feet of knees and elbows, apologizing as best she could. She brought her to a standstill at one of the center-aisle posts, nearer to Yvonne's liking.

"Look, I don't want to argue about this. It's a building, Mom. I understand that it's got some sentimental value . . . but the company that bought that land bought it fair and square, and he has a right to do with it what he pleases. Now I'm not moving from this spot. If you want to burrow your way up closer, then go ahead."

Unwilling to give Clare the final say, Yvonne tightened her face and gave Clare a look for emphasis.

"The chapel is more than just ours, Clare. Think of all the folks traveling on the highway who know their way home because of that old bell tower. I was a kid when Bill and Barb got married there, and just six months ago we celebrated their thirtieth anniversary in that very chapel . . ."

Yvonne wagged her finger and continued tapping each word into Clare's shoulder.

"Don't you remember when Henry died and Phyllis was so lonely and with those five kids? Elgin, bless his heart, came along and married her up in that church and moved them all out to his farm . . ."

"It's not so much an official church, Mom," Clare said. "And you seem to forget the ceiling tiles breaking in the middle of the ceremony and nearly killing the whole wedding party."

"Please, Clare, don't be so dramatic. Nobody got killed . . . a couple of tiles, was all." Yvonne was not to be corrected. "Think, Clare, of all the babies that have been christened . . . it's just hard to understand how we can smash that all to pieces," she babbled to an unsympathetic audience.

Clare closed her eyes and bowed her head in exasperation.

"Anyway, this spot is much better," Yvonne offered.

What was frustrating, Clare knew, was that her mother didn't actually care about everybody else's story. She was never going to stop badgering Clare with the usual fairy tale about how she had fallen in love with her husband Ray on that hill. The instant Yvonne caught wind that the building would be destroyed for land development, she had intuited that its destruction would knock down the last hope for Ray's return. Never mind that some viewed the site as sacred. Even though Yvonne hadn't mentioned Ray's name yet tonight, Clare knew what she intended and knew what was inevitably coming.

"I'm not in the mood tonight, Mother," Clare said, her resentment festering. "Don't go there."

"You're never in the mood, are you?" Yvonne sniffed.

How true, when it comes to you rewriting history about Ray, Clare thought.

Mayor Kohlhepp shuffled back and forth on stage behind the folding tables beside the podium, repeatedly checking the time on his wristwatch. The angered masses in front of him were in large measure his lifelong collection of relatives, friends, and associates, and he was plainly reluctant to throw himself on their mercy. Clare caught him giving a particular searing glare to the back of the room, where she realized Chief Grady might be, given the noticeable police presence around the room. All of them prepared as if for a LA-style riot were clearly meant to be symbolic, but knowing Jared, he'd find it a useful training exercise.

Clare located Jared. An awkward lust came over her, and she hoped her mood wasn't transparent.

The sound of the mayoral assistant's gavel and exuberant taps on the shoulder from Yvonne yanked her back to reality, with great relief.

The roar of the crowd diminished to a raucous hum, and then bit by bit it petered out to an agitated silence as the city council members meekly took their seats. Clare watched the panel shuffle papers, sip water, and clear throats for the ensuing onslaught. On any other occasion, Danfield eagerly bequeathed this group the power to dither about community decisions. But now, when it came to the steeple, the citizenry seemed to believe they could still demand their money back, as if they were returning a defective baseball mitt to Marwood's hardware store.

The ink had dried many, many years ago on the city's uncontested purchase of the dilapidated residential acreage on which the bell tower stood. Since then, the land had languished undeveloped and had changed ownership, and it was unclear at what point the sleeping giant of the town's attachment to their bell tower had been awoken.

The city's original comprehensive architectural plans had

played out in the back pages of the *Danfield Press*, getting equal billing with the obituaries and the classifieds for cattle sales. On lazy, steamy summer evenings and sub-zero winter afternoons, the misguided committee plodded forward. They applauded one another handily when they thought of the idea of placing limits on housing starts to control population growth, and they marveled at their own ingenuity when they took fact-finding trips throughout Wisconsin looking for ideas to bring home to Danfield. The few interested citizens trickled in and out of the planning meetings, seemingly content to observe and enjoy their free cup of coffee and an oreo.

At last, without any measurable citizen input, they managed to engineer a proposal for community revitalization that they believed would maintain the integrity of the town's look while engendering a community flair that could snag tourist tax dollars to fuel the local family owned businesses and lifestyle. Now the mayor and his team just had to figure out how to fund the proposal. And like a teenager viewing his first automobile repair bill, they nearly collapsed. Thus they were quite thrilled with the sudden arrival of Huntington Contractors and its offer to rescue them by buying the land and assuming the responsibility for the project.

The elephant in the room was this: had the demolition of the steeple and bell tower ever been lawfully agreed upon? And it had. But that it might not have been lawful was just the rhetoric from the emotional masses who didn't want to lose their sacred place and who had slept through this one major detail. Believing they could "make nice" and get the developers to change this one thing, they operated weakly on the premise that the location and the visibility of the steeple to the traveler was a part of the public domain and couldn't have been negotiated in a contract. But smiles, Bibles, and plates of cookies had no impact. According to the organizers of the movement to save the historic buildings, one minute the collective population had been under the belief that the buildings would remain intact during the town's renovation. The next minute, a bulldozer and a crane were preparing to run roughshod up the steeple road regardless of the public sentiment. That was the final straw for a group of citizens who were tired of being ignored. They watched, waited, organized without detection, and then gathered their collective butts for a sit-in on the first attempt at demolition. It took the mayor, the council, and Huntington so much by surprise that they had delayed the demolition, which had jump-started a more massive appeal.

Fueled by a front-page story, the battle had grown faster and more broadly than a late spring Kansas tornado, soon gracing the radio talk show circuit and the local evening news and soon finding new foot soldiers in neighboring communities.

Tonight, on the other side of the podium from the council, sat the heroic, awkward-looking Art Samowski, lone representative of the Huntington Group, braced for an impossible battle against public sentiment. The dutiful spokesperson, worn thin trying to put a positive spin on the revitalization project, would likely be pelted if he were to trot out any more "pretty" little adjectives as long as the bell tower remained on the chopping block.

"Please take your seats." The mayor's assistant again hammered on the wooded platform to officially introduce the Honorable Mayor Kohlhepp.

"Fellow citizens, we need to begin our meeting this evening," the mayor said and then cleared his throat. "I appreciate everyone coming out tonight."

The hushed but simmering assembly waited.

"As we all know, our gathering this evening is to discuss our community development plans." He pointed his pen toward the architectural rendering displayed on the overhead. The crowd murmuring bubbled up again. The mayor raised his hand. "I know that this is a troubling issue for the community, especially in light of other recent events," he continued.

Clare was thankful for his mention of Mary, however minimal it was.

"Why don't you say it like it is," called a voice from the crowd. "We're screwed!"

"Let me finish!" The mayor scolded. "We need to come together and agree on what we're going to do, and we can only do that with cooler heads. We're better than this." His voice crackled irritably, audibly rattled by the dissension.

"But you sold out our bell tower, Mr. Mayor," another voice from the crowd bellowed. "How can we be calm about that?"

"We were all here to make these decisions," said Councilman Harris Baumgartner in defense of the mayor.

"It's a pack of lies," wailed yet another voice, and several people raised their fists and cheered, including Yvonne.

Clare glanced again at Jared, who was motioning firmly to his men and monitoring the crowd. What should have been a gigantic brow beating seemed again awfully close to a lynching.

"Please," Mayor Kohlhepp said, seeming to find his strength. "Let's have a civil discussion about this. Let me first introduce the legal representative for Huntington Contractors, Art Samowski, to clarify to you all exactly what Huntington plans here."

He motioned to the far end of the stage. Art Samowski rose, sparking additional murmurs. From a distance, the forty-five-year-old Gregory Peck lookalike, was noticeably much grayer than he'd been on his first arrival in Danfield.

Clare understood Huntington's strategy of minimizing its appearance of being a corporate giant, but to send a single person to this meeting made the developer seem as though it had abandoned caring about the town's feelings at all. Yet Art was a good choice, an affable personality during the earlier council negotiations, and through her intermittent encounters with him, Clare had come to believe that, in spite of Art's considerable legal talent, his being chosen as the spokesperson by Huntington was designed to appeal to a small, meek community. Tonight, that appeal was all that might save him. After walking up to the podium, Art busied his hands and finally scanned the crowd at large.

"We want this to work for your town," he said, and the haughty whispers and murmurs began. Clare could see the sweat on his brow.

"If you'll just allow us a chance to show you the benefits of the development in this area," he went on.

"He's full of shit!" Yvonne shouted, and other people in the crowd began to shout with her. Clare turned and stared.

"Mother!" she said. "He's just trying to explain."

"They already explained," Yvonne said, loudly. "And look what happened!"

"Now listen here!" Art said and pounded the gavel over the yelling, hard enough to bring the room to a dead silence. "We've talked about all this. No one made any objection to the idea of losing these structures until it actually came down to it. This town had been tearing out old residential structures in the same area for years, and I understand that some of those buildings were even older than the building in question. Nobody said a word then, did they?"

"Maybe not a word loud enough for your liking," a voice said into the silence, and Clare was surprised to hear that it was Derek's employer, Franklin Marwood. He was standing all the way at the front of the crowd, close to the podium. "All you up there know," he continued. "That building—the 'structure,' as you're now calling it—is the heart and soul of Danfield."

Even though he was on the side of the mob, Clare was relieved that Franklin at least seemed to be bringing some calm to the proceedings tonight. "Franklin, let me finish," Art said, quieting down as well.

"Art, you can't treat us like a bunch of unsophisticated country bumpkins. We don't care what a big development company thinks of us. It may look like a dilapidated old building to you, but to us it represents generations of tears and laughter. That slivered old wood marked our birth as a town and hosted many milestones in our city's maturation."

"Please understand that we don't wish to diminish your feelings about this building," Art responded. "I just want to point out that in all of our contract negotiations, no one ever talked about this bell tower. Until everyone got organized into a human roadblock, not one person ever mentioned it as hallowed ground."

"Then you weren't listening very closely. We never dreamed it wasn't one of the primary structures to be protected," said Franklin, at last beginning to get heated. "Don't you see that?"

"Franklin, how many times did we meet for coffee?" Art asked. He looked around the room. "I've been in this town for some time, making these plans, and so many of you have been so gracious to me. I haven't been sneaking around behind your backs on this. We made it clear what we intended."

Art and Franklin stared at one another, eye to eye, the mob waiting in the background. The mayor and the council sat mum rather than accept responsibility for this blunder, which was largely their fault.

"Can't you incorporate the bell tower into your plans?" Franklin asked, pointing to the projection of the revitalization project. "Just give us this one thing."

"I don't want to trivialize anyone's emotions," Art said. "But we've already started this project. Any changes at this juncture would mean spending hundreds of thousands of dollars. We've already had to lay off workers because of the delay. Some of you standing in this room, as a matter of fact."

Immediately the rumbling began again.

"Please, please," Mayor Kohlhepp said, walking to the podium, a fully soaked hanky in his hand. Art nodded to the crowd and made it back to the safety of his seat with nary a toss of a banana peel.

"I think we've done all we can for tonight," said the mayor. "We've all got some stake in this. It's a problem that just cannot be solved with anger. I'm confident we can find a solution . . . " His voice trailed off, and his weary body stepped off the podium without any kind of official send off, scattering the council members through the back curtains like roaches struck by the light.

NINE

The crowd moved out as Clare, separated from Yvonne, elbowed her way through the mass exodus from the civic center. She was moving in the direction where she'd last seen Jared. She could hear people angrily talking as they left and knew that few of them had accepted Mayor Kohlhepp and Art's reasoning on the issue. Throughout the meeting, she'd wondered if there was anyone in the crowd who, like her, had remained silent, and why. Maybe they'd been buoyed by the prospect of a community facelift, or maybe they were less concerned about saving the splinters of an old building and more concerned with avoiding the greater anguish of pitting neighbor against neighbor.

The crowd was beginning to thin, and she caught sight of the back of Jared's uniform. Ever since their date the other night, she'd been thinking about how badly she wanted to apologize for her sour mood at dinner and for having broken the crime scene barrier. She wanted to make sure he knew she hadn't been in the woods specifically to go snooping around the site, even though when she'd seen the opportunity, she'd taken it.

Obviously wrapped up in a conversation with someone—she couldn't see whom; they were just out of view behind a pillar—Jared had yet to notice Clare who was waving to catch his attention. From his posture, however, his hands in his pockets, she gleaned that he was much more relaxed than he had been when she'd seen him at the back of the hall facing the angry crowd. Because he'd shared a few details about his former tumultuous days in Milwaukee, Clare had listened enough to know that he would consider tonight's ending, without a major conflict or multiple arrests, a success in spite of the long faces. Clare pressed closer.

"Clare, my dear." Martha Watkins put a gentle arm around Clare's waist. In a pale green pair of sweat pants and a holiday sweater, she seemed as cheery as if she were at a church bingo night.

"Oh, Mrs. Watkins," Clare said. "I see you made it out for the fiasco."

"Like anything else, we'll survive this, dear."

"Tell that to my mother."

Martha laughed. "You know your mother just wants to hold on to the good memories. You can't blame her for that."

Uninterested in discussing Yvonne's eccentricities, Clare ignored Martha's comment and kept her eye on Jared, who was still chatting amiably with some blond female. Clare could not see very much beyond his broad shoulders, but she could see the woman's hair flapping in the wind.

"Speaking of good memories," she said, turning to Martha, "how is Derek?"

"I'm great," Derek said, and she turned sharply at the sound of his voice. He was there, from somewhere, a strange lack of expression on his face, but Clare could tell he was under some definite strain. Martha quickly patted his cheek. They stood for a moment, and then Martha turned her attention to another chatty neighbor, and Clare and Derek crowded together. Clare embraced his wide body affectionately, as best as she could.

"I'm surprised to see you here," Clare said. "This can't be a whole lot of fun for you tonight."

"It's better than sitting home alone. Like you said, I need to be out and about. Keeps the press from hovering at my house. They're less interested if I'm not hiding."

"I'll bet either one of us could think of something more uplifting than this," Clare laughed. "But I agree this is probably better than being by yourself. Coach has got to be glad he's home."

"Yeah. I don't think he liked being cooped up at the station, but they sure gave him a lot of attention."

"If you give me a second, we could go to the NiteLite for a couple of beers. Get your mind off of things," Clare suggested. "I just need to make a quick stop to drop Yvonne at home."

Clare took another casual look in Jared's direction. Then she looked again, her blood suddenly cold. Behind the shadowy pillar next to Jared, she recognized Courtney Martin, her silhouette now clearly outlined in a halo from the center's spotlights.

"Clare?" Derek questioned.

She turned back to him; he was glancing about the crowd try-ing to find Clare's line of sight. "You look like you've seen ghosts. Are you feeling okay? You look pale."

"I'm okay, really," Clare said; she knew she didn't sound like it. "So how's the investigation going?"

"What do you mean, how is the investigation going?" Derek asked, his brow puckering.

"I mean, how are the interviews about that night going?" She knew this was a terrible time, but something about the sight of Courtney Martin talking to Jared made this urgent for her.

"We're talking about this right now?" Derek asked, his body stiffening. "You've already heard this from me. I had to go back to the station. We've gone over what happened that night a couple of times. That's it."

"The two of you need to find something happy to talk about," Frank Watkins said, coming up to them. "Derek, don't you think Clare's heard enough about this case already? This is a crazy enough night."

"It's not Derek, Mr. Watkins," Clare said. Derek said nothing.

"We should be going, dear," Frank said, nudging Martha, who'd returned from her conversation. "It may dip below freezing tonight, and I'd like to get home and get a fire going. Derek . . . we're leaving, if you want us to drop you back at home."

"You can drop me off, Dad," Derek answered, somberly.

So he wouldn't be going out to the NiteLite with her after all. Frustrated, she accepted Frank's bear hug good-bye and Martha's cheek-to-cheek nudge; then she reached out to pat Derek on the back as he grudgingly lumbered away with his parents.

She waited a moment and then looked back at Jared and met

Courtney Martin's gaze. Courtney's eyes widened and she stiffly stepped away from Jared as she saw Clare start to walk toward the two of them.

Clare and Courtney had had a less than amicable youth together. Their grade school scuffles, though they never quite deteriorated into any kind of physicality, were loaded with verbal friction and threats of bodily harm. Such taunting landed the pair at the school principal on a number of occasions. Eventually, tired of the same old merry-go-round, they started to avoid one another completely on the playground, which eventually evolved into a distant politeness and mutual tolerance as adults. But now, Courtney was walking toward the exit of the civic center, avoiding her without even a word passing between them.

Jared turned to see what had interrupted his conversation and caught sight of Clare approaching. He tried to put a cheery look on his face.

"You look a little crazed," he said.

Clare felt a stab of discomfort that he apparently thought she looked more crazed than Courtney.

"Just tired of bumping against everybody," she said. "I'm surprised the fire marshal didn't throw half of us out of here. Shouldn't you be arresting somebody for this nonsense?"

"We're lucky we didn't have to break out the riot gear," Jared said.

She looked at him. "I'm surprised Courtney felt up to being here."

Jared cocked his head. "I suppose she just wanted to be around people."

"Courtney? You haven't lived in this town long enough to

know that she wouldn't have anything to do with most of the people in this room if she hadn't married Russell."

"There's that unfriendliness again," he said, "whenever it comes to Courtney."

"I just find it interesting that the chief of police was having a conversation with a potential suspect," Clare said, looking him dead in the eye.

Jared's smile dropped. He motioned for them to step hastily out of earshot.

"Courtney Martin, a potential suspect?" he asked. "I just spent weeks with that family trying to find a little girl."

"I'm sorry," Clare said. "I shouldn't have said that. This isn't about you."

"You should be sorry," Jared said. "That was unnecessary when I've only been visiting with everyone about the events of tonight. That wasn't a private meeting."

"I just didn't word that right, believe me," Clare said. "But you, yourself, said the investigation wasn't closed. And everybody knows that the parents are subject to the highest scrutiny in . . . impossible situations like this. I just want to understand."

"Why?" Jared asked, exasperated. "Why do you need to understand? The rest of us don't understand yet."

She kept staring at him.

"I realize that you've a bit more knowledge than the average citizen about criminal psychology," he continued. "But I want to get to know you, Clare. Not fight crime with you. You don't need my opinion about the decisions you make in your banking career."

She stiffened; he was trying to use her feelings for him to change the subject.

"It's a small town," Clare returned, gingerly. "Nothing here happens in a vacuum like it does in the big city."

"You have to think better of me," Jared said. "Is it impossible to believe that Mrs. Martin and I were talking about trivial things? Maybe the bell tower, or maybe the weather, or maybe how she was doing under all this pressure?"

"I'm sorry," Clare said. "I jumped to conclusions."

"You did," Jared said almost playfully and then continued the poking with a bit of a smirk on his face. "And I'm too worn out from tonight, or I would drill you in return about why you're so set on pressing me about why I was talking to Mrs. Martin. If you remember I let it go when you hopped all over the crime scene."

He leaned in toward her as he said this and she suddenly wanted his embrace. She resisted.

"It just seems that none of this makes sense," she said. "And you're right, my head does spin when it comes to police issues. And when it comes to her."

"Don't you think it's time we took a really long weekend, you and me? We've done all the wining and dining this little place has to offer, and I'd like a change of scenery. You have to admit Wade's Café was a great distraction," he said, trying his best to change the subject. "Maybe a couple of days up in Door County?"

Even now, with Jared so close to her, and his ideas so appealing, she couldn't completely stop thinking about Courtney, how suddenly she'd left the room when Clare had seen her talking to this officer of the law.

"There you are, Clare!" her mother called out. "I've been looking all over for you." Yvonne walked up and looked right past Jared. "You said you would be just a minute."

"I ran into the Watkins, Mom. We should probably go now."

"Good evening, Mrs. Paxton," Jared said.

Yvonne gave him a cool nod.

"Come on now, Clare. I'm freezing."

"Jared, we'll talk about it later," Clare said.

Clare moved her mom swiftly to the car, hoping Yvonne wouldn't think too hard about her last statement. But her mother didn't disappoint.

"Talk about what later?"

Clare cringed.

"We were just having a conversation."

"You're just going to get yourself in trouble with that guy."

"Trouble? He's the chief of police. People think quite a lot of Jared, including Mayor Kohlhepp. You act like he's a worthless bum."

"He's slick, that's what he is. He'll just take advantage of you and then break your heart. And I'm not too fond of Mayor Kohlhepp's opinion these days either."

Clare had to laugh.

"Where do you get all these ideas? Jared and I have dinner once in a while, and yes, we've become friends. I don't know how to convince you that he's not a monster."

Yvonne grew silent. Around and around, Clare thought, first outbursts between the two of them and now the silence. And then, after the silence, the subtle dribble of nonsense that continued all the way until she dropped Yvonne at the curb.

TEN

Clare leaned against a waist-high stack of semi-gloss paint cans and craned her neck to watch Derek change a fluorescent light bulb in the ceiling of Marwood's. Most managers would have had one of the workers do this kind of busywork, but Derek took a particular pride in keeping things shipshape.

"How about getting out for lunch?" Clare asked.

"I brought my lunch today," Derek said.

She lightly kicked the ladder. "Turkey, processed American cheese, rye bread, an apple, bag of chips, and a diet root beer. How am I doing so far?"

"Go ahead and make fun."

"I am not making fun. Oh—and a little mayo on the top and mustard on the bottom. Right?"

"Say that a little louder so the whole store can hear, why don't you," he grumbled. She knew that he would have shooed anybody else to the slippery sidewalk.

"I'm buying," Clare said. "You can save it for your dinner tonight or lunch tomorrow." Derek stepped down each metal rung of his ladder with a powerful thud until he'd reached halfway.

Clare was always impressed by Derek's dynamo work personality. He was more authoritative on the job, addressing customer needs amiably and without breaking a sweat while dealing unequivocally with problems. Franklin Marwood, who had proudly unearthed Derek's hidden talents, gave his high-school protégé his implicit trust in manning the store in his absence.

"All right, snooty girl," Derek said. "Could we do this without the drama? I just like to bring my lunch on hectic days."

"I know you do, when you have a busy schedule," Clare said, grating some at Derek's creature-of-habit tendencies. "But I need a break, and we didn't get much of a chance to talk last night at the bell tower hoopla. If you really want your lunch, I'm sure we can sneak it into the deli."

She saw Buddy Webster coming a moment before he butted past her.

"Hey, Clare," he said.

"Hi, Buddy."

He gave her two seconds' worth of smile, looked up at Derek on the ladder, and waved a set of instructions at him.

"Derek, I'm struggling to get this garage door kit to work properly."

Derek shot Clare a wait-for-me expression, and she remained hovering on the linoleum aisle while he came down the rest of the way from the ladder and walked Buddy methodically through the instructions. This quality, she acknowledged, was what made Derek the stellar hardware store manager that he was.

"Give me a minute," he said as soon as Buddy was gone. "I'll meet you out front."

He rubbed his hands together, motioning that he was heading to the washroom, and then parted the swinging doors to the employee-only back room.

Clare seated herself on the cords of firewood near the salt bags at the entrance to Marwood's while she waited for Derek. Every time the automated entrance door slid open, the harsh cold stung her face; temperatures had plummeted in anticipation of the fall season's first moments of real paralysis, as promised in this morning's weather report. And even though the opaque watery substance had yet to become an official flurry, Clare knew the grocery stores would soon be cleaned out of canned goods and bread. In the distance she could hear salt trucks eagerly revving their engines at the pivotal ends of Main Street.

Clare was similarly ready to explode, but unlike the weather, she hadn't a clue of how to rid herself of her nervous energy. It didn't help that she hadn't gotten much sleep, though she'd dragged herself to bed completely exhausted. Having finally slipped into a few hours of deep sleep, she awoke feeling groggy and with a throbbing head, immediately reflecting on the gratuitous glasses of wine she'd had late last night after returning home from the civic center fiasco.

She questioned her reaction to the energy-charged evening on a number of fronts, and she hoped she wasn't the only one troubled by the prospect of fistfights breaking out between enraged citizens and city council members or Art Samowski amid the larger town crisis. The more she thought about it, through her gnawing headache, the more the mental picture of Jared and Courtney talking in the shadows of the civic center upset her. Even though Jared had put her in her place—rightly, she thought—Courtney's quick escape and Jared's calm defense of himself combined to annoy her. She couldn't shake her uneasiness about the whole Martin saga. It seemed the whole nightmare deserved more than a collective broken heart and occasional whispers about the precious little child, as though Mary might still come skipping down the street whether anybody lifted another finger in her defense. But here she was, looking at Marwood's community bulletin board, once peppered with multiple Mary Martin "child missing" posters, now only bearing the one that remained pinned to the top right corner, partially torn and flapping feverishly every time the automatic door slid open. Clare silently seethed at the short-lived memories about a child whose case had not yet been solved.

She wondered how anyone could stand Courtney, who was running around just days after hearing of the assumed death of her child, seemingly unaffected. Clare went over in her mind the many incidents of Courtney's willingness to use her daughter as a door prize to control her husband, as well as her continuing unabashed sexual flirtations with selective members of the male population.

"One more squeeze of that caulk and I'm going to have to make you buy it," Derek said, suddenly hovering over her. She looked down and realized she was crushing a tube of caulk in her hands, which was now nearly ready to ooze through its seams. Derek tossed it in the metal bin at the end of an aisle reserved for defective products and dollar-sale events.

"I'll pay you for that," she said and reached for her purse.

"Come on," he said. "Let's go to lunch before you cost me my job."

She knocked him with her leather glove on their way out the door. He'd have to be caught pouring a can of gasoline across Marwood's floor with his pants down, a matchstick between his lips, and a notarized confession in his pocket before Derek Watkins would ever be stripped of his livelihood. They loved him that much around here.

They sat in the deli. Clare warmed her hands around a cup of soup, but remained on edge.

"How is stuff for you?" she asked. "Really."

"What do you mean, stuff?" Derek asked, looking up from his food. "Did you actually drag me out to talk about 'stuff'?" He mimed a pair of quotation marks somewhat cheerfully.

"Come on, Derek," Clare smiled back. "Why are you so irritated by just having lunch with me? I want to know how you're doing. I know things have been a little difficult. Is it tough to be back at work?"

He drew a relaxing breath.

"Everybody is pretty good." Derek ignored her query about working. "You know Dad gets a little stiff this time of year and he hates taking anything for it."

"Good old stubborn Frank," Clare acknowledged.

"Glad to have Coach back to normal." He stopped just short of mentioning the incident. "He's one funny dog with his pile of junk he collects from around the neighborhood. Saturday mornings are like a garage sale; everyone comes to find their things."

"How about you?" Clare pressed. "We haven't chatted about you, personally. For example, I haven't bugged you in a while about whether you're dating anyone."

"Dating?" Derek asked. "That's out of the blue."

"It is," Clare reminded him affectionately. "But I could wait forever for you to talk about your love life."

"So, all this for my dating life," Derek said with a smirk puffed beneath his broad cheekbones.

Her antennae perked up; he wasn't immediately denying anything. Aside from his parents, she was one of few able to broach this subject. After a moment of calculation, he leaned toward her and spoke in a hushed tone.

"I'd like to not broadcast it," he said. "But Karen Forczek and I have been doing some stuff together. I wouldn't exactly call it a love life."

"She's great!" Clare said. "How long has this 'stuff' been going on?"

"Clare, keep it down!" Derek hissed. "I didn't say anything because I'd like to not make a federal case out of it. You know she's got a son, so our privacy is a big deal."

"Okay," Clare said, keeping it down. "When have I ever made

a federal case out of you dating someone? But Derek! The Forczek boy is a great kid. And your parents would love Karen. She's really a sweet girl."

"There you go now," he cautioned. "She is a very sweet woman. But we're just hanging out, taking it day to day. It's nothing right now, and I just don't need all the pressure."

Clare knew how his parents glowed at the mere sight of him conversing with a woman, but he always claimed he'd only bring home the *one*.

"Let me think about this," Clare said. "Sam is ten now, isn't he?"

"He is," Derek said. "Which means?"

"You said all that stuff about being a Big Brother—taking him fishing. How did that go over my head?"

"I meant that stuff the way I explained it," he said. "With Sam's daddy Jack clean out of the picture, Karen was in the store one day, telling me how she wished Sam could do more things with a grown man, like play ball and outdoor stuff. So I offered. We started to go fishing, and sometimes he'd come over and we'd work on my car, or build something. Kinda like I said, the Big Brother thing. Somehow we all started doing stuff together, the three of us. Then Karen asked me to a movie. Just me."

"How'd that not make the six o'clock Danfield news?"

"We drove over to a theater in Menomonee Falls, that's how."

"That's great, Derek. You know, she really is a neat person. I never could figure out how she got tangled up with that Jack. He was never her type."

"He's pretty much scum," Derek said, standing up tall, proud that he was able to be a better example to Karen's son than Sam's deadbeat dad Jack. "He never wanted her to have that child. She doesn't even go after him for child support because she's hoping he'll just stay out of their lives."

"He lives up north somewhere, doesn't he?"

"Karen thinks he does, but she doesn't know for sure. At some point soon she'll be able to move for full custody for abandonment, but she wants to wait until after a bit more time has passed rather than battling it out now when Jack could have a say. Although it's unlikely he'd do that."

Just discussing the scummy Jack brought her circling back to Courtney again. Derek was nearly done with his sandwich.

"I didn't mean to upset you last night about Mary," she said.

"Not the best timing," Derek replied.

"It wasn't."

"I'm supposed to be quiet about everything until the case is closed," Derek said quickly.

"If you read the newspaper speculation, the case could close pretty quickly, but I don't sense they are anywhere near being done with this," Clare said, nudging him slightly for some morsel of the truth.

"I suspect they'll do anything to get the media hysteria to die down," Derek offered, to Clare's dissatisfaction.

"I was so surprised to see Courtney last night," she said. "If it were me, I'd be wrapped up at home in my bedroom."

"No telling what people will do during tough times," he quickly flipped back.

She was beginning to fume again; it was so similar to what Jared had told her.

"It just seems like there is something we should be doing," she said, trying her best to control her worry. "I know people were affected by all this. But now it's like everyone has given up."

He frowned, confused. "What do you mean?"

"I mean, where's the outrage?" Her tone spiked. "For the past six weeks, this town has been paralyzed by fear and sorrow. And now, boom!" Clare clapped her hands together. "They find some evidence at last, and the whole case is quickly becoming one for the history books. Meanwhile, Mary's wacky mother is running amuck. Where's the grief, for Christ's sake?"

Clare's handclap brought the lunch-hour crowd in the deli to a brief pause before the chattering began again.

"What would you like people to do, Clare?" Derek asked in a flat tone.

"I want to know what happened to her!" Clare said. "I want everybody to get as riled up about what happened to Mary as they are over that silly steeple! You were there last night!"

Derek moved closer to her side and laid his bulking left arm across the back of her stool.

"It's an accident," he said quietly. "Just a horrible, horrible accident. People might be quieter about it now, but they aren't going to forget her. Nobody can."

Feeling unappeased, she asked, "Do you really think it was an accident?" and immediately felt worse about saying it to her friend who'd found the crime scene.

Derek took his arm off her chair and frowned. "Yes, I do," he said.

"Why?" Clare demanded. "Because the police said so? Because they haven't mapped out any other possibilities?"

He didn't answer; she didn't know if it was because he didn't have anything to say about it, or if he was deliberately trying not to say something to her that he'd regret.

"Think about it," Clare continued. "There were no signs of

an intruder when Mary first disappeared. Unless the police are masters at keeping secrets, it doesn't appear that there is any key evidence, which would in this case mean hair or fibers from anyone who wasn't supposed to be in that house. And did you know that a vast majority of child molestations and murders are committed by somebody close to the victim?" Clare felt a bit foolish repeating that mantra again and again when nobody seemed to be considering the possibility.

He looked around nervously at the crowd; many of the patrons of the deli were gaping at them, knowing that the two had been friends forever.

"Clare, why are you talking like this?" he asked quietly. "How do you know what all the evidence is?"

"The question is, why aren't we all talking like this? Why, like we said earlier, is the newspaper drawing straws for something to write about? A child may have been murdered in our town!" Clare slapped Derek's arm. "There, I said it! It's been eating at me and eating at me."

Derek grimaced as though he could lose his lunch. He stood up, took dollar bills from his wallet, laid the ticket and cash by the register, and walked out without waiting for change.

She caught up with him on the street walking back to Marwood's.

"Don't just dismiss me," she said. "I've needed to talk about this. This bothers me. We're friends. Can't I just tell you what's on my mind?"

He halted his brisk walk back to the hardware store and turned to look at her.

"I'm not dismissing you," he said. "I just don't know what to do with this—this inquisition of yours."

His piercing glare lasted just seconds before he continued down the sidewalk.

Clare couldn't discern whether she'd frightened him or pissed him off; his actions had to be more than just his natural inclination to avoid conflict.

"What do you mean, inquisition?" she demanded and then walked on behind him.

"You're like the emotional police," he growled. "Nobody feels as bad about Mary as I do. I found the spot where she died, if that's what happened. That doesn't mean that I agree with you that somebody murdered her!"

"But look at the evidence—"

"Stop!" he shouted. "I have to get back. We can talk about this later."

She hadn't the heart to embarrass her friend even further by chasing him down the sidewalk. It was obvious from how fast he was going just how ready he was to be rid of her.

ELEVEN

The sidewalk was developing slick spots where flurries were accumulating and the salting had missed. Although she was bubbling at the seams all the way to the office, Clare had no choice but to amble at a snail's pace without her snow boots. She arrived back at the office from her disastrous lunch just in time to witness the tail end of the Staudlemeyer mortgage closing. Her branch manager, Tom Pollenski, was looking in on the events in the conference room.

"Tom, thank you," she said, walking up to him.

"Not a problem," Tom said. "I didn't think you'd mind if we went ahead without you. The Staudlemeyers said they would've waited, but I could tell they were excited about getting the keys to their first house. And no one knew where you were. You okay?"

"That's fine," she said. "I'm glad you went without me. All these years of having to rent and move, I wouldn't have wanted them to wait a moment longer." She let his query about her well-being dangle.

Clare was as comfortable with Tom Pollenski handling the mortgage documents, as she would have been doing it herself. Her direct report and sidekick, Tom, was quite proficient at managing the sales and operations of the retail staff on a day-to-day basis. Clare rarely involved herself at this level anymore, except for exceptional cases. The Staudlemeyers were one of those.

The thirty-seven-year-old Rita and Will Staudlemeyer were a statistical anomaly: a couple who'd kept the loving spark between them long after their triumphant teenage marriage at seventeen. They were six years older than Clare, and she'd witnessed the dawn of their romance and its metamorphosis into a long-standing happy union. With their much admired, deep-seated respect for each other, peppered with the laughter of their children, theirs was a life that would be irretrievably lost without the other.

The Staudlemeyers' loan application had initially been declined because of their skinny credit file and a few dings dating back to their youngest child's illness. Clare stepped up to bear witness to their good-as-gold character in defense. She put her own neck and signature on the line and hadn't any worries about handing them the keys to their first home. Now, she'd skipped out on that moment to interrogate her best friend about his feelings on a local murder.

Rita and Will immediately flocked to Clare when they noticed her standing outside the doorway.

"We are so grateful," Rita beamed, as bright as a child on Christmas morning.

Will gleefully wrapped his arms around his wife from behind. "We're gonna let our oldest, Grayson, christen the place with the first brush of paint."

He motioned to their crew nestled quietly in the lobby seating area, among them the grown-up Grayson, who was home for the occasion from his second year in college on a well-deserved engineering scholarship.

The Staudlemeyer couple chattered on about all the good things that would happen because of Clare's one good deed. She was warmly affected by their enthusiasm, but still feeling bothered from her lunch with Derek, and from the annoying internal observation that the Staudlemeyers' loving household represented everything Mary Martin didn't have.

"Go, go," she finally said to them, smiling. "You have lots to do. I'll see you on moving day."

Still shamefully numb, she watched them gather their jovial family and leave. She could tell Tom was worrying about her. Hoping that the Staudlemeyers hadn't picked up on it as well, Clare walked over to her office off the lobby knowing that Tom would leave her be.

She spent the afternoon busying herself to avoid thinking about the Martin fiasco and all the little things that were starting to unnerve her. She slogged through a halfhearted meeting with Stuart over marketing objectives and then made a somber attempt at next year's budget. Unable to fully focus and effectively busted mentally, Clare made it to the end of the day without having produced anything substantive.

She had to admit she had been virtually out of action for much of the past week. And she knew, on some level, that her emotions about Mary appeared extreme. Derek certainly made it clear that he thought so. Yet even given that, this apparent disinterest on the part of the town regarding what had really happened to Mary was hard to get beyond: the taking of a child's precious existence should, at minimum, be investigated, not just accepted. And the more she thought about Derek's willingness to accept the official story—and about how he'd treated her earlier today when she had been the one he turned to—the more it gnawed on her. His behavior went against certain well-known truths about Derek's character.

Once, when they were thirteen, she'd been hanging out at Derek's family garage with Derek and a group of their mutual friends just after their junior high football game. Derek and some of the team members were still in football uniforms, soiled with mud and grass stains from the game, and everybody was grousing about the thrashing they'd just taken by a team from the northern city of Tomahawk.

Suddenly, their friend Darden Hickman still wearing his team uniform rushed in and tried to hide in the far corner of the garage. He'd come across the opposing team celebrating in front of the Burger Stop on Main Street and had climbed on the roof with a bag of oranges, which he started tossing down at his rivals. One of the oranges had connected with a headlight on a car owned by an opposing team members' parents, and Darden was looking for cover.

A very calm Derek immediately towered over him. He told
Darden to fess up to the police. Even now, there'd be a manhunt
for the culprit Derek said, as he piled on some ribbing in the process. He painted a grim picture for Darden: sirens on every corner,
parents sweeping the neighborhood with flashlight beams, while
Clare and all their friends snickered in the background.

Confessing wasn't an option, the terrified Darden said, and
so Derek frowned and thought. Then he motioned for Darden
to follow him. They first headed to Darden's house to clean out
his piggy bank. Then they bicycled to the auto parts store to pick
up replacement parts for the headlight and snuck in the middle
of the night to the hotel where they knew the opposing team
would be staying in order to replace it. Derek and Darden then
gathered Clare and the rest of their friends, secretly, at the hotel
in the morning, to watch the surprise on the faces of the visitors
when they saw that the light was magically no longer damaged.
The visitors were more than surprised except for one telltale sign:
Darden, without Derek noticing, had written "sucker" on a piece
of masking tape and put it across the headlight as soon as it had
been repaired, and it was all Derek could do to muffle Clare and
her friends' howls of delight at the effect.

Where was that person now? Clare wondered. Now, Derek's wanting to disconnect from everything surrounding the Martin case
rather than understand the events felt like a departure. It wasn't
just a departure from his childhood, but from the person he'd
become, the orderly guy she watched at the store earlier, helping
Buddy Webster sort through baffling garage door kit instructions.

Now, this friend, who could reorder the strangest of predicaments while they were growing up, was pushing her away.

She couldn't take it anymore; she went to the storeroom, where she knew LuAnn had been saving all the recent newspapers.

She worked methodically, pulling out every article she could find on Mary, beginning with that first horrifying day of her disappearance. She began to organize the papers, propping them against metal shelves, while she sat on a storage box filled with old loan documents.

"What I like about you is that you're always willing to dig in and get your hands dirty with the best of them," Lee Graber's voice echoed.

"Ahh!" she shouted and lurched to a standing position. "I'm sorry, I didn't hear you coming!"

Lee stepped forward, ready to catch her as she struggled to find her footing. "Sorry, sorry; I didn't mean to sneak up. LuAnn said she saw you come in here. Hatching up some great ideas for growing the business?"

Clare immediately mused over LuAnn's lack of better things to do.

"Just trying to see if I can spark a few ideas," Clare blathered.

"Great, what are you thinking?"

"I'm just in the early stages of trying to figure out what I want to do," Clare went on. "No earth-shattering epiphany to report yet."

Lee inched closer while Clare pretended to neaten. She folded several sections over each other to cover the front page of the day Mary's story first broke. "Let me help you move this all to the conference room," Lee said. "You shouldn't be stooped over in this drafty storeroom. You're making me feel like I haven't given you a big enough office. Unless of course you're done for the day?"

"I am," Clare said. "I'll clean this up later."

Leaving the mess, as she knew he saw it, Clare hustled her boss to the door and into the hallway. She quickly turned off the lights and closed the storeroom door behind her.

It was past 5:30 and LuAnn was already gone for the day. Lee motioned her back to his office and she followed, impatiently thinking of the papers she'd left in the storeroom.

She took a seat quietly while Lee aligned the papers on his back credenza. He then tested the back of his chair for a tight spring before taking his seat. He drummed his fingers on top of his wooden desk, and Clare concluded that he had no real agenda, again, that he probably just wanted to talk to someone.

Long ago his lean, large face and billowy white cotton hair had earned him the designation "Quaker Oats." In spite of the fact that the hair on his scalp was now scattered like crabgrass and kept neatly trimmed by his barber, his facial features still bore an uncanny resemblance to the cereal icon. He enjoyed the comparison and kept a collection of plantation-style hats to wear at outdoor community events.

"Everybody seemed to be relieved we skipped our Monday morning meeting, as I suggested we do after last week," Lee finally began.

"I think it was a good idea, with all the distractions," Clare concurred.

"Last night's event at the civic center might have overtaken any reasonable business discussion again. Boy—this bell tower thing has gotten out of hand, hasn't it?" Lee pensively massaged his chin.

"Next week we'll get this thing back on track. Do you think you could go over the systems upgrade again?" Lee asked.

She stared right through Lee to a speck on the wall—now Lee, too, had moved on from his "bite you in the butt" mood about Mary to being more concerned with the steeple.

"Clare?"

"I'll be happy to go over the systems upgrade again," Clare said.

"Are you okay, Clare? You look a little under the weather."

"Oh, I'm good," she said. "I didn't sleep much last night."

"I'm happy that we closed Will and Rita's loan. That was a worthwhile effort on your part." Lee commented.

"Great folks, aren't they?" Clare asked.

Lee nodded. "Don't mind keeping that loan in our portfolio at all," he said.

He began to drum his fingers again. Clare started to get up.

"Yeah, go ahead," Lee said, shooing her away with a hand gesture. "It's been a long day. I'm thinking about getting out of here in a minute, you should too. You look tired."

"Good night, Mr. Graber," she said and turned to leave. Then she turned back to her boss. He was tinkering with his back credenza again, trying to maintain even gaps between his piles of whatnot.

"Lee," she said. "Do you mind if I ask what you think about this whole Mary Martin thing?"

Lee folded his arms across his stout mid-section. "It's just a downright tragedy," he said. "Terrifying to think about. It's a shame . . . all of it."

"It's a wonder that little girl was as happy as she was," Clare said, warily.

"True," Lee concurred with an immeasurable unease. "There was so much trouble with the parents."

She waited, hoping he would weigh in a bit more heavily on the Martins' exasperating relationship; he didn't.

"It's strange," she said, getting riled again like she had at lunch. "That's all we seem to be feeling about this—a little sad, a little frustrated, just a little. We think she was kidnapped and now we think she's dead, but we really don't have an ending to it all. And it feels like Courtney doesn't seem to care."

Lee frowned at her.

"We all have to figure out how to get on with life," he said. "Many of us will never know what it feels like to outlive our children. As unlikable as the Martins are as a couple—I know you feel that way; I do as well—we'll have to support them in their time of need."

"Don't you think there's more to finding some resolution to this whole thing than just deciding to support the rotten Martin marriage?" Clare asked as an invasive comparison to Ray and Yvonne's relationship sprang to her mind.

"My dear Clare," he said and stood up. "Sometimes there are no answers. It's like our faith in God."

He put his strong hands on her shoulders and squeezed softly. "This may not be ours to question," he said. "That doesn't take away the ache, or the human need to want to make sense of it all."

She waited as he tucked his hands into his suit pockets.

"I'm sorry, Mr. Graber," she said at last. "You may be right about the need to just accept things as they are. I think I'm just tired." She made herself smile. "I'll see you tomorrow."

She exited down the dimly lit hallway before he could heap more sage advice on her. She waited in her office until she saw him wheel out of the bank parking lot from her office window before she returned to the storeroom. She packed up the papers and went to load them into the backseat of her Jeep.

At home, she squatted on the floor between the couch and the coffee table. Armed with a bottle of Sprecher Beer and a frozen pizza, she gathered momentum with each scissor snip at the papers she'd taken from work, slicing out every article pertaining to Mary's disappearance, however small.

Haunted as if she had seen it just yesterday, Clare drew a hallowed breath when she located the first headline about the disappearance, and she wiped her palms, smudged with newsprint and pizza grease, across the thigh of her blue jeans without thinking. Annoyed, Clare ran to her laundry room, washed her hands, and tossed on a clean pair of flannel pajamas.

Back to the living room floor, having had a moment to digest that first headline, she reviewed the article for its factual content, but found it not terribly enlightening. In terms of its speculative content, she found it much more interesting this go-round than she had when she'd torn through it on that hot August day.

That first article mentioned the separation between Mary's parents and said that they had "banded together in their time of sorrow." This completely glossed over the facts as Clare—and most people in Danfield—knew them, and there was no observation from the police whatsoever about the fact that Russell and Courtney, at the time of the kidnapping, were estranged. An innocent reader could easily misconstrue, based on this article, that the Martins' turbulent relationship was nothing more than a blip in an otherwise stable marriage.

Clare bit her lip. She scanned through a number of editions, all of which reiterated the same timeline for the first day's events, when the kidnapping had been discovered. Courtney and Mary had just returned home from a late summer family vacation sans Russell, after their formal separation. She claimed to have put the child down for a nap and then stepped outside to the garden. Then she had gone to Mary's room about ten minutes before Mary would have normally woken up. The toddler safety railing was still in its protective upright position, but Mary was gone from her bed.

The home, located in the prestigious Willowy Lane Estates—a pre-nuptial gift from her father—was large enough that it took Courtney some time to become alarmed. It appeared to have taken her nearly twenty minutes to report to the police that Mary was missing. But that was handily excused as Mary was getting older and deft enough now to climb the railing and busy herself in the well-secured second floor until Mommy came.

She compared all of the accounts. None of the papers mentioned anything that indicated a forced entry. That limited things to Courtney, no matter how she diced the sequence of events. Since the formal separation, Russell had been banished from the property, apart from his carefully crafted visitations while they awaited the permanent custody arrangement with the divorce, and Courtney was the only person who still had key access to the home.

Clare leaned her stiff back against the couch, thinking about the ongoing drama of Courtney and Russell. Each, during their very public breakup, had made raucous claims about his or her prospects for winning primary custody though it was widely believed they'd legally share parenting when all was said and done. Neither could substantiate that the other was an unfit parent, though the hyperbole fueled speculation. But it was Courtney whom the town had singled out for treating her daughter like a possession. She was much less likely than Russell to hug or to console Mary when she stubbed a toe or scraped a knee, while Russell doted on his daughter with a gentle but disciplined hand.

Clare massaged her aching neck and flipped another beer top to medicate her memories of Mary skipping happily in the comfort of her father's weathered hand. Affectionately known around the community because of Russell, Mary was adored for her outgoing, bubbly charm. She thought about the times when she'd seen him swing and toss Mary and her silly laugh would spill joy on the people passing by. She tried to put her personal feelings aside and to think, as objectively as she could, about any reason that might preclude Courtney from being the only realistic suspect. But then the woman in Clare made her pause. Surely Courtney wasn't capable of putting her own daughter in harm's way. Or was she capable of it? Did she do something unspeakably bone-chilling to her own daughter just to keep her away from her estranged husband? It was no secret that Mary was—on occasion—suddenly not available for Russell's turn when he came to pick her up. Nevertheless, Clare couldn't quite go there with the idea of Courtney being that kind of monster. She felt the idea bubbling sickly deep in her soul. It was almost enough to make her prefer the belief that it actually had been a horrific accident caused by an animal attack.

Emotionally raw, she found it easier to wallow in a snippet of common reality between she and Courtney rather than to continue falling back on these theories, even if she was doing it for Mary's sake. She and Courtney at the very least shared an unrelenting contempt for the small town around them. Although, the notion that they could be anything alike was almost enough to make a girl spit, Clare thought.

TWELVE

P ast the prospect of any semblance of a good night's sleep, wired on alcohol and tobacco and her prejudice toward Courtney, Clare finally got up, stepped into the hall bathroom, splashed cold water on her face, and then went back to searching the articles with renewed vigor. The papers reported the volume of blood at the scene as the single most critical piece of evidence, and the most solid argument in favor of Mary's demise. Regardless of any guesswork the reporters had done, she certainly knew that any competent crime scene investigator would consider significant blood loss to be solid enough circumstantial evidence to declare that Mary couldn't still be alive. At four years old and as tiny as she was, it would have been impossible for her to lose that much blood and survive. Yet the blood alone wouldn't be enough to point to any new facts. She sifted again through each account, searching for something equally critical hidden in the obscure details, something that could connect to the blood, or that could lead to some kind of solution.

Clare went over her memories of her own visit to the crime scene. That desire for a career in law enforcement and her high-school summer jobs at the police department before her internship at the bank, had given her a sense of the morbid realities of investigation. Her clerical duties that had included stints in adult crime prevention classes, where graphic crime scene photos were required course viewing became a precursor to the horrors and the harsh realities heaped on her and her classmates at Northwestern. And so she pretended she could look at this objectively like it was data and not—possibly—a neighbor girl's remains. But no amount of previous knowledge and training could keep Clare from becoming nauseated when she thought about the amount of blood that had been pictured in the newspapers. She imagined it filling that space she had seen by the creek. She leaned back on the couch and took slow, easy breaths to dull her urge to dart to the bathroom. Even the most seasoned law enforcement veteran, she was reminded, wasn't immune to the effects of working God-awful crime scenes.

She palmed the beading perspiration on her forehead and tried to clear her thoughts, to be as objective as possible. Hours later, in the still of her living room, under the dim light source of a tiny desk lamp and sound-muted television, Clare was combing through the clutter. Her brain, swimming in a sea of speculation, quieted for a single thought that came like a divine click. Had any of the newspapers mentioned anything about bone or tissue? Had any of them mentioned its absence? The lack of even the most minuscule physical piece of evidence—hair, nails, a toe, or a finger, or a scrap of skin—would be too suspicious to ignore. Yet that suspicious absence wasn't being dealt with at all either by the press or by the authorities, at least not as far as Clare could determine.

She knew she desperately needed to sleep, but she was too engaged in following this thread of thought to bail on it now. She went through the articles again, sifting them for any hint of conjecture about whether the lack of tissue at the scene might be significant. Finding nothing, she dug again, focusing on every police department interview in her possession, but they were all silent.

One of the earliest articles dealt with the K-9 unit that had been brought in from the police department in the neighboring city of New Berlin. The German shepherds had been given multiple assignments, beginning with Mary's bedroom. Their task was to track Mary's scent in every direction, looking for paths that were inconsistent with her normal pattern. But besides her play pattern—the spots where she had been picked up and dropped off by Russell and the other vehicles she had ridden in on the property—nothing exceptional was noted. The K-9 unit had searched the woods around the crime scene, but there were no hints as to how Mary had gotten to the creek.

She found herself fondling a close-up photograph of the blue suede shoes. A lone shoestring was dangling in the chilly creek, and she studied it, as if it might tell her something more. It was distressing to think that this sanitized photo was what the citizens of Danfield were clinging to. This particular gore-free picture brought to mind bright, cheery images of Mary and all that she represented, images that stood outside of reality. Clare wanted the bigger picture to be exposed, for everyone to truly bear in mind how horrifying Mary's demise might have been.

From her cross-legged position on the floor, she wriggled to get feeling back in her feet and ankles. She lifted her stiff, sore body to the couch behind her and toasted the dead space in front of her with a swig of her tepid beer in honor of her beloved city of Danfield and its love of feeling better at the expense of justice.

Her chest tightened, and all the reasons she had for escaping her hometown came to her again. But at the same time, she knew that her distance from Danfield gave her an objectivity nobody else had.

She heard footsteps and a knock at the front door and, feeling startled, she turned and knocked over a half-full bottle of Sprecher, but was able to stop it before it could spill across the clippings. She could see Jared's outline through the translucent valances on either side of the entry door. She glanced down at her gray flannels from the laundry room dash earlier, a junky sweatshirt, and heavy wool socks, and quickly found a hair clip on the coffee table. She was tucking up some of the wayward strands of her hair when she cracked open the front door.

"Jared, what are you doing?" she asked. "It's really late."

"It is late, and I'm freezing, and I've got a great bottle of wine," he said.

He opened his wool coat to give her a peek of an expensive cabernet. She was too wired to be impressed.

"Would you be offended if I said I didn't feel up to company tonight?" she asked.

"I would feel offended if I couldn't finagle a few moments with my favorite girl. And I can't imagine anybody looking sexier than you do at this moment."

Clare was amused by his attempt to smooth over her awkward appearance. For a brief moment she felt an urge to be taken in by him, but the papers she'd abandoned inside weighed on her more heavily. She offered him a halfhearted, loving grin.

"I'm usually better than this," Jared said. "I must be losing my charm or something."

Clare couldn't relax.

"I'm just exhausted, that's all," she said.

"Actually, you look distracted. We left each other hanging last night at the steeple show. I'd rather not leave things that way."

"I'm fine about last night," Clare said, though she wasn't actually fine about his interaction with Courtney after the town meeting.

Without realizing how it had happened, he had managed to nudge his way successfully into her foyer. "Come on," he said. "You're obviously stressed and I could use some company. Not only am I good at making you feel better, I'm harmless."

The tug-of-war between wanting his company and needing him to go intensified. He softly closed the door and took a seat on the third step of the stairs just behind them, setting the bottle of wine on the wood floor.

"Sit." He patted the stairway carpeting.

"Jared, look at me," she said. "I just feel like collapsing tonight."

"If I were a paranoid kind of guy, which I am not, I might be reading something into this. But since I am a complete gentleman, with a great bottle of wine, I would think you'd find it a bit harder to resist my overture for a simple nightcap."

He lifted the bottle of wine from the floor as a last gesture.

"You certainly can't fathom not getting your way can you?" she asked, feeling oddly amused.

Clare took the bottle from his hand, fingering the label. She took it to the kitchen, moving quickly past the papers in the living room.

"Trust me, lovely Clare," he said, following her. "If I had my way, we'd be looking through brochures of Jamaica and buying bikinis and suntan lotion."

"Oh, okay," she said. "We're past the part about just needing a few minutes of company?" She turned on the dim light above the sink to keep the focus off her attire.

Clare's avant-garde kitchen décor pushed most small-town decorative limits. With the help of Derek, Clare had happily driven the French-country from each of the smallest room in her house. She had traded the nostalgia of wood floors for trendy ceramic tile and dressed up drab cabinetry with open glass panels. Her cupboards, jazzed up with multicolored stoneware, were a Crate and Barrel showcase. The metal contemporary bar stools with steaming-coffee seatbacks were among her fondest accent pieces.

"I love this kitchen," Jared said.

"Every time you see it, you seem surprised," she said.

"If I'd had a few more invitations I might be used to it by now."

"You've gotten plenty of invitations, but it appears you've been too enamored with all those police chief duties to take me up on all of them."

"Duly noted," he affirmed.

She pulled out a stepstool to reach the red wine glasses, while Jared moved comfortably to the drawer with the corkscrew.

"A girl needs time to think about trips and things," Clare said.

"Take all the time you want," he said. "As long as it's before February. We ought to be knee deep in snow about then."

She wearily obsessed about the logic of her attraction to Jared. No matter how he viewed their humble surroundings, he'd achieved once-in-a-lifetime status, even given his tiny constituency. Danfield could be a lifetime appointment, and if she followed her attraction to him, she'd live out her biggest fear: becoming another Danfield casualty. But here he was, chipping away at her heart the way he always did, making her wonder.

"I find it interesting that you don't consider us worlds apart," she said, and she instantly regretted it. "Any of us in Danfield, really," she qualified.

She fastened herself onto a stool behind the island while Jared poured, fixated on his smooth handling of the wine bottle. He offered her a glass, leaned against the counter by the sink, and eyed her as if he would gobble her up at any moment if she would allow it.

"You persist in getting an answer to that big-city-boy and small-town-girl thing."

"It's not quite that at all," she said flatly. "I'm talking about our town of Nowhereville, Wisconsin."

"No?" Jared paused for a sip of wine. "If I dare guess from what I've gotten to know about you, you've got this fear that it'll look like I'm rescuing you. It's that officer and a gentleman phobia. I can see the anguish when you push your mother around on the subject of me." He paused cautiously. "Thank you, by the way, but it's high time we go to her house for some official declaration that might appease her. Isn't that what you do, appease her?"

The way he was flinging mud at her with a caring tone and remarkable ease was becoming annoyingly sexier with each word.

"Your psychoanalysis of me is quite fascinating," she said. "And in spite of my phobias and my pushy mother/daughter relationship, you're still here. Showing up late in the evening for your last stop on your way home."

"Look, don't beat up the messenger. I'm not giving my opinion on whether you have a right to be agitated by her. But in addition to her quirky habits, it's apparent that you can't stand the fact that she's living in the past and pinning all her hopes on something that's never going to happen. And, from what I see, it's fairly obvious that you're panicky about still living in this pretty little town ten years from now. Whether you live here or not is really not the point, is it? I can find my way to places like Steven Wade's Café. Got an hour? It's just a stone's throw to a great art show on the shore of lake Michigan in Milwaukee. It's not so bad around here after all."

She certainly had not been this explicit with Jared about the chinks in her armor. That the newest resident to Danfield, barring births, was somehow qualified to have an opinion on Yvonne's well-worn legends about her husband Ray was a reminder that Clare's life had become all too much a matter of public interest.

"I still don't see what a simple vacation getaway has to do with my mother," she said to hide what she was really feeling about his declaration that he wanted to be with her. "You're certainly dishing it out tonight. What happened to you coming in to make me feel better?"

"It wasn't my intention to lecture you about your mother," he said. "Just to sweet-talk you into a little R&R somewhere that

includes morning walks with sand between our toes and afternoon massages." He looked at her. "Since my charm isn't working,
maybe I have a point? Take some thoughts from the outsider with
a fresh perspective. Yvonne's mistakes aren't yours. If she wants
to live in the past, let her. If you aren't careful, the kind of man
you've envisioned holding her mentally hostage will be the only
kind you think the rest of us are. Me, I really just want to get to
the beach so we can really analyze the hell out of this and talk
about that law enforcement degree you abandoned."

Jared closed his lawyer-like summation with a smooth swallow of wine. The look on his face didn't seem condemnatory so
much as it did full of hope and desire. As with any attraction,
her mind flashed as she pondered. With the glass-half-empty
mentality that had plagued her her whole life, was he the one?
Was he worth an unabashed long weekend? Worthy of being
her best friend? And she felt confused, suddenly, about why she
kept resisting the urge to wrap herself in his big-city-boy arms a
bit tighter than their trysts so far had allowed her to see if they
could be a real couple.

But not tonight with her woolly socks on.

"Do we need to hit this subject any harder?" she asked. In
her weakened and exhausted state, Clare felt helpless. She didn't
want him to know right now that she might desire his affection.
That would make him right about something, whatever it was
he'd come here tonight to be right about.

"Just because you desire a little romance doesn't mean you're
not a strong woman," he said.

"As I recall, when you got here, you said you needed company.
Maybe we should focus on *your* glaring weaknesses," she replied.

"Well, aside from the fact that I desire to be in your company as much as you'll let me, a life on the force can be quite isolating."

She felt freakish for coming to life a little at the thought of his police work.

"I can't imagine how this whole Martin case must be weighing on you," she said.

His body stiffened at the shift in the conversation.

"I'm not talking specifically about the Martin girl," he said.

"But it has to be all-consuming," she said. "It's like nothing that has ever happened around here before."

His body language clearly showed he was demonstrably resistant to the shift.

"I'm sorry," he said. "I just wanted to put it all down tonight, really. Then I just start in harping on about you and Yvonne. It's not fair to you."

"Don't apologize," she said. "These are all the important things going on in our lives. This is how we'll get to know one another. Isn't it? My family life, your work life?"

"Don't take what I'm about to say to mean anything regarding how I feel about Mary," he said. "But I've seen death and dying and the horrible things that happen to families when bad things happen to young children. There is no response that puts it in a nice, neat little box for you, for the family, for the media . . . for anybody."

"I'm sorry," she said. "I forget sometimes about all those horrific things you've had to experience in your career. I know you are doing the best you can."

He was staring down at his boot, tapping her trendy kitchen tiles.

"I just don't want Mary to be forgotten," Clare added.

"I'm going to let you get some sleep," Jared said. "What do you think about a date at one of our places on Saturday night? We'll grill some hamburgers and rent a movie. And we won't talk about work."

"I'd like that," Clare said, returning the olive branch.

He reached out his hand and Clare fell in behind him to the door.

He turned to face her, exhibiting a sadness that she couldn't read, a sadness that she realized she'd overlooked during their brief visit.

"Thanks for letting me in," he said.

"Anytime, big-city guy."

His eyes wandered toward the living room, and she followed his questioning glance. The light over the coffee table, however dim, splattered the articles about Mary like a neon sign.

"Looks like I'm not the only one who takes work home," Jared said.

"Oh, it's not as bad as it looks," she said.

She reached up and palmed his face in her hands. Their mouths drew slowly closer, oblivious to the last twenty minutes of slowly heating conversation. Their lips parted together perfectly, and Jared gently pulled her closer, his hands at the small of her back.

Clare interrupted the growing physical tension by blanketing his lips with her fingers.

He resisted pulling away. "If you're making the point about who's the stronger person, it's you, hands down."

"It's not a contest," she tried to assure him.

"Better to go before the gentleman in me turns into a helpless beggar," Jared said. "I'd have to arrest myself."

He left her standing in the bitter breeze with the remnants of his lips' imprint just to the right of hers.

THIRTEEN

The bank management team had adjourned a little over an hour ago. Clare had never really been able to focus throughout the meeting. Instead, she wrestled with the memory of her smoldering moment with Jared and had mental flashbacks of the photo of Mary's blue suede shoes. It didn't help her mood today that she had fallen asleep in the living room last night and had been awoken, startled, by the blanket of crumpled newspapers in her lap. Detecting her short attention span, Tom Pollenski had periodically jostled her with his shoe under the conference table. She was annoyed that he was amused. It wasn't like Tom to be a nitwit; it was rare, though, for her to offer him this much material for his enjoyment.

At the meeting's conclusion, Clare had made a beeline to her office, eager to escape prying conversation. Sensitive to the stabbing rays of sunlight and the clients glaring from the bank lobby, Clare promptly closed the interior and exterior blinds to her office.

Mired in her funk, sitting listlessly in her office and holding her fourth steaming cup of coffee—which was doing little more than adding jitters to her sluggishness—she was oblivious to Parker approaching across the lobby; he landed in her doorway before she could focus.

Feeling a bit self-conscious, Clare began pushing her hair into place, straightening her posture, and fussing with the papers on her desk that she'd been moving around to no avail. "Sorry," she said. "I wasn't expecting visitors."

"Obviously," Parker offered, rather softly. "You look like hell. Have they been working you that hard?"

The remark felt as annoying as Tom's behavior had been earlier.

"Can't a woman just have a bad day and not have everybody remind her of it?"

"Did I forget to add that even messy looks good on you? It always did," he said. "Just a loyal customer in to make his deposit before the weekend. Thought I'd say hi."

"Loyal customers don't make it an issue when their bankers look like hell on occasion," Clare said lightening up.

"I'm just expressing a little concern for the line of us out in the lobby," he said, seemingly guarded about sounding too worried. "If you're coming down with a cold or the flu, you should go home. There is a lot of that going around, and the rest of us don't want it."

"Feel my forehead. I'm fine. Just a little tired."

Parker stepped all the way into her office.

"What a night the other night," he said. "The fight over the steeple."

"I knew in my mind how the whole thing was going to play out," Clare said. "If it wasn't for my mother, I wouldn't have gone."

"I saw the both of you huddled around one of the pillars. From the looks of it, the two of you were having quite the conversation," Parker said.

"Was it that obvious?"

"I tried to wave at you guys. I just couldn't get your attention. Tough to get between you two anyway."

Parker's comments were an unnervingly poignant reminder of his familiarity with her mother. Clare flashed warily to Jared's synopsis of her tug-of-war with Yvonne just last night, as if it were normal for everyone to jump off the sidelines uninvited to weigh in on Clare's ongoing battle.

Without waiting to be asked, Parker took a seat in front of her desk.

"It's been four whole days since the last food offering at the shop from some bank person," he smiled. "The guys were on watch all morning, but nothing came. I took care of it though."

Obviously he wasn't here to discuss the donut deliveries, Clare realized.

No matter how frustrating he was being right now, Clare had spent too many years avoiding Parker to ever really be angry with him. In many ways, she owed him. Aside from the fact that he was the perfect guy to a heartbreaking degree—a fact that many people had mercilessly shoved in her face—he had always been loyal and unfailingly kind to her in spite of her neurosis about her small-town surroundings.

Having had Parker all to herself at one point, she was cognizant of the many reasons for his popularity. No matter what he said or what he wore, he was easy on the eyes. It was his looks alone, his genetically enviable beefcake physique—which he maintained meticulously—and his wavy brown hair that earned him hunk status in Danfield. Elderly church ladies were susceptible to fluttering in his presence. But the physical was merely a bonus for a guy well respected for his business sense and his quality workmanship. Blessed with a healthy dose of brains and street smarts, Parker melted the stereotype about attractive guys.

Aside from his admirable traits, though, Clare was most simply captivated by his large, round, russet eyes.

"First *you* want to beat me up about my appearance, then about my mother, and now I'm in trouble for not bringing you donuts this morning," she snapped. "Did you just come here to make me feel more miserable?"

At least she'd gotten a hug and kiss and a great glass of wine from Jared for all his harassment last night. But in the light of her office, as beautiful as Parker could be, Clare hadn't the oomph to handle this at work today.

"Sorry," he said. "I don't mean to be talking in circles. That's your clever little way of dealing with things," Parker said with a slight smile. "Actually, I stopped by with good intentions. He then furrowed his brow, uncharacteristically. "I feel like I blew you off the other morning. We're worlds apart these days but we don't have to be. I made fun of you and your mom that morning too . . . but I didn't mean to stop you, if you needed to talk about something. Everything I said is only meant in good fun. You know that right?"

For a brief moment, Clare felt an uncomfortable pang that zapped her momentarily to a distant place in their past.

"Honestly, I really don't know what I wanted," she said. "Every time I turn around Mom is reminding me of what a fool I am when it comes to my choices involving men. Like she's the relationship queen."

"Yvonne does take a strong position about men, doesn't she?"

"Like nobody's business. And lately, listening to it, it's like nothing about my past is really settled."

"Clare, you can't keep second guessing yourself."

"But I botched us up," Clare blurted out. "You and I have been through a lot together but we barely wave at each other. I guess nothing makes sense to me right now . . . including me showing up at your shop." Clare stopped herself before saying *including everything about Mary.*

Parker was as noticeably uncomfortable as Clare about her last remark.

"Clare, I don't know what Yvonne said to get you all tangled up in knots. You've always obsessed about what she says. But it didn't matter then . . . and it shouldn't now. Things never turn out the way you think they will, but hopefully it all ends up for the best. What other option is there?"

They had spent years avoiding one another, and now here he was, in her office, saying this. Clare had nowhere to hide.

The noises from the lobby began bleeding into their untimely conversation.

"You've lived through a lot of my ghosts, Parker," she said. "I can't seem to change the things I need to, or to hold on to the things that are important."

"Important to who? To use your words, I thought you had your own yellow-brick road to follow. Why do you care what anybody else thinks?"

Did she detect some bitterness in him, still? As well there should be. There were times when she couldn't have spoken as openly as they were doing right now, when their emotions were still raw, since that unforgettable day trip to Lake Geneva when they were nineteen. He spent the whole day acting awkward and then confessed that he was trying to propose marriage. And while she had spent many years believing that this day would naturally come, she had sadly already begun to understand that she could never give him what he needed.

"You know, I'm not cold hearted," she said, "just because I don't want four or five children and a life where seeing the world is an afternoon glancing through *National Geographic*."

"This again?" Parker asked. "You're already free of us. What is eating you? It's gotta be something more than you and your old boyfriend not waving at each other." His tone was a lot more forgiving that his questioning stare.

"Sorry," she said, cupping her face, careful not to muss up every last bit of her makeup. She wished she could articulate what created such a feeling of fear. It made her sound crazier every time she tried. Even stranger to her was her spur-of-the-moment urge to confess that she had harbored a love for him like no other for many years after the breakup. But that would have been unfair for both of them.

"You have to give me more credit, Clare," he said looking eager to lighten the mood. "Have I ever branded you one way or another? This has got to be the part where you start talking in circles and I do the guy thing and shrug my shoulders. Just don't throw anything at me."

They both had to laugh to break a moment of embarrassment.

"Clare!" LuAnn burst into their emotional bubble. "Mr. Graber is waiting for you."

"Oh," Clare glanced at her watch. "Please tell him I'll be there in five minutes. I'm with a customer."

The three of them knew that calling Parker a customer was a stretch, but LuAnn nodded and pranced away anyway. LuAnn, unlike Yvonne, liked the idea of Clare with Jared over the likes of a garage owner.

Parker stood up to go.

"All I really came to say was that you can come see me anytime, just as a friend," he reminded her. "No gifts are needed. No need to talk about old stuff. And I didn't mean to pick on you so much today, or the other day. You have to admit you make yourself an easy target sometimes—but you seem quite willing to fight back. In a nice way."

He headed toward the doorway leaving her feeling bereft by his last statement. "Parker . . . all this . . . has got to be confusing for you, and you're offering me friendship?"

"Don't give it another thought, Clare. What's done is done."

"Here we were," she said. "This handsome, young, and popular couple. Our destiny seemingly foretold at sixteen. To have several beautiful children, to live a life with all our material needs fulfilled by this nice little Wisconsin town. You should have seen Rita and Will Staudlemeyer just yesterday—the picture of happiness. Could have been us, right? But look where we are. You've become a very successful businessman, but you're living a single life, without all the babies you wanted to have. Here I am—the girl whose only hope was to see the world—whose hottest time, until recently, was scuffles in the produce department with her mother."

"Like I said, the great part about our conversations is that I don't even have to say anything to participate," Parker smiled.

"Sorry, I guess I better let you go," she said. "LuAnn is likely to come storming back in here and take me by the ear."

"We should get together," Parker said suddenly. "I'm thinking just hang out, find out about what's going on with each other again. It's been awhile."

"Awhile?"

"Years," he said. "It's been years." Parker tucked his hands in his pockets.

She was suddenly thankful she needed to run. "I'd like that," she said, and she waved to his well-toned buttocks as he crossed the lobby and escaped through the front exit.

It was two miles, Clare figured, from the bank to the bell tower. Much of what was left of the recent, luscious snowfalls lay under the blue sub-freezing sky, carved into mounds by the hefty, steel snowplows. Clare slogged briskly through the crunchy, icy walkway that would grow increasingly more dingy from human, animal, and vehicle traffic until the next blizzard refreshed it. She had donned her favorite ski cap, wrapped her neck in a gray scarf, and bundled and zipped her calf-length wool coat tightly around her body to prevent skin burn. She'd tucked her wool pant legs

into a pair of snow boots to cover her nylons, however unfashion-
able it was. She squinted from the piercing, wintry reflection of
the snow in spite of the protection of her Ray-Bans, sporadically
dabbing her watery eyes with the tip of her gloves. These irritants,
coupled with a biting wind chill, were not yet enough to deter
Clare from making the trek.

Her ears were tugged by the cries of sheer joy that burst from
the children who were across the street circling the gazebo on the
grounds of the city's central park.

Seeing the handful of toddlers and preschoolers chasing and
leaving miniature sunken snow-prints around huddling, frozen
adults brought a smile to Clare's face. Each frosty, gleeful mouth-
ful of air triggered the happier moments in Clare's life—remarkably, the ones that least often involved her parents.

Parker had heard the best-laid-plans speech she'd blurted out
to him in her office plenty of times before. But since she had
come back to Danfield, she had only offered him glances, glares,
and nods, until today, when she said it all again out of the blue.
Why now? Why today? Why the other day with donuts? With
each snow-crunching step, Clare was growing more and more
uneasy about the whole conversation, especially with his offer to
reconnect.

She wasn't sure why she was spending her lunch hour walking
toward the steeple. If anything, she looked for the brisk air to jolt
her from her ever-darkening mood and another sleepless night.

Lips frosted and lungs working to warm each crisp breath she
took, Clare took the sharp turn up the hallowed path of Steeple
Hill. A weatherbeaten piece of plywood warned her about the
minefield of ice patches ahead. Obediently, she sought out the

safer sections of the old disintegrating steps of gravel, which
were sandwiched between a staircase of railroad ties. Each section veered and rolled in an asymmetrical path up the hill's steep
incline, purposely ordered so as not to make the hill attractive for
skiing or sledding. She thought of the annual incidences of broken limbs and crumpled bodies among those foolish enough to
disregard the warning, and she stepped carefully herself.

Nearing the midpoint, Clare slowed her pace and caught her
breath in the cold, dry air. She found solace in the timeless, his-
torical proclamations carved on the river-rock fence that lined
the pathway, seeing the inevitable yearnings of youth through the
hearts and the arrows. Some of the language in the carvings was
familiar to her, but much of it was an echo of a more distant
past that she could only imagine. Some of the inscriptions gushed
about successful unions, while others bemoaned the elusiveness of
the fountain of happiness.

With each reedy inhale, she looked at the carvings and thought
she understood how inexpressibly beautiful the red steeple and
bell tower must have been in that vibrant past. Even in its deterio-
rating state, the aura of the memories stored here had the power
to captivate her, and she felt some of the wrath her mother and
others felt in the face of "town revitalization." She had endured
all the jabs of being heartless, but she privately empathized with
the emotions etched before her, and she didn't need this second
to dissect the credibility of Yvonne's reflections about Ray. She
did think that although many brought their yearnings and wishes
about love to this sanctuary, most of them, it seemed to Clare,
didn't do so for the likes of a Ray Paxton, whose only good characteristics lived in Yvonne's imagination.

Clare dared to envision all the couples who had professed their love until eternity on this stage. Burgeoning youth made first connections; babies began lifelong friendships; still others hoped to mend their shattered dreams. There were reunions, renewed vows, baptisms, and among all those wonders, broken hearts. This incredible hunk of brick and mortar swelled with hope, with inspiration, and with its unending ability to shoulder life's sorrowful moments. But just like many human hearts, it was crumbling and in need of repair.

She felt tears freezing on her cheeks and realized she couldn't block out Yvonne's depiction of herself and Ray on this hill. She was disturbed that this was her connection to the place. Like most of her feelings about her father, she wished she could acknowledge them for what they were and then let them go completely. She didn't want the burden of knowing that her father was a bum; she just wanted to be done with him. Clare had never unconditionally idolized her departed parent, as many children in broken families did. Instead, it frustrated her that everybody in her community spent their lives trying to shield her from the fact that Ray was a liar and a drunk and a deserter, as if disguising it made it not true.

The cold, biting wind left her immobile and she gazed again at the steeple's magnificence. It wasn't that she was unable to cherish snippets of the past, but life to Clare had always been devoted to tomorrow, even if she didn't know how to get there. Parker was history. Ray Paxton was still a figment of a father. And right now Clare's mind was on one bright little girl who was supposed to be the future. Mary Martin had not had a chance to leave her mark on the steeple wall. Where was the warm fuzzy feeling for that?

FOURTEEN

Frequenting the NiteLite bar and saloon was as fundamental to living life in Danfield as the making of cheese was to a Wisconsin dairy farmer. As Clare would come to lament, her father Ray Paxton had introduced her to pub life when Clare was a naïve preschooler, dangling her feet over the barstool at the early hours of the day when only the ne'er-do-wells dared congregate. Later, she found it as comfortable to come to the NiteLite without an escort as she would have felt attending Sunday services, starting with her first attempt to get in alone by using a forged ID, an illicit exercise that ended with her being hugged instead of carded by her bouncer friends.

It was a rite of teenage passage to have a few Wisconsin-brewed Miller beers at the NiteLite. The NiteLite's unending constituency made it the second most-hallowed landmark in the city. It was never without a friendly local face, including those who had long since traded their alcohol for club soda or the like.

Tonight, the parking lot was already bulging with an eager happy-hour assembly, many of whom would be jonesing for their toast to end the workweek. As had come to be the Friday night tradition, trucks and motorcycles were parked at unorganized angles and with complete disregard for the faded lines of the parking spaces. It was a wonder that they could make it on and off the property without a scratch.

Though she had long relinquished her status as a regular, Clare still instinctively eyeballed the crumbling asphalt for familiar faces, including the one she was hoping now to find. She carefully maneuvered through the oil-stained lot for a spot among the rank and file, left her Jeep between two Ford pickups that nearly blocked the street entrance, and opened the door to the smoky glare.

Inside was a cross-section of attendees from Wednesday night's rumble over the steeple, though Clare imagined that tonight, the bell tower wasn't foremost on their minds. Though it would undoubtedly get a fair shake in conversations throughout the evening, tall cool ones, a pack of Marlboros, and enough quarters to keep the pool games and darts flowing were all more pressing.

Clare wrestled through the sea of winter coats and jackets for a free hook along the narrow hallway that led to the restrooms. Impatient at finding a spot, she flung her wool coat horizontally across several others. Peppered with hellos and jabs, she bumped and squeezed herself through the crowd toward the bar until she made it to a free stool next to Derek.

"Didn't expect to see you," he said, rolling a bottle of Miller between his hands. He gave a presumptuous two-finger signal to a bartender.

"I don't really *need* a drink," Clare said. "But if I went home now, I'd be asleep in an hour."

"No Jared tonight?"

"You know we're not joined at the hip, yet. He's probably doing his police chief thing and I'm too tired to make an effort tonight. We have plans for tomorrow night, anyway."

Tug Wharton, the bartender, interrupted her, pressing his overpowering physique against the rustic counter as he stretched his weathered, ample palms on the surface.

"Well, Clare," he began. "Where have you been, my pretty lady? Was beginning to think you were moving away on us again."

Clare loved Mr. Wharton, the father of her childhood friend Sara, and understood he meant the annoyingly well-worn sentiment lovingly.

"Just trying to stay sober and out of trouble," she said. "It makes you wonder why I am here."

Tug's sturdy face grew a comforting smile, one that had grown older and wiser throughout his tenure at the NiteLite. She couldn't get herself to give him one back.

"That bad, huh?" he asked.

"Just a bit battered and bruised and hiding from it all the same, Mr. Wharton," she said.

"What'll it be, then?"

"I'll take a tequila, if you have it."

"Coming right up." Tug slapped the counter, twirled a shot glass until it nearly lipped the edge of his counter, and ended with his signature drizzling of the agave liquor. She could see Derek eyeball the beer he'd just ordered for her.

Besides having served as the bartender for the past thirty years, and as part owner of the bar for some of that time, Sullivan "Tug" Wharton was a member of the city council and an elder in his church. Above all, he was most proud to be a grandfather of seven. Branded with his nickname in early childhood, he became Tug quite simply because he yanked with brute strength at everything in sight. Born burly and strong, he tugged his mother's curtains, cow tails, boats, and the like, and he was the unofficial tug-of-war champion at every playground and picnic.

Oddly enough, he hadn't had a drop of alcohol for the past fifteen years. One day, he'd realized how much time "the drink" took from his family, and instead of staying for a round after his shift ended, he'd headed home.

"How's Mrs. Wharton?" Clare asked about his wife Maggie.

As he answered, she watched him roll back a cooler cover, flip a beer top, and after serving it fling the empty into the trash in one motion. "Fat and sassy as usual," he said as he moved up and down the bar. "The girls are all in town this weekend. I'm thinking I'll have a chance to get some work done in the garage. You never know what five women are going to get to fussing about."

Clare knew how it worked in the Wharton household. She had grown up a close friend of his daughter Sara and happily blended in with the chaos as much as the Whartons would allow her. With four girls and no sons, Tug had become quite adept at surviving in his female-dominated world.

"If Sara is coming to town, I've got to see her," Clare said and perked up at the chance to see her girlfriend. "Maybe Mom and I should stop over this weekend."

He laid his warm hands over hers on the bar. "It's good to see you. And they'd love to see you too, Sara especially."

While Tug moved on down the bar for reorders, Clare turned back to Derek, who seemed amused by the whole exchange.

"He's such good guy," she said. "I don't know how he can watch everybody turn into a bunch of bumbling idiots without having a nip himself now and then. Just consider for a moment his sober bird's-eye view of half the population of Danfield. He has to be cataloging every little wrinkle, every liver spot. Imagine the book he could write about us. He'd make a fortune."

"That's a comical thought," Derek mused. "It wouldn't be pretty to see how we were graded over the years, much less see it in print. Thankfully he's not one to gossip."

"Speaking about gossip, I was thinking about lunch the other day," Clare said.

Derek leaned back, as though he'd known this was coming.

"Yes, we have to talk about 'it,' smarty," she said. "But I was thinking about Karen. We should do something together, the three of us. Or the four of us."

"Don't know if we're ready for the double date thing," Derek was quick to answer.

She believed his hesitation was as much about the idea of socializing with the chief of police as it was about any scrutiny of his dating life. She knew keeping company with Derek wouldn't be at the top of Jared's list either, but it was an important inroad for Clare.

"Better still. We'll have you over to Yvonne's. If I can offer one of her few redeeming qualities, nobody makes better fried chicken. You and Karen being there could reduce the static in the room where Jared is concerned."

"That's it . . . throw us under the 'Yvonne' bus so you can bring Jared."

"Don't look at it like that, it would be good for both of us."

"Maybe at some point," he said guardedly.

"I just don't think you should hide this thing with Karen."

"Nobody is hiding anything, Clare," he said. "Actually, Karen is coming tonight with some friends."

She motioned to Tug for another shot and a beer chaser.

"Already?" Derek noted.

"I promise I'll behave." Clare shifted in her seat. "Before she gets here, I need to hurry and explain the point of my conversation the other day."

"You don't have to, Clare," he said. "I know emotions are pretty high about that whole thing. You must think I am totally naïve. Let it go, okay? It's Friday. Just let it be Friday."

Encircled as he was by a sea of bodies, she knew Derek was without an immediate escape route.

"I know you don't want to hear this, but I'm not ready to call it an accident," Clare said anyway, leaning in.

"You're jumping straight to a murder!" he said in a harsh whisper.

"No, you keep putting the word *murder* in the conversation or supposing I'm pointing my finger at one person. I am simply stating the obvious. I just want to know something. Don't you?"

"Who around here didn't think the worst when Mary first went missing?" Derek reminded her. "Now that we found the spot about Mary . . . I am not focused on one outcome like you seem to be. You may not say that she was killed but it sure feels like you are thinking that way. That idea wasn't at the top of my mind until you pushed it the other day. Couldn't it just be a bad accident? I figure the police know what they are doing."

"I am not even saying it's one outcome. Doesn't some of what I said make sense?" Clare asked. "Just a little?"

"No, Clare it doesn't! I keep saying it doesn't!"

"What's eating at you about this, Derek?" she asked, emboldened by an alcohol buzz.

He furrowed his brow deeper. "It makes me feel bad to think about it at all let alone like that," he bristled. "Clare—I'm telling you to knock it off!"

Their distorted reflections, and the eyes of a few onlookers, hung in the mammoth distressed mirror behind the bar. She took a deep breath and a long slow swig.

"You could be right that I've let my imagination run wild," she said with a sense of regret that she'd riled him so badly again. "I just hope we can all come to a conclusion we can live with. Okay? It's been a long tiring week. I'll give you that. Let's let it be Friday."

The tension had mounted between them like at no other time in their friendship.

She brushed the back of his blue corduroy shirt. Visibly awash with relief that the inquisition was over, Derek motioned to Tug for another.

The NiteLite had reached near fire-code capacity. She secretly resented her sisterhood with the lot of them, but she hadn't the nerve to express it. She didn't aspire to be on Tug's list of has-beens, whereas her neighbors here wore that status like a badge of honor. Some aspects of the Danfield drive to be included as a regular—like one of the twenty, thirty-year veterans around her—were stomach churning when she was sober. They were palatable enough now, when she was riding her own alcohol fix.

Karen Forczek and her friends weaseled their way through the crowd toward the bar and into Clare's line of sight.

"Karen!" Clare called. "Girls' night out, I see?"

Barely able to hear, Karen leaned in. "I love that little guy Jack, but sometimes a girl has just got to be a girl."

"I just heard about you and Derek," Clare said, leaning closer. "I'm really excited."

"It's not time to be making any announcements," Karen said happily. "But he's a good guy, Clare. Jack really loves him. I hope Derek and I are doing the right thing, spending so much time together with him. We're trying not to be an 'item' in front of him just yet."

They both swung around to see Derek anxiously waiting. Given his slim track record with long-term relationships and his drive to keep his budding romance a secret, Clare knew he'd been trying to picture how he would handle Karen in this adult public setting without Jack in tow. Clare realized he might actually have other things making him irritable besides the Martin case.

Karen seemed to know enough to be subtle and moved ever so gently to his side. In a crowded room such as tonight's, he had little option but to stand close. Reacting in his own awkward but gentlemanly way, he moved her to his stool and the rest of her friends around them. Pleasantly amused by their cautious but instant level of comfort together, Clare beamed at them in a sisterly fashion. In the blink of an eye, her dear hulking friend had been transformed into a romantic as she had never seen him.

Not needing to invade their moment any longer, Clare settled her tab, offered her stool to one of Karen's girlfriends, and began to look for the best route out of the bar.

But in one swift gut-wrenching kick to her stomach, she gaped, as the cacophony of deafening chatter and blaring discotheque music quieted in her mind and her disbelief grew.

She could feel the spike of Courtney's laughter from across the room. For the second time in a week, she saw the grieving mother, this time wearing skin-tight blue jeans, a form-fitting cashmere sweater, and enough jewelry to replace a month of Sunday giving. Courtney was waving every one of her bodily calling cards to the fools all around her.

Derek was trying to get Clare's attention. She pretended not to notice and waved good-bye. Then she began to veer toward the game area at the back of the bar, fully aware that her motives were not in check. She barged in front of a pool shot in progress.

"Clare, honey, you need to move over a bit." A regular bar patron named Gary tried to move her out of the way of the table.

Clare moved forward a couple of paces, but not far enough. The two guys pawing Courtney were vaguely familiar and undeniably tradesmen, much like her soon-to-be ex. It was as much puzzling as it was infuriating to watch Courtney's thirst for the socially unsophisticated, given her utter contempt for Russell. Clare could tell Courtney was aware of her.

"Clare," Gary said, taking a firmer grip on her shoulders. "Maybe not the best time."

She stood speechless and without regard for the uneasiness of those whose games she'd halted.

Courtney finally turned to her, shifting her shoulders dramatically. "Here for a little pool, Clare?" she smiled. She nodded at the flustered Gary. "You might want to step aside and wait your turn."

"What are you doing?" Clare asked.

"I can't see that it would be any of your business," Courtney swiftly snapped back.

"How's Russell tonight?" Clare asked, unrelenting.

Gary tried again to intervene. "Let it go, Clare."

"How should I know how Russell is?" Courtney held up the third finger on her left hand. "In case you didn't know, we're not together anymore."

"Just a couple of weeks ago you were hanging all over him in front of a camera, talking about how friendly the two of you were. Something about how your missing daughter had brought you close again."

"You bitch," Courtney whispered. She nudged her two boy toys aside.

"Now that Mary's gone, I guess she's not cramping your life-style anymore," Clare continued.

Instead of springing to attack, Courtney veered around the edge of a pool table, within striking distance. Clare was by no means fearful of Courtney, but she felt a surge of nausea as the oxygen around them seemed to be sucked away.

"What do you want?" Courtney asked flatly.

"I want to see a little sadness," Clare said.

The stinky heat of too many bodies in the room and the effects of her rapid alcohol consumption caused beads of sweat to form a clammy sensation on her skin beneath her blouse. She could see herself drawing Courtney's blood with her fingernails and wondered if the drinks in her would allow her to carry it off. Courtney, on the other hand, looked fresh and poker-faced.

"I don't owe you any sadness," she said. "I don't owe you, I don't owe Russell, and I don't owe anybody a fucking thing. Keep going and make a fool of yourself. You can't touch me!"

"Hey, hey, with the foul mouths, ladies!" Tug was suddenly in the poolroom archway, wringing a dry rag from the bar.

She withered under Tug's intervention, but wished for some vindication in front of this corral of witnesses. She wished to be swallowed up by the tired wood-paneled walls. They weren't little girls in the schoolyard anymore, but Clare still wanted to strangle her.

"What's going on?" Derek lumbered over, within inches of the two of them. Like the wave at a baseball game, a hush rippled deeper into the room. Derek waited, gripped Clare's shoulders from behind, and guided her in another direction. She had little choice but to be grateful for the interruption.

"I'm okay," she mumbled.

She pretended to shrug away Derek's hold of her, but let him move her through a parting sea of inebriated citizens, grateful that he had a firm grip. Then the exit door swung open, and, struck by the glare of the parking lot lights, she painfully gulped the frigid air.

The litany of regrets she suddenly felt was as painful as her pounding headache. She knew that the rumor of her run-in wouldn't play well with Mr. Graber, or with the bank board.

Derek walked with her through the twenty-degree wind chill of the parking lot, stabilizing each stumbling step she took before she ran into parking pylons or vehicle mirrors. "What happened in there?" he asked.

"Nothing, Derek," she said. "We were just having a conversation."

"Some conversation," he growled. "More like something is not right with you."

"Now you get the picture?" Clare asked.

"I get the picture that something is not right with your incessant interest in Courtney," he said. "But right now I don't want to know what's going on."

"I've been trying to explain," she slurred. "But I guess nobody wants to be uncomfortable."

"You are meddling where you don't belong," he said. "Forget that you have to have an opinion about everything. I've never quite seen you like this . . . tied up about something that has nothing to do with you."

"You . . ." Clare stumbled again and was momentarily unable to finish her train of thought. ". . . You better get used to it."

They were at the Jeep. She reached out to grab the door handle, shaking her finger at him with her other hand.

"No you don't." Derek snapped up the keys and steered Clare to the passenger side.

"I'm fine now," Clare argued as Derek helped her into the passenger seat. "I just needed some fresh air. You, you better get back in there with Karen."

"Should I drive your truck?" Karen asked from somewhere in the lot. Derek tossed his keys to her and rambled around and got into the driver's seat.

Clare went over and over her thoughts for the silent, dark drive home. They'd covered each other's backs all their life; but until now, they'd never been this angry with one another.

Derek parked the Jeep in front of her house, the headlights from his truck shining on them from behind. He held up her keys.

Clare opened her hand for them.

"None of this is directed at you," she said, sheepishly. "Thanks for getting me out of there. Sorry about interrupting your date with Karen."

He waited for her to take the keys and then his large frame stood curbside until she had closed and bolted the front door. She felt, rightfully, like an ass.

FIFTEEN

The inside back door to Yvonne's kitchen was cracked open enough to allow the warm winter sunlight to splash through the full-length winter storm door across the scuffed checkerboard tile floor.

Yvonne hadn't noticed Clare sitting in the Jeep in the rear driveway, where she had paused to try to build herself up to deal with their verbal jousting as she watched her mother puttering around in the house. Her mother was wearing her twelve-year-old pink housecoat, worn ragged from a million washings and peppered with beaded fuzz balls. The top tip of the left pocket had pulled away and flopped over as a result of the tissues Yvonne stuffed it with. Yvonne, having turned down innumerable offers from Clare to stitch it, wore it like a badge of honor. She was wearing the pink and green slippers Clare had bought her last Christmas to replace the old pair that had suddenly vanished. Clare still endured Yvonne's occasional nagging about their whereabouts, and she wished that she had tossed the housecoat in the Salvation Army bin along with them.

She got out of the Jeep and entered the house, yanking the creaky, rusty-springed storm door and ambling up the concrete steps. "Is there a reason why you think I might not be sleeping at seven on a Saturday?" Clare asked, moving irritably through the outdated kitchen of her youth. She regretted every noise she made; it only served to remind her of the foolishness of last night. It had been quite a feat earlier just to get dressed in her Northwestern University sweats and a baggy, long-sleeved T-shirt.

"Can't a mother just want to fix her daughter some breakfast?" Yvonne asked, brandishing her inimitable signature pout.

Clare stooped to sit on the wooden bench beside the door to remove her wet rubber boots, irritated at her mother's insincere tug on what normal people might consider a heartstring. She shuffled in her sock feet to one of Yvonne's scuffed, maple-stained kitchen chairs, where she plopped down her jacket and scarf.

"Once in while I'd like to sleep in a little," she said. "That's all."

She was unwilling to admit that Yvonne's early-morning phone call came as a welcome diversion from her unsuccessful attempts to get a few winks. After a night of tossing and turning, her body ached, and she felt sure that her lingering lightheadedness would subside after a few greasy calories, which Clare had no energy to prepare in her current state.

"I hope you brought your appetite," Yvonne said, glowing as if she were a culinary queen.

"Smells good," Clare said. "As long as I'm here, might as well have a few bites." She snapped off half a piece of bacon, fending off her mother's protest to wait until it was ready. Then, jittery still, she poured herself a cup of coffee and lifted the *Danfield Press* on the counter and scanned it for evidence of the incident at the NiteLite, delighted that Yvonne had not yet broached the subject. Had Yvonne been privy to it, she would have blurted it in her morning phone call before Clare could have even lifted her heavy eyelids.

"The Wharton girls are in town," Clare said. "I just heard last night from Mr. Wharton."

Yvonne put the bacon in the oven on low and made the griddle sizzle with pancake batter. Clare's stomach growled with delight and churned from nausea simultaneously.

"Uh huh," Yvonne said.

"You know already?"

"Maggie called yesterday. We're invited to a barbeque tonight." Yvonne set the table and poured glasses of orange juice between flipping the pancakes.

"I thought maybe we could go by this afternoon, actually," Clare said. "I just want to say hi to the whole gang. I don't want to barge in on their family dinner. Sara and I will likely make our own visit. Isn't it a bit cold for a barbeque anyway?"

"You know Tug would barbeque anywhere, anyhow," Yvonne said. "Unless we were in the middle of a twelve-inch snowfall, there wouldn't be much to keep him from his grill. Maggie says most storms aren't a diversion either."

Clare listened tensely to the familiar words. Tug's grilling habits were becoming as well known as his tugging folklore, and Yvonne always found it necessary to repeat the obvious.

"I just thought we could go over there later this afternoon, so they could have dinnertime with the family," Clare continued.

"I'll be making some potato salad," Yvonne said, not to be swayed. "Martha and Frank might come by too."

"Sounds more like a summer picnic."

"Why don't you come by and pick me up at six?" Yvonne asked, beaming with total disregard.

"Mom, you go when you need to. I'm not planning on making an evening of it."

Yvonne flipped the last pancake onto a plate and took the glass baking dish from where it had been warming in the oven. She removed its foil cover and set breakfast on a hot pad on the table.

"I suppose you have something better to do this evening?" she asked.

"I do, Mother," Clare said, sitting down to breakfast.

"You should make some time for this," Yvonne said, sitting down with her. "These are our good friends. How often do we see them all together anymore? We are all like ships in the night."

They both spread butter and poured syrup on their pancakes while Clare inspected what had become of her mother's appearance: the wrinkled brow and sagging eyelids, the lackluster silver-brown hair. Yvonne had become what Clare could describe as a gleeful co-dependent. The once beautiful woman of her childhood had begun her physical deterioration at the point of Ray's disappearance. But it went beyond her premature aging; Clare had long ago concluded that Yvonne hadn't a clue how to live each day without putting Ray on some pedestal when she should be admitting to his abuse and abandonment. And better than that, Clare thought she should never speak of him again and maybe even consider dating someone new herself. Those who viewed her as a fiery personality were in deep denial or sadly mistaken, in Clare's opinion.

The hallway of Paxton family photos remained a constant source of annoyance to Clare. Yvonne's shrine was clearly an example of the unfinished family for Clare. As late as Clare's high -school pictures with her mother fifteen years ago, the two of them had borne an uncanny resemblance, except for their hair color, and Clare remembered the heap of compliments she and Yvonne had gotten for their signature long, wavy hair and slender builds. But the woman in the photos did not resemble the person seated across the table from her this morning. Clare had long let go of the notion that if Yvonne simply loosened her braid, colored her hair, and touched up with a little makeup, she could unearth the feminine beauty she had been.

"I'll be there at some point," Clare said.

She and Yvonne shared the quiet space with the elephants in the room while they finished their breakfast. She wondered whether her mother was as worn thin by them as she was.

"We'll be there, all right?" She wanted to make sure her mother heard that "we."

Yvonne heard her, but kept chewing as if she were dining alone.

"You can meet me over at the Whartons," Yvonne accepted at last.

Since the breakup of his marriage, Russell Martin had gone back to living in the two-bedroom brick lake house that had once been owned by his grandfather. A dollar and deed transfer passed the historic home to another generation, and Russell had become the official caretaker, no matter which relative occupied the house until his inevitable return after the separation.

Clare admired the miraculous accomplishments of Russell's slow, steady process of restoration. Either through the work of his own hands or through work done under his direction, the small, historic structure had been revitalized by a new roof, refurbished shutters, and a repaved front stone walkway. Every coat of paint and every replacement doorknob followed a blueprint to maintain the integrity of the house's roots.

Clare was not surprised to find Russell out back. Whether he was cleaning gutters or polishing a rifle, Russell was eternally in motion. His slow methodical movements could not diminish his penchant for always whittling away at some task, however small. But his meticulous attitude regarding life's physical details stood in odd contrast to the lack of care he'd applied to his own personal appearance; at least until his daughter's birth. In fact, his devotion to Mary was unlike any other relationship he'd had. When it came to Mary's care and fathering, it seemed to Clare that Russell became suddenly more clearheaded and engaging than he had ever been. Like Riley Jean Ridder's comments at her antique shop that Mary's birth had turned him into a man, everybody saw it. This likely aggravated his relationship with Courtney, who ceased to be the center of Russell's universe when Mary was born. It was an unattainable leap from being a Richardson daddy's girl to sharing Russell's unadorned lifestyle, a leap that would have been unthinkable without Russell's fawning over her. Their hot-and-heavy animal courtship was simply the only thing the Martins had in common.

Today, Russell was splitting wood. As Clare approached, he glanced at her, questioningly, then he rested his axe on the chopping block and moved in her direction.

"Clare," he offered wearily. "Everything okay?"

"Yeah, it's fine," she said. "I just wanted to see how you were doing." She shuffled toward him through the muted-rainbow of fallen leaves that were dying under pockets of the recent dips into freezing temperatures. "This has got to be a tough time. I wanted to see if you needed anything."

"Just chopping a little wood is all," he said.

She was here on a mission, but she hadn't yet formulated an exact plan. Her body was still a bit jittery, but better after the Yvonne breakfast. Her eyes focused on the lake behind Russell while she figured out how to wade through the natural silence of his wordlessness.

"This has always been one of the best locations on the lake," she said.

With his hands stuffed into his back pocket, Russell glanced back over his shoulder.

"Grandfather Hank would have just as soon been sitting out back and looking at the lake as anywhere," he allowed.

"It's amazing what you've done to this place," Clare said. "He would have been proud."

"It's looking better," he said, this time glancing back up at the house.

"Got any coffee, Russell?" Clare said shivering.

No matter how much he could have learned by living with Courtney, Russell was green when it came to the world of hospitality. He glanced back to the woodpile. "Uh, yeah," he said finally. "But it's been on a couple of hours though."

"Whatever you have would be great," Clare said quickly. "Just something to warm me a bit."

He hesitated and then turned back toward the house. Clare followed him around through the garage and in through the doorway to the small kitchen.

Surrounded by antiquated but clean and workable appliances, Russell poured the black thick substance into a mug he lifted from the dish drainer on the counter. Clare had no real need for his bitter cup of coffee, but she sipped it with interest anyway. Neither of them took a seat. She glanced through archways that led through to the dining room and to the small study. It no longer had the vast feel of their youth, but its memorable style had been keenly preserved.

Russell's grandfather wasn't much for the chattering either, but he had put on a heck of a summertime pig roast. From the few times Clare and her friends had been invited, she remembered a collection of kinfolk who had come from up north, but who otherwise rarely visited. Russell supposedly visited them during school breaks. His family led a relatively obscure existence, with lifestyles that were neither notorious nor remarkable and that didn't stir much small-town chitchat.

"I just wanted to see if there was anything I could do, Russell," Clare said. "I know how hard it must have been to take the doll from Mrs. Ridder for Mary."

Russell nodded. She tried to interpret the vacancy in his eyes.

"I appreciate your offer," he said, looking at her with a hard and edgy look for a split second. "You know . . . I was just thinking about her when you saw me."

"I know how much you loved her, Russell."

"That was a good idea to buy it for her no matter what happens. I don't think of stuff like that."

Clare pretended to not notice his discomfort in the conversation.

"How's Courtney?" she asked. "Both of you have been through so much."

"Don't see her much anymore. Especially since . . ." His voice trailed off for a moment. "The divorce is almost final."

He crossed his long, lanky legs and tapped his fingers on the countertop molding behind him. Even if Russell wasn't her type, Clare identified with the women who frothed over his men's cologne-poster physique especially because of—not in spite of—his rumpled, messy attire. The infatuation wouldn't last infinitely, given his dirty fingernails and his unscrubbed laborer's elbows, but it was obviously enough to spellbind the likes of Courtney, in spite of their long-term differences.

"You two seemed pretty close after Mary's disappearance," Clare said. "I thought maybe you had second thoughts about splitting up."

Russell tossed his head side to side in reply.

Clare, her mind freshly imprinted with the actions of his wandering wife, was dying to shout that he was better off without the slut, but thought better of hurting Russell even more. Instead, she followed Russell's steady stare toward the lake out the window over the kitchen sink.

"It was all a pipe dream, Clare," he said after a while. "A joke . . . we should have never done it."

Clare was taken by his clarity.

"You tried, Russell," she said. "I know people bugged you because you were opposites. But that doesn't matter."

Russell reached for a mug to occupy his hands. Clare shifted closer to the laundry room.

"Oh, we were more than just opposites," he interrupted, with an unexpected spike of anger.

Clare pounced. "I know it's not my place," she said. "But I never thought she was good enough for you, Russell. I think that's why your friends said things. She never appreciated you. Everybody knows what a great dad you were."

He shuffled sideways and crossed his arms over his chest.

"Yeah . . . well," he said slowly. "I can't blame it all on her. I knew how different she was."

Clare was disturbed that he had an ounce of defense for her, even now.

"She could have treated you better."

"That ain't it. Everybody talked bad about Courtney like she wasn't a good mother. She loved Mary." He spoke as if he actually understood the woman who'd left him. "She just wanted her to have a better life than . . ."

"Than you could give her." Clare spoke more quickly than she wished she would have. She turned and set her cup on the counter.

Behind the laundry gate, little stacks of underwear and socks lay neatly folded on top of the washer. Mary's jeans and jacket were tossed unceremoniously over the dryer. Her heart broke at the thought of him still washing her things, or that he hadn't the strength to put them away just yet. She glanced back at Russell and nodded toward the laundry room.

"Would you like me to help you?" she asked empathetically. "With this?"

"No . . . not yet." He walked and stood in front of the room, as if he were protecting his only connection to Mary. It was as if he held her by virtue of hanging on to her things. "I'm not ready yet," he said again.

"That's got to be so hard."

"Not until after we have the funeral," he said. "But my family will help. When it's time."

"When is the funeral?" Clare was discomfited by his use of the word "funeral" the moment she queried him for this detail. Her desire for more information had shamelessly trumped the question of whether this type of event was really in the works just yet.

"We don't know yet," Russell said. "We're still in the process of figuring out whether she can be legally declared . . . dead."

Russell bowed his head; he appeared to struggle.

"Russell, I am so, so sorry," Clare said. In her mind, it seemed certain that Mary was gone, except for a few loose ends that had to be tied. But she couldn't bring herself to say this out loud.

"They're still finishing the investigation," Russell said. "But it isn't much like there's a killer on the loose, anymore."

Clare looked up.

"I guess they've determined that for sure?" she asked. "That's the official stance from the police department?"

"They aren't saying for sure just yet," Russell said, hesitating. "But it looks that way."

"Everybody knows they look at family," Clare said carefully. "That had to have been particularly hard."

He looked weary, and Clare knew she was pushing his limit.

"Especially for Courtney," she went on. "She was with Mary at the time. And no signs of struggle . . . they must have scrutinized Courtney pretty well."

"But there wasn't anything," he said quickly. "She came forward and cooperated and all."

Russell stood at the center of the kitchen and rubbed his idle hands together. Somehow he made it clear that he was done talking. It dawned on Clare that he might not care to rehash this anymore right now to satisfy someone's curiosity.

She felt a pit in her stomach for any parent who had to imagine the scenarios surrounding the death of their child. She flashed back to the days when her father Ray went missing, and the uncertainty that seemed to grip the neighborhood for a period of time. There was a lot of chatter about what might have happened to him, but Clare always knew in her heart that Ray had willfully walked away.

It was a leap to compare the initial groundswell of concern among the neighbors between that shown to a grown man and that shown to Russell's baby girl. If anything, Clare viewed the hysteria surrounding Ray as an act of support for Yvonne. But Mary was too young to pack her own bags and flee, and she deserved more than a prayer that she had passed peacefully.

Clare offered Russell a hug. In return, he pressed her back like a man unaccustomed to showing affection. They let go, and Clare pushed open the back door to the garage to exit.

"Clare, nobody should be blaming Courtney," Russell added

as she left. "I know people thought bad things about her. But we were both to blame. I knew better too."

"Okay," she said. "I understand, Russell."

She closed the door behind her, troubled both for Russell's sake and for her disturbing memories about Ray.

SIXTEEN

At the moment Jared pulled up to her curb and she heard his car door shut, Clare looked out her second-story bedroom window while she threaded her second earring through her earlobe. She watched him take his smooth, assured steps up her front walkway. He was smartly dressed in a cream-colored turtleneck, dark blue corduroys, and her favorite leather bomber jacket, his neck wrapped in a checkered scarf.

He was unlike any off-duty cop she'd ever encountered and tonight he looked delicious.

Interestingly enough, Jared had taken her offer for an early but brief visit to the Whartons' somewhat enthusiastically. After the stop at the barbecue, they would return to Clare's for a movie at home.

As much as she wanted to see her friend Sara Wharton and introduce Jared as a date, Clare hadn't yet apologized to Mr. Wharton for having a few too many drinks at the bar and for his having to break up her little scene with Courtney. She wasn't concerned about him bringing it up as much as the possibility that it could come up in Jared's company or that Yvonne could grab hold of the incident. There was no telling how that would play out.

She waited for the bell to ring, and then she headed downstairs and opened the door to the cool, crisp air. Seeing how well he looked, Clare was pleased she had chosen her favorite taupe sweater, blue jeans, and brown, Chicago-style boots.

"You look nice and completely overdressed." She said, motioning for him to enter.

"And you look fabulous," he said. "If I close my eyes, maybe we won't be in Danfield for a couple of hours."

She happily accepted his compliment.

"There's the protest I was looking for earlier, when I told you about this thing," she said. "We don't have to go do this. I could pretend I have an ache of some sort and find some other time to see these people."

"You know what I mean," he teased. "A stop at the Whartons' would be great for us." He hung his jacket and gray-patterned wool neck scarf on her coat rack.

"Dreaming of fancy getaways isn't going to make it any better," she said. "If you're going to be a lifer, you'll have to start accepting our very simple, unadorned lifestyle."

Clare intentionally shuffled them toward the kitchen for a bit of relaxing before going to the Whartons' house.

She knew he wanted to be formally introduced to Yvonne in a dating sense, not so much to get her approval but out of a gentleman's obligation. She knew it would make him more comfortable to meet her, while she was selfishly dreading the commentary Yvonne was sure to make around the Whartons and anyone else who might be there.

"Tonight is plenty fancy for me," Jared said. "But I do want to make sure you'll survive dragging me along. Unpopular police chiefs have a way of bringing down the mood."

"In this group, don't worry. I called Maggie, and she's delighted. And you know Tug pretty well."

"He's one of my few supporters," Jared said confidently. "I stop for a cup of coffee at the NiteLite a couple of times a week if I can. Tug is a good guy."

"You'd be surprised to know how many fans you have. But it's not like you to worry about what anybody thinks."

"True enough," he said. "If you're okay, I know I'm okay."

Clare pulled out a couple of cold beers and flipped the tops directly into the garbage, thinking she'd have to make it right with Mr. Wharton. They took their pre-party hour to the living room, which by now had been cleared of all the newspapers on Mary. They maintained a physical distance, but Clare was in tune to the silent sizzle between them.

"Look, don't worry about my mother," she said again, as though she believed she could take that same advice. "With any luck, she'll behave with all those people around. It's a short visit, in any event. I'll give you a last chance to skip it altogether."

"I do like the idea of staying in and having a private evening," he said. "On the other hand, I'll relish our coming out, so to speak. It's a win in any event, as long as you aren't worrying about your mom."

"We'll only stay for a short while," Clare said. "A drink and a couple of hors d'oeuvres. Then we'll be back and snuggling at home."

"I like the snuggling part," Jared said.

She smiled at him and got up to tidy the room and get the fireplace ready for their return. He kept talking, and she responded casually. As her soft wintry-jazz CD played in the background, Clare's thoughts wandered to her afternoon visit to Russell's. She finished the fire and stood by the window, tracing her growing frustration in the distorted moisture's frosty reflection. How alone he must be without little Mary as the center of his life. He was taking the high road of defending Courtney's motivations, while he was the one left with a laundry room full of memories.

"Clare?" Jared was saying. "If I were a paranoid man, I'd be worried about your level of enthusiasm all of a sudden."

"What?" Clare said abruptly.

"Enough thinking about your mother, okay?"

"Thank goodness you're not a paranoid man," she said.

"I'm not inclined to be." Jared confirmed. "In law enforcement we steer toward a 'healthy' dose of skepticism, no more, no less."

"And you're patient too," Clare said affectionately. "Really patient. About us, I mean."

He grinned. "Did I jump to conclusions with my smartness? Do I hear commitment in your voice?"

Still thinking about Russell, she nearly brought up the case, but thought better of it.

"What you're hearing is me telling you that we ought to get

going," she said. "So we can get back to starting a fire and rolling that movie."

Clare took her bottle of beer to the kitchen counter. Jared tossed his empty into the garbage. She gave him a quick peck on the cheek and then hurried them out the front door.

They could hear the bursts of talk from the Wharton household spilling all the way to the curb. An unsuspecting guest might turn tail and leave, but Clare kept moving, clutching Jared's arm on the frosty porch steps. The clan was all together at last and the evening was only in its early stages; she couldn't help but feel a certain amount of familial excitement about it.

They entered the household without knocking, raucous as it was. So far, there were a few neighbors, the Wharton sisters, Maggie, and Tug.

"Oh Clare, come in!" Silvia, the eldest of the Wharton girls, sang out. She enveloped Clare in a welcoming hug. Peppered by loving glances from the lot of them, blanketed by the holiday scents of days gone by, Clare gathered in all the reminders of her home away from home. However crazy it was, she'd loved the Wharton household growing up.

"Everybody made it out," Clare said.

"We're all here, and we're about to blow the roof off," Silvia's voice reverberated. She hugged Jared as well; she was the only one who'd never left Danfield and already knew him. "Now Jared, I'm just warning you, we're really not insane people, just a little nutty all together! Come on in."

Clare and Jared shuffled to the corner of the kitchen where the room was awash in an assortment of topics.

"Hello, Clare!" Maggie embraced her. "In you come! Tug, will you get Jared's coat?"

The two men clasped hands as Clare greeted two more Wharton sisters. The fourth, Sara, was by the counter, mired in the task of preparing pre-dinner snacks and Clare could see her awaiting the best friend hug, saving it for last.

"There you are!" she called when she saw Clare. "And hugged by the best of them."

"Wouldn't have it any other way," Clare said, embracing her long-lost friend as though it were just yesterday.

"Where's Yvonne?" Sara asked.

"She ought to be along any minute," Clare said. "I thought she'd be here by now."

"How are things going?" Sara asked. "You're still here! Last we spoke, you were hightailing it back to Chicago."

"Haven't I been reminded of that lately," Clare said.

"I assume, then, that you've made peace with being back?" Sara asked directly.

Clare had missed the familiarity between them. They had grown close during high school, and Sara, more than any of her girlfriends back then, knew the realities of Clare's home life. Though Sara now lived in Cedar Rapids, Iowa, and though the two had fallen out of regular contact, they could resume their friendship in an instant.

"It's a big leap to say I've made peace with it," Clare said. "But the job is pretty good. Lee is a great guy to work for."

"Pretty phenomenal that you could pick up where you left off at the bank," Sara smiled. "Now you're a muckety-muck, according to Dad."

"One bright spot in the scheme of things, right? But not my first love, as you know."

"I know very well that you'd have the beloved law enforcement degree if you hadn't come back to Danfield. And we'll get to that, but for now I'd like to finish the nickel tour. I've got to get caught up on the Danfield soap opera."

She knew Sara had a short attention span for career chat, which was only confirmed when Sara halted her food prep and made a hand gesture: *more, more.*

"What exactly do I need to say about my mother?" Clare offered rhetorically. "It's still the same old thing. We can't seem to call a truce. Sometimes I want to believe it's not that bad. But really, I think I've just found better ways to deal with her. Or not."

She knew Sara understood what she wasn't saying; there were things better left unsaid in the midst of a cheery gathering.

"Then it shouldn't be much for you to get back to school." Sara knocked Clare's hip with her own.

"What do I need a degree for?" Clare asked, tongue in cheek. "Conceivably I'll have a shot at bank president in the next ten years. Who knows, maybe I could run for a local office."

"Okay, Clare, if you're going to be sassy about it," Sara replied. "Let's have some fun here. Tell me about this Jared guy. That's what I really want to know. Maybe it's the real reason why you're not getting off your butt? Dating the police chief? Mom says he's stirred things up around here, but he's a pretty good guy. I know Dad likes him a lot."

"We're getting to know each other still," Clare said awkwardly

"I wouldn't say we've made it to serious yet. With both our careers and his trying to revamp our sophisticated police department, we rely on spontaneity for the bits we get together."

Clare thought about how to characterize their relationship, even to a good friend like Sara. She hadn't prepared for the emotion of sharing him publicly or how to articulate her thoughts about him. She didn't relish the thought of Yvonne scrutinizing them. On some level Jared had been happy that they'd not jumped into the dating game for all to see a year ago, though lately he'd been pushing to make their "steady and gradual" more normal.

She caught his look from across the room in the kitchen where she and Sara were fussing with the food. With a beer in hand, anchored comfortably in the guy corner, he'd broken from a seemingly powerful conversation with Tug. Sara caught their affectionate glances.

"I'd say that looks like it's a tad serious," Sara teased.

"It's the alcohol talking," Clare pressed back.

"Right."

She looked away from Jared, enjoying the intrigue between them she couldn't explain; it transcended the milling sea of bodies.

"Here, girls," Maggie said, arriving to hand each of them a tray. "I'll finish the preparations. Out to the living room. It's getting a bit crowded in here."

They headed for the front room, which had ballooned now with more visitors. One of the daughters was welcoming Yvonne through the front door. Another daughter took Yvonne's hot potato salad from her and began passing it relay-fashion through the crowd to the kitchen. When it reached its destination, Maggie peeked out from the kitchen.

"Yvonne, glad you made it okay!" she called. "Tug could have come and got you."

"I got a ride," Yvonne said, rolling her eyes toward Clare. "Tug's got his hands full. With the salad and all . . . and I knew it would be crowded out front."

Clare moved toward the fireplace, out of Yvonne's path and toward where Jared and Tug had formed a growing male grouping, but Sara intercepted her.

"I'm not going to let you off that easy. Dad just introduced me, he's so intense and nice looking . . . So tell me more about the handsome police chief?"

Yvonne was moving up on them.

"There isn't much to tell," Clare said. "Like I said, we've kept it pretty casual, but we see each other when time permits and the mood strikes us. I'd say we're pretty good friends," Clare stopped short of expressing her true feelings and offered Sara a bit of a girly grin. If she could have snapped him from the room at this moment she would have. Sara wasn't the only one eyeing their interaction in the room full of eager-to-gossip neighbors.

"Good friends? Good grief, girl! A successful, handsome city boy—I'd say he was the perfect white knight for a girl like you. And you don't need any more guy friends. It's really hard to make babies if you know what I mean," Sara laughed.

"Another time," Clare inserted. She turned; Yvonne was right beside her.

"Mom," she said. "Can I get you something?"

"You know, Sara," Yvonne said, "he's never really come and introduced himself properly to me."

"Mom, enough," Clare said. "You've met Jared on a number of occasions."

"He seems like a very nice man, Mrs. Paxton," Sara kindly defended.

"I suppose," Yvonne replied. "If you like city boys."

Clare threw Sara a glance to leave it be. She turned her back to Yvonne and edged closer to what had become a mixed gathering at the fireplace.

The laughter and the chatter that had been flowing between friends and neighbors came suddenly to a standstill.

"It really is a shame," Tug said, finishing a statement.

"What's a shame?" Clare asked.

"I'm just talking about how sad this has been about Mary," Tug said, causing Clare to stop for a moment and listen in. "Russell and his daughter were inseparable. He's even more of a loner now. His boss was telling me that he's been much more withdrawn, even with the family. He wasn't a social guy to begin with. Talented with his hands, though . . . and good to that little girl."

"And Courtney," a neighbor interjected with displeasure. "She's just the opposite. Trotting around town with all kinds of guys . . . looking down her nose at the lot of us."

Clare watched Jared's eyes and watched the people around the group nodding.

"It's true," Clare said. "Russell is pretty much alone now."

Jared took a swallow of his beer.

"Maggie and I keep talking about that picture of her pretty blue suede shoes," Tug said. "Just lying there all clean and innocent of the tragedy. My wife and I just can't get the picture out of our heads."

At first she was simply relieved that there was some conversing on the matter of Mary that she hadn't instigated. But Mr.

Wharton's summation bashed a million little splinters in the dime store analysis. The image of the shoes was suddenly before Clare. Something he had said: *clean and innocent of the tragedy.*

"Hey, hey with this stuff at our beautiful party," Maggie was scolding. "Must be better things to discuss."

Tug engulfed his wife in bear hug. "Gosh almighty. You are so right, my lovely. Let me assume a role more suitable to my talents." He nodded and made a beeline for the cooler to dole out more alcohol as the group with the short attention span eagerly fanned out.

Clare, however, remained momentarily, enveloped by Tug's last words as if someone had knocked the breath out of her. "Mr. Wharton, let me help you with that."

Clare threaded herself through the party to gather her thoughts and to grab before there could be any more comments about Courtney on any level.

Clean and innocent of the tragedy. There had been some blood on Derek when he'd arrived at her house that night. He had talked about a pool of blood, about Mary's blood-soaked clothing. Clare mentally scoured the bundles of journalistic post-mortem that lay hidden in her hallway closet: all of them, to the best of her recollection, agreed on the presence of the blood. She'd already considered the lack of tissue samples at the scene. Now her mind was racing over this: why would the shoes be free of blood and not the clothes?

Clare pulled back the front door. Tug was bent over the cooler on the front porch pulling out beer and wine coolers. "Can I take some of those and pass them around the room?" Clare asked.

"No, no, you get back in there. It's chilly out here," he said. "This is my job."

"Mr. Wharton, I want to apologize for Friday night," Clare jumped in.

He set down his collection of liquor on a little table and shut the cooler. "Clare, don't say another word about that. It's done. I didn't even have to eject the two of you," Tug's face was bright, fatherly, and with an unmistakable grin that told her that he might have been amused by the exchange.

She patted her steamy cheeks as though they might be noticeably gushing perspiration because it wasn't just her apology she was thinking about.

"Oh, Clare, you're not upset about it are you? If you saw what I see day in and day out in that place, you wouldn't give it another thought. And I haven't seen you and Courtney spar like that since you two were little girls." He leaned into her. "She makes my blood boil too sometimes."

The front door opened and Jared came out.

"You guys need to get back in there," Tug said. "I surely don't need this much help slinging beer." He headed back in with his arms full.

"You about ready?" Clare asked.

Jared smiled. "You're kidding," he said. "Don't you want to hang around a while longer?"

"No, let's go," Clare said. She forced a smile. "I promised you a quiet movie night alone."

"This has turned out to be fun. You'd break everybody's heart if you left now." Jared affectionately pressed his lips to her temple. "I never thought I'd be turning down a well-deserved moment alone with you," he said. "But you never get to see these girls together like this. Come on."

Her thoughts were racing over the newspapers in her closet, most of her subconscious trying to remember exactly what they'd said. With the part of her brain she had left, she wondered if she should just tell him what she'd just realized and decided against it for now.

"My mother seems a bit agitated," she said for some excuse that might pry him from an evening he deserved.

"Look, don't worry about me," he replied. "You said she would behave in a crowd, and she is behaving. I could tell by your glances a while ago that I had become a topic. No bottles were thrown; you two maintained your composure. I'll take that as a positive sign, for now."

He frowned at her. "You've just been taking this Martin case so seriously," he continued. "I dreaded your reaction to that conversation, but look . . . you walked away with Tug, and now everybody has moved on to something more appropriate."

She stopped thinking about the case for a split second; her whole mind snapped into focus. He was grinning at her, like he pitied her a little.

"Okay," she said, wishing she could share his good mood. "We'll hang a little longer. But I'm not staying all night so you can play the martyr and then hold it against me."

"Try to forget about what you're worrying about," he grinned, eternally confident. "I'm fine, Yvonne's fine. This is wonderful. But if you are not feeling good? You look a bit pale."

"I think I'll go in the kitchen and get some water," she said.

They both headed back inside to mix with the company.

She poured herself a glass of ice water and held it against her cheek, thinking about the newspapers, as the party swung on without her. Had it not been for Jared, she'd have bolted through the back door.

The evening dragged on through Tug's famous barbeque ribs and chicken, and the household's feast of mouth-watering homemade pastas and salad creations, and a dessert collection that could have put renowned caterers to shame. The Wharton girls grew more boisterous and competitive spirits flared. Clare remained in the background, watching Jared enjoy a social hour making new friends.

They were quiet for the short ride home and the walk to her front doorstep.

"Looks like we have to save movie night for another time," Clare said at last.

"Seriously, Clare," he said. "Just give me a minute and I'll get that fire going. A late movie would be perfect—even better with a little nightcap?"

She watched his immediate disappointment spring into a passion for saving the evening, no matter what she had to throw at him.

"You were the one who decided we should stay at the party the whole evening," Clare said, annoyed. "It's late now."

He dared to shake his head happily. "I stand guilty, but it turned out pretty good. It ended up being a great time to get to know some of these old codgers a little bit better. For a minute there I didn't feel like the lonely old chief."

Clare knew full well that Jared deserved a relaxing night with the neighbors and a chance to soften his image. It had been an evening that technically couldn't have been better for the two of them.

"Do you really care about stuff like that?" she asked.

"Clare?" he frowned. "Don't we both?"

She felt his questioning stare.

"I really need to get some sleep," she said. "I'm more exhausted than I thought."

"I asked you earlier if you felt well. Now that I think about it, you spent a lot of time hanging out in the kitchen away from anybody after I suggested we hang around. I guess I shouldn't have suggested we stay longer."

"I'm just not up for a later night," she said. "I'd fall asleep on you in a half hour."

"That would be okay too," Jared said quietly.

They stood there in the doorway for a while.

"I'm sorry," she said. "I promise you a rain check."

His face fell.

"All right," he said at last. He pulled her hands over the threshold of her front door, offering her a last confused yet gentlemanly gaze. Then he let them go.

For a split second—thinking about what Sara had said about him, her white knight—Clare nearly yanked him back. She knew full well she'd squandered the evening with Jared. But she let him go, watched his car turn off and disappear, and then, yawning, she went to get her newspapers out of the closet.

She lay, finally still, in the darkness of her bedroom; her eyelids were much heavier than they were an hour ago when her eyes had been burning a hole in her kitchen ceiling. She wanted to sleep so that she could pull her thoughts together in the light of day, but the late-night scrounging for some cohesive thought had left her wired and more confused. The beers after Jared left didn't help either.

It wasn't until Mr. Wharton had unfurled his remark about the clean shoes that certain ideas began to jell. "Why would there be shoes at all, not to mention no blood on them?" She had said it aloud as soon as she had thought it, shattering the silence at her kitchen table, spilling her Miller in the process.

Ordinary accounts were puzzling contradictions this go-round, more about what was *not* said than what *was* said. Vivid writings about the outer banks where Derek had tangled with Coach for his attention left little to the imagination. Bloodstained articles of clothing were described with horrific detail. Yet material questioning and analyzing the unblemished shoes seemed remarkably absent.

Clare lay in bed thinking, hearing the echo over and over: why were they there?

Aside from the insanity of a child with shoes on at naptime, her thoughts about the tight-lipped police department brought her full circle to her feelings for the man she'd left unsatisfied and confused at her front door earlier. They should be lovers stretched out on her couch as the movie ended, talking about these major issues in their community. But instead she'd found herself quite interested in a guy who couldn't just be her boyfriend—that by itself was a milestone, as Sara had tried to impress on her. He was a guy who couldn't help her untangle this mess in her head.

Tucked beneath her chilly bed sheets, she thought about her inability to coordinate her recent weeks of confusion about the Martin matter and the resurgence of her thoughts about living in Danfield, which hadn't troubled her this much in a long while.

SEVENTEEN

Yvonne stepped gleefully down the front walkway in her charcoal gray suit, which was usually reserved for funerals and other special occasions, as Clare peered through the frosted passenger window, feeling the all-too-familiar twinge of irritation. It would be the second time in two days that she would nurse a splitting headache in the company of her mother. She was exhausted; she'd gone through every column inch of the papers again for hours. To the extent that she trusted the journalists, she'd found what she'd expected to find: there had been no mention of blood on the shoes, and there had been no mention of the complete strangeness of finding Mary's shoes in the first place. In other words, it seemed all but impossible that Mary's assumed death could still be seen as an accident. But what was she supposed to do about this discovery now? She wasn't the police; this wasn't her case to solve. Surely somebody had noticed this besides her. But it wasn't any clearer what she should do in the light of day as she had hoped.

Her head was pounding and Yvonne was opening the door; now was not the best time for her to think about it.

"I'm so pleased you called me to go to church," Yvonne chirped, settling into the front seat.

"Nothing to get too excited about, Mom," Clare said.

Yvonne was not to be deterred. "I can be excited that my daughter wants to go to church with me."

"You can," Clare affirmed.

Without further discussion, Clare savored the brief silence until they rolled into the parking lot of the First Assembly of God. Apart from its sparkling stained glass windows and its palatial stone steps, the simple wood structure was quite visually unremarkable. But the church had sustained a loyal constituency since the late 1800s, and the town had bestowed on it a status comparable to that of the bell tower, right on behind the NiteLite. In addition to the faithful, the nonbelievers in the community also participated in the weekly tithing to support a multitude of events. It was a venue for Scout troop meetings and women's bridge clubs, and beyond prayerful Sunday services, the First Assembly had played host to many a wedding and holiday concert.

"I thought the Wharton family put out a nice spread last night," Yvonne said. "Don't you, dear?"

"They really did," Clare replied with little emotion, having anticipated an inquisition.

"And everybody had such a great time. You stayed longer than

I thought you would," Yvonne entered gamely. "We could have gone together after all."

Clare's instinct was to express how well Jared had enjoyed the affair, but she wasn't after a tussle today and let it go unaddressed.

"What do you say we go out to Mae's Diner after church for some breakfast?" she asked, locking the Jeep's doors.

"That would be lovely!" Happily diverted, Yvonne trotted up the front steps.

Clare felt as conspicuous as she had during her recent showing at the NiteLite on Friday; she had become less involved both with church and professional drinking since her return to Danfield. While all the remarks and waves were kind, her absence had not gone without notice. Just like the Wharton party, she could only hope that her little tap dance with Courtney the other evening hadn't been broadcast to the congregation by those who found comfort in both places.

Sitting beside her mother, with the sunrise splashing its majestic tinted sparkle across the congregation, Clare clung to her jaded view of churchgoing that she'd inherited from Ray. Except for a handful of times, as Clare recalled, her father had stayed home from church to sleep off his drunken stupor. She remembered leaving him at home, hacking over a cup of coffee with a smoldering cigarette butt dangling between his fingers. While Yvonne put on her "hopeful hat" that Ray would come along every Sunday, Clare prayed each week that he wouldn't join them, and she was embarrassed on the rare occasions when he did. After Ray had left, the whole church routine became less interesting to her.

After the service, she exited onto the front steps into the piercing morning sunrise, having unwittingly experienced a few moments of religious euphoria in spite of her thoughts of Ray and Yvonne's faux doting glances and pats to her thigh, as if she were a well-behaved child.

Mae's Diner wasn't much to look at inside or out, yet it served up the best biscuits and gravy and mouth-watering pancakes. The diner had been so successful from its founding that the residents of Danfield were helpless to keep it a hometown secret, and members of neighboring communities made the regular weekend trek to sample Mae's legendary breakfasts. Folks consciously abandoned their diets and risked their waistlines for the deliciously sinful homemade fare. Even Courtney's parents had found their way from time to time to belly up with the common folk for a sampling of the signature homemade rye bread and blackberry jam.

"Oh, look!" Yvonne waved and pointed through the diner's parking lot at some people she recognized. "This is great, Clare."

"I always forget how popular this place is," Clare said, scouting for parking options.

"I wonder if we'll see Mae today," Yvonne said. "I heard her arthritis was getting worse."

Though Mae Buhler had long ago relinquished the physical work of running the diner, including her famous berry picking, to the younger members of her clan, the eighty-seven-year-old founder still regularly frequented her establishment. For three to four hours a day and longer on Sunday, Mae came to mingle with her friends. Following her playful kitchen inspection to ensure the authenticity of her succulent crepes and such, she could be found sipping a cup of her signature blend of coffee at the end of the wooden counter.

Clare and Yvonne were lucky to make it to the screened-in porch, sealed already with storm windows, for their wait to be seated. They were flanked inside and out by the diehard regulars who'd wait for upwards of an hour for their turn even in the chilly temperatures. Between the tiny space heater in the corner of the porch and the warmth from the sea of bodies huddled together, they were comfortable. Clare sipped a complimentary cup of black coffee and nabbed nibbles of homemade sweet breads from a rotating basket to squelch the grumbling in her stomach through their forty-five minute wait.

"We should do this more often," Yvonne said when they had finally taken possession of their menus.

"Maybe we will again sometime."

"Everybody is excited to see you, too, Clare," Yvonne continued.

"Don't you think you're a bit overboard today?"

"I certainly do not."

"You're acting as if I just rode into town," Clare said. "I see most of these people on a pretty regular basis." Clare made sure her tone was not too aggravating.

"Not singing hymns. Not at Mae's. There's a difference, you know."

"I know, I know. That's why I thought this was a good idea."

"And there is nothing wrong with my boasting about my beautiful daughter," Yvonne reminded her.

Clare was out of ways to get Yvonne to tone it down and just smiled, reluctantly.

The waitress scurried back with the coffee. Clare ordered the special egg scramble and rye toast while her mother ordered the blackberry pancakes.

"You do look wonderful today," Yvonne continued. "But a bit tired. I hope you got some sleep last night."

"I got plenty of sleep," Clare lied.

"You know, I'd love to see a young man in your life," Yvonne said. "Just the thought of being a grandmother . . ."

Clare swallowed Yvonne's comment on the heels of Sara's poke last night about getting a man who wasn't just a buddy.

As far as Clare could read, Yvonne wasn't even considering Jared as a potential cause of her tiredness. Clare again, decided not to acknowledge it in lieu of more pressing thoughts.

"Mother," she said. "Do you remember that night at dinner, when Vivian called with the news about Mary's disappearance?"

The waitress freshened their coffee, and Clare waited irritably while Yvonne paused to tinker with the milk and sugar balance again.

"Of course I do, honey," she responded at last.

"Did anything strike you as unusual about the whole thing?"

"Well, I don't know what you're asking," Yvonne said. "It was devastating news . . . I remember that."

Breakfast arrived, and Yvonne burrowed into her pancake prep. Clare fiddled quietly with her plate.

"I'm just thinking about how nasty everything was between Russell and Courtney at the time," Clare said after a minute. "But at the news conference, they seemed pretty chummy."

"Of course they came together for the sake of their missing child, dear," Yvonne said. "Aren't you going to eat, Clare? Your food is getting cold."

Clare nibbled on her toast. "Maybe I'll take it with me."

"You can't eat leftover eggs," Yvonne said. "You're worrying me. Now come on; enjoy this wonderful treat."

"It just seems they went from clawing each other's eyes out to holding hands," Clare said. "I think that's a bit much. Russell might have misread the signals. You know how much the divorce was tearing him apart."

Yvonne made another purposeful scan of Clare's plate and returned to devouring her own breakfast.

"Who knows what people do during tough times," she said.

Clare wondered whether Yvonne was reminiscing about her own marital compromises. Her mother would be damned before she would ever offer a disparaging word about her marriage or Ray. Just once, Clare wanted her to admit it had been crap.

"Do you remember what they said on the news about what Mary was wearing when it happened?" Clare asked.

"Oh, I wish I could make pancakes like these," Yvonne said.

"Mom, do you remember?" Clare asked again.

Clare sat waiting during the interminable silence that was only abated by the sounds of silverware clicking against their plates.

Yvonne wrangled joyfully with the last couple of bites of her pancakes. "Let me think. She had on a pretty blouse and skirt, if I remember correctly. It's just so horrible to consider. This is really not good breakfast talk, Clare!"

Clare signaled for the check.

"Do you remember her shoes?" she asked.

Yvonne's expression changed. "Of course," she said. "That picture in the paper. Those blue shoes of hers just sitting on that rock, all pristine looking. Just like her mother always dressed her. No matter what people say, she always looked so nice with Courtney.

Honestly, that Russell had her all scuffed up like she was a little boy sometimes."

"But looking at the clothes and shoes, she seemed a bit dressed up for a nap, don't you think?" Clare said.

"Well, I don't know," said Yvonne, flustered. "Who would think of something like that?"

Clare left enough cash on the table for the bill and the tip.

"It doesn't seem like proper nap-time attire," Clare said. "At least it wouldn't if it were my kid."

They got up from the table and headed to get their coats from the rack. Yvonne waved good-bye to some acquaintances.

They were walking through the parking lot, dodging the Sunday traffic.

"If you'd ever had children yourself, you'd know these things," Yvonne said suddenly.

Clare stopped walking for a sec. "What things?"

"What's got you so excited?" Yvonne turned and asked, and they both started moving again. "About what Mary was wearing at her nap time? Does it matter now? It's such a sorrowful time for the family and you're worrying about her clothing! Clare, let's not spoil this beautiful morning talking about Mary Martin, of all things."

Clare waited until they got back in the Jeep. Then, key in the ignition, she turned to stare down her mother.

"Tell me, Mother. If they never find the person who did this to Mary, are you going to feel nervous?"

"I don't think it was a person who did this," stammered Yvonne. "I thought the police were acting like it was a . . . like it was some kind of nonhuman mishap."

"And this mishap just carried her out of her bed? Wearing shoes?" Clare had to push her harder on her discovery.

"Clare, you know exactly what happened. She climbed out of her bed and got out of the house. She was an active four-year-old. Boy, if you could have seen yourself at that age—it was hard chasing after you all the time. It's no time to be bashing the parents."

"We're not talking about me," Clare snapped from the ridiculous notion that a small child stopped to put on her shoes if she had climbed out herself, "And I'm not bashing anybody!"

Her head was pounding from too much caffeine this time. Yvonne watched her and waited.

"I'm just wondering," Clare said, with difficulty. "What if somebody really did take her from her bed that day? Doesn't it make you nervous that they're still around somewhere? Worse still, living near us? Among us?"

Yvonne said nothing. Eventually Clare started the car. They were quiet all the way home. At least they had talked about something besides Ray, or Jared, Clare found herself thinking.

"Come on in for a while," Yvonne said as she stepped onto the curb. "I'll make us a fresh pot of coffee."

"I'd explode if I have any more coffee. I think I'll go home and take a nap," Clare said.

"That's a good idea, dear," Yvonne sashayed up the walkway in the same manner as before.

Clare got home to find everything on her kitchen table just as she had left it last night, including the smell of evaporated beer. She was frustrated and drained enough to let it lie, and she curled up on the couch and drifted quickly into sleep.

Derek could often be found tinkering in his garage on a late Sunday afternoon. There was always oil to change or new seat covers to install or tools to reorganize. When it wasn't his automotive projects, he could be found invested in his love of woodworking. Eyeing him with quiet affection, Clare paused at Derek's wooden garage door to observe him restocking his shelves. It reminded her of their teenage years, when he would undertake tasks as simple as stacking wood for his father and turn them into minor works of art. He put the same endless energy into polishing shoes as he did into the upkeep and waxing of the family's vehicles. Even the stray cat used to get an extra-thorough brushing every spring when his coat began to shed feverishly on all of Derek's mother's furniture. He was happiest when everything was in place. His propensity for orderliness was among the characteristics that had cemented his long-standing employment at the hardware store, and it was a trait Clare figured would have been more of a woman magnet than it had turned out to be.

At last Derek turned in her direction.

"Clare!" he said, juggling a can of paint thinner. "You snuck up on me. How long have you been standing there?"

"Long enough to realize I need to hire you over at my place. You would cry if you saw my messy garage."

Clare entered and set the six-pack of Miller she'd bought on his workbench.

"I've seen that mess," he smiled. "If I thought you were sincere and might keep it tidied up, I'd do it for nothing, again. But seeing as though you might be mocking me, I ought to charge you double this time."

Derek had never charged her a cent. Theirs was a friendship of bartering the physical for emotional. While he had leaned on her on many occasions for self-confidence, Derek was credited with being the doer in their relationship.

Clare peeled off two cans and put one in front of Derek.

"Thanks."

They both popped their cans in unison and drank in silence. Clare picked up a lug wrench as though she had found a violation of his order, and Derek lifted it from her possession before she could harp about it. He neatly replaced the wrench and the spare tire in their rightful spots in his trunk before shutting it, and then he zipped around the garage closing cabinets like he was preparing for takeoff.

"I thought I'd see you at the Whartons' last night with your parents," Clare said finally.

"I did stop by in the afternoon for a bit to say hi," Derek explained. "I had plans already in the evening."

"With Karen?"

"Yeah. We took Jack and one of his little friends to see a Disney movie."

He grabbed a couple of stools and placed them near a space heater at the opening of the garage.

"Things are going really well for you two," Clare said. "Did you bring them with you to meet the Whartons?"

"No, grabbed them after my stop. We aren't flaunting anything just yet. It's just better for Jack if we don't make too big a deal right now."

"About Friday night," she said suddenly. "I didn't mean for you to be in the middle of that. Courtney has a way of making me so angry. And so you know, I apologized to Mr. Wharton last night. I felt awful that he had to see that."

"I was trying to keep you out of trouble," Derek said. He leaned over and pressed his index finger into her shoulder. "I could see that look in your eye all the way from the bar. You were a bit crazed."

"I know you were trying to help. And you should know I appreciate your stepping in. I'm sorry for pushing you away."

Derek got up to grab another beer.

"I am going to say it, Clare." She turned to look at him; he waved his massive hands in front of his chest. "You seem to be obsessed with Courtney more than usual lately," he said. "We'd just talked about her at lunch the other day, and then you started right in at the bar with me."

"I'm frustrated, Derek," she said. "And worried about you, if anything."

"I can see that," he said. "And as a friend, I love you for that. But you being mad at Courtney won't bring Mary back."

Clare felt her temperature spike. She tried not to say anything about what she was beginning to suspect, about the suspiciously clean shoes. It really worried her that he seemed so willing to separate himself from that night at the creek and the fact that the shoes had no blood on them when he had found the clothing. Had it occurred to him? Did he know? Was he just fed up with the whole case and didn't care?

"Don't you ever just get a feeling?" she said. "Like something isn't right, but you can't put your finger on it."

"I've always left that to you, I guess." He smiled. "Lord knows I'm not psychic, Clare. And I know that you've had all that law enforcement schooling, but neither are you, in this case. I think it boils down to how easily Courtney crawls under your skin."

She started to object; Derek's face stopped her.

"She always has," he continued. "Courtney is not my favorite person, but Courtney is Courtney. I know you see her as some evil person in all this, but I don't know how you can connect her snootiness with Mary's dying. Just try to forget it and let the police tell us what happened."

"What if they don't tell us what happened?" Clare snapped. "What if our simple-minded little town is incapable of seriously investigating the truth?"

"Do you mind if we don't cover every little thing you hate about Danfield?" he asked, tiredly. "I happen to like this place."

She didn't say anything; she didn't want to tell him what she was thinking about Courtney right now. He wandered his garage and Clare kicked at the hanging tire.

"Okay, okay," she said at last. "Let's just change the conversation back to Karen."

"Boy, if it's not one thing it's another." Relieved, Derek shook his head.

She led him innocently through the details of his romance with Karen; the handholding and the tortuous anticipation of their first kiss. He seemed genuinely pleased—and a bit more comfortable sharing than she had been with Sara when they talked about Jared at the party last night—measuring his success by the fact that Karen still liked him and trusted him around her son. He seemed stronger as he talked, as well. Somehow it made her a little sad.

After finishing her second beer, she left him with the last two cans to stock the icebox in his garage. She realized, as she walked back to the Jeep, that his pushing her to change the subject had actually worked; she had stopped thinking about Mary's death while she'd been discussing Derek's love life. But her gut began to gnaw again the moment she threw herself into the driver's seat.

EIGHTEEN

"Clare," Stuart Heyman nodded, cup of coffee in hand at the doorway to the conference room at the bank.

"Stuart," Clare mumbled.

John MacNeil scooted a box of donuts in her direction before she had a chance to organize her things on the conference room table. "I haven't touched the little chocolate cake donuts you like," he said.

"Thanks, John. Can't do the sugar just yet." She opted to grab an orange juice from the conference console that was oddly overflowing with fruits and breakfast treats again. Not being the first one ready before the meeting was becoming a routine Clare didn't like. She wished she could turn tail and run back under the covers with a sick day.

"Can I get you anything else?" LuAnn bussed in a fresh pot of coffee to swap out the nearly empty one on the warmer.

"If you'll just pass out the agenda and close the door behind you, LuAnn, that'll be good for now," Lee directed.

"LuAnn, what's all this food for?" Clare asked.

"In honor of the Packers, Clare," called Edmond Dutch's harsh voice. "Didn't you see the game?" She turned to look at him; he was even wearing a team cap with his dress suit.

"It's hard to miss what's happening with the team," she said having been completely oblivious. "But don't you think it's a bit early in the season for the dress up?" She was speaking rhetorically; in addition to the paraphernalia available at every sporting outlet, nearly every grocery, quick mart, or retail store was already sporting some item with the Green Bay logo. Still, she thought the morning meeting ought to have been a safe haven from it.

Lee Graber idly shuffled papers. "Just a couple more minutes guys, if you want to get your coffee refills. Clare, I'll give you plenty of time today." He cleared his throat. "I hope everybody had a good weekend. I myself did enjoy that game."

Clare suffered the opening minutes in relative silence. She was still thinking about her glaring realization about Mary's shoes. And she hadn't heard from Jared all day on Sunday, which didn't surprise her given the way she had acted at the party and how she had treated him afterward. She tried to force herself to focus on her presentation of the proposed system upgrade.

Fifteen minutes into the agenda, Lee gave her the go-ahead. She stood up and peeked out of the conference room to wave in her direct reports Tom Pollenski and Kayla Johnson, the operations manager, whose areas would be most affected by the changes.

She had already presented this material—as she and Edmond were both well aware—and she succinctly and with plenty of supporting documentation provided an abbreviated technical overview and timeline for the implementation.

"Given the amount of time we've already spent on this project," she concluded, "I don't see the need at this point to field follow-up questions during meeting time."

"Very good, Clare," Lee offered, ready to move on to the next item on the agenda.

"That's it?" Edmond broke in. "Because I have a question. What are we paying for this, now?" His ridiculous Packers cap had vanished somewhere.

"At this point, Edmond," she replied, tiredly, "do you think you could be a bit more specific with your objections? We're long past the decisions about the expense of this project. We need this. It's a very good system for a bank of our size."

"It seems we could buy a whole lot of print and media advertising with the money we'd spend on this," Edmond said. "Or get a bigger booth at the fair, whatever. We're a small bank. What do we need with something this elaborate?"

She closed her eyes against the mounting pressure in her head. "This elaborate?" she asked. "This is a bare-bones platform. What happened to the initial tax benefits we'll reap, not to mention shaking our reputation for being unsophisticated? If we don't do something, the banking regulators could threaten sanctions."

"Let's not play the regulator game," Edmund said.

"Edmond, we've already justified this," Stuart broke in gingerly. "I am very confused about your objection at this point. I can understand design changes if you have any last thoughts about that, but don't you think the train left the station as far as the decision to move forward with the major components of the project? We've got the full backing of the board of directors."

Clare cringed at Stuart's mild approach, but nodded at him before turning back to Edmond. "Edmond, if you think about it from Stuart's perspective alone, we'll have more flexibility and capability to make marketing modifications and limited runs with our materials if we can produce some of them in-house, which these systems will allow us to do."

"Savings that'll take years to realize, if we're not careful here," Edmond jabbed.

"Why are we having this conversation?" John MacNeil tossed in blandly. "Like Stuart said, we can't keep rehashing this."

"What do you want us to do, Edmond?" she snapped, exasperated.

Lee's brow furrowed. "Tom and Kayla, could you excuse us?" he asked.

Except for Tom and Kayla shuffling to leave, movement in the room came to an uncomfortable standstill.

Tom shot a glance at Clare—plainly he thought he should get to watch this—before closing the door behind them.

"Edmond," Clare said. "It is inconceivable to me that you're vacillating about modernization at this point. As Stuart said, this ship has sailed." She glanced over to John McNeil for a break from his interminable silence and then back to Edmond when he failed to respond. "We've chewed up and mulled over a litany of reasons for the umpteenth time!"

"Clare," Lee interrupted, calmly.

Clare wasn't ready to be interrupted. "Think about it, Edmond.

Decreased transaction time. Better customer information files. Less downtime so Mr. Harper won't huff and puff in line."

She waited for Edmond to respond; he eyed Lee's deepening brow and didn't say anything.

"What about all our chats about improving sales opportunities?" she pressed on. "Hand-written ledgers would be better than our current backup system! Weren't you listening?"

"Clare," Lee said, much less calmly.

"Look at all the major banks moving into our sweet little town!" Her voice elevated.

"I've got it from here, Clare!" Lee demanded as though he'd eject her with one more word.

She stopped, but glared straight at Edmond. Her head was pounding.

"We need to take this down a major notch," Lee began. "Where are we on this, guys? We've spent countless hours on the design, considerable effort on the vendor selection process, not to mention our presentation to the board. Can you shove aside the sweets for a second, John?"

John took his hand out of the donut box.

"Why all the concern at this juncture, Edmond?" Lee continued. "We should be talking execution at this point."

Edmond sat upright; just the sight of his face was starting to make Clare sick. "It just seems that as we make this tweak here and that tweak there, the exponential value, relative to the growing expense, is diminishing. As CFO here, I think it's important to the well being of this bank to consider the cost of these changes."

"Getting your head out of your ass is important for the well being of this bank," Clare shouted. "Why don't you start there?!"

"Clare! Enough!" Lee was standing.

"I beg your pardon?" Edmond stammered.

"I'm through kissing your ass!" Clare hissed a notch softer for emphasis.

"This meeting is over," Lee said angrily. "I want you all to come up with your pros and cons regarding this system upgrade, and we will reconvene later. I cannot and will not tolerate this kind of behavior among professionals!"

The management team, including Clare, began to collect their things. She watched Edmond approach Lee as though he'd have the last word in defense and then retreated with the rest of them.

Lee pointed to Clare. "Stay!" he said. She didn't need him to tell her twice.

Everyone filed out, and Lee closed the door.

"What the hell is wrong with you?" Lee asked.

As high-strung as she was at the moment, she blinked in shock; Lee Graber never used profanity. But then, neither did she in professional settings. It was certainly an unwritten "Lee" expectation for the management team.

"My office," he said. "You have the length of the walk there to cool down."

It was easier than she might have thought; as furious as she was with Edmond for sabotaging her presentation in some power play, she was well aware how abnormal her behavior had become. She had hoped her nap yesterday afternoon would help her frame of mind, but she still had major trouble sleeping that night. The case and the issues left unsaid during her visit with Derek in his garage kept running through her mind.

Lee closed the door of his office behind them, and she slowly eased herself into a chair in front of his desk. He sat down as well and said nothing. Again she thought she should have stayed under the covers this morning.

"I know, in general, emotions seem to be running particularly high these days," he began at last. "And you've put an untold amount of effort into this project. But your behavior today—"

"Mr. Graber, I was completely out of line, I realize," Clare jumped in.

Lee motioned her to stop talking.

"Clare, I've known you a long time," he said. "I have always admired your passion and your tenacity for getting the job done. But I cannot tolerate that kind of unprofessionalism. I don't care who put the bee in your bonnet. You come to me if it's that bad."

"I can't tell you how sorry I am," she said, looking down. "As soon as we're through I will offer an apology to Edmond and then to the rest of the management team."

He looked at her. "What's eating at you?"

She felt perspiration bead on her skin beneath her blouse.

"I think I just got a little bit excited to get the systems project moving," she offered.

"Really?" Lee asked. "All that for a bit of technology? No, I don't think that's it."

The moisture in her palms was sticking to the arms of her leather chair.

"Something is eating at you," Lee said. "Just while you've been sitting here, you look like you're going to explode. But it's not just today. I've been noticing a bit of an edge on you."

Suddenly she felt her emotions flip on her. She no longer felt sorry. She remembered talking with Lee—how quickly he'd shifted from sharing her concern, on some level, about Mary Martin, to being equally distressed about the bell tower. Now he was distressed that she had acted unprofessional in a meeting while giving a presentation she should never have had to give to an obnoxious man who had no intention of letting her give it. And now he wanted her to apologize, to explain why she was acting "crazy."

"I wasn't aware that I appeared upset," she snapped, bracing for whatever assault he offered next.

With his elbows on his armchair, Lee built a tent with his fingers before his chest and then mysteriously whittled away the next few seconds in complete silence, eyeing her.

Never before had she wished for a LuAnn interruption.

"Are you feeling okay?" he asked, and her emotions settled again.

She felt exactly how tired she was right now and how childish her last statement must have sounded.

"Actually, I don't feel so well," she said. "I feel a little achy . . . a little nauseous . . . I worry about my mother and . . . and all the other things that are tearing this town apart . . . "

Lee—her mentor throughout her banking career, the person who'd believed in her—continued to gain the upper hand again as he watched her some more while she sat in the chair and stared at her knees. She wished she could disappear.

"How about you say a few words to your teammates," Lee said, "and then you take the rest of today."

Drained of all reason, she lifted herself from the chair.

"You have a ton of sick days built up. Take tomorrow too. We'll touch base on Wednesday."

He dismissed Clare by waving her away.

NINETEEN

It was bad enough that she had to prostrate herself to Edmond
Dutch in order to save face with Lee Graber. But to dream
about Edmond in the middle of a clammy sweat on a Monday
morning was more disgusting than when she had dreamed about
Courtney or the blue shoes. Groggy still, she wrestled herself to a
sitting position at the edge of the couch, where she had fallen for
a brief but deep nap in spite of a morning talk show blaring in
the background, and began to pick up her train of thought where
she'd left off.

Some of this had to do with the scene at the bank earlier, but
the bulk of it centered on the shoes and what she had come to con-
clude about them. The notion that Mary had been wearing shoes
when she had died—shoes suspiciously without blood evidence

on them—meant that there was essentially zero chance her death had been an accident: someone had deliberately brought Mary to the creek. She'd felt Yvonne and Derek out about this issue; neither of them seemed ready to accept that conclusion. Yvonne she expected, but if Derek couldn't see the logic in her position, how was she supposed to expect the rest of Danfield to? What was she going to do with what she knew?

The knock at her front door startled her. Through the window she saw Jared's truck at the curb. Her first instinct was to hide, but there was no way to leave the room unnoticed. And here he was again, seeing her when she didn't look her best. She looked in the fireplace mirror, stabbed at her rumpled hair, and then went to the door.

"Jared," she said neutrally.

"Do you have a minute, Clare?"

"This is not a good time," she said. "I'm really not feeling well."

"I can see that. I just came from the bank. I was hoping to share a mid-morning coffee break. They said you went home ill."

"It's just some bug," she said. "I think I just need a good day to sleep it off."

Part of her brain was screaming at her: *tell him!* But once she told him, what would happen? She'd told him her suspicions about Courtney plenty of times and he'd told her, in so many words, that she was imagining things. This time she wanted to figure out her own information first. Until she did that, the idea of letting him into her house seemed uncomfortable at best, at worst a disaster if they were to burrow into Saturday night.

"How about if I come in and fix you some soup or toast," Jared offered.

"I couldn't think of food right now," she said. "But thanks. I really appreciate the offer. I've got plenty of stuff in the house if I get hungry."

He put a slight pressure on the door with his hand. "A cup of tea or something. I'd really like to do something to make you feel better."

"Jared, not now, okay?" she said irritably. "It's chilly in this doorway, and all I can think of is lying down again. I'm not really in the mood for company."

She saw his face fall, revealing hurt and defeat.

"All right," he said. "I'll call you in a couple of days to see how you are doing."

He turned and left her fading in the breezy doorway. She leaned against the inside of the door. She wasn't in the mood to be pushed today—not even by the guy who'd made inroads into her heart.

She reclined on the couch and stared at the ceiling for just a minute before sitting up.

Suddenly she didn't feel tired anymore and wasn't going to sit here watching daytime television. She kicked her butt to the shower, got dressed in her running clothes, and then left her Jeep in the driveway, walking the streets, headed for the Coffee Clutch. It was a reasonably long walk, but that would give her time to think. Further, it was just down the street from the bank, but she didn't care. Let them all see her there: Edmond, Lee, Jared, Courtney. She was sick of being analyzed and ready to head back to Chicago and ditch the lot of them.

Lisa Handover, the co-owner of the Coffee Clutch, was behind the counter.

"Just a plain old strong cup of coffee," Clare ordered. I know it's getting to be lunchtime, but do you have any quiche left over from breakfast?" Clare suddenly realized she was hungry.

"Sure," Lisa said, brushing her hands on her bakery-spattered apron. "How about a nip of chocolate and bit of cinnamon with that coffee?"

"As long as it doesn't weaken the jolt, why not?" she asked. "And gin, if you have it."

Lisa laughed as though she had heard it in jest. "I'd join you on a cool midday like this if I could get away with it. Can you imagine what a liquor license could do for our business?"

"Yeah, they'd all come crawling in from the NiteLite, and nobody would get anything done around here." Lisa's partner Diane peeked out from around the kitchen counter.

Clare took a spot at the window and distracted herself from her funk by watching the controlled chaos of Lisa and Diane. They baked, wrapped, and managed the help, and they waited on and chatted with each patron as if each were royalty. Famed as they had become, Clare remembered them as they had been: a couple of seemingly ordinary housewives looking for a few extra bucks to supplement the family household budget. Spurred by their fame at local fairs and festivals, Lisa and Diane baked themselves nonchalantly into a new tourist attraction. Without a large accounting firm or fancy lawyers, they'd penned out an uncomplicated business plan, signed a lease, and without fanfare, thwarted the efforts of the likes of Starbucks from cluttering the hometown landscape. Their success spurned township legislation that inhibited the growth of national retail chains.

Lisa brought over the coffee and quiche. "It's tough to get going on Mondays, isn't it?"

It was as if she'd just noticed Clare's casual attire.

"I'm just trying to picture a tipsy NiteLite crowd with a beer in one hand and a cinnamon strudel in the other," Clare said.

"It's a funny thought, isn't it?"

"I envy you girls," Clare brooded. "What's it like to do something you love every day?"

"It's not always a bowl of cherries. Do you think it's easy getting here early to make the dough and staying late to polish the counters?"

"Don't listen to her, Clare." Diane was always dying to get in her two cents where Lisa was concerned. "She loves every minute. Look around. We've hired all these people, and I still can't get her to go home once in while."

"Who's kidding who?" Lisa leaned in, nudging Clare in the arm. She headed back for more banter with her partner, and Clare turned to her coffee.

Bullet Broadmor and his two sons walked past the window and into the bakery. The twins, Kyle and Mason, carefully scanned the candy sticks as though they might err in picking the right flavor. Bullet connected with Clare's eyeing them.

"It's not what you think. I know it's a school day," the husky, heralded Danfield high-school ex-quarterback said, wandering to her table.

"Don't worry, I won't turn you in. If I were their age I'd be doing the same thing."

He chuckled. "Aren't you doing the same thing? Taking a long weekend I see," Bullet commented.

She smiled and didn't respond to his reference to her sporty dress. Like most who'd grown up in this community, Clare couldn't separate her classmate's relatively short, five-foot-ten stature from the records he'd set in his football days.

"They both had great dental checkups, and here I am giving them candy," he said in a playful whisper.

"I'm sure they're grateful for any sweet you'll give them," Clare said.

"I am pretty guarded about giving them too much sugar, aren't I?" His quirks about a healthy diet for his kids, an offshoot from his football training, were well known in Danfield.

"They're good boys, Bullet," Clare said.

Unexpectedly Bullet's expression turned sour.

"When something happens like it did to Mary Martin, you realize how important your kids are . . . how quickly they'll be grown and gone . . ." he shook his head.

Clare perked up. "It's hard to believe we may never know what happened," she said.

"Surely there has to be an answer," Bullet insisted.

"But what are we going to do if we don't get one?" She looked at him seriously. "What would you do, if you knew there was a murderer on the loose in this town?"

He blinked at her and then turned to his kids completely distracted by their chattering over the selection. "Okay boys, just pick one and we've got to go. Diane, how much?"

Bullet walked over to the counter to pay and collect his sons.

"Good to see you Clare," he said, waving without looking at her as he shuffled them out the door.

Her coffee cup slowly emptied as she bit her lip and thought. Bullet had been the first, in her opinion, to have an appropriate reaction. Bullet knew. His boys were everything. She had no doubt he'd be interrogating all of Wisconsin if anything had happened to them. But he hadn't mentioned any concern about what the town should do until the murderer was caught. So once again it came back to Courtney and Russell. Russell was always quiet; he internalized things. But why wasn't Courtney reacting at all?

Why did she seem content to chalk the death up to an accident and put everything to rest?

The idea for what she'd do next hit her all at once. She worked out the details in her mind, drained her cup of coffee, and paid the check. She walked home, dressed in something nicer, got in her car, and headed to the grocery store and then on to Yvonne's.

Yvonne was in her backyard, already in full fanny-farmer gardening gear plus a raincoat. She had already pruned the roses and topped off the hosta, and she was in the middle of raking out a flowerbed.

"Mom," she said. "Do you have more of your pumpkin cookies? Can we bake some? I brought some things for it."

"Clare?" Yvonne gaped from beneath patches of dirt on her face. "You surprised me with church and breakfast yesterday, and now you want to bake cookies. I'd don't think I've ever seen you this touchy-feely."

"Your garden looks great," Clare said. "Come on."

She started to bring the sack of groceries through the back door into the kitchen.

"Clare, I would love to," Yvonne said, rushing to catch up with her daughter at the storm door. "But I really need to finish this off. I'm way past the first frost. Can you wait just a little bit?"

Clare leaned out the door. "You're way ahead of the neighborhood," she said. "Certainly ahead of me. Everything looks pretty well done. I'll help you this weekend if you need me. Come on, bake with me. This is just a tiny, tiny favor," Clare begged in a sweet, sing-songy tone that surprised them both.

Yvonne snapped off the garden gloves, kicked off the work boots at the top step, and looped through the house to wash up while Clare took out the groceries and started putting the flour in the bowl. Yvonne rejoined her and put on an apron.

"It's the middle of the workday," she said. "Did you take the day off, dear?"

Clare decided not to respond to this. "Mother," she said. "I just got to thinking about how I've been acting lately. I've been so critical of Courtney, and think of the situation. There she was, doing her best, and suddenly her daughter went missing, and then what Derek found . . ."

"You want to bake cookies for Courtney," Yvonne said, frowning.

"I also bought the fixings for the famous Paxton potato salad," Clare said, making herself smile. "On the way over we'll stop by Mae's Diner and grab some fresh roast beef slices. I just placed the order."

This was the part of the plan she was most worried about; surely her mother would wonder why her daughter had pulled a 180 from accusing Courtney Martin of murder to baking cookies for her. But her mother only seemed confused for a moment before pulling out her baking sheets and taking over the flour mixing from Clare.

"This will be nice, Clare," she said. "This will be nice . . ."

It made Clare sad, in a way that her mother seemed not to know who she was at all.

In two and a half hours, they were pulling around Courtney's circular stone driveway. Clare gathered up the meat and salad that she had chilling in a shallow Styrofoam container. Yvonne proudly carried one of her favorite glass trays full of pumpkin cookies up the winding entry steps from the driveway. Clare felt her skin get cold as they walked closer and closer to the house, just as it had when she had come across the crime scene. This is where everything had begun.

"I hope she is home, like you said, Clare," Yvonne said. "I'd hate for Courtney to miss all of this."

Clare knew something about Courtney's schedule and was relatively certain she would be home. Courtney, on the other hand, was unprepared for the intrusion.

Looking every bit a high-society gal in a pair of leggings, a thigh-length tan sweater, and an ornate black belt around her waist, Courtney couldn't have been more perplexed. Her eyes narrowed at Clare, who she'd last seen under the dim light of the back room at the bar.

Yvonne was perfectly on cue.

"My dear Courtney," Yvonne said, raising the tray. "We have been so remiss in coming to visit. We've brought you dinner and some goodies."

Clare smiled in spite of Courtney's presence; her unfettered use of Yvonne was the most brilliant element of what she was about to do.

"We're truly sorry for your loss," Clare added, looking Courtney in the eye. "We won't stay long."

Courtney looked back and forth between Clare and her mother.

"You brought me food?" she said, visibly unsure. She eased the palatial wood entry-door wider.

Yvonne's eyes lit up at the glimpse of the interior. She marched forward. Then she grabbed Courtney with her free left hand and gave her a motherly smooch to the cheek.

"That'll be good," Courtney grimaced. She waved to a circular foyer table. "You can set everything right there."

"Courtney, your home is beautiful," Yvonne said, eying the entryway on her way past Courtney and around the circular foyer table toward where, by some Yvonne instinct, she knew the kitchen would be. "I must confess that I snuck a peek at the layout while you were still building. I just couldn't resist."

Courtney struggled to maintain the plastic smile on her face as she followed Yvonne, taking her ease in the house as if she were a frequent guest.

"Sorry," Clare smiled at Courtney, pacing her on the way toward the back of the house. "She just insisted. Yvonne thinks her pumpkin cookies are the solution to all the world's ailments."

Courtney ignored her. "Ladies, this is really nice of you," she said in a forbidding voice, directed at Yvonne's back. "I'm doing okay, really."

Clare could hear the clip, clip, clip of her heels hastening on down the hallway after them.

"You and Russell have just held up so well through all of this. Now let's see what we got here." Yvonne went through the containers of food, opening the lid of each to take a peek, while Clare and Courtney stood at the edge of the kitchen, tense and watching her.

Courtney lasted just seconds before she followed in Yvonne's tracks, resealing the plastic lids. "Really, Yvonne, you shouldn't have," Courtney said, careful not to muss her beautiful manicure. "My family is helping with everything. But I appreciate the gesture."

Amused by the two of them, Clare knew Courtney wouldn't lift a finger in the kitchen and was rumored to be a consumer of home meal deliveries and known to bring in chefs on occasion. Likely the hired help would be enjoying Yvonne's pumpkin cookies.

Yvonne pivoted.

"Your house seems wonderful, Courtney!" Yvonne interrupted. "Can I get a tour? I've just been dying to see how you decorated this place."

Yvonne wandered away from the kitchen counter and oohed and aahed her way through the table decor in the dining room and at the fixtures in the den as much as she could see of them through Courtney's beating her to block the archway.

Courtney glared at Clare and then glanced at her watch.

Clare silently remembered that one little suggestion she'd made to Yvonne and smiled.

"We could set up a time for you to do that, Yvonne," Courtney was saying, even as it was too late.

"Oh, let's just take a quick run through," Yvonne insisted. "We'll get right out of your hair."

Courtney opened her mouth to say no, but Clare knew that she was the only one who stood even a remote chance of stopping Yvonne once she got an idea into her head. She continued to cruise through the house, oohing and aahing louder and louder. Clare briskly trotted after her; it was important to keep pace with her and not to let Courtney get between them. Yvonne made an even swifter turn to the stairs, Courtney, her steps growing faster and faster, was close on both of their heels.

"Oh my, Courtney," Yvonne said when she'd reached the top, stopping so abruptly that Clare nearly knocked into her. "This is such a beautiful room!"

Clare knew in an instant that this had to be Mary's. "All the bright yellow daisies," Yvonne gushed. "Look at this, Clare! Pink-painted ponies . . . it's a castle theme!"

Clare quickly stuffed her eyes with the exact layout of the room where Mary had been taken.

"Clare," Courtney hissed in her ear. "You are way out of bounds here."

"I'm really sorry that we're racing all over your home," Clare said loudly, for Yvonne's benefit. "Yvonne's been dying to see this place."

"We are getting all the help we need from the police," Courtney snarled. "Stop sticking your nose where it does not belong."

Yvonne stopped looking at the room and turned to cast questioning glances at the two of them. Clare made a last survey of the organization of the room. Then stepped forward to put her hand on her mother's shoulder.

"Come on, Mother," she said. "We really need to go."

Other than the glance, Yvonne remained mum about the tension as Courtney marched them out of her house and to the front entry. "Do enjoy those goodies we brought," she chirped. "I'd be happy to make up some more salad if you like!"

Courtney followed them outside and around the lengthy circular drive and didn't even bother to fake a smile as Yvonne got into the Jeep.

Clare walked to the driver's side door, turned, and looked at Courtney. "We really do wish you well," she said simply.

"Really cute, bringing your mother, Clare." Courtney said. "Do this again and you and I are really going to have trouble. Legal trouble, if you know what I mean. I don't need your condescending crap!"

Clare had a couple thoughts come to mind but didn't dare start up in Yvonne's presence. "Great day to you," she said and got into the car.

"Oh, that was so nice, Clare," Yvonne began, "really and truly."

"Yes it was," Clare said, thinking about the layout of Mary's room.

"She got a little edgy at the end, did you notice that?" Yvonne went on, situating herself sideways in the passenger seat to face Clare. "And what was that she was whispering to you? Maybe it wasn't such a good idea that we took that tour."

"Like you said, it was a nice gesture."

"Did you see how beautiful that room was? Oh my . . . straight out of a catalog."

"Yes, it was very pretty," Clare said, thinking to herself that it really was.

"Why did the two of you never get along?" her mother suddenly asked. "Even when you were little girls."

She didn't seem to really expect an answer. Clare drove on in silence for a while.

"Clare, I am so proud of you to reach out to Courtney like that," Yvonne said. "You have really made your mother proud. She must be so, so sad. We'll pray for her . . . what do you think?"

Clare absorbed the final commentary without remarking and watched Yvonne shuffle out of the Jeep and up her walkway, feeling like the little girl whose mother simultaneously gave her the "good conduct grade" while giving the snob queen a pass.

"Clare?"

On a side street of Yvonne's neighborhood, under the dome light of her Jeep, focused on jotting relevant thoughts about the visit to Courtney's, Clare screamed and tossed her pad in the air.

"Oh! Parker . . . what are you doing?" Clare barked through the driver's side window glass. "You scared the crap out of me!"

Parker jumped back, completely unprepared for her shrill reaction. Clare couldn't fumble fast enough to turn the ignition in order to roll down the window and just opened the door instead.

"Okay . . . calm down. I thought you heard me pull up. What are you doing just a block from your mom's? Have you taken to stalking her now?"

She smiled. "Not funny, Parker. I just dropped her off and I am on my way home."

She held up her finger a moment, closed her door, and rolled down her window.

"So what do you want?" she asked.

"How about a beer?" Parker asked.

"What?" Clare was taken aback by his suggestion.

"You know," Parker said. "An alcoholic beverage?"

"It's Monday," Clare said.

"So? They have beer on Monday."

"Well," she said. "We could do that."

"Great. See you at the NiteLite in ten."

Before Clare could really figure out whether she wanted to go, Parker was off through the neighborhood maze, headed toward Main Street.

At each stop sign she glanced at how she looked in the rear view and over at her notes on the passenger seat, her mind still reeling from the Courtney visit. There were many more curious things to consider. Why did the room look so untouched? Why had the door just been open for Yvonne to see it and wander in? Why hadn't it been cordoned off, even?

Parker was already in the NiteLite. Once her eyes had adjusted to the dim lighting, Clare located him at a small table at the end of the bar.

"Is Mr. Wharton here?" she asked.

"Doesn't look like it," Parker responded.

"Can't honestly remember the last time I was here on a Monday," she said. "It's not so crowded."

"What can I get you?"

"Just a Pepsi, Parker."

"Really?

"Yeah. I really can't think of alcohol at this moment."

Parker drifted to the bar.

She wondered how she had gotten here. She and Parker hadn't been together privately since her return to Danfield.

Parker set down his Miller and a Pepsi for Clare and took the chair beside her. "Now," he smiled. "What were you doing sitting in your car by yourself?"

He seemed quite chipper compared to his stop at her office the other day.

"Certainly you didn't drag me to a bar to drill me some more about that," she said. "I pulled over to make sure I had everything after leaving Yvonne's."

"Hopefully having a drink with me isn't a drilling," he said. "A good spur of the moment idea, don't you think?"

"So what were you doing?" she smiled. "Spooking frail, weak women at dusk?"

"I would describe you as anything but frail and weak," Parker said.

She watched him pick the label on his Miller and massaged the condensation on her drink glass, pondering all the things left unsaid.

"This is strange, isn't it?" He suddenly seemed eager to cut to the chase. "You and I shouldn't be so uncomfortable. I've been thinking an awful lot about your stop out of the blue at the garage. Talking to you again at the bank . . . I am just still reeling from it for some reason. It's like I'm noticing you more and more, and you've been back for forever now."

"It was a bit unfair to have just bombarded you like that," she said. "Three years after I came back to town. I'd spent so much time planning my escape, and now my life is back here nursing Yvonne again. Who would have guessed that the two of us would be alone, like this?"

"Not sure why it has taken us so long," he smiled. "But I suppose there is some reason why I bumped into you all alone today."

She grinned. "Oh man, Parker! You still remember saying that to me when I was twelve?"

"How could I ever forget? It was the Country Fair field trip, I do believe."

Her smile faded. "I'm sorry I made it so hard for us to say hi again," she said wistfully. "It was up to me to reach out to you years ago. I wish I could tell you why I didn't."

"Since you've been back I've wanted to see how things were with you instead of hearing it through the grapevine," he said. "Really . . . none of this dancing around each other. I'm not the best with this kind of stuff."

"Don't say anything, Parker. I know I left you empty handed. And you handled things better than most guys would have. You just happened to meet me."

She had an urge to reach over and grab his forearm; she resisted it.

"Clare," he said. "We've been through the wars together. But we're big kids now. Yeah, I admit it was tough trying to understand your logic about giving up what we had to experience a life that sounded to me like uncertainty. I didn't want to deal with it for a long time. So you ignoring me when you came back was somewhat helpful, for a while."

"It's not fair," Clare fretted. "I really didn't mean to bring up all the hurt."

"I'm okay," Parker said. "But you can understand my surprise when you showed up. And the next thing I know, you're buying a house and taking up a serious career in Danfield. This from the girl that I secretly hoped just had an insatiable travel bug."

She suddenly sensed that he really wasn't okay with the past, no matter how much he was smiling while he chatted about it.

"Parker."

He motioned that he was not finished.

"I understand the whole Yvonne thing," he went on. "A little surprised she got to you like that. But I realized, for whatever reason, that you were making some kind of a sacrifice. That's a grown up kind of thing to do. And somewhere in there, it came time for me to grow up too."

"It doesn't make sense, does it?" she asked.

He got quiet, and she realized two things. First: she had owed him this conversation long ago. And second: telling him now that she really had loved him—that, with her absent father and whacko mother, he was really the only reason she had developed any capacity for love—would be a rotten thing for her to do.

"It doesn't have to make sense, Clare," he said finally. "That's what I am saying." He pulled his chair closer and picked up her left hand; she let him. He folded it between his two hands. "You're back now, and there is no reason why we can't be part of each other's lives. It's just too small of a town if we don't. Otherwise, I am just going to have to chase you out of town again."

She blinked, her hand between his hands, her eyes growing moist.

"Hey guys," came Jared's voice. "I heard there was a disturbance."

He was leaning on a chair opposite them, his eyes on her hand.

"No disturbance here," Parker laughed. "Just catching up on old times." He let go of Clare's palm and stood up, and he and Jared shook hands. "How about a beer?" he asked.

"No, just sit," Jared said, not looking at Clare. "I'm looking for some of the council members. We're meeting here to discuss this whole bell tower thing. We've got to get this under control and get some decisions made about how we're going to control the crowd and let the contractors do their work. We're catching wind of a town rally on Main Street; it'll be a whole lot of fun as long it doesn't interfere with the new construction start date."

She braced herself that Jared might turn to her, but he never did, and he spoke with the utmost ease, making no reference to her supposed illness.

"Looks like you have your hands full," Parker said. "I'll be glad when it's all settled."

"Me too," said Jared. "Anyway, you two relax. Here's Mayor Kohlhepp coming in now. Good to see you, Clare. Parker, I'll take you up on that offer later. We really ought to have a beer sometime."

She watched Jared walk away seemingly unfazed, her face, she knew, was white as a sheet.

"He really is a great guy," Parker mused. "We're lucky to have nabbed him from Milwaukee." He smiled and scooted closer to her. "Now where were we?"

"I probably should go," she breathed.

"Not that quickly," Parker said. "Look, I'd love to have you in my life again. In spite of our differences, we're two of a kind at heart. We'll never lose that. I know you'd rather not have been pulled back to Danfield by Yvonne, but I suppose you would have regretted it if you hadn't. Maybe you guys can patch things up. Who knows?"

"It's not really that important that Yvonne and I patch up anything," Clare said, shortly. "But you're right that you and I have waited too long to talk. I really need to go." She looked around the room; there seemed to be no sign of Jared or the mayor.

"What do you say we make a date when we have more time?" Parker smiled. "I guess I really should let you get going tonight."

"I'm sorry," she said. She was still squinting her eyes after Jared when Parker leaned in and barely brushed a kiss on her cheek.

Before she could say a word, he was off and out of the bar.

TWENTY

Clare started the coffee brewing before heading out to nab the paper off her porch, nearly stumbling over the box of crap she had lifted from Yvonne's garage following her departure from the bar last night. She had bet that Yvonne wouldn't have thrown out Ray's old hunting and camping gear, and she had been right. It was a wonder with the strangest of days yesterday—from being sent home to cooking for Courtney to the surprise visit with Parker—that she had the forethought to snoop for her father's things.

The front-page headline—"City Officials Powwow About Bell Tower"—immediately triggered Clare's guilt about everything that had happened yesterday, especially running into Jared while she was with Parker. Aside from its personal relevance to her, the article was aggravating on its own terms, as it appeared that the closed-door discussion would do little to deter a protest march and rally that apparently some of the town—including, maybe, Yvonne—had been planning under her nose. A bit more evidence, in Clare's mind, that their quiet little Danfield had suddenly been drained of all its normal mental capacity. Not the least bit amused, she tossed the paper into the bin near the hearth.

The one fortunate consequence of Lee Graber's edict was that Clare suddenly had nothing but time. Without so much as a goldfish to fill the void, she sat, experiencing a unique moment of aloneness. She obsessed over what Jared's impression might be of her strange behavior yesterday especially her huddling with Parker, as well as what his reaction might be at her visit to Courtney's, or what she'd figured out about the shoes. She wondered if she would have the chance to talk to him about it, or if he would listen if she did.

Buoyed by a muffin and a third cup of coffee, she went back to the task at hand, and dug through Yvonne's collection of Ray memorabilia for the things she would need.

There was a collection of photos in the box. Not surprisingly, most of them were of strangers, including a hodge-podge of hunting buddies she'd never met. She flipped quickly through this until she came suddenly to a photograph of her teenage mother and Ray—holding a baby. She stiffened and flicked the photo back into the box.

To preserve anonymity for what she was about to do, she drove to an Army surplus store she knew of in a neighboring city halfway to Madison, seething over the family photo the whole way. Then, with what would become her disguise in hand, she headed back to Danfield and to the park where she had been jogging just days ago now, near the crime scene.

It was still early enough on the weekday for the park to be mostly empty—except, of course, for the police presence Jared had assured her he was keeping at the scene—and she was able to dress in her hunter camo-fatigues, tuck her hair in a cap, and stuff her jacket with light foam to fatten and hide her female figure without the worry of being noticed. Then she headed back to the creek where Derek had found Mary's clothes and shoes.

In an effort to unearth anything that might spark a plausible explanation for the absence of body parts, she circled the area, working up and down the sides of the creek but staying outside of the police markings still strung between the trees. At one point she crouched outside the boundary and specifically eyed the rock where the pristine blue suede shoes had been. How had they got-ten there?

As the last of the leaves dangled in the cheek-biting wind, Clare scanned the site yet again. Of all of the unanswered questions she had, the lack of explanation behind the clean pair of blue suede shoes seemed the most remarkable. There were no body parts at the site, but there had been a pile of bloody, torn clothing. If Derek hadn't been the one to stumble on the scene and find the blood and clothes, she'd have wondered whether any of it was even true. The only clear fact seemed to be that Mary had been under Courtney's sole supervision—Courtney who hadn't even had her child's bedroom cordoned off.

On her third circuit of the site, she suddenly froze. There was a bright object clinging to a bush. She looked down—the creek was below her—and went closer. It was a pretty bow-shaped pink barrette that Clare immediately knew was Mary's. Who else's could it be?

She knew enough to minimize her movements lest she further disturb this area of the woods. With a baggie taken from a pocket of her camouflage-garb, she carefully enveloped the branch and softly shook the barrette loose. Instinctively she pivoted and scanned her surroundings for anything else that might be connected. She looked for some time, but found nothing.

She made it back to the Jeep, thankfully without seeing a soul. In the driver's seat, she banged her elbows and knees as she quickly changed back into her jeans and sweatshirt. Then she stuffed the entire disguise into a large garbage sack and put it behind the passenger seat on the floor.

Clare could partially see Jared from the waiting area in the administrative hallway of the station. His assistant Wanda had notified him of her arrival minutes ago, she knew, but he remained fully focused on some organizational matter as Wanda leaned over his desk. Clare waited, until the minute Wanda stood straight, walked away, and appeared to be finished, and then Clare darted past her in the hallway without waiting for an invitation.

"Just give me two seconds," Jared said, seeming surprised to see her. "I've got to finish this with Wanda."

She pulled Jared's door closed and leaned forward against his solid wood desk. "No, Jared, this can't wait."

He gave her a stern look and then stood and briskly walked to the door, which he opened to a waiting Wanda. Wanda followed him back to the desk where he discussed, in police code, her assignment while Clare leaned on his desk and watched the two of them. Wanda took her assignment papers, but hesitated to leave.

"Go, Wanda," he said. "It's ok. I've got it here."

While he remained standing at his desk, Clare turned to close his door again.

"Leave it open," Jared ordered.

"Just give me a minute, Jared," she said. "It's important."

He burned her with his stare, and after a moment she sat down, and then he sat.

"What are you doing here?" he asked, coldly.

"You've got to listen to me," she said.

"I'm listening," he replied. "What are you so fired up about?"

She ignored his condescending tone and wondered how much he'd been affected by seeing her and Parker.

Clare pulled the baggie from her purse. She laid it in the middle of his desk mat.

"I found this," she said. "It's Mary's."

"What do you mean, it's Mary's?"

"I was out hiking in the woods this morning," she began, but he raised his hand.

"I thought you were sick," he said. "What are you doing hiking in the woods?"

"You're not listening," she said.

"I'm listening all right," he said. "But I'm hearing that you went wandering around the crime scene again. I asked you not to."

"Did you not hear me that I have something of Mary's that could help the case?"

He pinched and lifted up the baggie. Then he walked back to close the door. He sat in the visitor chair next to Clare.

"How do you know this is hers?" he asked.

Clare was incredulous.

"Who else's pink barrette would be just yards from where Derek found her clothes and shoes?" she asked.

"But you've touched it."

"I haven't. Look." She pointed to the bag. "It's perfectly protected. You won't find my prints on it."

He stared at the bag for some time, his demeanor impervious, as his desk clock ticked in the background. She watched him. Finally, he took a deep breath and his shoulders relaxed.

"Clare," he said, taking another full, deep breath. "I am so tired and frustrated with this case. I'm sorry. It's hard to believe we missed something like this. This could be really huge."

"What do you think it means?" she asked excitedly.

He got up and returned to his office chair, taking the baggie with him. He set it on the middle of the desk as if it was a barrier between them, and he folded his hands.

"Thanks, Clare," he said. "It looks like we need to give the area another run through. This will hopefully be the big clue we've been looking for."

She stared at him, baffled.

"What exactly have you been looking for?" she asked again.

He stood up, walked to the door, and held it open.

"If you don't mind," he said. "I've got a lot on my agenda this afternoon. There's a protest march tonight, as I'm sure you've heard."

Suddenly, this was not the man who'd dropped spiced coffees off at her office or who'd been pining to whisk her away in a bikini.

"Jared," she said, feeling a sudden insatiable urge to touch him and find the spark in his eyes. "About seeing me and Parker last night. It was just a quick chat between old friends."

"I knew you two were high-school sweethearts," he said. "Not a big deal."

"You've been so great and I've been nothing but a bundle of nerves lately," she said, keeping her voice down. "Can we finally watch that movie, or something? I'd really like to make it up to you."

He looked down at her, holding open the door. "We'll figure out something in a couple of days," he said.

Feeling horribly conspicuous for the walk back down the narrow long hallway from his office, she was relieved when she passed through the secure doors to the exterior lobby and handed in her visitor badge.

All she wanted was to quietly down a tuna sandwich, fruit, and some chocolate milk at the malt shop downtown, but a surprising turnout for the preparation of the antidevelopment activities that evening spoiled her enjoyment. It felt like a Danfield High football pre-game tailgate party as she watched the giddy group of citizens, who actually believed they'd be able to halt a legal demolition, go to work papering old telephone poles and store windows with flyers. At any other time, this kind of fervor would have seemed admirable to her, but right now she felt a maddening urge to run out and scoop up their flyers as soon as they put them up with tape. Instead, she wadded and tossed her lunch papers and headed home to shower for a more lighthearted visit with Sara Wharton before her friend headed back to Cedar Rapids.

Mrs. Wharton was her typical ebullient self.

"Clare, I am so glad you left a message that you could see Sara before she went home. You guys can't really catch up when the family is all together. And the other night, it was maddening to try to string more than a couple of sentences together."

"Much quieter now," Clare said.

"But it was fun, wasn't it? We could have awakened a den of wolves. Though I'm afraid Mr. Wharton and I surely don't have the energy we used to, and neither do the neighbors, I'm sure. We are just plumb worn out, if you know what I mean."

"But you'd do it again in a heartbeat," Clare smiled.

"That's right," Mrs. Wharton beamed. "And your mother is such a hoot, isn't she?"

"Hey girl!" Sara said, coming down the stairs. She gently yanked Clare by the wrist back through the front door to a chic setup of chairs and a table at the corner of the front porch with a few outdoor heaters set up nearby. "You were serious about catching up," Clare said, looking at the preparations. "I just walked right by all this."

"So I was glad to hear you had the day off," Sara said. "Did I snatch you away from the office with the lure of my famed Bloody Mary?"

"I can't think of better reason to play hooky," Clare said. "I am really so sorry that I couldn't get here earlier like I had planned, but I'll take those Bloody Marys any time of the day."

She watched Sara and her mom cross paths to fill the wicker table with the spiked tomato juice and a plate of sweets. "Let me help with something."

"Nope," Sara scolded, lighting candles on the table. "Can you believe most of these goodies are left from the other night? And you know us Wharton girls could do with a few less calories."

"Sara!" Clare chuckled about the family's tendency to live large.

"It's true. For the last couple of days we've been foisting trays of stuff on the neighbors." She sat down, while Maggie hovered, and Sara filled three glasses.

"This is really great," said Clare. "Thanks, guys."

Sara and Clare tapped their glasses and each took a cheerful sip.

Maggie took the smallest drink for herself. "It's great to see you two together," she said and went back through the front door.

"So?" Sara burst out as soon as her mother was gone.

"So what?" Clare replied.

"Come on. Spill the stuff on this Chief Jared guy."

"Don't get all crazy on me," Clare said, thinking numbly about the scene at the station earlier. "Not much to spill. He's a good guy. He's smart, good looking, has a great job. That about sums him up."

"Seriously? I know there's more than a checklist; I got those tidbits the other night. My dad loves him and obviously Yvonne doesn't. Combined, that adds up to something special, right? And I saw you two ogling each other at the party. That wasn't just a 'good guy.'"

"Listening to you, it sounds like a Harlequin," Clare smiled.

"But," Sara suggested.

"There really isn't any but. You could say we have some chemistry, but timing is everything. He's still battling his reputation and me, I'm always still a foot out the door."

"Clare . . . really," Sara said. "Isn't it time you made a choice and then just ran with it? It's been nearly three years since you came back. And you can look at it a couple of ways. Either Jared gives you the best reason to live a better life in Danfield or you get your butt back to Chicago."

"You were never one to mince words," Clare said quietly.

"Neither one of us was," Sara said. "Look. I know we're both bad about regularly staying in touch, but we've always told each other the truth. We'll always be best buds. And I would be a lousy friend if I only said things to make you feel good."

"But look at you," Clare defended. "You *did* it. You slipped off to school, married the perfect guy, and had the most wonderful two children. Me—I have a Yvonne around my ankles."

"You're right," Sara nodded. "But life isn't roses all the time. I miss it here. I'll admit that sometimes. The other night was exactly what I yearn for about this town, and that included seeing you." She frowned. "I've never said this, but the first couple of years of my marriage were pretty rocky. I packed my bags so many times."

"Really?" Clare said, surprised.

"But, before we dwell on all the little squabbles. I woke up one day and I decided that Barry was what I wanted. I wanted that more than I wanted to be nineteen into infinity. For me, I really wanted to raise a family while I was younger."

"And you and Barry wanting the same thing at the same time makes all the difference," Clare said.

"It does, but I'm making the point that we had to fight for what we wanted. And Clare, you're too old to let this indecisiveness ruin you anymore," Sara continued. "You didn't get the best spin on parents, but after age eighteen, all your choices are your own."

"I saw Parker last night," Clare blurted.

"Yeah?" Sara said. "How's the old hunk? Who doesn't drool

over that Parker? He'll still have that dynamo body when he's eighty. I thought about having Mom ask him over to the party, but I wasn't sure if that would be comfortable."

"No," Clare said, "I mean I *saw* him last night."

"Oh no," Sara said, puzzled. "Like a date saw him? The gossips say you two have kept your distance. What gives?"

"Not a real date, so don't get too excited. We just had a drink at your dad's place. I should have known better about that spot because we ran into Jared. It was a last minute thing."

"That's not good," Sara said slowly. "But now I'm really confused. That's a guy you kicked in the teeth after stringing him along with a maybe for years. And a minute ago you mentioned you'd still dart from Danfield with the right motivation."

Clare nodded, brow tight.

"Man, you're a mess!" Sara laughed, and Clare joined her. They were loud enough that Maggie even peeked through the front window at them.

"I admit it," Clare said finally. "I am a mess. So let's talk about something else."

"Anything," Sara said. "But we're not done about this guy thing."

Clare hesitated a moment. "Has your mom mentioned Mary Martin?"

"Talk about a tragedy," said Sara. "It's hard to miss the national news coverage. I heard the guys talking in front of Jared the other night. He's got a lot on his plate, not to mention you."

"Sara, I can't get her out of my mind," Clare confided. "Everybody around here is treating this like an open-and-shut case. And you ought to see that Courtney flaunting it around town."

"She's always been a slut. That's nothing new."

"Seriously, Sara," Clare pressed. "It has to be more than that. Russell's flat out decimated and she's out looking for her next prey. No tears whatsoever. Something's going on."

Sara looked at her and she took a sip. She appeared to be considering.

"You really are chewed up about it," Sara said at last. "You don't really think Courtney could have had something to do with it, do you? Is that what you are suggesting? I'm thinking not with her own daughter. I don't like her either, but that idea is unfathomable. And, do you really think she sleeps around or just craves the attention?"

"Honestly, does either matter if your daughter is missing?"

"Good point. As a mother, it's an awful thought."

"But nobody wants to rile the rich beauty queen," Clare pressed.

"Dad says this Jared guy is really good," Sara mused. "That he doesn't have any vested interest in protecting anybody. If you think highly of him professionally, you should trust him to do his job."

Clare's face fell. She picked up the pitcher and refilled their glasses.

"Actually," Sara said, perking up, "I overheard Jared say to my dad that he liked you because you were a bit of a maverick around here."

"I've got some time yet," Clare poked back. "How about we nitpick your pretty little life a bit? I could use some dirt on those first couple of years of your marriage."

Sara laughed, they tipped their glasses together, and they began anew. Without faltering a minute, Sara and Clare covered everything from children to the tower controversy to small-town fashion and finally to the funny parts about having a mother like Yvonne.

"I hate to break this up," Clare said at last, looking at her watch. "But speaking of Yvonne, I promised to take her to the rally. We're having a whole twenty-four-hour happy spell, if you can call it that. I'd like to not mess it up."

"Good idea."

She got up and headed for the Jeep, with Sara following. Her friend waited until they were at the door.

"The Parker thing?" Sara began. "He's beautiful and successful, and God knows—as much as I do—what it took for you to walk away. You followed your heart, and so you need to think twice before taking him down your mushy road again."

Clare looked at the pavement.

"On the other hand," Sara continued. "Honestly, Jared is really a sweet, sweet guy and very bright, among other things. If you feel any spark for him at all . . . take a chance with somebody like that. He sounds like he's a bit of a snob about this place like you. With his talent, he isn't going to live here forever. And in the meantime, you guys can travel to places that don't allow baggie sweats and T-shirts."

"He does like some of that outdoors stuff too," Clare countered. In the back of her mind, she wondered, after the reception she got at the station earlier today, whether the happy future that Sara was outlining was even possible anymore.

"You know what I mean, smarty," Sara smiled.

"We can't wait this long to talk again," Clare said, growing teary. "I owe you a visit to Iowa."

"That you do," Sara acknowledged.

They firmly embraced. Clare gave one last wave before pulling the Jeep away from the curb.

TWENTY-ONE

I t wasn't until Yvonne was already approaching her Jeep, in bright red colors in solidarity with the evening's theme and with a Save-the-Steeple flag protruding from her coat pocket, that Clare realized she'd forgotten to move the plastic bag and her disguise from earlier—components of which she'd borrowed from the Ray memorabilia, things she wouldn't want Yvonne to recognize.

She bent behind the passenger seat where she remembered tossing the bag and felt nothing. Then to be sure she leaned across the console and groped for it on the passenger seat floorboard, but there was nothing there. Panic-stricken, she turned on the overhead light as Yvonne opened the door.

"Clare, what is it?" Yvonne asked happily. "No need to clean up for me."

She clearly remembered tossing her camo-fatigues on top of the plastic bag when she was hurrying to leave the woods but now all of it was missing.

"I had a bag," Clare said. "Just thought I'd left a bag I put together for Goodwill. Now I don't remember where I put it."

"It's not like you to be forgetful, like your old mom," Yvonne tittered, jumping into the Jeep. "There is really going to be a crowd tonight! We'll show them a thing or two."

Clare fanned her arms front and back, dumbfounded.

"It'll be great, Mom," Clare said distracted, staring at the place where her disguise had been. Finally she started the car and began driving. "Just don't get your hopes up," she said after a moment.

"Clare, don't be getting negative with me already."

"Really, I'm not, Mom."

All of their arguments about the bell tower that led up to this protest ran through her mind, most notably the one that said that, in a nutshell, if they demonstrated until the crack of dawn, it was all a bunch of noise and they hadn't a legal leg to stand on. But in keeping with her desire to maintain a truce, Clare thought it wiser not to rain on Yvonne's parade.

"It doesn't hurt to try," Clare added after a moment.

Yvonne glanced at Clare, almost disappointed that their talk hadn't turned into a quarrel. "Well, okay then," she said.

They drove in silence awhile. Part of Clare's brain was racing. She must have taken the bag with the disguise into her house. Normally she would have remembered something like that, wouldn't she?

"Oh, look," Yvonne chirped. "There are all the girls gathering in front of the Coffee Clutch."

Maggie Wharton and Derek's mom Martha, among others, were huddled next to the doorway of the bakery where Diane and Lisa had installed a temporary tent in front of their awning and set up a table of free coffees and hot chocolates in support of the rally.

"Mom, don't get out yet," Clare said. "I'll get you a little closer."

"That's okay," smiled Yvonne. "I'll just walk across. I'll see you down at the parking lot at the end."

She watched her mother hurry across the street in the direction of her friends until she was sure Yvonne was at the bakery. Then she rolled on slowly through the burgeoning crowd whose parade route would take them from the park entrance to the parking lot of the First Assembly of God church.

Clare couldn't shake her dreadful feeling about the missing clothing. She pulled into the side alley of the gas station and turned the overhead light on to look again. The bag wasn't on any of the floorboards or under the seat. She got out and cautiously paced the vehicle perimeter, opening each door and patting each floorboard.

She got back into the car and slumped in the driver's seat. She thought through the day and the only places the bag could have gone missing: the parking lot of the police station, at home during her shower, certainly not in front of the Wharton house while they sat on the porch. Her gut burned. It was an awful feeling to wonder who might have been interested in her disguise. As far as she could tell, Jared was the only one who knew about her whereabouts today.

Feeling ridiculously unsafe in her little hometown, hidden in the shadows behind the gas station, Clare quickly started the car and pulled out toward the sudden burst of cheering coming from Main Street, where the procession was about to start. She carefully crawled up closer to the church parking lot, lucking out and finding a spot at the corner of Peak and Main where a city worker was just departing.

For Yvonne's sake, she withstood the dueling bullhorns and nauseous signage—Save Our City Heritage—posted everywhere. The sea of citizens on Main Street, color coordinated in red, locked arms. She waved and fielded hellos working her way along the parade route, as the crowd mushroomed with each horse rider, walker, and convertible joining the march.

Walking behind the last of the picketers, freezing and wishing she were anywhere else, Clare honed in on several folks she did not recognize. She sifted out obvious media persons who were toting cameras, badges, and miscellaneous recording gear. In lieu of the obvious, more serious matter of a child abduction, the steeple story offered comic relief and fodder for late-night television. In Clare's mind, the media was making Danfield into a bit of a laughingstock.

"I would have expected you to be anywhere else," said Jared. She turned anxiously and found him smiling.

"I can think of a million other things I should be doing," she said. "What about you? Up to arresting a few aging protestors tonight?"

"Nice jab, Clare," he said. "You shouldn't worry about police brutality. They'll all do a few more of these and eventually fizzle out, and then the builders can get on with what they're doing."

She stared at him, incredulous at the change in his persona from earlier in the day.

"Look, Clare, you caught me at a bad time today," he began. "Maybe I was a little hurt about the constant wall you throw between us. Especially after I had such a great time at the Whartons' the other night—one of the few times we got to be seen out as a couple. And so you know, I certainly haven't given it a thought about the Garage Guy."

She looked across the church parking lot and noticed Courtney with her arms crossed, squarely facing the two of them. For a brief second Clare and Courtney locked glares. The hair on the back of her neck stood up.

"That was a joke about Parker. I call him Garage Guy to his face," Jared was saying. "Clare? You look like you don't feel so well. Really, why are you out here? I mind your blowing me off yesterday by saying you were sick, but obviously there's some truth in it. Why not be home crashing for a change? You'll feel better. I know you don't care about this rally."

"Yvonne needed a ride because of the crowd," she said distractedly. She turned toward him, trying to prevent him from noticing Courtney.

"There are a ton of folks who could give your mother a ride," he said. "I just saw her with dozens of them. Look, I'll let her know you left. Go home and get some rest. In a couple of days, I'll take you up on your offer for dinner."

She glanced back where Courtney had been; she was gone. Clare immediately relaxed. "I've got Yvonne," she said. "It's better that it come from me, okay? But thanks. I agree, I really should go home."

Jared tugged at her wrist and gave it a gentle squeeze. She accepted it without a stir, smiled, and headed over to where Yvonne was standing.

There was no reason she should have worried about Yvonne's reaction; Yvonne nodded her head happily at Clare's proposal to leave and then turned back with her friends so as not to miss any of the goings-on. In her haste to get out of the crowd and away from the prying stare of Courtney—what was she doing here?—Clare ran smack into Trevor Colson, the local area mortician.

"Trevor!" she said, startled. "Sorry!"

"Hello Clare," Trevor said. "You're in a hurry; have you had enough already?"

A year ahead of Clare growing up and bumped up another year due to his extraordinary IQ, Trevor was one of an elite group of math geniuses in Wisconsin, not to mention a whiz when it came to debates and spelling bees. Unapologetic about his thirst for higher education or about his desire to leave the area to get it, he took advantage of a scholarship for medical school in California. Veering at breakneck speed through graduate school, an internship with a coroner's office in California, and a stint with a mortician out west, Trevor ultimately moved back to work for Bradford and Sons Mortuary in Waukesha. It was no surprise that he'd become the director of the Danfield location within two years. Clare had always been friendly with him and had gotten to know his wife Molly, a native Californian. Molly herself was an honors graduate with a degree in internal medicine, but she had given up practicing to become the perfect stay-at-home mother, raising their daughters Lily and Bethany.

"Really I just don't feel well," Clare said. "I need to get home and get warm. How about you?"

"Wouldn't miss a stick of this. I'm just running out to my car to get a couple of blankets for the girls. You got to admit it's pretty neat, seeing everybody come together like this. I just saw your mom vying for her chance at the bullhorn."

"Too bad we all couldn't get out the bullhorn and get organized about Mary Martin," Clare grumbled. Then she paused: his expression had changed completely.

"Trevor?" Clare pushed.

"You just made me think back to those first couple of days when she went missing and we all pulled together for that prayer service and then when we all combed the area with the police. And now we've got that awful mess down at the creek . . . what a shame," he said.

When we all combed the area around Danfield. Clare got to thinking about Russell's possibly alluding to a funeral. "And the thought that Courtney and Russell may have to deal with having her declared dead," she said.

"Where would you get an idea like that already, Clare?"

"Nowhere," Clare fibbed. "It's just that we have no body and all the talk seems to suggest they'll never find one."

"Well, Clare," he said. "I can't help you there. We'll have to leave it to the experts to decide those kinds of things."

"Trevor . . . I suspect you have an opinion about what's happened to Mary with all your medical training. Look at all the information in the paper about the blood and clothing but there's no shred of human remains. And I'm sure you're in the know if there is about to be a funeral." Clare leaned toward him feeling breathless for spilling her frustration.

"This is crazy talk Clare! Really, right here, right now in this parking lot? First of all I'm just the funeral director. Chief Grady has a forensics unit for all that. And the County Medical Examiners office will make the ultimate determination whether to declare her deceased. Not me. Nobody talks to me about these matters. And secondly, this business about a funeral for Mary . . . if something like that were to be true . . . that kind of thing is between me and the family."

She was taken aback by his frankness.

Trevor shifted. "I've got to go get the blankets before the girls come looking for me," he said.

"Trevor stop . . . I'm sorry for attacking you like that. You do so much for the grieving families in this county . . . it's just that ever since Derek found the site, everything's been so hush-hush. How do we move forward as a community? Shouldn't we be talking about a memorial—is that a better way to ask that question?"

"There you go," Trevor said. "We wouldn't, until we know something definitive. Why are you so wrapped up in this? How come?"

Clare waved her hand toward the crowd. "Do you think this is a more important thing to be wrapped up in?"

"It's not a matter of whether this is more important," Trevor said. He waved toward the crowd as well. "This is life, Clare. And no matter what happens, we need to celebrate life's oddities . . . while we are living." He smiled at her, appearing much calmer, and speaking like a true mortician. "Now, my family is waiting and you need to go home." He tapped her coat lightly.

"Guys?" Jared intervened.

Both of them froze.

"Franklin Marwood is up on the podium for the big speech," Jared offered. "Trevor, Clare's gotta get home. She's been ill."

"Thanks Jared," Trevor answered slowly. "I'd hate to miss Franklin." He looked at Clare. "Good seeing you, Clare," he said quietly. "Feel better."

She could feel Jared staring a hole through her back.

"Thanks," she said and quickly split.

Choosing a well-lit route, she made the seven-minute walk back to where she'd parked her car, a million crazy thoughts drumming through her head, including the timing of Jared's interruption. As soon as she opened the driver's door, she saw the plastic bag—plain as day.

Frantically she reached in and pulled out a piece of her camouflage and then her cap and binoculars.

From out of nowhere, camera bulbs began to flash. Blinded by the glare, Clare couldn't make out a single human figure, in the ghostly dusk; in the voiceless onslaught, photographers continued to pepper her with flashes and clicks of shutters.

"What is this?" she shouted. "Go away! Get away from my Jeep!"

They never stopped, the faceless, shadowy, half-circle that surrounded her. Finally she tossed the camouflage and bag onto the passenger side, jumped into her seat, and drove quickly from the scene, cameras still going off.

Breathing heavily as she raced through the icy streets, she kept thinking one thing: *they were waiting for me.*

Before bolting the doors, Clare zipped around her house going room-to-room, checking all the closets and large cabinets. She inspected all the window latches, though they had already been secured in preparation for the coming winter. She didn't want to sleep in her bed and sat bundled in a blanket on the couch, listening for any creak or sign of movement beneath the street-lights. In a few short hours, she had gone from the high of reminiscing with her dear friend to being terrified for her life.

She couldn't call the police; Jared's behavior had been too erratic today for her to trust that idea. Parker wouldn't have a clue of what to do, and Derek already thought she was over the top. She mentally combed through the events of the last twenty-four hours. One new thing was certain: Trevor Colson was agitated about something. If Mary was about to be declared dead, the Martins were surely in contact with him about services.

In one easy move, she had let the chief take the evidentiary pink barrette; she kicked herself now for allowing it.

She hadn't a clue who had taken her gear and then put it back or whether they were the same people who'd just now snapped the pictures. She felt incredulous just piecing it all together, but was oddly impressed that her actions were starting to be of interest.

TWENTY-TWO

At 6:30 a.m., Clare emerged fitfully from her early morning dreamscape, having slept through the 6:15 radio alarm. Once she stirred, it took her just seconds to become fully aware of the mess of her life.

She hurriedly showered and dressed in anticipation of her follow-up meeting with Lee Graber. She hadn't spent a moment of her two days off dwelling on the question of how to make nice properly.

Patrolman Rick Maher's arm was in motion to knock when Clare opened the front door. Two uniformed officers stood behind him on the front steps in a stance that would have been utterly intimidating had she not known the three of them from around town as rookie officers.

"Rick?"

"Clare," he said. "Do you have a second?"

"Actually, Rick, I don't," she said. "I'm late for work."

Rick gently pressed her forearm as she tried to pass. She felt the burn in her stomach.

The neighborhood had been sufficiently roused by the two squad cars out front. Clare pretended not to notice the prying eyes in the windows of houses along the street and the sudden profusion of dog walkers on her sidewalk behind the bulky police troop.

"Rick," she said. "Is this really necessary right now? How about I come by on my lunch hour?"

"Clare, I have orders to ask you to come to the station," he said.

"Am I being arrested?"

"No," he said. "But we need to talk with you, immediately."

She folded her arms. "You can't legally make me go with you unless you have a reasonable suspicion I've committed a crime. What crime would that be?"

Rick sighed.

"You know I know this," Clare said. "Did Jared order you to do this?"

"We've got a few things to ask you and don't want to do it hanging around your house," Rick said. "It's just better if you come down."

He glanced behind him and Clare made note of the seemingly entertained neighbors who were trying to be inconspicuous as they watched her porch.

"You could have simply called," Clare said.

"Clare . . . " Rick began, apparently unprepared for a struggle.

"Rick, I have to get to work. I'll just follow you in my car and head over to the bank after that. I'll call Lee and tell him I'll be a little late."

He sighed again. "I'd prefer not to let you do that."

"Fine," she snapped. "Let's go see Jared."

She took the painstaking stroll, exaggeratedly swinging her arms to show the lack of handcuffs, to the police car.

The journey to the station was silent except for Rick radioing his position at regular intervals; she spent the time going over exactly what had been happening and working out some choice things to say to Jared when she got to him. The silence lasted until she saw the salivating press corps on the front steps of the station.

"This is nuts, Rick!" she said, disgusted. "Can't you take this car to the officer entrance?"

"Slow news day," Rick said. "Just stay with me."

Unlike last night's frenzy of silent flashbulbs, today strange voices bombarded her with random queries. Clare thought curiously about the media. If she didn't know exactly where this trip to the station was headed, then they shouldn't have a clue why she was being bussed to the station, let a lone be privy to it happening. Rick gripped her forearm to guide her through the reporters and up the front steps; she thought better of resisting.

Without one word of instruction, Rick continued to move her through to a narrow hallway. On the way, they passed lifelong friends, neighbors, some members from the religious community. No one said a word to her, and she tried not to look at them. He led her into one of the interrogation rooms and left her alone in silence. Five minutes later, Rick returned with an officer that Clare recognized as Lieutenant Vernon Joseph.

"Okay, Rick," she exploded. "I came with you and met the

press to my surprise. I'm curious about what Chief Grady thinks about that. Now what is going on? Lieutenant, is this really necessary?"

"That's what we are here to talk about," Vernon responded.

"Where's Jared?"

"It's just going to be us for right now," Rick said.

"No, I want to see Jared," she said. "I want him here in this room."

"Clare," said Rick. "Calm down. We have couple of things to discuss with you. Shouldn't take too long. No crime has been committed, but we have a few things to ask you."

"Explaining what shouldn't take too long?" Clare said, her temperature rising rapidly, she needed them to make the first move. "Your boss just sent you to pick me up in a police car in front of the whole neighborhood and the guys out front of your station were snapping my picture getting out of a squad car. Soon my face will be plastered across every newspaper in the county. So explain why I'm here."

Vernon walked over to an easel and pulled back the cover. Clare gaped at the audacity. It was covered in photos of her holding up the disguise at her Jeep, as well as photos of her walking through the woods to the crime scene in the same kind of disguise. How much had they been tailing her? And to create a display like this?

She had not yet come up with a motivation for her sack of supplies and clothing disappearing and reappearing, and then the scuffle with the press at the protest. It hadn't dawned on her to look at the paper this morning with her thoughts on setting things straight with Mr. Graber. She found it incredible that the pink barrette was bagged, tagged, and pinned to the center of the board.

"What is this?" she asked, shocked that her innocent discovery was being used against her. She was mildly comforted that her disguise was so good it wasn't readily apparent that it was her in the outfit, but nonetheless she was alarmed by the whole display.

"That's what we would like to know," Vernon said.

Clare didn't know which piece to react to. "Lieutenant, I need to make a phone call," she said.

"You aren't under arrest, Clare."

"I know that." Clare rummaged in her purse for a pen. "Get me a phone to call Lee Graber. I'm supposed to be sitting in front of him this minute at work. I can't have him hearing about this from somebody else."

"Hearing about what?" Vernon questioned calmly.

Rick handed her a cordless phone.

"Make your call," he said.

"Come on, Rick," she sighed. "Give me a moment of privacy, at least."

Rick said nothing. She took the phone and stood up. Neither Rick nor the lieutenant moved. Silently, she walked to the door of the interrogation room and stepped into the hall just outside. She left the door open and turned her back to Rick and Vernon, who were watching her from inside.

She dialed Lee's office, pressing her hand to her temple.

"Lee Graber's office," LuAnn said.

"LuAnn? This is Clare," she said, wincing at the thought of how this was going to spread from Lee's secretary to every corner of the bank.

"Oh, Clare!" said LuAnn eagerly. "What's going on?"

"Please put Mr. Graber on the line," Clare said sternly.

"He's not here."

"Just tell me where I can find him."

"Clare, he's on his way to the station . . ."

Clare hung up the phone. She took a deep breath and then stepped back into the room. "Guys," she began. "I really would like to see Jared."

Rick moved carefully to the table and slid out a chair for Clare.

"Calm down a bit, Clare," he said. "This won't take long to clear up. Just have a seat, please."

They stared at one another in a brief and silent showdown, as Clare considered the fine line between cooperating with an investigation and incriminating herself. She gingerly took her seat at the table, furious with Jared for not having the decency to be here after he'd sent the police to her door at dawn.

"Just tell me why I am here, guys," she said.

Rick walked over to the easel and tapped each item with his cheap ballpoint pen. "You tell us," he said.

Clare glanced at the headline for yesterday's rally photo for the first time: *RESIDENT SEEKS TO FOIL PROTEST.* Internalizing her emotions, she didn't know whether to laugh or to cry, it was so incredible.

"Tell you what? So you have my picture holding a pair of fatigues." She specifically pointed to the one photo taken at the rally. "I'm not trying to be glib, but I don't know what you want to hear. I don't know why you dragged me here this morning."

"See this?" Rick pointed to the baggie with the pink barrette. "Where did you get it?"

"Ask Jared," Clare began. "Ask your chief. I found it hanging on a bush and I brought it to him."

"Why?"

"What do you mean why?" Clare snapped. "I thought it might be a piece of evidence."

"Come on," Rick said impatiently.

"Jared knows all this," she said. "Surely you have the answer. Why pretend you don't? I thought it might belong to Mary Martin. I brought it here to him yesterday. If you recall a couple of months ago, there was a big community effort to look for evidence of what had happened to Mary. Do we not care anymore?"

"Clare, we're not trying to be difficult," Vernon said.

"Well then, tell me what you actually want to know!"

The two cops communicated with each other via some indecipherable nonverbal interface. She wondered why a rookie patrolman was the one Jared had chosen to interrogate her. Maybe he was practicing for real criminals, she decided. Rick returned to the easel and began to tap the pictures of her wearing or holding the hunting gear while Vernon remained completely silent.

"Here you are," Rick said. "Running around the woods near the Mary Martin crime scene. Forget, for a second, that you've repeatedly ignored the chief's order to stay away from this area. We've warned everybody to be careful here. Can you explain why the hell you're in disguise?"

Jared hadn't kept their conversations about the crime scene confidential.

"Jared can't order me to stay away from a particular creek in the woods," she said, "unless there's an active, ongoing investigation of a crime scene. Are you telling me that despite what everyone's saying about Mary Martin being the victim of some random animal attack, the police department is still saying they're actively investigating that crime scene but there is no activity going on out there?"

Vernon fidgeted, but said nothing. Clare watched him until she was sure he wasn't going to say anything about what he knew. Her playing along with this whole "interrogation" was looking like a bust.

Clare took one last run at them; she wagged her finger squarely at the photo of herself in the woods. "Are you trying to insinuate that this is a photo of me?" she said. "I don't see the resemblance. So I own some fatigues. So does half the population of Wisconsin. Not to mention Halloween is coming up. I'm an outdoors person."

Rick rolled his eyes. "Really, Clare?"

"Unless you tell me why it's forbidden to go to a creek in the woods that was supposedly the site of a random animal attack," she said, "then yes, really."

Switching gears, he tapped the baggie. "You say this barrette belonged to Mary."

"I don't know for sure," Clare answered. "But I thought it could be."

"And you found it in the woods?"

"I did. I'm hiking through there all the time."

"It's peculiar," Rick said. "There are hiking trails all around, yet you seem to accidentally end up in this particular spot. Twice. I guess that's what you'd have us believe?"

"Come on, Rick," she snapped. "Stop talking to me like I'm a stranger. You know me. What is this all about? I'd like to know why I'm here. You said I was not being arrested, yet your boss sends you to bring me by the station so I can be photographed for the whole town to see, as if I'm accused of some high crime. Why? So I own fatigues. So I found a pink barrette."

This time Rick backhanded the board.

"Look at this mess," he growled, unconvincingly.

"What mess?" Clare laughed. "Even if that was a photo of me, you still haven't told me what would be so damning about walking in the woods in fatigues."

"This isn't getting through to you?" Rick asked. He lifted one boot to the seat of a chair and leaned down on his knee, as if he'd caught one of America's most wanted. She thought she caught Lt. Vernon's eyes rolling at Rick's rookie theatrics. "We've been hearing a lot of stories about how interested you are in the Martin case," he said. "We've cataloged your movements around the crime scene. We're trying to figure out why you're so interested. Beyond all the dress-up games and so-called evidence you've dragged in, there are reports of your harassing a bereaved mother. And don't bother denying that. We've got a bar full of witnesses."

She nearly burst out laughing again.

Rick stood up from his perch and circled the room, awaiting her response.

"So there's no actual question," Clare concluded. "I'm afraid I have nothing for this little fishing expedition. If being a concerned citizen has gotten everyone all riled up, then I'm truly confused. If you don't have anything else to imply, I've got to get to work."

Rick paused for an interminably silent moment.

Clare got up and opened the door, exercising her right to leave freely, and made it halfway down the hallway before Lt. Joseph managed a tight squeeze of her elbow. There wasn't a prying eye to be found.

"You seem to think this is joke," he lit into her with his barely audible, high-and-mighty tone. "That you can come in here with your flip little answers. Message from the chief: Stop interfering with this investigation! If you're really up to something, we've got you coming and going. And don't think we won't make this interesting. Otherwise, stop giving the media a reason to get hysterical about this case. Do you hear me?"

"You're hurting me," Clare responded with her last ounce of disgust. "I suggest you let me go."

Clare shook loose when he didn't. She could suddenly hear Rick's footsteps following her out and trailing her down the hall.

She frowned, going over and over the interview and mugging by Lt. Joseph. He was a hotshot, Clare knew, and she'd deal with it later.

Lee Graber was sitting on a bench in the lobby of the station, fidgeting with his hat.

"Clare?" He sprung to intercept her. "Mrs. Graber saw you in the news this morning. They said you were somehow caught up in this bell tower protest business! What's happening?"

"Not here." Clare wanted to do this away from the station; the knowledge that Jared had been so adamant about keeping her away from the investigation that he'd been willing to put her name in the news was beginning to make her livid. "Can we just go back to the office? I'll explain."

Lee noticed Rick behind her. "Hey, Officer Maher," he called. "Do you have a quiet spot?"

"Sure," Rick said and pointed back down the hallway she'd just come from.

Had it not been Lee, Clare would have bolted, but he was the closest thing she had to a father figure. Begrudgingly she followed Rick back down the hallway.

"A conference room or something," she insisted. "Please."

Rick clearly understood her preference for a room without two-way glass and was apparently done with torturing her for the day on what she knew was Jared's order. He continued down the hall to an empty detective office and ushered them in.

"We're good here," Clare glared, and Rick grinned and closed the door.

"Lee, don't say anything yet," Clare quickly began. "I wasn't arrested—"

"Clare, why were you brought to the station?" Lee was clearly agitated. "Does this have anything to do with your behavior on Monday? You didn't say anything about any of this!"

"Mr. Graber, just hear me out," Clare said. "I'm not in trouble. They just had a few things to ask me. That picture in the paper about me messing with the rally was a joke."

"I cannot believe they'd haul you down here because you wanted to heckle the crowd," Lee said in disbelief.

"Forget the photo. They had questions about the Mary Martin investigation because I found a piece of evidence about the case," Clare said, caving. "And I am begging you to not repeat this to anybody."

"This has something to do with the Martin case?" Lee demanded. "What in the Sam Hill would you have to do with the Martin case?"

"Mr. Graber, I had nothing to do with the Martin case," Clare said, incredulous at the implication. "Some things have been blown out of proportion."

"What things?" Lee asked.

"You know Derek is my friend, and it's no secret he came to my house that night a couple of weeks ago when they found the spot with Mary's clothes," Clare said.

"I still don't understand how that puts you in the middle of this," Lee said tersely.

"Let's not talk about this here," Clare said, eyeing the detective's office.

"Here is as good a place as anywhere!" Lee snapped. "If you are in trouble, I want to know what the trouble is. Does Yvonne know what's happening?"

"Lee!" Clare snapped.

"I'm offering to listen and help," Lee said more quietly. "Why are you being so stubborn?"

He reached out to touch her shoulder; she shrank back from his hand. He waited while she caught her breath.

"First of all, Yvonne will know what I want her to," she began slowly. "This is not the place to explain. Somebody has misconstrued my curiosity about Mary's death, and my bringing in a possible piece of evidence, and they're trying to make something out of it. I don't know who it is . . . I don't know why. But I've struck a chord, somehow."

"Why do you need to be so involved?" Lee asked, frowning. "Don't we have a police department investigating? It seems that we have a damn good police chief."

She looked him in the eyes. "I don't feel comfortable talking about it here," she said.

He looked at her. She looked back at him. He sighed and began to pace.

"What I need to do right now is damage control while I wait for you to come clean," he said, as if to himself. "You were already on the news being taken into the police station. Those pictures in this morning's paper are incredible, you have to admit. Are there more pictures to come? Rumors about to run wild?" he asked in jest. "We've got a board and shareholders who don't need to be nervous about this."

"Lee, don't," she began.

"Clare, you are an officer of the bank," Lee said, looking her in the eye again. "It may just be for a week or so, but I've got to suspend you. No matter how wrongly, your name could be associated somehow with a little girl's murder. If something leaks out that it's more than you in a little bell tower tussle, you'll have more problems than you can shake a stick at. I'm sure it's just a bad nightmare that will be cleared up. But you understand my position."

"You can't possibly believe that I'm connected to this murder." Clare choked on her use of the word murder.

"Clare, enough," Lee said, more gently. "Of course I don't believe that. But clearly you've been knotted up about this."

He put an end to the discussion by opening the door.

"Go home and stay out of everybody's sight," he said. "When I can, we'll meet."

She had nothing more to say to him, and she knew him well enough to see how distracted he was at the thought of what the precious shareholders would think of his COO now. If anything, given the photo of her holding the fatigues, she was certain she'd be getting an awful beating about her opinion over the bell tower demolition.

He walked off without so much as an offer to drive her home.

She watched him go, numb. Then she turned to find Officer Maher again. If he'd brought her here, she decided, if he and his boss had contrived to get her name and face in the papers for literally no reason that she could see beyond blatant intimidation, then the least he could do was drive her home.

TWENTY-THREE

This time, Rick took her down and out of the station through the police garage, avoiding the possibility that the media was still lurking. She slumped down in the squad car and braced herself for a media swarm at the other end, but perked up when they pulled to curb of her house. There were no reporters or onlookers, which relieved her, but also confused her. The neighborhood had seemingly returned to normal. Without a word to Rick, she exited the car, darted around back, and went inside her house. She secured the patio door.

A shadowy figure moved on the periphery of her vision. Someone was in here. She grabbed at the door she'd just locked.

"Clare, wait!"

Parker moved into the light and grabbed her shoulders. On

instinct, she pushed him away. Then she looked at him, all the tension of the past hours suddenly draining out of her, leaving her helpless.

"Parker," she exhaled and grabbed him back.

"Clare . . . my God," he said, and she began to sob inaudibly. He held her for a moment and then pulled her away from him. "What did you do?"

"I've done nothing," Clare collected herself. "Why does everybody think that I've done something?"

"Come on," he said. "Let's think this through. Come sit down." He began to move them toward the bay window in the kitchen. She stiffened.

"Wait," she said. "Explain what you're doing in my house."

"Yvonne called me and then stopped by the garage," Parker said. "She was pretty shaken."

"I bet the whole neighborhood couldn't wait to call her," Clare said bitterly. "Why did she call you?"

"You forget I was almost her son-in-law," Parker reminded her. I've seen her more than you have over the years, especially when you were AWOL in Chicago."

"That doesn't explain why you're in my kitchen."

"She said she wanted me to take your house key . . . just in case. I called the station and they said you were about to leave, so I thought I'd wait for you here."

"Just in case," Clare said. "Great. Thanks, Yvonne."

She sat down at the table by the bay window, both oddly comforted and distressed by Parker's presence in her house.

"Why would you be involved in that bell tower business?" he asked flatly.

She stopped and stared.

"You really don't know?" he asked. Then he reached into his back pocket and lifted this morning's paper. He'd already folded the section around her picture.

She glared more closely at the photo she'd just seen on the evidence board in Rick's interrogation room: Clare, looking surprised beside her Jeep, the fatigues in her arms.

Clare shook her head, frustrated. She'd just done this with Mr. Graber. "Parker, just understand than I am not in trouble and I wasn't about to mess with the rally. You'll just have to trust me on this. I am home, I'm fine, and I'll take care of Yvonne."

"The trip to the station was because you wanted to protest about the tower protestors?" he asked. "That makes no sense."

"A big misunderstanding." Clare was intentionally brief. She could see his intuitive little mind working away.

"Clare," Parker began. "You recently tried, on a couple of occasions, to talk about Mary Martin. Is that what this is all about?"

"Why is that strange to you?" Clare asked. "I find it ridiculous that I seem to be the only one who's interested in what happened to her. Look at the rally last night; I'm sure you were there. We're more riled up about a pile of old dilapidated bricks than we are about the brutal slaying of a child."

"As your friend . . . you do seem to be fixated on that point," Parker said. "And you can't lump everybody in this category of not being interested."

"I can't handle this conversation with you," she said.

"Clare," Parker said gently. "Aside from the fact that you've decided that nobody in this town cares about what happened to Mary, except for you—what's your involvement? I understand that your law enforcement training makes you smarter than the rest of us. But last I checked, you don't work for the police department. Why did they want to talk to you . . . really?"

She was more concerned about the urge she felt to let him comfort her than she was about how direct he was being.

"Do you think we could let this go?" she asked. "I'm tired."

"You just got back from the police station, Clare," Parker said. "That's extreme for anyone. So enough with your tough act . . . I can't believe you don't want a friend to talk to right now."

"This is not about whether I need someone," Clare said. "Believe me when I say that this is all a misunderstanding. Someone's worried that I'm asking questions about this case. That's all."

"So it isn't about the bell tower?"

Clare looked away.

He sighed. "I know you pretty well," he said. Regardless of your interest in law enforcement, this is your buddy's problem, not yours. Don't you have any confidence in Chief Grady?"

Furious, Clare turned to him. "I found a barrette and took it to the station," she said. "That's all. That's the extent of my *playing detective.* I am just a concerned citizen who wants answers."

Parker folded up the newspaper and tossed it on the bench behind him. "You really aren't listening are you?"

She felt an insatiable urge to be destructive, but opted to hang tight, her hands clenched into fists.

"I'll quit worrying about Mary," she said in a hollow voice. "I'll just make everybody more comfortable." She felt tears spill down her cheek and wished Parker wasn't here to see.

"Clare," Parker said, softening, "my only hope is that this is some kind of cathartic thing you're doing because you need to get on with your life. After Mary, and after . . . everything. Both of us need to get on with our lives."

This infuriated her. Sara had said only the other day: Clare hadn't picked him. She had no interest in leading him on now, or in letting him dissect her entire personality because her mother had decided that he was the best person to call in a crisis—this person she'd left years before.

"That's it?" she said sharply. "That's your explanation for this thing that's obviously very important to me? Clare needs a shrink?"

Parker's face fell. He set the spare key on her counter.

"I have to go," he said. "And knock on my door any time, when you really want to talk."

She let him wrap her in a bear hug. Then she watched him leave through the backyard, apparently as eager as her to avoid the limelight.

Clare picked up her phone and sizzled over the furiously flashing caller ID display that had already captured fifteen messages that Clare attributed to her new notoriety in the paper. She opted to ignore them and stood in the front window, watching the street as she dialed.

"Mother, do me a favor," she said as soon as Yvonne answered.

"Clare!" her mother wailed. "You're out of jail!"

"Geeze-us, Mother," Clare said, wincing. "I wasn't in jail."

"But Nora said that—and the article about you—something about the tower."

"Nora nothing," Clare snapped. "Could you just do me a favor and get me a couple of things at the store? Can you do that . . . just help me a little?"

Yvonne agreed, and Clare ended the call and fell back against the end of the couch. Yvonne was the dead last person to call in a crisis, but she didn't know who else she could call right now. No

Sara, no Lee, no Derek, no Parker, absolutely no Jared. Imprisoned by her own four walls, she sat stewing, growing angrier at everyone she couldn't call with each passing minute.

All she wanted was to know was what had happened to Mary. Instead, *she* had become the story. She was thankful the article was about the rally, hoping it meant she had a prayer of saving face with Mr. Graber.

In an instant, she flung her couch pillow at the fireplace, only to topple her treasured Chicago vase and send it smashing to the wood floor.

She was sitting next to the fireplace, her feet among the broken shards when she heard Yvonne creaking through the back door and placing a sack of stuff on the counter.

"Clare? I brought the things from the grocery," Yvonne called out. "Are you okay?"

Clare ignored her, and her mother came around the corner.

"Oh!" Yvonne walked over to the smashed pottery. "This is your favorite . . . not mine, of course. But you love it."

"Just leave it, Mother," Clare snapped. "I'll get it!"

"What happened?"

Without responding, Clare walked past Yvonne to her tiny downstairs office for an envelope. She picked up some cash from the kitchen counter.

"Here," Clare said, handing Yvonne the cash. "For the groceries."

"Oh, honey," Yvonne sighed. "Don't worry, I had the money."

Clare stuffed the thirty dollars in Yvonne's coat pocket and sat back down on the fireplace. She started to write a note.

"Say something, Clare," Yvonne said at last. "You're worrying me."

"What business did you have to call Parker?" Clare asked.

Clare peeled off a note from the pad of paper, folded it, stuck it in the envelope, and sealed it. She placed an additional sticker across the seal of the envelope.

"Don't be mad at me, Clare," Yvonne said. "I couldn't think. I thought you were arrested. I didn't want to upset Derek, so I took a key to Parker at the shop."

"You couldn't just drive down and see how I was? Did anybody bother to say that I wasn't being handcuffed?" Clare demanded. "Why didn't you call Mr. Wharton or something?"

"Oh Clare, you know how you are with authority," her mother said. "I thought Parker could just figure out what was happening."

"News flash, Mother," Clare shouted. "Parker and I don't date anymore! Try over nine years ago! How could you possibly have thought that was a good idea?"

Yvonne was clearly hurt. "What is happening here, Clare?" she asked quietly. She leaned toward Clare, suddenly meek. "I'm sorry. I just wanted to help. Why did they take you to the station?"

"You need to listen to me carefully," Clare said, ignoring her, unwilling to explain about the barrette. "I need one more thing from you. And then—Mother—I need you to go on about your business." She motioned with her finger to her lips for Yvonne to be quiet. "If anybody asks you anything," Clare said, "tell them everything is okay, it's just little misunderstanding about the photo. You saw me yesterday. I was headed home to get some rest.

I don't know why the media cares about my fatigues. But I wasn't planning to get in the middle of your rally."

Clare heard a car door and leaned around the kitchen opening to the living room where she could see through the front window that it was Derek, coming up her walk. Derek couldn't be here now. She looked down at the note she had written with a slight hesitation and then turned back to Yvonne.

"Take this envelope to the station," she said. "Give it to Jared."

"What is it?"

Derek knocked on the front door.

"Listen to me," Clare grabbed Yvonne. "You don't need to know. Just help me. I promise to explain everything another time, but not now. Take this envelope and leave it at the front desk for Jared only! And whatever you do—" Clare gripped Yvonne tighter "—do not tell anybody it was from me!"

She guided her mother into the living room, past Derek as he was entering.

"Hi." She shooed Yvonne out the front door. "Good-bye, Mom," she said. "Thanks for bringing me some things from the store."

She waved Derek in and shut the door.

"I was just going to call you," she said. "I wanted to come over to your house this afternoon. Can I, still?"

"Clare?" Derek asked. His eyes gravitated to the smashed vase. "What happened?"

"You know, just a klutzy accident." Clare headed back into the kitchen to put away the groceries. "So can I come over later?"

"What's this I'm hearing about you getting picked up by the police this morning?" Derek asked. "I had to hear about it from

Frannie Dexter while I was reorganizing the snow chains. And right after that, my mom called. And there's this thing in the papers about you sneaking around wearing fatigues? Something about the bell tower protest?"

She was too tired to go over this with him, too. She opened one of her modernist cupboards and set a can of soup inside.

"It's nothing to worry about," she said flatly. "I'm sorry you had to hear about it from Frannie."

She turned her head; his expression was aggravated.

"Is that it?" he asked. "Why are the police talking to you? It isn't because you wanted to throw a monkey wrench into the rally? Is this about the Mary Martin case? Did they ask anything about me?"

"Derek, I'm tired," she said, wearily. "Everything is okay, but I need to lie down for a bit. I was going to call you and ask to meet at your house in just a little while, I swear. It'll be about 5:15, and I'll tell you everything, okay? Right this minute I can barely keep my eyes open."

In two steps he was beside her. He shut the cupboard door. She could barely turn; he had sandwiched her without breathing room.

"Derek, I'm tired," she said.

"You look tired." He continued hovering within inches of her. "Maybe you ought to start taking better care of yourself."

She swallowed. "Derek, you're making me uncomfortable."

"Why are you doing this, Clare?"

"Move away, Derek," Clare said. "Just move." She slapped his chest.

"I've begged you to stay away from this," he said, breathing down at her. "Haven't I? Does our friendship mean nothing to you?"

Suddenly he broke away. Watching her, he backed into the living room; she stood by the counter next to Yvonne's groceries and didn't move. Derek, her childhood friend, was looking at her; his eyes were full of panic, as they'd been on the night when he came to her front door, covered in blood and soaking wet. He threw his hands up and left hastily through the front entrance.

Completely unnerved, she felt another urge to throw something again. Instead she sucked up a deep breath and walked around to the front room. She grabbed her broom and began sweeping up the broken vase, frantically.

"Maybe I ought to start taking better care of myself," Clare whispered. "What are you talking about, Derek?"

Just a couple of weeks ago, Derek had fallen on her doorstep in need of her shoulder to cry on. She squeezed the broomstick to hold back the tears.

TWENTY-FOUR

The much-needed two-and-a-half hour nap took her to a deep sleep and left her feeling groggy. She was well past her 4:15 alarm when she acknowledged her beeping sports watch and got hold of her senses. She barely had time for a splash of cold water and a new sweater, and she was left with the drive from her house to Derek's to spruce up a bit from her makeup bag sprawled in the passenger seat. On the whole drive, she went over what had happened with him in her kitchen earlier: how aggressive, even threatening, his actions had been; how scared he had seemed of whatever she was involved in. For a moment she regretted the note she had sent Yvonne with earlier.

No matter how strangely he had been behaving earlier, Derek

was still a creature of habit, and she found him just flicking off the overhead light of his garage at 5:15.

"Hi . . . we got to talk," she said knowing that she was about to hurt him again. He turned. She exhaled in relief; he didn't look as panicked as he had earlier but there was something about how he was glaring at her.

"We finished at your house earlier. I didn't really expect you to come by," he said to her. "I think we've said all we need to say right now."

"So you don't want to hear me tell you about this interview at the police station?" she asked softly. "Or about getting suspended from my job?"

He didn't make a move to stop her from coming on in behind him.

She could feel the growing rift between them. Though he seemed more in control than he had been earlier—if he hadn't been, she would have been at a loss as to how to abort her plan— he was clearly still not ready to talk to her yet as they rambled through the side door and down a short hallway that led to his kitchen.

Through the silence of their shuffling they hung coats and scarves on the faux antler hooks in the hallway.

She always admired the uniqueness of his handiwork, the neat and organized outdoorsman-magazine layout that was a logical mirror of Derek's personality. The kitchen, as fulfilling as the first time she'd seen it with its darkened pinewood cabinets, the springboard for the warm, lodge-like feel throughout his house. The care and craftsmanship Derek bestowed on his family and friends extended to the remodel he'd done on this run-down 1920s Tudor that he'd acquired from an estate sale against the advice of his realtor. Though it was merely 1,800 square feet, his vaulted ceilings and his carefully crafted open floor plan gave it such a spacious feel that the same realtor had begun to use Derek's house as a showcase to inspire prospective buyers when he showed them his other degenerated properties.

"I don't think I've seen those pictures before," Clare said finally.

"There is nothing new," he said, without looking at what she'd pointed to. "All this has been here for some time."

It was already time; she paced to keep her anticipation in check. There were three photographs mounted on the stone above the mantle of his fireplace. Clare examined one of Derek and his parents, another rare photo with a couple of fishing buddies, and a third with him and Coach. Off to the side of the mantle was a freestanding picture of Karen.

"This wasn't here last time," she said, pointing.

"You're not here to check out my stuff," he snapped. "Could you get to the point? Could you tell me why the police wanted to talk to you?"

Clare heard a car door close out front. She moved to just out of view of the front door. Derek frowned at her, but there was a knock on the door, and he went to answer it.

"Jared?" he asked.

"Derek." Jared moved swiftly into the foyer and closed the door. "What's with the note? What's happening? Couldn't you have come to the station?" In his hand was the paper Clare had sent earlier with Yvonne.

Clare stepped out of the shadows. As soon as Jared saw her, his face began to grow red.

"Don't even tell me you set this up," he said.

"Set what up?" Derek demanded. "Clare?!"

Before she knew it, Jared had hold of her arm; she bristled. He yanked her into a spare bedroom.

"Explain yourself," he said.

"Knock it off, and that goes for Lt. Joseph as well." she said pulling free from his grip. "You need to tell me what's happening. Don't send police to my door and get my picture in the evening news! Is that why you followed me everywhere last night at the protest? So you could be sure I wasn't paying attention while you put the fatigues back in my car? Your cop minions sure made a big deal about my owning outdoor gear!"

She could hear Derek pacing in the hallway just outside the open door. Using his house for a liaison with Jared had become less of a great idea.

"How dare you have me hauled in!" she continued. "For everyone to gossip about? I got suspended from my job today, Jared!"

"I didn't know you'd get suspended," Jared said, as if he didn't particularly care at this moment. "And I was picking on you, Clare, because you've made this whole investigation about you. While I'm out there busting my ass, you've done nothing but spread subtle accusations about my work on Mary's case as if you are some authority. You are not! So far, you've done nothing but muck this up."

"Muck what up?" she asked, her eyes narrowing. "I brought you Mary's barrette and you didn't seem to be the slightest bit concerned. Next thing I know I'm getting browbeaten by your police force."

"What is this about a barrette?" Derek barked from the other side of the wall.

Jared stalled. Then he left the bedroom without saying a word. She followed him. He was standing in the living area, looking at Derek. Derek looked as terrified as he'd seemed earlier that day, at her house.

"Derek," Clare demanded. "What is happening here?"

Derek looked as though he'd been gagged.

"If I find out you had anything to do with this," Jared said and pointed at Derek.

"I didn't know," Derek said, his mouth suddenly dry.

"Do with what?" Clare snapped.

Jared began rattling his keys and fastening his jacket to leave, as though he couldn't stand the sight of her.

"Jared," she said. "I'm one of your biggest fans, remember? You know that full well."

He said nothing, clearly unimpressed. Clare snagged a handful of his jacket.

"You're using me, aren't you?" she said. "What was the dance about this morning, really? I deserve to know. What I don't deserve is public humiliation when all I am doing is caring about a little girl."

Jared made another cursory glance at Derek and then, in an instant, pulled free of Clare's hold. Her heart stopped and he pressed within inches of her face.

"You aren't paying attention," he growled. "That was nothing! If you get in my way again, Clare, the next trip to the station won't be just for a visit. Do you understand me? I will charge your ass with a string of behavior that I can trump up to ruin your life for a long time if you want to play this game!"

"Jared, that's enough!" Derek fired but he was obviously still verbally handcuffed.

Before Clare could respond, Jared was out the door.

She felt completely demolished.

Derek was standing in the hallway, leaning on the wall.

"There you have it," he croaked. "You wouldn't listen to me. Looks like you aren't listening to anybody. Not even the chief."

"I knew he wouldn't come to my house," Clare said, numb. "I wanted some answers about my being interrogated."

"So did a showdown in my house with the chief of police help you?" he asked.

She closed her eyes, counted to three, and turned to him.

"What was with the eye rolling?" Clare asked. "He treats me horribly and you just stand there? What is going on between the two of you?"

Derek rushed past her into the kitchen. She turned and followed.

"Derek, answer me," she shouted.

"He's right," Derek said quickly. "Who can talk to you when you're like this? You're a bulldog, Clare. You're off your rocker like I've never seen, and I know you. How is the new chief in town supposed to interpret your actions and do his job?"

"So now I'm a bulldog," she yelled, tears on her cheeks. "What the hell is that supposed to mean?"

"You want everybody to want what you want," Derek pressed. "Nobody's allowed to like it here. It's a sin in your eyes for people to want to live in a small town. It's strange sometimes that you think growing old with friends and raising a family in the same community is somehow abnormal . . ."

She stood in his kitchen, tears running down her cheeks, staring at her best friend.

"What does any of that have to do with Mary Martin?" she said finally with a raw voice. "What does any of that have to do with whatever's going on between you and the chief?"

Derek didn't say anything. She took her coat from the antler rack and left to drive home.

Out in front of her house, the Jeep sputtered in the freezing temperatures. Clare sat alone, sulking, in lieu of a complete meltdown.

But she couldn't erase Derek's expression of sheer helplessness. She turned the ignition and drove to the police station to find Jared again. She hadn't a clue what she would say, but knew she wanted to see him. Whatever was going on with this investigation, she knew he was deeply involved, but she was beginning to wonder if his involvement was only limited to his being the chief of police.

His parking space at the station was empty. Again ignoring a little voice that whispered she should head home, she hustled back to her vehicle and tried to calculate his whereabouts.

For the next half hour, she wandered the streets of Danfield making what she eventually realized were uneducated guesses about his personal routine. As she rolled by his house for the third time trying to remember the names of any restaurants he had said he liked, any social events he might have said he took part in, she realized how little she'd actually invested in his personal life when he wasn't with her.

At one point, after leaving the NiteLite parking lot yet again after no sign of Jared's car, she drove to her mother's house and parked across the street, spying on Yvonne's simple existence through the front window as her mother comfortably knitted in her pajamas and robe. She harbored a sense that life, as they knew it, was no more. In a rare moment, she sometimes felt like she ought to involve her mother in some of the new developments—a mother/daughter chat that had so far eluded them. Maybe someday.

In short order the spike of adrenaline that had fueled her last thirteen hours, since Officer Maher had knocked on her front door this morning, began to plummet. Cold and blanketed with exhaustion, she began to feel relieved that she hadn't bumped into Jared in her frenzied state. Driving toward home, half dreaming, she decided that she should set one of her last demons at rest for the night and drove to Courtney's house.

Like many in the town, Clare bristled at the opulence of Courtney's neighborhood, and she remembered the tug-of-war over the stark contrast of such a development—dubbed "Richville" by the locals during the city's permit process—with their much humbler Danfield. On a street perpendicular to Courtney's cul-de-sac, she found an unobtrusive spot across from the open-gated entrance of the mega-home division. Nearly dozing, she peered into the darkness toward Courtney's front walk, remembering the layout as she'd seen it the other day: the house where this had all started.

After some minutes, she was ready to flick the headlights on and drive home when she saw Jared in his unmarked police car flying down Courtney's cul-de-sac and into her palatial stone driveway. She stopped breathing and squinted across the distance into the darkness. She could just make out Jared's hurried steps up the tiered entry, his knock, and the sight of Courtney opening the front door to him, as if he had been expected.

She thought quickly: it must have been an emergency. There would be multiple squad cars on their way in just seconds. But she rejected the idea. If it were an emergency, Jared would certainly not have been the first person on the scene, in an unmarked police car, no less.

On instinct, she grabbed the fatigues in her backseat. She paused for a few seconds, considering the crap of the last day over them, but put them on anyway.

She trekked quietly up the slushy, rocky service road that ran behind the properties, designed by the architects of the subdivision to keep maintenance crews from cluttering the neighborhood street. When she got closer to the house, she left the service road and began to work her way through the lightly snow-covered lawn. She visualized the room layout from Monday's visit. The deck off the kitchen would be the easiest to get to.

She was crossing the wooden deck that lined the long bay window when she froze. Courtney came into the kitchen alone, wearing a revealing designer outfit that elicited a maddening spike of jealousy. Clare crouched, not breathing, beside the deck, watching Courtney gather something from the counters, until at last she walked back through the archway that led, if Clare's mental map served, to the den.

Clare stepped off the deck to follow the direction Courtney had gone in the house around through the landscaping. She remembered the large, glass windows from her notes, and she kept herself out of view of them as best as she could. She crept closer and closer, in remarkable silence despite the residual pockets of

snow and the leafless shrubs hidden beneath the fluffy cover, in
and out of the shadows of trees lit by spotlights. It was a small
comfort that the neighbors were acres away.

Jared was in the den. Clare watched Courtney come into the
room and gingerly set a tray of coffee and food on a stone table.
Jared frowned, as if her preparing him a snack were a distraction
from what he was about to say. They talked at an awkward distance until Courtney stepped closer, within a couple of feet. Jared
was speaking with hand gestures that Clare couldn't decipher.
Courtney appeared perplexed.

In spite of the anger she had for Jared right now and Courtney
forever, Clare was beginning to feel bad about spying on them
for no rational purpose. She stepped back, ready to return to her
vehicle, but stopped when Courtney buried her million-dollar
face in her manicured hands. Jared walked over and engulfed her
in his arms. As if Courtney would faint without his support, her
legs wobbling, she clung and he clung as tight and without a stick
of breathing room between them.

She bit her lip and tried to stay rational. It could be a sign of
movement in the case. But why was he here alone? What were
the two of them planning together, doing together? She resisted
the urge to run into the house to pry them apart, and carefully
resumed her trek back through the landscaping and over the service road. Her adrenalin spike had returned in full force—if Jared
saw her here, now, the interrogation this morning would seem
like nothing—but she kept going, and she made it to the Jeep
without being seen.

She threw the fatigues in the washer as soon as she got home
and then decided to wait up while they dried so that she could
pack them away in her closet as soon as possible.

Something was clearly happening, she mused as she surfed channels and waited for the dryer to buzz. But thus far the police department had remained remarkably silent on exactly what their investigation was focusing on. Clare wondered whether they were focusing on anything at all. All she knew, after today, was that Derek was certainly in the know, but unwilling to talk. All Clare could do was wallow in confusion, thinking about the secret meeting between Jared and Courtney and how little she really knew, it turned out, about the one guy who was to install a true order of law in Hicksville. All she knew, she realized, was that she had let him down, on a number of levels.

TWENTY-FIVE

C lare woke from a sound sleep to a loud, feverish knocking sound. Her eyes, instantly pierced by the bright
dawn that sprayed across the bedroom, began to water.
As difficult as it was to drag herself out of bed, Clare was impatient for any news.

Halfway down the stairs she was suddenly certain that the
knocking was coming from the back door and was therefore likely
to be Yvonne.

It was too early to deal with the picture in the paper. Stiff and
sore and emotionally drained, she was at her kitchen archway
before she recalled the mess of Martin-related newspapers she'd
started to look through and left on the kitchen table last night
during her catatonic state.

"Just a second!" Clare barked. As quickly as she could, she snagged a handful of papers from her fireplace hearth and sprawled them across the blaring Martin mess. Then she opened the door and leaned into the frigid morning air, where indeed her mother was waiting for her.

"Mother, I'm sleeping here," Clare said. "Couldn't you have called?"

"This morning is the final bell tower meeting at city hall," Yvonne said. "It's at nine. I thought you'd like to go, since you aren't—"

"Aren't what?" Clare responded curtly. "Aren't going to work?"

"I just thought you might be interested."

Clare surmised Yvonne was really here for the skinny on yesterday's headline and trip to the station. "Mother, I cannot imagine losing sleep to go to another city hall meeting on this subject."

Clearly unaffected by the rejection, Yvonne remained steadfast on the steps. Clare was painfully irritated by the biting winds at her feet, hands, and face.

"A cup of coffee then, dear," Yvonne said. "I'm freezing."

Clare widened the opening for Yvonne to squeeze though and secured the storm door behind her. "Have you ever noticed you've got remarkable timing when it comes to my sleep schedule?" She backed up to a stool by her counter to keep Yvonne from eyeing the newspapers on the table.

"Clare, don't be snotty. I thought you'd like to go. It'd give us a chance to chat," Yvonne hinted.

She frowned at her daughter. "Honey . . . how are you, anyway? I want to help with whatever is going on."

Clare ignored her on all measures. "What's in the bag?" she asked, pointing to Yvonne's sack.

"I brought you some muffins from the Clutch and one of those cinnamon coffees you like."

Clare felt a twinge of unfamiliarity; it wasn't characteristic of Yvonne to show this kind of sincere, unfettered mothering touch.

"If it's okay with you, I would like to go back to bed," Clare said. "Right now that's how you can help. I just need some sleep."

"Let me do something for you," Yvonne said gingerly, as if she thought Clare would crack. "You're not telling me what's going on. Why the silly mission to the station yesterday to deliver that note? And then what's that picture of you in the paper? You promised to tell me what was happening."

Clare was amazed it took Yvonne this long into her visit to bring up the picture in the paper.

"Mom, look, I'm good," Clare said. She pointedly glanced at her watch. "I'd really like not to be standing in my kitchen at this hour talking about muffins. Can we do this later?"

"I am not talking about muffins," Yvonne said, resolute. "We cannot just shove it under the rug."

Now it seemed more about Yvonne's reputation. "I have absolutely nothing to say about the picture in the paper. I don't know why it was taken or why anybody would think I'd do something like that. Please, Mother, it's just too early in the day."

"At least let me help around here. You go ahead and go back to bed. I'll tidy up for you and run a load of laundry. Maybe you'll be ready to talk in a while when I get back from the meeting." Yvonne said unbuttoning her winter coat.

"You'll be late for your meeting if you do all that," Clare said, nearly ready to strangle her. "Let's go to city hall. Maybe it'll be more interesting on a weekday morning, without all the crowds."

"What's all this mess anyway," Yvonne said, frowning down at the table. "What are these old, dingy newspapers?"

"They're nothing," Clare said, shrugging and attempting nonchalance. "They're just some work things I was going to catch up on. I'll get rid of them." She picked up the papers, casually. "Let me just change really quick. Give me that coffee and I'll have the muffin in the car, okay?"

Yvonne nodded. Clare tossed the papers on a chair in the front room and dashed upstairs with her coffee. In just minutes, she put on one of her better sweat suits, put her hair up in a clip, and applied minimal makeup.

She came downstairs to find Yvonne going through the newspapers with eyes wide.

"I thought I told you this wasn't important!" Clare barked.

"Clare, why do you have all these clippings on Mary Martin?" Yvonne scolded. "This is crazy stuff! What on earth are you doing?"

Clare snatched the papers away and sighed violently at Yvonne. "Mother, I am either going back to bed and you are leaving, or we're going to city hall. You pick. I don't need a lecture about my newspapers."

An emboldened Yvonne accepted Clare's offer by bundling up and heading out the back door, as though she was still unaffected by their running argument.

Clare drove them to the meeting in Yvonne's car, devouring muffins and coffee from the center console.

"These are pretty good," she said. "Just what I needed to get going." She wasn't going to admit to her mother that she'd eaten virtually nothing yesterday except a handful of stale crackers and some cheese late last night. Nearly a zombie by bedtime, unable to get the huddle between Jared and Courtney to evaporate from her mind, she finally busied herself by pulling out all the Mary crap from her closet at about two in the morning. That led nowhere, and the memory of Courtney and Jared's embrace didn't make her feel any better now in the light of day.

Yvonne had called her Mary Martin newspapers "crazy stuff." That left literally no one in her life who wasn't eyeing her with suspicion. She'd become a freak show, without even the credibility of her job to fall back on.

Clare parked and then she and Yvonne wove their way through the milling masses on the front steps at city hall, some of whom were powering through their last cigarettes. Unlike the meeting at the civic center, city business was normally conducted in this much smaller hall in front of a token handful of attendees. One could usually snooze through the routine agenda with a clear conscience. Today, however, as Yvonne explained, the save-the-steeple faction had become paranoid that the council was going to make a "final decision" about the tower in a "secret session" and had shown up in force. Clare rolled her eyes at their paranoia. "Imagine that, Mother," she said. "They've scheduled a peaceful meeting during normal hours, so that they can move forward with their lawful project."

Yvonne ignored her. Then she turned and broke into a smile. She'd caught a wave from her friend Thelma, who looked under pressure to give up the chairs that the group of them agreed to hold for Yvonne. Clare and Yvonne hurried over to grab two aisle seats.

Bernard Kohlhepp moved to the podium and pounded the gavel to bring the council session to order. He appeared much more composed than he'd been at the town meeting a couple of weeks ago.

"Mr. Secretary, please read the minutes from our last meeting," he began.

Clare appreciated the next twenty minutes of agenda items that had nothing to do with the bell tower. Lulled by the monotony, she drifted until Yvonne's elbow caught her side.

"We're having a sit-in," Yvonne whispered, warming Clare's earlobe.

"What?"

"We're having a sit-in. We just decided. To keep these thugs from destroying our town."

"Really!" Clare whispered back. "Who is we?"

"The ladies' bridge club . . . we want them to know we're serious." Yvonne glared at the council members droning on stage.

"Just the other night, you all rallied with your parade on Main Street and to the church, and before that there was the town meeting, and before that you blocked the first day of construction," Clare whispered. "I think they got the message that you're unhappy, Mother."

"Apparently they didn't," Yvonne said and cocked her head emphatically.

Shushing noises from behind them ended their escalating warfare. Clare got up to take her scowl to the back of the crowded hall for some air and a trip through the goody table.

She was taking a sip of the weak complimentary coffee when an arm wrapped around her waist.

"Riveting, isn't it?" said Parker. "What brings you to this wonderful highlight of Danfield civic affairs?"

She squinted at him; just yesterday he'd been peeling her off her kitchen floor.

"Yvonne's idea," she said. "And you? This certainly can't be as riveting as installing a new carburetor."

"There's my Clare," Parker teased. "Actually, the more elderly women among us have been going door-to-door around different businesses, trying to rally the troops one more time if today doesn't go the way they want. You could say I'm intrigued."

"Did they bother to tell you how? About the sit-in that's coming up?"

"That's what I've heard," Parker said. "Pretty bold, isn't it? I just thought I'd pop in to see how today's events unfolded."

There was a sudden shout from the audience, a familiar voice. Clare spun: her mother had sprung from her chair, pointing her finger at the council members on stage in solidarity with her fellow gray-haired agitators.

"That's Yvonne," Clare said. "I can't watch."

"Let her be," Parker warned, but she disengaged from him and moved to the marble entryway.

She worked out what had happened, listening to the increasingly loud and raucous shouts from the citizens: apparently the council discussion on the issue of the bell tower was essentially an affirmation of prior debate. The council and the mayor, having learned their lesson from the civic center event, conducted their abbreviated business without reacting to the growing number of shouts from the galley, as if the town hall had been entirely empty. The citizens of Danfield could have thrown lead balloons at the stage and still not riled the council. The silent clampdown on the dissent about the tower buoyed Clare's spirit; it might finally bring closure to the months of battling.

At the sound of the closing gavel, the entry hall began to flood like the Pamplona streets during the running of the bulls. Parker found Clare and put his hand on her arm, clearly intending to guide them into a corner. Clare gently shook loose.

"I guess I should go get Yvonne," she said.

"She'll be out in a second," Parker said. "Clare. I'd hoped to see you today. Have dinner with me tomorrow night?"

She started and leaned away. "Tomorrow?" she asked, fumbling for some response. "On Friday?"

"If that works for you. We keep saying we need to catch up. Let's actually do it. I thought I'd come get you after I finish at the shop tomorrow."

She stared at him, her feeling of exhaustion and ugliness intensifying such that she couldn't remember her last shower, but she was grateful that she'd at least brushed her teeth.

Suddenly Yvonne was between the two of them, frazzled and breathless. "Parker! You're here. And I see you have found our sweet Clare. Never mind all of that crap with the council in there; isn't she the picture this morning?"

For once, Clare was grateful that Yvonne's presence had stifled his date-like overture.

"She is," Parker grinned.

"Time to go," she said, leading Yvonne through the propped exit doors toward her car. "I'll call you later, Parker."

She didn't look back at Parker as they walked through the packed parking lot, ignoring Yvonne's glares.

"What's this again about a sit-in?" Clare began as soon as she started the ignition. "How far are you and the Gray Gang going to take this now? If you had supported this development just a little, maybe they would have tweaked some of their plans here and there. As it is, they're digging in their heels. No more, all right?"

"There's no point in trying to explain our love of that hill to you," Yvonne complained.

It only took the slightest nudge from Clare and a promise to keep absolute secrecy for Yvonne to spill her plans for the sit-in anyway. Her being sworn to secrecy didn't matter; Clare couldn't follow the plans whatsoever and remained clueless from the time Yvonne began talking until the moment she'd arrived home and Yvonne was backing out of her driveway.

As soon as she locked and leaned against her back door, she succumbed to a trance and crashed on the couch. She didn't stir until three in the afternoon. When she got up, she called Parker and thankfully got his machine.

TWENTY-SIX

Clare arrived a little early at the Bar Stool, a legendary hole-in-the-wall founded in the 1950s by a handful of drunken University of Wisconsin fraternity brothers. The converted old hay barn had remained minimally refurbished until the mid-eighties, when the county ordered the owners to repair multiple code violations or shut down. They complied with the letter of the law: except for the updated internal wiring and plumbing, the place still appeared as shoddy as the day it was founded.

Clare pictured those occasions when she and her nineteen-year-old buddies had ditched the NiteLite scene and headed west to this spot halfway to Madison. Naïvely believing that they were being sneaky, they passed badly forged IDs to the steel-engineer/

Friday-night bouncer, who must have suspected they were minors but who lifted nary a finger to check, in what turned out to be sort of a "don't ask, don't tell" arrangement.

She sat next to the retired jukebox near the end of the bar and watched for Parker. She had gone ahead and ordered two Miller beers.

It didn't take long, and she instantly recognized his outline against the misty spray of light in the parking lot. He strode over to her, playfully tapping the back of each empty bar stool as he passed.

"I cannot remember the last time I was in here," he remarked, eyeing the place as he walked up. "But I remember how you girls used to practically live here."

Overcome by a rush of nervousness, as though she were on a first date, Clare felt awkward eyeing the melding of his mature features and adult stubble with his boyhood good looks. "I should have known you would remember it that way. It was only once in a while, really."

"Let's call Sara and see if we don't get a different version," Parker insisted. "I'm a bit surprised you all aren't pictured along with those ancient family photos on the wall."

"Be careful with that selective memory," Clare laughed and stood up. "As I recall, you slugged down a few in this place."

He leaned a little closer, and Clare caught a whiff of a tell-tale scent that she could have found blindfolded. "Clare—you look great all grown up, if I haven't told you," he said. "We really should have done this sooner."

As they took their seats, the bartender brought the two beers and Parker handed him a twenty dollar bill.

She was bewildered by the electricity she felt between them.

Never mind her resolve: all the attempts she made at rehearsing this conversation last night went out the window.

"Yeah," she said, grappling for a response. "I agree we should have met sooner. But you look unchanged, really. It's almost like . . ."

"Like we've been zapped back to the past," Parker said. "Can you believe it's been nearly a decade?"

"It sounds dreadful, when you put it that way."

"Clare," Parker said. "I don't really want to dredge up the past. I just wish sometimes we could have left things between us a little differently."

She felt the strength in his voice and regretted the rift she'd put between them; he'd been nothing but a rock to her ever since their lives had been connected in their youth. "I don't know where to start, Parker," she said. "I was young and stupid."

"This is not about blaming you, Clare," he said. "You just wanted to see the world, and I didn't want to wait. I was so anxious for us to begin life together and for the family stuff to start while we were young. If I could have just been a little more patient—"

For years, she'd borne the burden of their breakup; to hear him blame himself now was a complete bombshell. "It wasn't your fault," she said.

"It was," he insisted. "I wanted everything my way back then. I never told you, but I had been crazy about you even back in grade school. I'd nearly made up my mind about our whole life by the time we connected as teens. It wasn't until we began going steady . . . Clare, I was ecstatic. But you, on the other hand—you wanted to experience other things, besides just Danfield. Certainly I ignored your desires and then, when you said no to my proposal, I was ruined. I felt like you despised me, believed you were throwing away everybody who loved you. I used to imagine I was your special sanctuary."

"You were my sanctuary," she said, her eyes watering. "Didn't you know that? Parker, where is all this coming from?"

He didn't answer except to say, "The Yvonne thing," he said. "And your dad . . . Ray, I mean. I understand that whole dynamic now."

"Parker? Why would I despise you?" she asked. "I don't remember things this way at all. You weren't mixed up with Yvonne and Ray in my mind. I loved you. I leaned on you more than you apparently realize."

He grabbed hold of her hand. "Something changed when I saw how you gave all of that up—your whole dream—and responded when Yvonne needed you."

"Stop, Parker," she said. "Especially with that stuff about my mother. She's just a crazy lady who blew up the illness she had in order to get me back."

"The point is that we all tried to steal your little wish to see the world," he said, looking her in the eye. "I used to get so mad when you went on and on with Bullet Broadmor about how he ought to get a football scholarship and experience something new. I always chalked it up to your hating marriage and wanting to leave because of your bad memories of Ray."

"You keep dwelling on my father," Clare said. "I don't remember putting him between us, or even mentioning him much."

"You don't have to mention him, even now," Parker said. "Everybody knew what a crappy guy he was. I guess I just wanted to be the hero Ray wasn't."

Clare remained incredulous that he was apologizing. He'd meant the world to her, but at the time, her longing for the world itself had meant more. And now—sitting here reliving that time—she realized she still hadn't gotten over that choice.

"We all tried to steal your dream," Parker said again. "Now . . . now you have to forgive us all and move on."

Clare brushed a mushrooming tear from the corner of her eye and smiled. "The good part about your rewriting our past is that you can leave out the fact that I'm a little nutty. I'm not exactly the poster child for commitment, no matter whose fault it is."

He sat there, guarded.

"This is the part where you tell me to grow up instead of making excuses for me," Clare said.

"I think I just did," Parker said and finally eased into a calming smile.

"Nobody stole anything from me," Clare said gently. "Especially not you, Parker. You may not like this, but the best thing would have been if I hadn't come back when Yvonne called." She smiled. "The next best thing would have been our having this conversation a lot sooner."

"I guess I could have helped you with your nuttiness instead of trying to fence you in before you were ready," Parker said, continuing to shoulder the blame. "Things could have been different."

She reached over and took a firm grasp of his forearm. "For my whole life, I let my mother interfere with my dreams," she said. "I never included you in them. I assumed I had to kick the whole town loose to have a life. I know now that was not true."

He didn't say anything, just smiled. She noticed the music from the bar speakers, finally; she'd been deaf to it during that conversation. Now a sappy love song was playing, and she had a strange flashback to what could have been.

She leaned in and buried her head in his shoulder as the rift between them melted. "We always had a chance, didn't we?" She lifted her eyes to meet his. "Dance with me. It's silly, but I feel like being seventeen for a moment."

He pulled away to arms' length from her and looked at her with his beautiful eyes burning right through her. "You and I, we'll always have something special," he said.

"We do now," Clare said, breathless with anticipation.

"This was long overdue," he said, his voice level. "But we got through it. We don't have to tiptoe around one another anymore."

"Parker, you look so serious," she laughed. "Look at me, I'm happy. You don't have to feel bad anymore. This is a beginning for our getting to know each other again."

Clare tried to stand again to dance, but Parker remained, arms out, maintaining the distance between them.

"Cathie Gilbert and I are getting married," he said.

She stood still for a long moment before sitting down.

"You remember Cathie, don't you?" Parker asked.

She looked for words. "I do . . . a little," she said. "She's . . . honestly . . . I don't really know her."

"Clare, you're shocked," Parker said, clearly embarrassed. "It wasn't my intention to surprise you. We just needed to clear the air so that we both could get on with life. And . . . and maybe in some way we can be a part of each other's life in other ways."

Staring blankly, Clare wondered how she could not have known this. Yvonne, who Clare had sensed pushing for a reunion just yesterday, hadn't mentioned a word.

"I guess it's sort of crazy that we've kept it as quiet as we have," Parker said, far too casually. "Mostly people have seen Cathie and me as great buddies more than anything else. And so many people around town thought you and I would connect again, no matter who I dated."

"I think a lot of people thought that," Clare said hollowly, as if he should have pined for her forever.

Parker hadn't a word in response.

Clare tried to salvage a bit of her pride. "But look how long I've been back in town, and nothing has happened. Cathie Gilbert— honestly, all I remember is that she was a couple of years behind us in school."

"After finishing college here locally she jetted to DC for a couple of years. She's a physical therapist." Parker kept the explanation moving.

"That's great," Clare said dully.

She connected with his concerned expression.

"Clare, I never thought it would be this hard because we ended it so long ago. But the memories are there . . . just like this old place." Parker took in their surroundings. "But I am glad we got a chance to talk, instead of you hearing it through our friends."

"I agree," she said quickly for fear of crying. This felt almost like a death. "And I think it's incredible that nobody has caught on to this by now."

"Look, Clare, I've watched you these last couple of weeks. You're at a standstill. I don't even want to go there with this Mary thing, you're a big girl and I'll let you handle that. I've seen you around with Jared, wondering whether it was going anywhere. He's great. I actually like him and what he's done for this town so far."

"So you've moved on," she said, wincing at the mention of Jared's name right now.

"We both have, haven't we?" he asked. "I don't beat myself up about losing what we had anymore, and I wanted to tell you that I didn't resent you. I waited so long for you to show up at the garage like you did a couple of weeks ago. I thought you'd rip me a new one, if anything. And now . . ." He thought for a moment. "Ultimately we have to be friends," he demanded.

"It's too small of a town if we don't," Clare said, just to keep from bawling like a baby.

He looked at her. She didn't feel like dancing anymore.

"Clare, I need to run," he said at last.

"I know."

"I'll follow you back to Danfield," he offered.

"I'm going to hang out," she responded.

He put his arms out, wanting to hug her. She offered him her cheek.

She remembered nothing of her drive back to Danfield an hour and a half later, rehashing every recent moment with her high-school lover.

Totally wrecked, she decided to make a day of it and turned by the police station. Many of the officers had left for the evening or were on patrol, and Clare slipped in without fanfare. The evening desk clerk nodded at her and buzzed her through the secured door, but not before giving her an evil nosy look in the light of what had happened here earlier in the week.

Jared was leaning back in his chair, fully relaxed. He waited for her to turn the corner of his office door before sitting up.

Clare held out her wrists. "I've come to turn myself in."

"Sit down," Jared said, amused. "I ought to have you arrested."

"Let's not go there."

"How would you like this to go?"

She watched him watching her from his chair, remembering how he'd looked through the window of Courtney's den that night.

"I know I've pushed the limit," she said. "But whether you like my reasoning or not, I'd like to have my life back." Clare petitioned.

"You will," Jared affirmed with confidence.

"Poof! Just like that," she said. "So that means you'll call the newspapers, and Mr. Graber, and tell them all that I'm not guilty of any sinister scheme; Although, you went to some trouble to make it look like I was."

"At some point I may be able to do just that," Jared said. "It all depends on you."

"Tomorrow would be good for me," she said.

"Clare, you keep interfering with an ongoing investigation," he said simply. "Let me determine when to let you off the hook."

"An ongoing investigation, huh?" she laughed. "You know I'm not the center of attention where Mary's murder is concerned. We both know that my questions about Mary and my 'finds' are dead on. If my curiosity is a problem for you, why not just satisfy it? What's the ridiculous secret you have to trash my reputation to keep?"

Jared tossed her an incredulous expression. "If you would have just let me do my job . . ."

"I didn't mean to demand that you owe me the full details of the investigation," Clare said. "I just don't want any crap about needing to throw the book at me to keep me quiet."

"Okay, I won't give you any crap," Jared said. He rose and fiddled with something on his file cabinet. "How's Yvonne? You guys planning something for the holidays?"

She could feel the wrath of a beleaguered police chief doing his level best to whisk her away.

"I'll forgive you for using Yvonne to change the conversation," she said. "But I get to ask you why you hauled me to the station on Wednesday. I get that you want me to back off, but I want you to tell me why. Because I was snooping around the woods? Because I found that barrette? What is it about what I've done that has you so eager to hush me up?"

"Clare," he snapped. "I need you to stay away from the Martin thing. That ought to be all you need to hear."

"I couldn't be farther away from it, with the way you're keeping me in the dark," she complained. "Even when it comes to whatever you're cooking up with my best friend Derek—"

"That's it!" Jared shouted, butting the cabinet with the palm of his hand. "This is not about you, damn it! Go home, Clare!"

She shuddered. She could feel herself pushing him to the brink and pushing him away and knew she was out of control. Realistically, she'd asked for things from him that were none of her business, but she kept on and on.

He covered the new dent in the metal with his hand and kept his eyes down.

One of the evening police officers stuck his head in. "Okay, boss?"

"I'm good, thanks," Jared said.

"It's about Derek, isn't it?" Clare said softly. She felt her stomach grow hollow, remembering her friend's increasing distance from her, and his uncharacteristic behavior since his gruesome discovery at the creek.

"We're done here," Jared said tersely.

She left. On the whole long walk down the hallway to the front door she went over and over in her mind everything that had passed between Derek and Jared during their confrontation at Derek's house just days ago. Hunched in her driver's seat, deep in obsessive confusion, Clare nearly missed the sight of Russell Martin exiting the station.

She rolled down the passenger window. "Russell?"

Startled, Russell leaned in and then recognized her. "Hey, Clare . . ."

"Sit for a second," Clare said and motioned for him to get in. "I want to see how you're doing."

"It's a bit cold to be sitting in the parking lot," he said, his shoulders slumping.

"It is," she said. "But come on . . . just for a second."

"I really have to go," Russell said, but he opened the door anyway and lifted one foot to the passenger floorboard.

Beneath the dome light of her Jeep, Russell was noticeably dressed up in a pair of black denim jeans and dress boots. He was still wearing his flannel vest, but for once a very neat, unwrinkled variant of it. His hair and nails were as trim as Clare had ever seen.

"You've done something different," she said, approvingly.

"Different?" He looked down to eye his appearance seemingly just as surprised as Clare, "Oh yeah. Just taking care of business . . . me and Courtney have some things to discuss."

Clare didn't have a response to the sad prospect of his tidying up for Courtney.

"How are things progressing with the case," she asked, changing the subject. "Do the police have anything at all yet?"

"Not really," Russell said, his voice cracking. "We're just all racking our brains to figure out what happened to my baby."

"Just let me know what I can do," she said and smiled. "Anything, Russell. I'll be there for you."

Russell turned and looked her square in the eye.

"I heard you got in a bit of trouble for me," he said. "Clare, everything is okay. They're doing everything they can to help us find an end. Maybe they never will. Please don't lose your job and stuff. It really will be okay."

It was one of the longer speeches he'd ever given. The fact that he was trying to console her touched her.

"You're a good man, Russell," Clare said. He smiled and lowered his leg from the floorboard to the pavement.

"And Courtney," he added. "She'll get on and I'll get on, and we'll both remember our little girl . . . don't hate her, Clare."

Something fell from his pocket to the pavement.

"Russell, you dropped something," she said.

"Oh, thank you . . ." He leaned over to pick it up. It was Mary's pink barrette.

"I found that!" Clare yelped.

Russell looked her in the eye again.

"I know you did," he said. "Thank you. They gave it to me to keep . . . something of Mary's."

She tried to keep her voice calm. "There wasn't any evidence on it, I guess?"

"Nothing," he said plainly.

He dropped the barrette back into his pocket. Clare was speechless and gaping. He waved, walked over to his truck, got in, and took off.

TWENTY-SEVEN

Functionally frazzled, admittedly on edge, Clare battled her front door lock as if it too was scheming against her. She darted inside and caught the ringing phone just before it could go to the answering machine.

"Yes?"

"Clare!" Yvonne shouted. "Clare, I need you to come over right away! The washer—it's terrible—there's water everywhere, just everywhere . . ."

"Hang on." Clare tossed her purse and keys on the counter, hurrying to secure the front door to stop the cold air from getting in. "Tell me what you have done so far."

She held the phone away from her ear as Yvonne was wound

up and quite loud, explaining exactly what had happened in excruciating detail.

"Mother, just shut off the water," she said finally.

She listened and then waited for Yvonne to come back to the phone.

"It's not working," Yvonne said. "Or, I'm not sure I'm doing it right. One of the two. Clare, stop being difficult and come help me!"

"As long as you turned off the washing machine," Clare said, "just do nothing and call the plumber in the morning. What am I going to do at this hour?"

"Please!" Yvonne begged. "I need you to come over, Clare, please . . ."

Completely incredulous about the evenings' events, Clare tossed the phone in its cradle. She sat there for a moment in the Jeep, thinking about the situation, filtering out Yvonne's hysteria: leaky washer, water spilling everywhere, complete disaster. She thought about Derek and what Jared had unwittingly revealed at the station. She went back in the house, placed another phone call, and got back in the Jeep.

She yanked open her mother's back door to see the end of her mop and backside sticking out from the laundry room.

"Did you shut off the water?" she called. "It looks like you have it under control . . ."

"Can't a mother in need call her daughter?" Yvonne chirped.

Clare narrowed her eyes and prepared to respond, but was stopped by a knock on the door. It was Derek, fully prepared with his shop vac and assorted plumbing and cleanup tools.

"Thanks, Derek," Clare smiled. "I figured you'd be better at this than me." He glared at her with complete skepticism. "No problem, Ms. Paxton," he said to Yvonne. "I'll have it fixed up right away."

"I only wish my daughter could be so polite and willing," Yvonne jabbed.

"I called him, didn't I?" Clare said. "What do I know about leaking washing machines?"

"Ladies . . . please," Derek said.

He was clearly uptight with her. She watched him as he evaluated the situation and shut off the washer's water valve. She was quietly attempting to decipher every oddity in his demeanor while rummaging in her mother's overstuffed linen closet for towels to toss to Yvonne, who was slopping through the pool of water.

"Not my good towels, Clare!"

"Step aside, ladies," Derek said finally, "I got this."

Derek came between the both of them, sucking up the water with his shop vac. It was like he was breaking up the brats on the playground, Clare thought.

"Mom, go find some old sheets then so we can dry this," she said. "I'll let you know when we need you in a minute."

"I can help," Yvonne protested. "Just tell me what to do."

"It's not flooding anymore, but we gotta let Derek get this cleaned up before we figure out what to do about your washer."

She endured Yvonne's glance. Then she waited as her mother journeyed out of earshot. She began to wring out the saturated towels in the kitchen sink while Derek pulled out some very large, dry shop rags and tossed one over to Clare. She dropped to her hands and knees to sop up the residual moisture; starting around the washer so that Derek could take a closer look.

She wanted to know . . . she needed to know.

"Sorry about the other night," Clare began tentatively.

"Not a big deal, Clare," he said. "Normally I'd think something was wrong. But everything you do is nuts lately. So we don't need to discuss it."

"Derek, don't be hurt," she said, quietly. "But this whole thing isn't about me, is it?"

From his hands and knees, Derek quizzically glanced in her direction, tightly gripping his wrench.

"Think about it," she said. "Except for a few nosy fools in the neighborhood, who's paying attention to me? Why would Jared go to lengths like this to keep me out of this case?"

"I don't see anybody else making headlines lately," Derek said warily.

"Exactly, I'm the lone interested citizen bystander," Clare dared jab, "who got suspended from her job for asking innocent questions."

"I don't think falsely luring the chief of police to my house gets you a lot of sympathy from me, Clare," he sniped.

"Look, buddy," she said loudly. "Think about it. My only connection to this case is you. Whoever wants me to be quiet and stop investigating, it has to be because I know you."

"I am not having this conversation," Derek said flatly.

"Oh, so you're not talking to me now!" Clare shouted.

Yvonne burst from around the corner, where Clare immediately knew she'd been eavesdropping. "Clare! Derek!" she wailed. "What's happening? Somebody tell me what is happening!"

Clare fingered the moisture streaming down her beet-red face.

"What did you forget to tell me that night you came to my house?" Clare shouted. "Damn you, Derek, what have you done!"

She suddenly drew in her breath and got quiet. Derek was

kneeling and holding some kind of tool, almost a foot long, at his side like a weapon. He was crouching just inches away from her, at her feet. In his eyes was a look of sheer confusion.

Their silent standoff lasted an eternity until Derek eerily let go of his tool, shattering the silence with a bone-chilling thudding sound on the soggy linoleum.

She and her mother stared as Derek stood up. He walked off through the back door, leaving behind his shop vac, his rags, and his tools. He had never been capable of leaving a mess in his entire life.

"Clare," Yvonne began, in a whisper. Clare spun around at her.

"No, Mother! Just no!"

Yvonne backed away.

She carried the heavy wrench in one hand, using the other on her steering wheel, all the way to Derek's house. When she arrived, she banged on his door mercilessly. He opened it immediately, as if he had anticipated her following him.

She pushed open the heavy solid wood door.

"Here, you forgot something!" she shouted, brandishing the wrench.

He reached out to grab it, but Clare raised it and pulled it back, as if she was fully prepared to use it.

Next, he tried to grab her arm.

"Don't touch me!" Clare shouted. "I'm not moving until you tell me what's happening."

Suddenly Karen Forczek stepped out of the front hall and into the doorway.

"Clare, what are you doing? Give me that!" Karen reached for the wrench.

"Sorry, Karen," Clare said, pulling it back again. From a safe distance, she shook it at Derek. "It's because of you that Jared's been on my ass," she hissed at her friend. "Tell me! Why's he so worried about you? What have you done?"

In spite of the frigid wind tunnel sweeping past and down the hallway, sweat seemed to gush from every pore of her body. Clare wasn't sure whether to be frightened, to be empathetic, or just to jump in her Jeep and escape completely.

"Clare, you need to go now," Karen said. "There's nothing you can do here."

"Nothing I can do here? What does that mean?" Clare snapped. "What happened to Mary, Derek? You were so upset that night . . . you haven't been right since. What did I miss?"

Derek lunged; this time he got a grip on Clare's arm. He yanked her inside the house while attempting to slam the front door shut. Her blood running cold, she lost her grip; the wrench spun away. In one uncertain moment, Clare fell back in a tumble against the coat rack, knocking her head against the wall.

"Clare!" Karen rushed over to help her. "Derek, this has got to stop!"

Clare floundered, woozy and uncertain. Her eyes were filled with the sight of her friend, standing above her with the wrench in his hand and his expression blank.

She was getting to her feet; Karen was helping her up.

"You can't do anything here," Karen said. She gripped Clare's arms. Clare knew she was shaking. "Listen to me, Clare. You have to let this go."

She could feel the bruises forming where she had hit the wall during her fall. She looked at Derek calmly looking back at her. His expression said a thousand "I'm sorrys," but he just stood there.

"Clare!" Karen admonished more sternly. "Be his friend and walk out of here. We only have one chance to get this right. If you can just see it in your heart to listen to me . . . then just listen to me. This will all work out."

She looked at Karen, this woman who was here with Derek. Karen seemed as weary as the two of them, but she acted like the strong one. Clare looked deep into Karen's eyes and asked them what had become of her childhood friend.

TWENTY-EIGHT

O nce she had bolted herself inside her house, hopeful
that Yvonne hadn't handed out any more house keys,
Clare instinctively headed to the kitchen to find something to drown her sorrows. No sooner had she flipped the Miller
top than she became overwhelmed with nausea. She barely made
it to the toilet.

She vomited for another fifteen minutes, off and on, in the
downstairs bathroom before sheer exhaustion made her pass out.

Sometime in the middle of the night, she peeled her body off of
the chilly tile floor. She made it to bed and didn't stir until the

next morning. Her skull was pounding and she pressed her fingers as hard as she could into the back of her head.

With each painful breath, Clare examined the clothes she'd worn to bed, massaged her unwashed face, and smacked the nasty taste in her mouth, feeling altogether as though she'd been left to die in the dessert.

She imagined Derek calling with an apology and an answer for this horrific nightmare as her faculties slowly awakened. She realized that there was a whole lineup of people who owed her an apology, people she didn't have the stomach to care about just this minute.

She dragged herself downstairs, wobbly and groggy at best. She plodded through brewing the coffee and grabbing the paper. She spit the first sip in the kitchen sink; the taste didn't mix well with last night's upset, aspirin, and morning toothpaste just yet.

She felt filthy and imprisoned.

Her attempts to take a cursory inventory of her life or to imagine the unimaginable—what Derek might have done—felt ridiculous and finally became maddening enough to bring a halt to her self-assessment.

She started to clean, as much to express rage as to restore some sense of order. She started by boxing up the Mary clippings. Then leaving the box in the middle of the living room, she cleaned around it, tearing through the whole house. From the kitchen cabinets to the interior walls, Clare dove into every crevice. Intermittently she broke for runs to the Salvation Army, the dry cleaner, and the grocery, wearing her raggedy worst. She hoped the oversized hooded ski jacket and wool cap would make her unrecognizable. In the event they didn't, she tried to seem as if she was ill so anyone who recognized her would keep their distance. Clare ignored the glances and what appeared to be whispering that was more than likely about the front-page camo-fatigue photo. She rested in short, uneasy bursts.

The work stiffened her joints and magnified every pain—physical, emotional, and otherwise. Finally done, she brought a sack upstairs to bag the old clothes for the garbage and then stripped herself for the final cleansing of the day in her shower. Under the hot water, she tried to reach and massage the aching bruise on her head. It didn't stop aching. She bent to reach for her legs and feet and suddenly felt breathless with cramping. Near nauseous again, Clare slumped to the shower floor. Hot water steamed over her head and neck while Clare sobbed uncontrollably.

After ten minutes, she was able to get up and shut the water off. She found her way to warm pajamas and a midnight snack of scrambled eggs and toast.

It was Sunday morning. Clare was sitting at Yvonne's kitchen counter uninvited, a Styrofoam cup from the Coffee Clutch in front of her. The mess from the washer that had spilled into the kitchen was gone, to a meticulous degree that she knew only Derek was capable of. Her mother was away at church. On her way over, Clare had stuck a note in the crack of Derek's front door, a lengthy account of their life and friendship. She didn't apologize for hounding him, her mind on his threatening behavior. But she did goad him into coming clean to her with whatever he'd done.

"Hi, Mom," she called when she heard Yvonne opening the back door.

"Clare?" said Yvonne, frowning as she came in. "You could have gone with me this morning."

"I know, Mom," Clare replied.

Yvonne took off her wool coat, long since worn to rags, and laid it with her purse and keys around the corner in her living area. If she had had an ounce of energy, Clare would have grabbed the coat and retired it with the junk clothes she'd trashed from last night's cleansing.

"I'll make you some breakfast," Yvonne announced.

"I'm not hungry," Clare offered, though the twinge was beginning in her belly. She moved politely to the laundry room door while Yvonne rustled through her cupboards as though she hadn't heard Clare's no.

"Looks like Derek got things taken care of for you," she said.

"I tried to call the other night," Yvonne said.

"Mom," Clare said. "I want to apologize for being short with you. There was no need for me to be frustrated about the laundry leak."

Yvonne paused politely for the historic gesture.

"That's all right Clare," she said finally. "You were obviously tired."

"I was exhausted."

Both of them wallowed, speechless, in the uncharted territory of harmony.

"Let's eat something," Yvonne insisted. "You must really be hungry."

To the relief of both, Yvonne began her breakfast preparations again. Clare took the newspaper from the corner. The front-page headlines were screaming about the sit-in at the bell tower on Monday morning.

"Ugh," Clare groaned.

Yvonne leaned over. "Great! With all that press, maybe we can get somewhere."

"You guys really have given this your all, haven't you?" Clare observed.

"And we're not done yet," chirped Yvonne.

"Certainly you've stalled the project," said Clare. "But I'm not sure for how long."

"We are going to stop them, Clare," said Yvonne. "How can they look a group of old ladies in the eye and take our steeple and tower? It would be great if you could come and join us."

"All that's going to happen is that you'll push back the demolition for a couple of hours," Clare said. "While they cart all of you ladies to jail."

"Clare, would you be positive?" Yvonne sighed. "They won't arrest us."

"I don't care if they arrest you," Clare said. "Let 'em, if it's that important to you guys."

Obviously not appeased, Yvonne turned around from the stove to face Clare squarely with her hands on her hips.

"How about offering some constructive ideas instead of being against us?" she demanded.

"I just did," Clare said. "You may have to let them lock you up to prove your point. That'd be a heck of a photo-op for the old tower." She tried to change the subject. "I am actually feeling hungry . . . let's eat. And then maybe we could run out and do some antiquing today?"

"You didn't come here for food or to go antiquing, did you?" her mother asked, angry.

"I came here to apologize, okay?" Clare sighed. "I'm trying.

How about you make a little effort here instead of standing there with your hands on your hips? I just don't want you girls to be let down with your sit-in. No matter what, you aren't stopping them tomorrow . . . I'm just suggesting that you have fun with it. Who cares if they lock you up for a few hours?"

"Here we go again with your nastiness," Yvonne said. "Some apology this has turned out to be!"

"I'm really just trying to help," Clare said quietly. "If you can't stop them, maybe you could find something nice about the new development. It'll spruce up the square for generations to come—"

Yvonne shook her finger. "You don't get to have an opinion or pretend to be helpful! You don't even like it here, Clare! You don't like this town or anybody in it! I can't understand for one minute why you came back here—"

Yvonne's face turned sheet white. Clare stared at her, the pressure slowly building in her mind.

"You want me to come to your protest!" Clare finally blew up. "Oh, I'll be there—like I always have been, you seem to forget— with a bag over my head if I have to! I guess you'll need me to bail you out again? Maybe you could make up some story about them beating you in the jail cell or something to get sympathy from everyone."

"Ah, get a life," Yvonne spit back.

"While we're at it," Clare continued, "news flash, Mother! Ray's not coming back! He was a piece of trash, and no crappy kiss on that hill is going to make it worth the twenty-five years you spent caring about his ghost!"

"He was my husband!" Yvonne said, beginning to unravel.

"Where is he?" Clare flew around the small space of Yvonne's foyer, living area, and hallway. "I don't see him!"

"He was a good man, Clare!"

"And what about your daughter? If you spent half the effort you've spent pining for him and the stinking bell tower on my getting a simple degree in Chicago . . . isn't that what parents do? Want their kids to get an education and a stab at a better life? All my life, I never once measured up to Ray's ghost! I suppose you would have been happier if I'd have been a drunk like him! How sick is that?"

Yvonne began to bawl like a fanatic, swatting the dead air between them like a boxer in the last minutes of consciousness.

"You think I don't know he was worthless? Give me a little credit, damn you! I regret every day . . . every single day that I messed up your dreams! I see your loathing looks . . . "

Yvonne's tears and spittle sprayed the heated space between them as Clare stared at her mother.

"But I am not the bumbling old lady that I know you see when you look at me . . . I know what he was, and there was a good man in that beat-up old soul. Unlike you, I look for the good in people . . . There was always hope, Clare. Do you know what hope is? That's what I tried to give you. There was always hope that he would come home and not be the miserable old coot that he was . . . that he would make it all better for both of us . . . "

Her mother breathed heavily for another moment, trying to get her composure. "He was good when I met him, Clare, and he loved me," she said finally. "He was good when I met him . . . and when he found out I was pregnant with you . . . it happened."

"You got pregnant with me at the tower . . . " Clare barely whispered the thought.

It was a lousy, lousy brick her mother had just thrown.

Yvonne buried her face in her hands. There was no sound

except the noise of Yvonne's weeping and Clare's shallow breaths. Her mother's exposé of Ray—their whole worthless moment of truth, actually—was long overdue, and it gave Clare far less comfort than she'd imagined it would.

She broke their silence with the noise of her bundling to leave. She could feel Yvonne's eyes on her, wondering how to keep her from walking away again, this time for good.

"Clare," her mother said weakly as she went out the door.

TWENTY-NINE

Had Clare not already been staring impatiently at the ceiling at 5:30, the hovering news helicopters would have woken her up anyway. She could hear the earliest team of activist organizers testing the loud speakers somewhere near the bell tower hill.

She languished beneath her warm winter comforter until the last possible moment to get ready, envisioning a microcosmic event, something analogous to a Wisconsin State Fair opening: a year-long wait for that first cream puff.

After leaving Yvonne's, she'd spent Sunday in her pajamas, awash in news shows and a pile of movie rentals, buttressed by intermittent pockets of self-loathing. At midday, nagged by the box of newspapers she'd never moved from her living room floor during her day of purging, she dared to sort through the debris of the Martin collection one more time. She sifted and questioned an activity that she realized was swiftly becoming the eternal scourge of her life.

Now, in the chilly, pre-dawn darkness of Monday, she finally pushed off the comforter and turned sadly to her investigative box. Covered still in her sleepwear with her trench coat and snow boots, she went into her backyard and mounted the leaf pit. Breaking a host of municipal burning violations, Clare set the whole mess of newspapers aflame. She huddled with a mix of coffee and bourbon and watched the tiny black specks of ash escape and take flight to the neighbors' yards.

Clare, back in the house, took a last few sips of her doctored coffee, changed into daywear, and began to bundle up to go out for the sit-in's official start time of 7:00 a.m.

She was impressed at how prepared the women protesters were. There were some two hundred and fifty of them, surrounded by a crowd that had already ballooned in support. It felt like a holiday parade. There were T-shirts on sale for just a dollar, long-sleeved and white with an etching of the bell tower in red. She backed up to the curb, leaned on an icy lamppost, and watched key members of Danfield's new activist community move in to buy shirts in bulk from the local entrepreneurs before going back to work dispensing the shirts and pushing the swelling crowds as evenly as possibly along Main Street.

Clare shouldered the quick jabs and thumbs up from a few brave souls about the newspaper picture, but by and large today was notably about the steeple and not about Clare's rogue activities. The wrath would surely come another day.

She looked on in silent wonderment as the sea of protestors swayed to the backdrop of "Amazing Grace" that churned out of a temporary sound system. The core group of elderly women was comfortably situated on inner tubes and other rubber substitutes in a chain, linked by twos and threes, that ran from the south end of Main Street up Steeple Hill. Behind them were the menfolk carrying sleeping children, the younger women, and the disengaged, forced-out-of-bed teenagers who had been tasked with wandering in and around the older women, delivering hot coffees, chocolates, and an abundance of eats.

At some distance the executives of the development company and their construction crews were preparing their bulldozers and equipment, their efforts at developments and fellowship with the town now over. There was a small knot of city officials who were standing quietly nearby. Clare suspected they were lonely. She silently understood their plight.

Exasperated by it all, Clare contemplated the diverging philosophies of nostalgia and progress as they converged on the small-town battlefield. She felt like the only one affected by the biting winds in a showdown that carried a preordained ending.

But like the dried, blackened ash that Clare had left for compost in her backyard, life was not without its enduring ability to purge itself of all sorts of sins. Blanketed by the terrible argument with her mother about Ray, Clare sought some redeeming value in all the madness. Maybe this was some Danfield day of reckoning, something about which she was too clueless to reap the benefits.

Promptly at 7:30, the police stirred and began to work their way into the crowd. She could see the conflicted expressions of the officers, many with opinions that were in stark contrast to their obligation to uphold the law. Thankfully, those in authority had checked their weaponry at the station.

The streetlights began to dim beneath the burgeoning sunrise and a cloudless, chilling blue sky. She happened to look in the direction of Marwood's, across the block. Derek was there, looking back at her. They watched each other for a while, silently. She thought about the note under his door and her bruises from her fall, and she knew she might not be able to forgive him for not being able to tell her whatever he had to tell. She looked away.

She distracted herself from the dark feelings she had about her friend with eavesdropping on the chatter of the crowd. Absent was the anger and madness that had brought them to this day of final protest. In its place were whispers of hope. All the rhetoric and near fistfights had done nothing but unify a community; even though they had to know, Clare now realized, how inevitable it was that they would lose their beloved bell tower. The developer-Grinch would steal nothing from the town. Clare imagined the folklore that would result from today; it would last for generations, possibly more important in the end than saving the steeple would have been.

"Martin? You sure?" asked a female voice from somewhere behind her, and immediately Clare's thoughts focused.

"Yeah, Russell put a sign up yesterday," said another voice. "Looks like he's going somewhere to start over. Some guys were buzzing about it yesterday at the NiteLite."

"That makes no sense."

"I checked it out! I ran by his house and there he was, packing up a U-Haul. I tried to talk him into staying and that we'd help, that we needed to at least have a going-away party or something. With all that's happened . . . we can't just let that poor guy go off on his own."

"That's crazy," Clare blurted; the two women looked at her. "That's his grandpa's place he's leaving behind," she explained. "He just loved his grandpa. Why would he sell it to just anybody like that?"

The women looked at her, maybe remembering her picture from the front page.

"It's crazy, but it's true," one of them said, finally deciding Clare was safe enough to include in the conversation. "You should have seen how determined he was. He was all ready to head out this morning . . . I guess he figured we'd all be too busy to make much of a fuss about it."

"That whole Mary thing is so sad," said the other woman. "How could anybody get over losing their baby girl like that?"

Clare turned; something in what the women said was tugging at her. Derek was no longer standing in front of the store.

Russell wouldn't leave his grandpa's place for no reason. That was all he had left, that plus a town full of friends and support he couldn't replace. There was—she realized, remembering in sudden clarity the details of every interaction she'd had in these past weeks—just one likely reason that Russell would ever ditch his grandfather's stronghold.

Her gut was burning as her brain calculated what had suddenly become obvious. Mayor Kohlhepp was slowly moving to the middle of the pack in the street, juggling his bullhorn in preparation for a last plea. Someone turned up the music in an effort to make him work for their removal.

She began to walk in the direction of her Jeep as she worked out her next moves. Frantically eyeing the crowd for Derek, she found him in a spot parallel to where she was standing, feverishly looking about the crowd as well; Clare suspected he was looking for her. So as not to be seen, Clare crouched lower and darted through the alleyways.

On the way to her Jeep, she looked ahead at a Kwik-Mart convenience store lot filled with police vehicles and heavily armored SWAT members. She suddenly stopped and ducked behind a parked car; Jared was there in the driver's seat of a cruiser. Talking to him, in the driver's side window of a car facing the opposite direction, was Courtney. Her heart pounded in fear and she quickly got into her Jeep and then U-turned and twisted her way back through the city's side roads toward Russell's. There was no traffic and she ran stop signs and red lights undeterred. A couple hundred yards from his house, she rolled to a crawl to get as close as she could without being detected.

The remarkably small U-Haul the women had described was there, attached to a battered old van that was ready to roll out of the driveway. She could just see Russell at the far end of the dock that extended well out over the lake. He was carrying a rifle and he was tossing something into the water.

She abandoned her Jeep in the middle of the street, ran past the van, and down the gravel driveway around the side of the house toward the dock.

"Russell!" she called.

Russell turned. He went ghost white as soon as he saw her.

"Go, Clare . . . just go!" Russell shouted. "You can't be here!"

He began to move feverishly up the ramp toward her, the rifle in his arms. Clare froze. Her eyes darted left and right. Out of the corner of her eye she could see his back deck. There was a small child's suitcase, and leaning against it was the doll with the blue shoes that she had helped him buy.

She heard the van door opening and turned in time to see Mary Martin standing there.

"My God, Mary!"

"Mommy," Mary screamed, looking over to the side of the house.

In symphony, from every direction, police vehicles and bodies converged. Tires screeched, metal collided, and multiple footprints stomped through the slush. Among the approaching officers, she caught sight of Derek.

"Clare, get away," hollered Jared from somewhere within the madness. Then everything began to blur and whirl around her.

She turned and began to run toward Russell because she knew, on some instinctive level, that she was the closest now. Surrounded, Russell, now unable to follow through with his escape with Mary, retreated like a cornered mama bear in the direction of the dock, readying his rifle.

Courtney was up nearer the house, charging toward Mary Martin, who stood rooted and terrified next to the van. There was the crack of a rifle shot from an officer firing behind her, and Courtney screamed and fell to the ground, her leg twisted under her. And all hell broke loose.

"Don't shoot," Clare waved and yelled back to the sea of law enforcement; she'd realized they thought Russell was readying to aim at her.

Clare watched Russell point his rifle toward his head. A hush fell over the wooded area. In Clare's mind, she could no longer feel her feet moving beneath her.

"Russell!" Clare screamed, knowing she wouldn't make it to him in time. They all knew, she knew. She screamed, her fever pitch scream burning from every ounce of her being.

Russell's heaving body fell to the ground; his brain matter spread over the trees and the dock. She was unable to halt fast enough from the galloping momentum except to slide powerlessly beside him, what was left of him.

The police arrived, swarming over her and patting her down for injuries. She swatted their arms away.

"Russell . . . no, Russell," she whimpered, gasping to take air into her lungs. She wanted the officer who now stood shadowing her view of Russell's body to move away. She couldn't speak; she couldn't feel a thing as the police tried to bring her numb legs into a standing position.

Derek was bent over on the back deck, gripping his head as they moved her to the front of the house.

In a burst, Clare pulled away from the officers and charged at him.

"You couldn't talk to me?" she screamed. "About what? About what! Damn you, Derek!"

She slapped him as hard as she could on the face before the officers could regain control.

"You don't know, Clare," Derek said, nearly weeping.

The officers forcibly moved her and put her in the back of a squad car. She let them; she felt like she had just seen a family member die. As the officers drove her away, she pressed her face to the squad car window and watched the trees near Russell's house whip by.

At home again, en route to an alcoholic coma, she heard the back door open, but remained slumped on her living room couch, wrapped around an armchair pillow, completely fatigued. She had yet to change from her blood-splattered clothing. There was a minimally iced Styrofoam cooler of beers on the coffee table; she lapped at the last of her third Miller, tossed the empty in a grocery sack on the floor, and grabbed another nearly room temperature beer. She watched TV while she waited for the intruder. Jared's press conference had already come and gone, but the networks were replaying the most horrific highlights and then regurgitating their unsubstantiated guesswork, trading fact for sensationalism.

"Clare?" asked Derek from the kitchen archway.

She popped open her fourth beer and flicked from channel to channel without acknowledging him.

"I need you, Clare," he said.

She heard his breathing and his weighty shuffle to get closer.

"I don't blame you for being angry," he said. "I couldn't involve you . . . I couldn't involve anybody."

She tossed her partially consumed beer can onto the heap of the others and groped clumsily for another still not knowing what his involvement was. Didn't care.

"Don't do this," Derek said. He was there, leaning nearer.

"Get away!" Clare roared. She tossed her full beer at him. It banged to the floor and spewed the foamy liquid on his pant leg. He didn't move. Her handprint was still on his face from their last go-round.

She lunged at him, shoved him, and pounded violently on his chest.

"Don't," he said, holding his hands back.

"You better fight, buddy," she screamed. "Or get the hell out of my house! Why aren't you in jail now? They're saying on the TV that you're being considered an accomplice! Did you come over here to involve me some more now?"

"Let me explain," Derek said weakly.

"No! Let me explain!" Clare said at the top of her lungs. "We sat right here that night!" She slapped the couch. "You came here all distraught about Mary dying . . . and now she's alive, and Russell is splattered all over the woods! Were you lying the whole time? What in the hell did you do?!"

Derek looked at the floor and whimpered. "I didn't lie to you, Clare."

"You don't have an answer," she yelled, "do you?!"

"Russell thought I saw him at the creek that night," Derek said. "I'd seen his truck on the way out to go fishing, but didn't connect it."

"What is this about? So you saw his fucking truck! Why all the hiding? I could tell by talking to Jared I'd been thrown under the bus. It was because of you all along!"

"You had nothing to do with anything except getting yourself in the way!" Derek suddenly exploded. "You kept on being nosy, no matter what I said!"

"Getting in the way of what?"

"He came to me—"

"Who? Who came to you?"

"Russell! For Christ's sake, let me finish!"

She took a deep breath and glared at him through the dark living room.

Derek breathed raggedly before going on. "It was just after the news broke about me finding that scene at the creek. Before he knew I hadn't made any connections about his truck, he'd said too much to me. He wanted everyone to think Mary was dead so he could move away. He just wanted away from Courtney. He just wanted his baby girl . . ."

"And you didn't tell anyone?" Clare was incredulous. "Are—are you saying you helped him kidnap Mary?"

"No, Clare! He had Mary already; at first I thought she was safe. Then I was worried about how he was acting, that he'd do something to her if I said anything to anybody."

"All I heard from you was how hard I was being on Courtney," she said, her voice shaking, "that she wasn't the slimy slut I'd made her out to be . . ."

Derek put his fist into the stairwell wall and then crouched on the floor. "I couldn't tell you," he said. "I didn't tell anybody what he was saying to me . . . for just a few days."

"Why?"

"At first he was so broken up and I felt sorry for him. He was just crazed about Courtney's messing with his visitations, always having an excuse about why Mary couldn't go with him to his house. He said he had a lawyer and that he would come clean about having taken his own daughter, but that he just had to figure out exactly how he'd defend himself against Courtney first.

Then everyone kept talking about what was happening, and I started to push him about why he was still keeping silent . . . it turned threatening. He kept saying he'd never let anyone take Mary away from him again . . . ever again!"

"Why couldn't you come to me," Clare asked.

"You have to understand," he said.

"Understand what?" Clare asked. "What could Russell have possibly said that kept you from doing the right thing?"

"I don't know, Clare—I couldn't think. I wasn't sure what to do . . . but if Mary was still alive, I didn't want him to hurt her."

"You couldn't tell Jared?"

"He knew it involved Russell," said Derek. "He knew from the beginning . . . and then he kept after me. I told him long before you had him over to my house that night. He's held my arrest and worse charges over my head if I didn't stay quiet and cooperate and continue my routine with Russell. Clare . . . that included not talking to you."

She pointed over to the TV again. "They say they're going to arrest you," she said. "For aiding and abetting a kidnapping? Do you know what that means?"

"The press are out of control, Clare, please don't pay attention to that," Derek said. "You just went through this very thing. I'm working with the police. I'm headed there now. It'll be messy but I'll work it out . . . somehow."

Her sight blurred, looking at him now. She knew it would take hours of purging before she would be capable of understanding the grungy, slovenly guy that stood, weakly, before her.

"I need you," Derek said.

EPILOGUE

A montage of spring flurries feathered the melting, icy grunge of the first weeks of spring. For hours on the eve of her second good-bye to Danfield, Clare had observed the silent slumbering snowfall with neither jubilance nor fear, with neither anticipation nor anxiety. She just watched through Yvonne's windowpanes hearing nothing but the tick, tick, tick of the antique grandfather clock.

It was astonishing how elaborate Russell's plan to kidnap Mary Martin had been, given how much of a reputation he had for being easygoing and kindhearted.

Mary had been hidden by sympathetic kinfolk near the very rural northern edge of Wisconsin, bordering Canada, and had only been brought back into town for the final preparations for

Russell's departure. At first, after Derek's discovery by the creek, the medical examiners uncovered the telltale signs concerning the condition and age of the blood evidence. Then there were the issues like the lack of tissue evidence and the oddity of the shoes having been at the scene in the first place. That and the inconsistencies from the New Berlin Police Department K-9 search, had started Chief Grady and his detectives on their frenzied search, a search that Jared knew he'd have to keep out of the papers if there was any hope of finding the kidnapped girl. The forensic results gave them hope that Mary might still be alive and some clues that might link the kidnapping to Russell.

From the cache of blood-filled vials and the abundance of syringes gathered by the Danfield Police Department forensics unit in the aftermath, and the needle marks on Mary's arm, Jared and his detectives—armed with results from the county medical examiners' office—finally concluded that Russell used his experience with animals and being raised on a farm to create a supply of blood in order to concoct a death scene.

Clare shuddered whenever she thought about it, wondering when Russell had started drawing his daughter's blood, what he had thought about what he was doing.

There was talk that the funeral director, Trevor Colson, had in fact met with an inquiring Russell about death certificates and funerals. That accounted for Trevor's jumpiness at the rally. She remembered running into Russell all dressed up that one evening when she'd stopped at the station to see Jared and he'd just been given the barrette. Maybe he'd come from Trevor's funeral home. Clare could only imagine.

For months after that day, Clare had nightmares. Most of them—most commonly in slow motion—revolved around the image of Russell, his rifle in his hand, throwing that mysterious object in the lake. It turned out in reality to be a bundle of his grandfather's war mementos, which Clare privately believed to be his parting good-bye to the place and his hero. She couldn't remember the actual moment of his death at all.

As could only be foretold in the tradition of indiscriminate Wisconsin weather, Clare spent her last day in Danfield that April with the other wedding guests, enjoying the sparkling 55-degree weather, just hours after a late season snow flurry had feathered the slowly melting winter ice the previous night. The gorgeous Cathie Gilbert exiting the church on Parker's arm was an exquisite sight in and of itself, Clare thought, and would have been so under any weather conditions, but as it was, framed beneath a colossal blue sky, the event was granted a particular wonderment.

Showing up at the wedding was the least Clare could do. After Parker's heartfelt proclamation, she and Parker had barely seen each other, beyond slightly improved neighborly interactions whenever they met by chance, one last donut delivery to the shop, and a single early breakfast at Mae's so that Clare could say her perfunctory good-byes. Whatever their youthful connection had been, Clare chalked their adult friction up to their delay in saying hello again. For them to have anything else would require Clare to commit to Danfield. In any event, it became rather fruitless to pass on or to shoulder blame. Maybe she could have delved deeper into the sheath of anger that had shadowed her since her return to Danfield, an anger that had resulted in her deliberate ignorance toward a community that she felt had skipped on without her. But to do that would have required true self-analysis.

Decidedly restless, Clare sipped punch in the back of the reception hall and signaled to Yvonne, again, that her mother had ten more minutes to wrap it up. Her mother had spent the last three hours of the reception making the rock star rounds as if she'd never see anyone again. Yvonne fielded nearly as many compliments as the bride, and Clare included herself among the ones who were markedly impressed with how Yvonne had actually cleaned up for the event, sporting a new hairstyle, makeup, a French manicure, and blond highlights over her formerly gray-speckled hair. "It was the *frosted* look," Yvonne informed Clare.

In the days leading up to the wedding, Clare silently witnessed a steady metamorphosis that had brought Yvonne within striking distance of her late-forties. Only a genie could correct the years of neglect, but Clare was beginning to recognize a profile or a posture or a certain smile that mirrored the good-looking image of her mother that was etched into her memory. Clare supposed that Yvonne wasn't motivated to impress anyone or to become a babe again, but that she was likely demonstrating that to do so was within her power, an exhibition that might end the Ray discussion between them forever.

Jared must have been watching Clare near the punch bowl. As soon as he saw her looking at him, he came over.

"Hey," he said. "Not even a good-bye?"

"I think we've said our good-byes," she replied. "Not really much to say, is there, Jared, that hasn't already been beaten to death?"

"I'd love to hear how you are doing once you get settled," Jared offered softly. "I want the best for you. You must know I want you to be happy."

"Sure," Clare said, neglecting to respond in kind. She knew he still wanted something more from her, and she remained singularly focused on changing her surroundings as soon as Yvonne finished her good-byes—even if she actually returned his sentiment in her thoughts.

"Clare?" he said. "Are you all right?

"I'm fine," she said.

But she wasn't fine where Jared was concerned. It had been several long months since the events of that life-shattering October day, and in addition to her dreams of Russell at the dock—and her mental block of that single horrifying moment where he took his life—she was consumed many times by dreams of Jared, Courtney, and Mary, all huddled together while Jared attended to the bullet Courtney had taken in her leg. Each time she dreamed it she would wrestle and jerk until she awakened from the sweaty slumber.

"Please don't be angry anymore," Jared said. "It's all going to be okay."

"I suspect we're all getting what we deserve," Clare said.

A big whoop came from the reception tent.

"Glad we could work out a deal to have Derek's charges of obstruction reduced to community service," Jared said.

"He was so relieved; you'd have had another protest otherwise," Clare responded crisply.

She hadn't yet mustered a thank-you to Jared for keeping Derek's life intact following his formal arrest the day after the Russell firestorm.

"You really could have trusted me," Clare whispered. "And you know that. I told you he was my friend, and that I could have helped. All this would be different." Actually Clare wasn't sure it would have been, given that Russell had done the unthinkable.

Clare was suddenly sensitive to the breeze off the lightly flapping tent openings and the way it moved Jared's hair. She allowed herself to imagine that their hearts were having one last private dance, concealed beneath the distance of their sober conversation. Aided by her last drops of alcohol, before she gave it up all together, she had trudged again and again over everything that could have been different between them.

"I had a chance to keep her alive," Jared said. "Derek was my line to Mary, and the more you got involved, the more likely you were to make Russell realize how closely we were watching him. So we turned you into the perfect decoy."

"I get it," Clare said. "I don't understand but I get it."

"It kept her alive," Jared insisted.

"Russell would never have killed his daughter," Clare said flatly.

He stared at her; she stared back. Then he leaned forward and Clare gently moved away from his attempt to hug her good-bye.

"Please," Jared said. "I explained to you . . . nothing happened with Courtney until after the case. It was just comforting her and Mary at first, and after that it's just been dinner now and then. Frankly, I don't know where it's going but it wasn't while you and I were together, and I never imagined that I'd pursue it. It's not like I'm her type anyway—the civil servant type."

"I don't care about you and Courtney," Clare said, lying only a little. "You could have trusted me. It's that simple."

"We were very real, you and me," he said.

"I'm okay, Jared," she said, offering him freedom—regrettably—and nothing else. "You can go."

Jared nodded. Then he went back to join his waiting entourage: a dancing, joyful Mary and Courtney, leaning on a cane.

Courtney smiled, happily, seeing her police chief coming to gather his girls.

Yvonne interrupted her thoughts. "You sure we shouldn't stay just a little longer?"

"We've really got to get going, Mother."

Clare watched Yvonne peer wistfully as Parker and Cathie got into their limo, Cathie wiping floating rose petals from her dress.

They were walking out when she felt Derek's arms engulfing her with his infamous bear hug, bringing her smile back after her encounter with Jared. It must have been the hundredth bear hug he'd given her over the winter as they slowly worked to make amends. Reparations with Derek were the most substantive link she had to her past.

"Clare, you'll be back for ours?" Derek said, referencing his wedding next spring to Karen.

"Assuming you're not in solitary," Clare beamed.

"Not funny at all."

"Wouldn't miss it," Clare said, more quietly. Her tears began to well up. It was still strange, though welcome, to see how assured his stance was now, with Karen, even given all he'd gone through. Derek's transformation from chubby-cheeked and lumbering to the handsome yet exacting man that he had become had finally been completed now, twenty-five years later, by Clare's willingness to let him be someone she had no need to coddle. They would be friends forever, a fate born on the day in the school cafeteria when they had met long ago.

But she still hadn't totally forgiven him.

The band blared again for the post-reception celebration. She smiled at Derek again. "Good-bye," she said. "See you soon."

She wondered whether she would ever come back to Danfield again if were not for Derek. She suspected Yvonne thought as much, too. Neither knew that she wouldn't be ready to see him for an awfully long time.

Yvonne and Clare stopped quickly at Yvonne's for a quick change of clothes and to grab suitcases for a mother and daughter trip to Door County before Clare would head on to the apartment she'd rented in Chicago. Selling the house a month ago freed her to clear up her duties at the bank and to begin the motions of getting back to a place in her life that might include college. Right now, she was thinking less about whether she would ever set foot in a classroom again and more about everything cluttering her to-do list before her departure.

"Hey, hey, Clare, pull over," her mother begged, beside herself with glee. "Look at the start of the beautiful brick walkway!"

Pulling over at an angle in some residual, melting slush, Clare and Yvonne stepped out for one last catalog of their past. If Clare hadn't known otherwise, she would have believed Yvonne had wanted it this way all along.

The whole town had been watching, whenever the weather had permitted that patchy, dreary spring, while eager contractors began work on the redesigned revitalization project. The new plans included the preservation of the bell tower. The modifications came at a hefty premium, but after the chaos of the sit-in calmed down—and in the aftermath of the unbelievable fact that Mary Martin was here, alive, after all—the town officials, a few wealthy families, and the developers agreed to sit down and revisit their plans. As the legend would later be told, Clare knew, the closed-door session only concluded after the jail cells were overflowing with gray-haired women, including, proudly, Yvonne. No one would ever know whether the catalyst for the compromise had been Russell or the heart and determination of a small Wisconsin town.

"Give me just a sec."

Yvonne slipped up a couple of steps to the construction guard and laid down a plastic yellow rose.

"It is beautiful," Clare smiled.

In an effort to give Yvonne her due, Clare forestalled commentary and paused for her short ceremony.

"We should run, Mother. We've got a storm coming in behind us."

Yvonne kissed her fingers and touched the rose before silently obeying and returning to the Jeep.

Clare drove on and glanced in the rear-view mirror at the fading picture of Danfield. She smiled at the sudden memory of Lee Graber's parting words, pontificating about life's twists and turns and keeping the door open for what he considered to be her inevitable return to the bank. "A vacation cures everything," he said, when she told him she was quitting and moving away.

They had gotten out of the city limits and onto the highway before Clare noticed that Yvonne had begun knitting. Although their mutual yelling and accusing had come to a complete halt, they hadn't spoken again about Ray or attempted to mend their differences.

What Clare believed from their critical lone summit was that they both craved contentment, if they actually had anything in common at all. But no matter how stark their differences might be, Clare permitted herself to stop wrestling with the question of whether or not to miss Ray. Yvonne could pine for him if she wanted, and Clare could set aside her guilt for never having waited for him to come home. With the help of Lee, she found the maturity to let go of her compulsion to remind Yvonne how much better off they were, really, for having lived without him.

Resisting a queer urge to laugh out loud, she thought about Yvonne's gift to the bell tower: a plastic flower that could never die. Maybe it represented Ray. She knew Yvonne would remain faithful to a memory of possibilities, fictional though they might be. Somehow she could see through her mother's eyes now what Ray had been to her: a lifelong love affair, a lover that never cried, never fought, and never abandoned her again for some other love.

Clare, in contrast, was content without a lover just now. Instead, strangely, she had the one photo she hadn't burned in the backyard fire that day—the picture of the blue suede shoes— nestled in the glove box beside her. It was the one small item Clare could not yet throw away. That the image of the shoes had spurred her to such an enormity of action meant some kind of promise in and of itself.

"What are you making this time, Yvonne?" she asked.

"Oh, Silvia Wharton's having another baby," Yvonne said. She held up an undecipherable green patch, presumably meant to become a bootie or sweater at some point. "She's not going to know the baby's sex. This will be a good color whether it's a girl or boy, don't you think?"

"Perfect," said Clare.